Praise for *The Fourth* from people just l

WOW!! WHAT A page turner! I received the manuscript for *The Fourth Awakening* via email late in the evening. I printed the first fifty pages, figuring that was all I could read before I fell asleep. But the 50th page ended with them in the car and Walker saying "We really have to go." and Spence asking "Why?"

I tossed and turned for 20 minutes making up all sorts of scenarios of why they needed to go right now. Then I decided to heck with it and got up and to read the rest. I was glued to the screen until I finished the very last word at 9AM. You CANNOT release this book to an unsuspecting public without two things:

A) A warning sign such as: CAUTION, once opened, this book cannot be closed until the last word is read. Reading this book will bring about great change in your life, whether you are ready or not.

... And...MOST IMPORTANT

B) A list of resources where people can get help to get back on track when knocked off by what they read, because there's no way not to be affected by this information!

For the past several years, I have had moments of intense clarity when the fog cleared away and I could see clearly, then the fog moved back in. I continue to search for ways to have that clarity for longer periods of time. Are you teaching the methods that Michael Walker would use to have that level of awareness? I want in!

– SYBIL TEMPLE, LOUISVILLE, KY

A VERY UNUSUAL concept... thought provoking and a fantastic read from beginning to end. I seriously could not put it down. Usually books bog down somewhere but this one never did. I just wanted you to know how much I enjoyed it. My mother-in-law started to read my copy before she could get her own, and I was chomping at the bit to get it back. Thank goodness she reads fast. I can't wait for the sequel!

– SYLVIA McCARTHY, CHARLESTON, SOUTH CAROLINA

LOVED THE BOOK. Really, really loved it. The cat and mouse game of it was superb in execution. And this comes from an avid reader of Ludlum, Follet, Uris, Grisham and Archer. For the uninitiated into the weightiness of the subject matter, it was perfect. And what a great read to initiate them.

– DEB MEYER, OELWEIN, IOWA

WHAT A GREAT read! The story kept my attention and was entertaining. It had a great pace, and enough twists and turns that it kept me wanting to read more to find out what happened next. The most remarkable thing about this book is that it has the potential to reach a wide audience. As a general reader but also someone who strongly believes in the power of thought, I couldn't believe how well it hit the mark in both cases and always left me wanting more.

I kept thinking of *The Da Vinci Code*. Dan Brown's brilliance is in his ability to use history not only to support a very controversial theory, but to make many readers wholeheartedly believe in its truth. This book does the same. It uses historical references to illuminate changes in human development that are not a result of independent thoughts or actions, but of a collective consciousness. The way the authors explain this history doesn't leave me questioning if "enlightenment" is a possibility. It leaves me questioning how anyone could deny that humans and the world developed in this very way.

Many congrats to the authors who have accomplished all of this with such craft. It is an important message to be shared, and moreover, a brilliant idea to write a fiction book about a very real concept everyone wants to share. I look at so many "self-improvement" books, and shut down. This has the ability to speak to so many different readers and change so many lives, including mine, that I am truly impressed.

— ANNE OWENS, NASHUA, NEW HAMPSHIRE

I WAS RIVETED from the first page and knew right there I wasn't going to get much else done until I read the entire book; and, frankly, that's *really* odd for me because, while I'm avid reader, I'm always reading several books at the same time and they're always "practical, how-to" non-fiction type works that I almost never read cover-to-cover.

The Fourth Awakening was a totally different experience for me because I was so caught up in the story that it wasn't until I was a couple chapters in that I realized the authors were actually sneaking in some vital spiritual lessons at the same time. Not to get too esoteric, but as I continued to read, I found a sense of calm and connectedness wash over me where I realized it was time to return home to my true passion: inner exploration of universal Source.

So, if you're looking for TRUE inspiration (not warm bath motivation which quickly fades) that feels like a hug from God, stop whatever you're doing, buy this book, clear your decks for the next 12 hours, read the first 5 pages and prepare to embark on the most enjoyable journey you've ever taken. It can change your life. To YOUR joy!

— JOSHUA SHAFRAN, CAPE CORAL, FLORIDA

THE FOURTH AWAKENING

≈

Rod Pennington

&

Jeffery A. Martin

INTEGRATION PRESS, LLC
CHARLESTON, SC

THE FOURTH AWAKENING

Integration Press
2245 C Ashley Crossing Drive - Suite 102
Charleston, South Carolina 29414

ISBN: 1-57242-000-6
EAN: 978-1-57242-000-7
Library of Congress Control Number: 2009926636

Cover Designed by Cathi Stevenson
Interior Designed by Gwen Gades

THE FOURTH AWAKENING

≈

Rod Pennington

&

Jeffery A. Martin

PART ONE

The Choice

"Life is like a game of cards. The hand you are dealt is determinism;
the way you play it is free will."

Jawaharlal Nehru

CHAPTER ONE

"The road to enlightenment is long and difficult.
Bring snacks and a book to read."

ANONYMOUS

"NELLIE! WHY DO you even bother to carry a cell phone when you never answer the darn thing?"

As usual, with the phone buried in her purse, Penelope Spence hadn't heard it ringing. The familiar baritone on her voice mail brought a smile to her face. Mark Hatchet, Managing Editor of *The Washington Post*, was the only person on the planet who still called her by her old college nickname of Nellie; to everyone else she was, and always had been, Penelope. It was ironic that he should call. She had been thinking about him recently, hoping he would have another assignment for her; maybe this time he had one with a bit more meat on it.

"Call me. It's important. Don't go through the switchboard, use my cell." Penelope frowned. It was an odd request. She dialed his number and he answered on the second ring.

"Mark Hatchet."

"Penelope Spence."

When they were journalism majors at Columbia, they had worked on the school newspaper and been less than friendly rivals for the best stories and the editorship of the paper. After college, as their careers moved in different directions and real life settled in, they became the kind of old friends who stay in touch and talk a few times a year.

"Thanks for returning my call so quickly," he said, a bit stiffly.

"So, what's the big story this time? Problems with the strawberry crop in Georgia?"

"No, a little better than that." Mark's voice was strained and he seemed to be choosing his words carefully. She could hear other voices in the background.

"Want me to call you back?"

"No," he said. "Hold on one second." The background noise faded and Penelope heard a door click shut. "I can't really talk right now, but I have a potential story for you."

"Potential? What does that mean?"

"The story is big enough that it can't go to print without multiple confirmations. So far, no one has been able to get even a single person to go on the record."

"What's the story?"

"Not on this line."

"What do you mean, not on this line?"

Normally their conversations were light and breezy, but not today; he was deadly serious. "Someone may be tapping my phone," he said.

"What have you been smoking? No one in their right mind would tap the phone of a senior editor of a major newspaper."

"Don't be so sure."

"Okay," Penelope said as she sat up straighter. "You've got my full and undivided attention."

"I sent you a package by courier. Inside are an envelope and a cell phone. Do not open the envelope or show the contents to anyone under any circumstances until we've talked. And don't mention this conversation to anyone."

"That sounds ominous."

"This is serious enough to cost me my job if any of this gets out."

Penelope stood up and began pacing in a tight circle. "You're kidding, right?"

"No. I don't want to go into any details until you have the package. But it is critical that no one else sees the contents until we talk. Okay?"

Penelope's brow furrowed so deeply her eyebrows touched. "Okay. But you're starting to scare me a little bit."

"Don't worry," he said with a forced laugh. "There are some issues in play here that I'll explain when you have it in front of you. This is right up your alley."

"What alley is that?"

"A government cover-up at the highest level," Hatchet answered with a laugh. "Let me ask you a question. When was the last time you had a front page byline?"

Penelope felt a tingle of excitement. "It's been awhile."

"Well, this may be the story you've been wishing for. Promise me you won't open it or mention this conversation to anyone until you talk to me."

"I promise."

The phone went dead in her hands.

The path not chosen. After winning a Pulitzer for investigative reporting at the tender age of twenty-three for exposing corruption in the South Carolina Statehouse, Penelope could have gotten a job with any paper in the country. In fact, many sent out feelers and lunch invitations to see if she would jump. Instead of punching her ticket to a big-time newspaper in New York or Washington, her wedding to Bill Spence was only a few months away and she decided to stay in Charleston and get married.

Their wedding was the social event of the season. With a guest list that included two former presidents, and an assortment of senators and congressmen, to change her mind at such a late date would have been the death of her mother.

Two days short of the anniversary of her Pulitzer, her first daughter, Carrie, was born. *The Post & Courier* let her work part-time, for awhile. But with three children born in just under four years, she found herself declining more and more assignments. They kept her technically on the staff for a few years, mostly for the prestige of having a Pulitzer Prize winner on the masthead, but eventually even that illusion vanished.

A couple of decades later, after Bill left and she had decided to take another shot at reporting, she was so far removed from journalism that the paper didn't even offer her a job. Advertisers weren't buying ads like they used to and they already had a newsroom full of ambitious J-school reporters who were half her age, and a fraction of her salary. Since her divorce, Mark had been her only lifeline.

While Penelope was raising her family Mark had risen through the ranks of several major newspapers. He ended up behind the big desk at

The Washington Post with some of the best reporters in the world at his beck and call. Over the years he had thrown her a few stringer assignments when he didn't have a reporter in her area. None of it was front page, above the fold stuff, but between her trust fund and what she was getting from her ex-husband each month she was doing it more to stay in practice than for money. Plus, no matter how thin the subject material of the story, Mark was always thoughtful enough to call personally instead of having one of his editors contact her. It was a nice courtesy to an old friend.

≈

PENELOPE SPENCE TRIED to roll the tension out of her neck as she sat cross-legged on her mat. Her morning yoga session, as usual, had been fine. Fully rested from a good night's sleep and before the events of the day began to weigh on her she had been able to clear her thoughts and have, for a moment, that feeling of deep inner peace she had grown to crave. Now, as she tried to relax, her meditation wasn't getting anywhere as the conversation with Mark kept bubbling to the surface and was simply too much for her to overcome. With a sigh she stood up and, arching her back, bent over and put the palms of her hands on the floor while her knees locked. It was nice to feel the old flexibility returning. She wasn't as limber as she had been in her old college dancing days, but a year of yoga stretches had really paid off.

Penelope turned on the radio. The "Oldies" station was playing one of her favorite Eagles songs—*Seven Bridges Road.* Closing her eyes, the incredible vocal harmonies swelled and she began to fall into the music. Just then, her eyes flew open.

She dialed a ten-digit number with a 415 area code that was answered on the first ring. "Hi, Mom." William said.

"Hello, dear." Not being particularly technology savvy, she always had to pause and tell herself it was Caller ID and not their close relationship that allowed her only son to know it was her. "Did Sam get out again?"

"Are you a part of the doggie psychic hotline? We are out looking for him right now."

"We?"

"My new friend Nathan."

"I see."

William put his hand over the mouthpiece of his cell phone but

Penelope was still able to hear him. "It's my mom. She knew we were out looking for Sam...yeah, I know. Freaky, huh?" The muffling went away as William turned his attention back to his mother. "You have any suggestions?"

"Did you try down by the lake at Golden Gate Park?"

"We're driving by Stow Lake right now."

"No, not Stow Lake. Is there a North Lake?"

"Yes, there is a North Lake, but that's at the other end of the park from my place. He's never gone that far before."

"Humor your old mother."

"Okay. North Lake it is."

Penelope loved all of her children, but she had a special bond with William. He was the youngest and last to leave the nest, and she had always felt he needed her a bit more than the girls did since he and his father were estranged.

"For once you were wrong," William said with a quick laugh. "Sam wasn't *at* North Lake, he is smack in the middle of it. By the way, Nathan is now officially terrified of you. Come here Sammy!" There was a pause and a rustling in the background. "I have a very wet and happy dog in the backseat I have to deal with. I'll talk to you later. Bye, Mom. Love you."

"Goodbye sweetie. Love you too!"

Over the years she'd occasionally had visions that involved her children or other close family members. Sometimes they were right, like today; other times they were false alarms. Recently, as she had gotten more committed to her twice daily regiment of deep meditation and yoga, instead of hit or miss she was almost always spot on.

Heading down to the kitchen, she found an invoice on the counter from the pool man and another one from Blue Flame for a refill of her propane tank. Natural gas wasn't available on her street when they built their home and Penelope refused to cook on an electric element. Being only four feet above sea level and located next to the Ashley River placing the tank underground was out of the question. Instead it was behind the house next to the swimming pool. The twenty-five year-old privacy fence around it had dry-rotted and the yardman had recently mentioned that he thought it needed to be replaced before it became a fire hazard.

Penelope sighed. The big house on the river with the swimming pool no one used anymore had a quiet sadness about it. When the kids were growing up it was the place all of their friends chose to hang out and the walls echoed with music and laughter. Her three children, Carrie, Kelly and William, had all gone off to college and never come back. As each bird flew from the nest the noise level dropped, until now the only laughter came from the ghosts of happier days.

Penelope heard the rumble of the FedEx truck in front of her house. Wiping her hands in anticipation of having to answer the doorbell, she was surprised when the door burst open. In marched her best friend Joey Rickman dressed in full gym regalia, with every item she was wearing carefully mismatched. She had the red, white and blue shipping box in her hand and tossed it in Penelope's general direction.

"Your FedEx guy is cute."

Penelope shook her head as she stopped the box from sliding off the end of the kitchen counter. "He went to high school with your son."

"Oh," Joey said with a shrug as she headed toward the refrigerator. "Thought he looked familiar."

The two women had been friends since kindergarten and their lives had followed very similar paths. After Ronald F. Rickman, Esquire had packed his bags and announced he was leaving Joey for a woman less than half her age, she went through her own personal 12-step program. When the initial shock wore off instead of attending boring meetings, or turning to a higher force, she discovered Dr. Schwartz. If it could be tucked, sucked, lifted, injected, peeled or stretched, Dr. S was always there. She bragged that she had spent enough on plastic surgery to put one of the good doctor's kids through college. Ivy League college.

For those who had not seen her in a few years, the transformation was startling. For the 24 years of her marriage she was Josephine Middleton Rickman, President of the local Junior League and, like Penelope, a member of both the Daughters of the American Revolution and the Daughters of the Confederacy. She was the wife of one of the most successful trial lawyers in the country and a pillar of Charleston's high society. Now she was a tight gym rat with a head-turning body that looked a minimum of ten years younger than the DOB on her driver's license.

Penelope opened the box and dumped the contents on the kitchen counter. She checked inside to be sure it was empty before tossing the box aside. "What have we here?" Joey said, biting into an apple.

"You remember Mark Hatchet?"

"Our age and single; of course I remember him."

"Single is not the word I would use. Between wives may be more accurate."

"Well, I just happen to be between husbands."

"He has an assignment for me."

"God, I hope it's more interesting than that last one. What was that? The Vidalia Onion Festival, or some nonsense? A week, all expenses paid, in beautiful Vidalia Georgia at the height of mosquito season."

Penelope shrugged; beggars can't be choosers. The onion article made the Sunday travel section and won her a byline in *The Washington Post*. For many reporters, getting an article published in a major paper like the *Post* would be a career moment. For her it was another step back to the world she had grown to miss but that didn't seem to be missing her.

Because of Mark's vow of silence, Penelope hadn't mentioned anything about this when Joey called earlier to confirm their dinner date. Still, Penelope had been secretly hoping Joey might drop by. She hadn't liked the tone of Mark's voice, nor the way he had shrouded it in such mystery, and she could use the moral support.

Scanning the contents of the box spread out on the countertop, Penelope found a disposable cell phone and a large white envelope heavily sealed with transparent packing tape. Attached to the outside of the envelope was a handwritten note with instructions to call an unfamiliar phone number with the enclosed cell phone before opening the envelope.

Looking over Penelope's shoulder and reading the note, Joey said, "Yeah, right," as she reached for the envelope, but Penelope slapped her hands away. "Excuse me!" Joey exalted as she returned to foraging through Penelope's refrigerator. "Here's the reason you're losing so much weight, you have no food."

Penelope picked up the phone and began dialing the number.

Hatchet answered before the third ring. "It's me. Are you alone?"

"No, Joey is here."

"Hi, Mark," Joey shouted, opening a cupboard and finding it just as sparsely stocked as the refrigerator.

"Have you opened the package?"

"I haven't been given permission yet."

"Like that would ever stop you. I won't bother to ask you to send Joey out of the room since I know she'll weasel all of this out of you anyway." He took Penelope's silence as affirmation and continued. "Inside the envelope is information that is so closely held..."

"Is it classified?" Penelope interrupted.

"What do you care? Senator Horn got you Top Secret clearance as the world's oldest intern."

"Ha. Ha. Very funny. I haven't done any work for the senator since he announced his retirement. Besides, there are rules that have to be followed to get clearance not to mention lots of scary documents I had to sign. I really don't want to spend my golden years in Leavenworth."

"Trust me, Nellie. There is nothing in the envelope that will get you into legal trouble. Everything inside is a matter of public knowledge and came straight off of the Internet." Mark Hatchet paused, then added, "And in the off chance it does get you into any difficulty, the *Post* will stand behind you."

"That's reassuring. Will you come see me on visiting days?"

"Of course and I'll even bring you cartons of cigarettes and chocolate bars you can share with all of your new friends... Look, if you're not interested, just return the envelope to me unopened and I'll find someone else."

"Relax. I didn't say I wasn't interested. After our earlier conversation I'm just trying to figure out what you're getting me into here."

"What I've got is the name of one man and the name of the black project they're doing at a hush-hush department of Homeland Security."

"Homeland Security?"

"There is a division called Emerging Technologies..."

"That would be Noah Shepherd's department."

"And that's why no one will ever play Trivial Pursuit with you, Nellie. Do you know him?" Hatchet asked.

"No. I've never met him but the senator had me do a complete profile on him a few years back."

"Find anything interesting?"

"Garden variety upper-level bureaucrat. Yale Skull and Bones type. His father and grandfather were all in the government, if I remember correctly."

"These days he's one of the big players in town. Shepherd may be the most powerful person in Washington that no one has ever heard of. He's positioned himself so he gets the first look at all new technology that comes around and then cherry picks the stuff he wants to keep. Many of his projects are cutting edge, high-tech psychological warfare kinds of things. He is a big-time behind the scenes player on the Hill and at the White House."

"So, what does Shepherd have to do with all of this?"

"He's slapped a lid on this story and nobody, and I mean nobody, is talking about it."

"If no one is talking, how did you find out about it?"

"I have a source..."

"Ha!"

"What?"

"You've been sitting behind a desk for the past five years. Where in the world would you get a source?"

"You'd be surprised, especially if you knew who it was."

"So, who is it?"

"If I won't tell my boss, I sure as heck won't tell you."

"Okay, so you have this imaginary friend who gave you this story that no one else is able to confirm..." An early warning signal went off in Penelope's head. "Hold on," she said. "You must have fifty reporters who would walk over glass for something like this. Why me? And what's with this phone?"

"The phone is one of these cheap disposables you always hear about in bad movies, except these weren't so cheap. I needed ones without GPS and I had to..."

Penelope had spent enough time interviewing people to know when they were trying to avoid answering a direct question. "Wwwhhhyyy. Mmmeee?" she said slowly, carefully enunciating each word.

"Are you kidding me? You're one of the best investigative reporters I've ever known."

"You have a slew of top reporters on your staff who are better connected than I could ever dream of being."

"I needed someone I know and trust."

"And?"

The phone went silent for a few moments as Mark Hatchet gathered his thoughts and selected the right words. "At the personal request of the President of the United States; the heads of Homeland Security, the CIA and the NSA; the House and Senate leadership of both parties; and the Chairman and ranking member of the Senate Select Committee on Intelligence *The Washington Post* has been asked, in the interest of national security, not to pursue this story. My publisher has agreed to honor the request."

"Well, that certainly explains why you didn't want to go through the *Post's* switchboard. This Shepherd character must know where a lot of bodies are buried to get that kind of support for a cover-up." Penelope smiled wryly, as she put more of the puzzle pieces together. "Let me guess why you're risking your job over this story. I'm betting the Grey Lady up on Times Square isn't feeling quite as patriotic as your publisher?"

Penelope could almost see the color building in Mark's face. The slightest mention of *The New York Times* was always enough to set him off on a sputtering diatribe. Today was no exception. "They hadn't heard anything about it, but as soon as they got the request they put three reporters on it."

"Gee. And you mainstream media types can't understand why everyone hates you. That still doesn't answer my question; why me?"

"I have it from my unimpeachable, imaginary, source that they are transferring the guy who holds the key to this entire story to the brig at the Charleston Naval Weapons Station which, according to MapQuest, is less than 10 miles from your house."

"So it's not my worldly charms and brilliant reporting skills but geography that made you think of me?"

"Please. You're one of the best reporters I've ever known."

"And you're one of the worst liars I've ever known."

"If you're not interested…"

"Don't get huffy. I didn't say that."

"Okay. Before you open the envelope, I need to know if you're in or out."

"In."

"Don't even want to think about it for half a second?"

"Nope."

"This could be dangerous."

"Don't care."

"We're talking Homeland Security and secret projects."

"I got that part."

"You're not only going to be up against the entire federal government but also some of the best reporters in the business, and they have a head start."

"So why don't we get started?"

"And you understand my position...."

"You haven't seen me in years. Didn't like me the last time you did. You have no idea where I got this information. I, in no way, shape, or form, represent *The Washington Post*. Yet strangely if anything happens you guarantee that I'll have *The Post's* backing."

"That's my girl."

"Ouch!" Penelope turned to see Joey sucking her left index finger. While Penelope was distracted, Joey had claimed the envelope. In her haste to get it open before Penelope turned around, she had stabbed herself with a paring knife.

"Give me that before you hurt yourself," Penelope said as she sat down the phone. Grabbing a cutting board and the razor-sharp knife from Joey, she sliced the end of the envelope off and pulled out a file folder. It was filled with about 30 pages of background that looked like it came straight off of a home printer. She picked up the phone and tucked it under her chin.

"All right, I've got it. What am I looking at here?"

"This is all I was able to piece together before the order came down from upstairs to stop looking. There was a super secret project with the code name 'Hermes'. Rumor has it they were trying to use a combination of drugs and who knows what to build some kind of super spy or something, until things went south."

"Don't those government types ever learn? What happened?"

"That's what you're going to have to find out. Apparently, Homeland Security, under extreme pressure from your old buddy Senator Horn, cancelled the project six months ago but the people involved kept it going. Now the rumor is they have made some kind of breakthrough."

"What kind of breakthrough?"

"I have no idea. Only a handful of people have the details on the project."

"And no one is talking?"

"Not only are they not talking, no one can find any of them."

"What?"

"For all intents and purposes, they have all vanished."

Penelope felt her earlier bravado crumble and be replaced with an uncomfortable knot in her stomach. As she pondered the possibilities she felt goose bumps rising on her arms. "You don't think?"

"I don't know," Mark said softly. "But considering how much effort is going into this cover-up, we can't rule anything out."

"How many people are we talking about?"

"Over 30 ultra-high clearance people have simply vanished, including a Nobel Prize winner. No one has seen or heard from them in nearly six months."

The knot in Penelope's stomach wasn't getting any smaller. Suddenly, her desire to get back into big-time journalism was being hotly contested by her survival instincts. If this story was big enough for someone in the federal government to order the assassination of over 30 people to keep it quiet, then what was the death of one reporter — more or less? She rubbed the goose bumps on her arms and drew in a deep breath. This could be as big as Mark thought it was; it could also be too big for her.

Hatchet knew Spence well enough to understand exactly what her sudden silence meant. He knew she was itching to get back into mainstream journalism, and he would put her on staff immediately if she was willing to relocate to Washington or New York. But that was never going to happen. Still, despite its obvious risks, this could be a career defining story for both of them. He hated putting her in harm's way, but with his normal resources blocked she was the only one he trusted enough to even consider for the story. "So, what do you think?"

Penelope's mouth was so dry she reached for her bottle of water and took a sip before trying to answer. "Boy, I'm not sure about this, Mark."

"I understand completely. Look," Mark Hatchet felt if he could just give her a gentle nudge she would do what he wanted. "Do this for me. Just go over to the brig and try to talk to this guy, and if it doesn't feel right, walk away... Okay?"

"I don't know."

"If you can get him to talk, heck if you can even confirm he's in the Charleston Brig, I'll guarantee you'll make the front page of the *Post*, and probably every other newspaper in the country."

"You always knew how to sweet talk me."

"Who is this guy?"

"His picture is in the file."

Penelope rummaged through the folder until she found a professional-quality head and shoulder picture of a man who looked familiar but she couldn't quite place. Fit and a bit John Wayne-ish; he looked like the guy you'd want to do your estate planning, but not necessarily someone who'd be a ton of laughs in Vegas on a long weekend. Turning it over, she read his biography. Her eyebrows went up and a small whistle escaped her lips when she read his name.

"Oh my!"

CHAPTER TWO

"If you believe you are enlightened, you are actually a little bit crazy."

TAISEN DESHIMARU

"YOU'RE SLIPPING, NELLIE," said Hatchet with a laugh. "That took you about thirty seconds longer than I expected."

"I did background research on a bunch of his people for the senator."

"I thought that might be the case."

"Are they the ones who are missing?"

"Yup."

"And he's the one they're taking to the brig?"

"Yup."

"Yikes!"

"Tell me about it," said Hatchet with a small laugh.

"He's got to be a zillionaire."

"And then some."

Penelope's mind raced and she felt her fingers tingle. "The heck with the other stuff. One of the world's richest men being held by the federal government is a huge story by itself."

"Really?" Hatchet said, his voice dripping with sarcasm. "That never occurred to me. You've got a real knack for this journalism stuff. Have you ever considered a career as a reporter?"

Penelope ignored the jab and studied the picture more intently. "A man in his position and with his wealth hardly seems the type to be involved in government conspiracies."

"I wouldn't be so sure. Walker has his fingers in a lot of pies, not only in Washington, but in Europe and the rest of the world as well. Whatever this Hermes Project is, the government cancelled it. Apparently, Walker decided to bankroll the entire operation with his own funds."

"How much money are we talking here?"

"You can ask him when you talk to him. But his research and development budget is larger than the gross national products of half the members of the United Nations."

"Is this Walker guy dirty?"

"Never been even a whiff of scandal."

"Funny. Why haven't I seen anything about this in the press?"

"Because, Nellie, thanks to my imaginary source, you're the only one who knows he's been detained and knows where he is."

"I'll leave now..."

"Whoa, Nellie."

"You know I hate that."

"I know. But he may not even be there yet, besides visiting hours are over. It's too late to get anything for tomorrow's edition, and I don't want this to break with an online story or to tip our hand. I want to be the only paper in America with this on its front page Sunday."

"I'll go see him first thing in the morning."

"Until then, keep this completely under your hat."

"What about Joey?"

"What about her?"

"Well," Penelope said with a glance over her shoulder in the direction of her friend. "She's been reading the file while we were talking."

"Hi Mark!" Joey shouted again. "How come you never fix me up with any guys?"

"Oh lord," Hatchet said with a sigh. "I did mention I could get fired over this, right? Can you keep her under control?"

"Nope. Gave up trying years ago."

"Super."

"Relax. Who is she going to tell?"

"You guys talking about me?" Joey demanded.

"Yes," Penelope said with a laugh. "We were just talking about how good you are at keeping your mouth shut."

"I am?" Joey answered dumbfounded. Penelope's eyes grew big and she gave Joey a look usually aimed at an unruly two year old. Recognition exploded on Joey's face. "I am. Absolutely. Secrets are us."

"God help me," Hatchet said with a sigh. "Keep me posted." The phone went dead.

"You, young lady," Penelope said shaking a finger in Joey's direction, "are not getting out of my sight for the rest of the day."

"Slumber party!"

≈

JOEY HAD INSISTED on going home to shower and change before going out for dinner. Reluctantly Penelope had agreed. Penelope took a sip from her chamomile tea, then typed rapidly on her laptop. She wanted to know as much as she possibly could about Michael James Walker. Up until six months ago he had been a public relations dynamo. There were literally hundreds of stories about him and his company, then absolutely nothing since last fall. "That's odd," Penelope muttered to herself. She checked Yahoo, MSN, and several other search engines getting more or less the same result. She printed off some background material about Walker and Walker Industries and added it to the folder.

Picking up the photo of Walker she carefully studied his face. Strong-willed, of that she was certain. But whether he drank too much and smacked women around, or went gaga over kids and puppies, without more information there was no way to tell. Remembering what Mark said about 30 plus people missing, it was easy to assume the worst.

Turning her focus back to her computer, Penelope clicked a bookmarked website. A request for her name and password to the FBI National Database opened. With previous stories Mark assigned her, there had been no risk of a conflict of interest between *The Washington Post* and the senator. This was very different and she felt her toes approaching a line she preferred not to cross. Leaning back in her chair she checked her watch and couldn't believe how late it had gotten. Checking her hair in the mirror as she reached for her car keys she noticed the book, *Power of Thought*, that was lying on the nightstand by her bed. Someone in her yoga class recently was talking about the Law of Attraction and Penelope decided to check it out.

"What the heck?" She thought to herself. Simply wishing for something to happen and having it magically appear sounded like New Age poppycock, but with the bizarre things that had been happening in her life recently she was willing to give it a try. Closing her eyes, she visualized herself arriving at the restaurant where a premium parking place, one in the shade, would be waiting for her. She continued, visualizing herself being grateful to finish dinner and return to a car that wasn't scorching inside.

During the short drive to the Sunfire Grill, any thoughts about parking places were released and replaced with a thousand questions about her conversation with Mark. He had certainly piqued her curiosity. She pulled into the lot just as someone was pulling out of one of the few shady spots. She smiled and shook her head.

Joey had sworn on her ex-husband's grave she would be there no later than six forty-five. Since Ron Rickman was still very much alive and Joey had never been on time for anything in her life, Penelope was confident she would still be the first to arrive. She was right; Joey's car was nowhere to be seen.

Penelope looked up when she heard the blare of a car horn, and watched as a fire engine red BMW roadster squealed into the front parking lot. With the top down on the sleek little sports car, Joey was able to fully extend her left arm and wave at the driver of a late model pickup truck who was using his horn to offer a personal critique of Joey's driving skills. Joey Rickman had two unfortunate weaknesses; a lead foot and a lousy sense of direction. She never seemed to know where she was going, but was always in a hurry to get there.

Bounding from the Beemer, which was now parked straddling the white line between two sun-drenched parking spaces, Joey pushed her windblown mane of vivid red hair out of her face. Her green eyes twinkled. "I don't believe that man has an ounce of Southern hospitality in him," she said with a wry smile.

"You were supposed to be here 10 minutes ago," Penelope said as she gripped the handle and pulled the restaurant door open.

Joey batted her eyes. "And when have you known me not to be tastefully late?" she said breezing past her lifelong friend. "Besides, you just got here yourself."

"How do you figure that?"

"You were still outside." Penelope shrugged; Joey was right.

In the lobby, Penelope glanced at Joey who was already getting fidgety. She had seen that look many times before and knew what it meant, nicotine withdrawal. With Charleston's recent ban on smoking in all public places, they would be dining on the deck today. Penelope made eye contact with the night manager Jennifer who was busy placing menus in front of a middle aged couple in the main dining room. Penelope held up two fingers and pointed toward the patio. Jennifer, seeing that Joey was with her, nodded to indicate she understood and turned her attention back to the table she was seating. As they passed through the bar area Joey paused and spoke to the bartender who was wearing a white blouse and black vest pinned with a name tag that said "Allison". Like so many in Charleston's service industry, Allison looked too young to be drinking liquor much less serving it.

"Sweetheart," Joey said sweetly. "In a few minutes you're going to be getting an order for a dry martini. In this case, 'dry' means you can show it the bottle of vermouth, but don't you dare pour any in the glass."

The part-time bartender, a full time student at the College of Charleston, was a stunning beauty. She had flaxen hair and widely spaced blue-green eyes that could make any male with a pulse say and do embarrassing things. She turned her attention to Joey. "Yes, ma'am," she said with a smile bright and warm enough that she might have been able to save the Titanic by melting the iceberg. Joey Rickman led the way to the patio while reaching for a cigarette.

"That child called me ma'am."

"So?" Penelope said as she pushed open the door to the patio.

"Did you forget your Southern-to-English dictionary again? We both know 'ma'am' means that 'B' word that rhymes with witch."

"I thought she was being polite and respectful of her elders."

"Elders!" Joey fanned herself. "Gracious. How old do you think I am?"

"Since we were born three days apart, I have a pretty good idea. I'll be happy to blurt it out for you if you would like."

"That won't be necessary, ma'am," Joey said as she looked around to see if anyone was listening. "You know the first thing a Southern lady learns how to do is deliver an insult with a smile."

"Oh, Lord," Penelope said. "Here we go again." Her voice changed to a monotone. "You can say anything catty you want about someone if you smile and add, 'bless their heart.'"

"Exactly."

"You are totally deranged," Penelope said, then added with a fake smile, "Bless your heart."

Joey patted Penelope's hand. "That's the spirit."

Once seated in the wrought iron chair, Joey tapped the end of her Benson and Hedges on the glass tabletop with one hand while fumbling through her purse for her lighter with the other. Penelope eyed her friend critically. "You really should give those things up."

"Oh, please," Joey said, rolling the wheel of her solid gold lighter. "Allow me one small vice."

"One? Ha!"

Joey stuck her tongue out at Penelope. Sparks shot out from the flint of her lighter, but there was no flame. She tried several more times before finally giving up and returning her cigarette to its package. "Why is it my lighter never seems to work when I'm with you, but works just fine any other time?"

"Maybe because you're always on your best behavior when we're together?" After a short pause, the two old friends both giggled. For over 40 years they had been thick as thieves with "good behavior" never their default mode.

"I think you've hexed my lighter."

"And how do you suppose I was able to do that?"

"I have no idea. All I know is strange things have been happening around you since you started this yoga stuff. That has been annoying enough; I mean, why can't you do Pilates like everyone else?" Joey said as she shoved her lighter back into her purse.

Jennifer approached the table with two menus in hand, placing one in front of Joey and the other in front of Penelope. She pointed at Penelope, "Water with lemon and no ice." Turning her gaze toward Joey, "Double Grey Goose vodka martini, dry." Both women nodded.

Joey smiled sweetly. "Could you bring me some matches?"

"I'm sorry, Mrs. Rickman but they're on back order and we're all out."

"Of course you are," Joey said as she gave Penelope a sideways glance.

Jennifer nodded. "Your server will be Allison. She's new, so bear with her a bit. She's working the patio and the bar."

Joey dropped her cigarettes back into her purse and glared at her lifelong friend. "So far I've been supportive of your little spiritual quest for self-fulfillment, but now it's starting to affect my day." Joey shook a threatening finger in Penelope's direction. "Watch it!"

"Demented," Penelope muttered as shook her head.

"So what's our plan?" Joey asked as she held the menu at arm's length to avoid the indignity of having to put on her reading glasses.

"What plan are you talking about?" Penelope asked as she pushed the menu aside without opening it.

"How are we going to get into the brig to see this guy?"

"Who is this 'we' you're referring to?"

"Me and you."

"Ha!" Penelope said with a laugh. "I'm going to the brig. You will be spending the day at the Piccolo Spoleto planning meeting."

Joey Rickman winced. "I'd forgotten about that."

At that moment Allison appeared carrying their drinks.

"Filet rare with creamy grits. House dressing on the salad," Joey announced as she folded her menu closed.

"I'm feeling decadent. I'll take the portabella sandwich with a side of the parmesan risotto," Penelope said as she handed her unopened menu to Allison.

The server acted as if she wanted to frown but didn't seem to quite know how to go about it. She started flipping through the handwritten notes she had tucked in her order book for quick reference. Her eyes were showing a hint of panic. "Will you excuse me for one second?" Allison turned and dashed toward the door leading to the restaurant.

"Was it something I said?" Penelope asked. Joey just shrugged. She had no idea what had sent the waitress/bartender scrambling for help. Allison emerged through the door with Jennifer in tow.

"Allison told me you wanted to order risotto?"

"Yes," Penelope answered with a smile.

"You mean the creamy grits?"

"No, risotto."

"Ms. Spence, we don't have any risotto."

"Ah, sold out."

Jennifer carefully measured her words before speaking. "Are you sure you don't mean the grits? They are very similar."

"Jennifer, I come in here twice a week and I love the risotto."

"I've worked here for over three years and we've never had risotto on the menu."

"Just bring her the grits," Joey said as she patted Penelope on the hand. "Having a senior moment, are we?" Joey said, as she fought to keep from laughing. "We've been eating in this restaurant together for the past 15 years and I've never seen you order risotto before."

CHAPTER THREE

"Do not think you will necessarily be aware of your own enlightenment."

DOGEN

WITH PENELOPE EITHER on her computer or reading and rereading the background information about Walker it had been an early night for Joey. The lack of lively conversation and a shortage of vodka had forced her to turn in before ten. After morning coffee on the deck by the pool and with a promise not to mention anything about what Penelope was up to, Joey headed to her meeting while Penelope got ready to visit the Charleston Consolidated Brig.

It was a crisp Chamber of Commerce-pleasing Saturday morning in Charleston, with clear blue skies and a temperature still under seventy degrees at 9 a.m. By noon it would be warm enough to hit the beaches but not too hot for strolling around in the historic district or perusing some outdoor malls.

Penelope had to go down several rows in the brig's parking lot before finding a space for her Prius. She mentally kicked herself for not visualizing a better spot. Inside the clean, modern building she was third in line waiting to speak to the guard at the desk. When it was Penelope's turn, before she could speak, she heard a deep male voice bark, "Name."

"Michael Walker."

"Your name is Michael Walker?"

"No. I want to see Michael Walker. My name is Penelope Spence."

Flipping his clipboard to the second page, he ran his finger down the page and checked the "S" section twice. Without looking up he said, "Sorry, you're not on the list," while sliding a printed piece of paper in Penelope's direction as he'd done a thousand times before. The second item on the sheet had been highlighted with bright yellow marker.

2. Visitation planning. Visits to prisoners should be coordinated ahead of time by the visitor and the prisoner via mail or phone. This allows the visitor to be approved for a specific day and have their name added to the list for that day. The approved visitor's name will be added to the list the brig provides to the Perimeter Gate for that day. It is strongly recommend that you not make any air reservations until you are sure visitation for a specific day has been approved and coordinated.

Penelope glanced at the sheet. "I'm not a visitor, I'm a reporter." For the first time, the Chief Petty Officer at the desk glanced up and made eye contact. He was a burly man who looked like he had allowed himself to soften of late, as he approached his thirtieth year in service to his country. With the enthusiasm of a man marking time until retirement, he sized up the woman in front of him, decided he wasn't impressed, then turned his focus back to his clipboard.

"You want to see a detainee?"

"Yes."

"Are you his legal representative?"

"No."

"Are you his religious advisor?"

"No."

"Then you're a visitor, and your name is not on the list."

The biggest enemies of reporters are gatekeepers. It is the gatekeeper's job to keep the nosy press out and, since failure to perform their assigned task can result in job termination or worse, some can be quite formidable. "May I speak to your superior officer?"

"Yes, ma'am," he said with added emphasis on the "Ma'am", making it sound like a pejorative. She wondered if he had read Joey's Southern-to-English dictionary. "Please have a seat over there." He pointed to a small anteroom with six straight ladder-back chairs aimed towards an office containing a lithe and fit female Commander in a crisp white uniform. Turning his attention back to his list, the guard called, "Next."

Penelope was unsure if she was supposed to take a seat and wait to be acknowledged, or knock on the door. Always one for the direct approach, she tapped lightly on the frame of the open door. The officer, without looking up from the document she was reading, held up a finger to indicate Penelope had made the wrong choice. As the seconds turned into an awkward minute, Penelope finally turned and sat in one of the uncomfortable chairs. The Charleston Brig certainly wasn't going to win any awards for customer service, but considering the clientele she wasn't sure she should have expected more.

Finally, after reading the document, signing her name to the bottom, and dropping it in her "out" box the officer motioned for Penelope to join her. Before Penelope was situated in one of the two chairs that were of the same vintage and comfort level as the ones in the waiting area, the officer barked crisply, "I'm Commander Durkin, how may I help you?"

"I would like to see one of your detainees."

"Your name?"

"Penelope Spence."

The Commander scanned a piece of paper that appeared to be the identical twin of the one at the front desk and said. "I'm sorry, but you're not on the list." She reached for a form with "Item 2" highlighted and started to push it toward Penelope."

Penelope held up her hand. "Already have a copy, thank you. I'm a reporter, and I would like to speak to one of your detainees, Michael Walker."

Immediately defensive and guarded, Commander Durkin raised her head and studied Penelope. Her eyes were a fierce blue, almost bird-like. "Reporter, you say?" The Charleston Consolidated Brig, which was used by all branches of the services for petty crimes and misdemeanors, had also held some of the world's most dangerous terrorists. The brig had a checkered history with the press. They didn't much like each other and neither side was timid about expressing their reasons. The press thought the brig was covering up some kind of torture chamber and the brig thought the press was jeopardizing national security. Reaching for a different list, Durkin scanned it twice.

"What news organization do you represent?"

"I'm freelance."

"I see." The Commander became less and less impressed with each passing moment. "Unless you are a detainee's lawyer or religious advisor, you must be approved in advance..."

"I've read Item 2," Penelope said curtly, wishing she could tell the Commander she was working on a story for *The Washington Post*, but the satisfaction she might receive didn't justify jeopardizing Mark's career. "What exactly do I need to do to get my name on the list?"

"You're wasting your time, ma'am."

"And why is that?"

Commander Durkin checked the sheet of paper in front of her again. This was neither the time nor the place to make a mistake. "We don't have a Michael Walker currently residing in our facility."

"Would he be on your list if he arrived late last night?"

"This list was updated at 6 a.m. this morning."

"And it includes all of the detainees, including those in the high security wing?"

With the mention of the high security area, Commander Durkin's internal warning mechanism clicked from 'Yellow' to 'Red'. "This list includes all current detainees as of 6 a.m."

"Would you be willing to verify that for me?"

"Ma'am. This list is less than four hours old and it is current. There is no Michael Walker in the Charleston Consolidated Brig."

Penelope had played chicken with gatekeepers many times before. She felt a rush that had been missing from her life for entirely too long, and decided to drop the bomb no gatekeeper ever wanted to hear.

"You're willing to stake your entire military career over a single phone call?"

A thick silence settled over the room. The Commander's first job was to protect the gate. The second was to protect herself. Commander Durkin blinked. She reached for her phone and dialed an extension. She turned away and spoke too softly for Penelope to hear. Returning the phone to its cradle she said, "There is no Michael Walker in the Charleston Consolidated Brig."

Penelope studied Commander Durkin for several seconds to see if her body language gave any clues as to the veracity of her comment. The Commander was one tough cookie; Penelope knew what it was like to compete in what was usually considered a man's world. She could envision her with stars on her shoulders one day.

"May I speak to your superior, please?"

"Captain Fredrick does not work on Saturdays, but I'm sure you can make an appointment on Monday to see him, ma'am."

Penelope knew when she was beaten and rose to her feet. "Thank you very much. I won't take up any more of your time."

Back outside, as Penelope pulled her keys out of her purse and headed back to her car she kept working the possibilities over in her mind. There were a limited number of options. Walker either was or wasn't in the brig. If he was there, then either Commander Durkin was lying or someone was lying to her. Either seemed plausible. If the government was holding Walker incommunicado, then his name would likely be omitted from anything put in writing. On the other hand, if he wasn't there, then Mark's great tip from his all-powerful source was a dud.

She was so immersed in thought as she drove out of the brig's parking lot that she failed to notice the black Suburban with dark tinted windows pulling out behind her.

CHAPTER FOUR

"There's a world of difference between truth and facts.
Facts can obscure the truth."

Maya Angelou

PENELOPE WAS RELIEVED that traffic was light on I-526. Known as the Mark Clark, it was named after the General who signed the ceasefire agreement with North Korea in 1953, and who served as president of The Citadel from the mid-1950s to the mid-1960s. The highway was a loop of interstate that skirted north of Charleston, allowing people traveling from Savannah to Myrtle Beach the opportunity to avoid the congestion of downtown. Without having to focus so much on her driving, Penelope allowed her mind to work overtime on the task at hand.

She doubted Mark could have gotten it completely wrong; that would have been out of character. He checked, rechecked and verified everything. He could have been misinformed, but he referred to his source as "unimpeachable." Odd choice of words, even for Mark. As Penelope continued to work the angles over and over in her mind she noticed a huge green directional marker that read "I-26 Columbia".

"What the heck," she muttered to herself. "What else do I have to do?" She turned on her right blinker, headed west on I-26, and had gone less than a mile when a foreboding sense that she was not alone in the car hit her like an unexpected chilly breeze. Penelope checked her rearview mirror to be sure there wasn't an axe murderer in the backseat. It was empty. "Get a grip Penelope," she said as she shook her head and refocused on her driving. "I have a good feeling about this. Senator Horn is going to be in his office and there is no one else in the car but me." She checked her rearview mirror again, just to be sure.

Not wanting to be on the road without some traveling money, Penelope exited at Ashley Phosphate and headed toward the Bank of America branch on Rivers Avenue. There were more cars lined up in the drive-through lane at the ATM than she had seen on the Interstate, so she wheeled her precious little hybrid car into a parking space at the front door of the branch. Since it was a Saturday morning and there were so many people waiting to use the ATM she thought the branch was probably closed, but it wasn't. It turned out to be one of only a handful of Bank of America locations in Charleston with Saturday morning banking hours.

≈

A T THE COUNTER *I absently reach for one of the two checkbooks in my purse as I try to shake the feeling that I am not alone. I can feel eyes on me, but turning around, no one is there. Still these odd pulls and tugs make my skin crawl. It was similar to a few minutes earlier in the car only much stronger. I write the check on autopilot as I struggle to understand the emotions and sensations that are sweeping over, around and through me. Maybe I am overwhelmed by being back in the game. Maybe I am losing my mind.*

≈

"M AY I HELP you?" the tall, athletic African-American teller said, as she smiled in Penelope's direction. Penelope placed her check and driver's license on the counter top. The teller examined the check, front and back, and compared the photograph on Penelope's South Carolina driver's license to her face. The picture was three years old and she had dropped nearly 15 pounds in the interim but it still looked enough like the person whose name was on the check to satisfy the teller.

"Would you like that in large bills?" she asked in a surprisingly high voice that didn't match her physique. It seemed like an odd question for a $300 withdrawal, but Penelope nodded that large bills would be fine.

Penelope waited as the teller, for some reason, moved to a different part of the bank. She again allowed her mind to wander. This assignment had dredged up all of the old doubts that had kept her awake at night. Had it been too many years since she had done something like this? How could she compete with reporters who were younger than her children? Obviously this Walker character was involved in something shady or he wouldn't be under arrest; he was wealthy and connected enough for very little to be out of his reach. Did she really want someone like him to even know her name?

Pulling her cell phone from her purse, she dialed the last phone number she had for Senator Horn's Columbia Office. Not surprisingly, being a Saturday, it went straight to voice mail. "What in the world am I doing?" she thought to herself. "I'm planning on driving two hours to arrive unannounced at what would likely be an empty office..." Her chain of thought was broken as the teller began counting $100 bills out on the counter. "Excuse me, what are you doing?"

The teller looked a bit perplexed. "I'm sorry; I thought you said you wanted large bills." Looking over the counter at the check Penelope had handed the teller she was stunned when she noticed the amount on the check was $3,000, not $300. "Where is your brain, Penelope?" she muttered to herself. Instead of making a scene or inflicting further embarrassment upon herself, she decided to redeposit the funds on Monday at her usual West Ashley branch.

"I'm sorry, you're right," Penelope said with a self-conscious smile. The teller hesitated for a moment to be sure, then finished counting out the bills, stuffed them in a narrow white envelope and pushed them in her direction.

After climbing behind the wheel of her Prius, Penelope shook her head. She wasn't sure what was stranger, what had just happened or what she was actually planning to do. Her mind and emotions continued to churn for the two hours it took to drive from Charleston to the Columbia office of Senator Clayton Horn.

In Penelope Spence's mind, politicians pretty much fell into four categories: True Believer, Corrupt, Ambitious, and Serious. The True Believers, whether from the left or the right end of the political spectrum, are the most interesting. They hold strong views which they defend loudly while being impervious to logic or counter arguments. They're always a great source for quotes and fun to poke sticks at by asking loaded questions at press conferences. The most common are the Corrupt and Ambitious types. They're difficult to tell apart until an indictment is handed down.

The rarest form of politician is the Serious. These are men and women who get involved in politics because they love their country and want to give something back. Unlike the rest, they know how to keep a secret. Senator Clayton Horn was a Serious politician. After four terms in the House of Representatives, the good people of South Carolina had seen fit to elect him five times to be their U.S. Senator, each with a larger majority.

With more time on her hands as her kids started to troop off to college and no prospects of gainful employment in journalism on the horizon, she volunteered to help the senator in his last re-election campaign. To her surprise, instead of stuffing envelopes or making phone calls, he hired her to do opposition research. When the campaign ended, he kept her on as a part-time staffer doing background checks from her home in Charleston. Over time her duties expanded to include even more sensitive assignments, including research involving the senator's role on the Select Committee on Intelligence. Getting a Top Secret clearance took some time but was less odious than she had imagined, mostly because all she had done for the previous several decades was raise her family and serve on various charity boards. The required additional 'codeword' levels were another matter entirely. Thirty-six hours of labor for her first daughter had been a snap compared to that process. Horn had already announced that his last campaign would indeed be his last campaign. Penelope found herself being used less and less as the senator's retirement date got closer and he groomed another senator to take his place on the Select Committee.

It had been over a year since Penelope had visited the senator's office. While strongly hoping he would be there, she had no delusions that he would actually be in. The sign on the door indicated that his office was closed on Saturday, which wasn't a good omen. Bracing herself for the worst, she tried the knob on the door and found it unlocked.

Inside was the familiar large room with a half dozen desks, each with stacks of file folders on the corners and computer monitors in the middle. Her previous visits had been during normal hours when the office was a madhouse of activity. Now it was eerily still. Having heard the door open, a grey-haired woman popped her head out of her office; Penelope recognized her immediately as Joan Inman, the senator's long serving chief of staff.

"I'm sorry, but we're not open..." she stopped dead in mid-sentence, stared and blinked. "As I live and breathe," she said with a not too thick but nonetheless charming Southern accent. "Penelope Drayton Spence? Is that you?"

"Hi, Joan!"

Inman held Penelope at arm's length and examined her from head to toe. "I swear; I hate you. You look better now than the last time I saw you. What has it been, a year?"

"At least that..."

"We were just talkin' about you," her Southern accent, like a pot of grits bubbling on the burner, was getting thicker by the second. "Clay! Clay! Look who's come here for a visit!"

Senator Clayton Horn stuck his head out of the office next to his chief of staff's to see what was causing the commotion. The senator looked much older and more tired than the last time she had seen him. There was less hair on top and more lines on his face. He still had those gentle brown eyes that made you trust him instantly, but his skin appeared drawn and had a sallow, grayish cast. There had been rumors that he was in failing health, and seeing him firsthand confirmed them. Instead of being in a suit or blazer, the senator was wearing a golf shirt and Dockers. He always felt a responsibility to wear a coat and tie whenever he was doing government business, so he obviously hadn't expected to see anyone today.

Upon seeing Penelope, his eyes brightened and a huge smile broke across his face. He embraced her with arms that were more frail than she had remembered. "We were just talking about you!"

"That's what I told her, too."

"You are lucky to catch us," the senator said with a warm smile. "We decided to stop by and pick up some stuff at the last minute."

"If you had been five minutes earlier or later, you'd have missed us completely," Inman cooed. "That would have broken my heart."

"What can I do for you?" Horn asked.

"I have a couple of questions for you. Then maybe a favor to ask."

"If there is anyone I owe a favor to it would be you." Senator Horn motioned toward his office and then to one of the comfortable chairs directly across from his massive Carolina pine desk. After they had settled in, the senator's voice softened. "I heard about you and your husband."

Penelope waved it off. "These things happen."

On the wall behind him were framed pictures of the senator with various other politicians, world leaders, and prominent South Carolinians. The one in the center of the maze was a much younger Clayton Horn, probably taken when he was still a congressman. He was in the Oval Office, shaking Ronald Reagan's hand. Sharing the center spotlight of the photo array was a more recent picture of the senator with the Reverend Billy Graham.

Penelope smiled when she noticed that she had made the wall of fame. Up in a corner near the top was a picture of the senator taken at the Rickman's years earlier during a fund raising event. To the senator's right were Josephine, not Joey, and her ex-husband; to his left were Penelope and Bill. They were all beaming and happy. What a difference time made.

The top of his desk was reserved for pictures of his children, grandchildren, and an adorable infant with a pink ribbon on her bald head, who Penelope assumed was a great granddaughter. Joan Inman joined them and perched herself on the corner of the desk, continuing to beam.

"So to what do I owe this visit?"

"I'm working on a story."

"Good for you," Joan said, almost clapping her hands. The senator, on the other hand, became much more serious as his grin melted into a smile.

"What kind of story?"

"I'm looking into the recent activities of Michael Walker."

Horn didn't flinch. "I see."

"You previously had me do some background research on him but since then there are some rumors floating around."

"There are always stories circulating around Washington. I wouldn't put too much stock in an unsubstantiated rumor."

"With your help," Penelope said with a smile, "maybe we can put this one to rest quickly. How well do you know him?"

"Mr. Walker is a very wealthy man and a generous political donor. I would suspect that everyone in Washington knows him, or would like to. Why do you ask?" The smile was completely gone.

"Have you ever heard of the Hermes Project?"

"Why do you ask?"

Always answer a question you want to avoid by asking another question. Political Speak 101.

"You didn't answer my question."

"Nor did you answer mine."

Penelope knew they could parry and thrust all day, but in the end the guy with nearly four decades in Washington wasn't going to be tricked by any questions he didn't want to answer. Penelope had a weak hand, and it wasn't getting any stronger sitting across the table from someone like Horn. She had already shown her two best cards by mentioning Walker and the Hermes Project and Horn hadn't even blinked. Now she only had one good card left, and it might be a joker if Mark's information was wrong. At this point she had nothing to lose and decided to go all in.

"I have been told, from what is considered an unimpeachable source, that Michael Walker was recently detained and transferred to the Charleston Consolidated Brig because of his association with the Hermes Project. I was there today and spoke to a Commander Durkin, who denied that he is being held in their facility."

A heavy silence settled over the room for a few moments. Senator Clayton Horn, never taking his eyes off of Penelope Spence finally said, "Joan, will you excuse us?" After 39 years of working together, the senator's chief of staff knew exactly what the tone of the request meant. She immediately got up and closed the door behind her as she left the room.

"An unimpeachable source," he said, with a laugh. "This is all very interesting, Penelope. Where did you get this information?"

She had obviously hit a nerve. Horn was the ranking Republican on the senate oversight committee that controlled the spending and kept an eye on all of America's intelligence-gathering agencies. He and the other members of the committee had the authority to write whatever number of dollars they felt were needed into the annual federal budget for these agencies. Last year they had written $173 billion dollars on that line and it was approved by both chambers, without debate, and by unanimous consent.

"You know I can't tell you that. What do you know about the Hermes Project, Michael Walker and his being held incommunicado?"

"Can we go off the record?"

"I would prefer we stay on the record."

The senator rose from his chair and extended his right hand. "Then it has been good to see you. As you know I'm not running for re-election so I guess we won't be doing any more fundraisers." Penelope knew exactly what the senator meant. He was grateful for her past generous support, but there were limits to his gratitude.

Penelope didn't move. The problem for Penelope was the senator now knew all of her cards, and she didn't know anymore than when she walked in except that Mark Hatchet's information had been correct. There was a Hermes Project and wealthy industrialist Michael Walker was involved. Plus, Walker was probably in the Charleston Consolidated Brig. If she refused to go off the record now, with the brig denying they had him, the story might end here.

"Okay," Penelope said, her shoulders sagging slightly. She dropped her notepad and pen in her purse. "We're off the record."

CHAPTER FIVE

"Do the things you know, and you shall learn the truth you need to know."

LOUISA MAY ALCOTT

"SO, PENELOPE, WHO gave you this information?" She just shook her head. "For someone living in Charleston, you are remarkably well informed about something that is going on in Washington. This would mean you have an outside source. You need to be aware I could find your source if it becomes important."

Penelope smiled as she wondered who was bluffing now. The senator read her face perfectly. "Since you deal in the written word, it has to be one of five print news organizations. *The New York Times* and *The Boston Globe* are out since they are still nosing around this story, and they would have assigned a staff reporter who would have presented his credentials. That leaves *The Washington Post, Wall Street Journal,* or *L.A. Times.* Since they know their competitors have not honored the government's request to back off the story, they would not want to be caught flatfooted if all heck breaks loose. It would be in their interest to continue working on the story, but they would need to turn it over to someone outside their organization to give them plausible deniability. It would have to be someone good and someone they trust." The senator's eyes bored into Penelope Spence. "Someone they had a personal relationship with." Penelope shifted uncomfortably in her chair. "Someone in one of these three news organizations is going to have a connection to you. Since I influence a large portion of their budget, how long do you think it would take for a certain federal agency to find that person for me?"

Senator Clayton Horn, even in his later years and in declining health, was a formidable force.

"I gave my word..."

Horn held up his hand. "I will not ask you again to violate that trust. I just need you to understand that if I can find your source in less than an hour with a single phone call, so can people who may be less friendly. And I must warn you, by working on this story without the protection of a major news outlet you may be placing yourself in grave peril. There are many people who will go to great lengths to keep what Michael Walker is working on out of the public domain."

Penelope leaned back in her chair as she absorbed the senator's words; he was not a man of hyperbole. What in the world had this Walker character done? "Many is a pretty ambiguous word, senator. Who exactly would go to such lengths to keep this story quiet?"

"By reflex, all of the intelligence agencies want everything classified. They would slap a 'Top Secret, compartmentalized' stamp on the lunch menu at the CIA cafeteria if we let them. But this is different. The rumors surrounding a possible breakthrough in Walker's research have put a scare into some very powerful people."

"For example."

Horn chuckled. "Where to start? First, there would be many of the religious leaders, worldwide. Anyone who is currently in power in any of the governments of any country in the world and, of course, all of the wealthy people on the planet would want this suppressed. There are around seven billion people currently residing on earth, and I would guess that Walker, and to a lesser degree you, should consider about a billion of them as your mortal enemy. Myself, included."

It took Penelope Spence a moment to allow all of this additional information to sink in. Senator Horn was not prone to exaggeration, which lent power to his words. "Why do you include yourself in the group?" she asked softly.

"As you may know, I consider myself a religious man, and I believe what Walker is doing to be sacrilege. I'm the one who put a stop to the project."

"Really? Why?"

"Before I answer that, let me ask you a couple of questions. Do you consider yourself a religious person?"

Penelope Spence leaned back in her chair and studied the senator. He was famous for his strong beliefs, but this seemed an odd question even for an openly devout, born-again Christian. If Penelope had been asked that question two years ago she would have answered with a confident, "no." While she considered herself spiritual and believed in a higher force, the nature of organized religion had always left her cold. But lately she had been feeling a tugging. At first she thought it was the sudden change in her life situation that had rattled her self-confidence, but with each passing day, the pull became stronger. "Yes," she heard herself say.

"Do you attend church regularly?"

"No."

"Is there a reason?"

"Senator, I'm not sure…"

"Please. Just bear with me and this just might turn out to be your lucky day. Is there a reason you don't attend church regularly?"

"I just don't think much of organized religion."

"Why is that?"

Penelope sighed. "Organized religion, with its rigid dogma and antiquated sexist and ethnocentric rules, just doesn't appeal to me."

Senator Horn nodded his head in agreement. "You're not alone. Did you know the fastest growing faith organizations in the United States are non-denominational fellowships where the goal is to speak directly to God without going through the rules of a traditional organized religion?" Horn didn't wait for an answer. "Have odd things started happening to you, things that can't be explained logically?"

"Senator…."

"Please, this is important."

Penelope thought about the risotto, knowing the location of her son's missing dog, and a series of similarly dramatic events that had occurred recently. "Yes, senator, they have."

"That's what I thought. When your name came up this morning for the first time in a year, I knew I would be seeing you soon. Penelope, Michael Walker and the Hermes Project may have set events in motion that, if not stopped, could mean the end of the world as we know it."

The hair stood up on Penelope Spence's arms. Senator Clayton Horn was a devout man. He didn't drink, smoke, womanize or gamble. The worst that had ever been said about him was that he occasionally sang too loud in choir practice. When he took the floor of the U.S. Senate, all conversations ceased and reporters reached for their notebooks. He was a serious man that everyone took seriously. For the senator to verbalize this level of concern to a reporter, even off the record, was stunning.

"What exactly is the Hermes Project?"

"That's on a need to know basis."

"What can you tell me?"

"You can't expect me to honor your clearance when you enter this office as a reporter. At this point, everything I'm going to give you is either a matter of public record or something you could get with a "Freedom of Information Act" request." Horn paused, leaned back in his chair and continued to study her, and the situation carefully, "As I'm sure you know, the government funds thousands of small-scale research projects every year. What you may not know is if we consider the research to be vital to national security we can take control of the project and move it to a top secret lab. In addition to our federal facilities, there is a group of large and small companies that further this type of research for us."

"One of them is Walker Industries."

"They are among the largest. They are currently involved in projects for the Department of Defense and Homeland Security that are so classified they are only referred to by code names, even in our closed committee meetings. Obviously I can't talk about any of those projects with a reporter."

"Are these the 'black' projects I occasionally hear whispers about?"

"That's a bit overwrought. The government is involved in some secret research projects that are performed by private and publicly held companies, with strict oversight."

"What type of research were they doing at the Hermes Project?"

"It was just your basic, garden variety university research grant that started to show some potential, and Homeland Security turned it over to Walker Industries. At some point, Michael Walker took a personal interest in it and then all kinds of strange things began to happen."

"What kind of things?"

Horn shook his finger at Penelope. "I'm already telling you more than I probably should. But knowing you like I do, you'd ferret out the rest soon enough." Penelope felt her cheeks darken slightly from the compliment, though she knew Horn was probably playing her like a well tuned piano. He hadn't spent decades in Washington to have a conversation like this out of the goodness of his heart.

"I received some reports that I found particularly disturbing, and over the strong objections of Homeland Security and some of the others on the committee I used my influence to have the project cancelled. Walker Industries was not happy about this and not only advised that we continue with the research, they recommended strongly we substantially increase the funding. In addition to an impressive list of scientists, Walker himself and an Assistant Director of Homeland Security's Emerging Technologies Division appeared before my committee to try and convince me to withdraw my objection."

"What was your objection?"

"Sorry, that's a bridge too far," Horn said with a shake of his head. "I'd made up my mind and am still convinced it was the right decision. When we cancelled the Hermes Project, I thought that would be the end of it. But Mr. Walker decided to finance the entire project from his personal funds. When I found out what he was doing I moved to reacquire the project..."

"Reacquire?"

"Yes. We always have the option to take back a project even if it has been cancelled."

"Then why haven't you taken this project back?"

Senator's Horn's nostrils flared with anger. "Until two weeks ago, we hadn't been able to locate Walker or any of the original people involved with the research."

"Two weeks? I was under the impression he was arrested just a few days ago."

Senator Horn's cheeks flushed and his eyes narrowed. "I can't comment on that other than to say there have been some complications in detaining Mr. Walker."

"What does that mean?"

"We've had some difficulty holding him in various detainment facilities."

"His lawyers were able to get him out?"

"If only it were that simple."

"What does that mean?"

"It means we've had some difficulty holding him in various detainment facilities."

"Okay," Penelope said with a shrug. "So he was ordered to the Charleston Consolidated Brig?"

"No comment."

"Walker really has gotten under your skin, hasn't he?"

"I think Walker orchestrated the entire defunding of the project just so he could get personal control of it."

"Is he that smart?"

"I think he intentionally provoked me because he knew how I would respond." Horn ran his fingers through his thinning hair. "If I had my way, Walker Industries would lose all of their government contracts. But, his lawyers shielded the corporation from any punitive action and our legal staff hasn't found a way around it, yet."

"I'm guessing he won't be getting any more contracts from your committee."

"I only have one vote on the committee, and I'm a lame duck." Horn sighed as he regained his composure. "He played me beautifully, but I have to admit some of my colleagues on the other side of the aisle seem to be enjoying this a bit too much. As strongly as I feel that Hermes should be buried in a deep hole and forgotten, there are those who believe just as strongly that it is too important to be kept secret."

Horn again nervously ran his fingers through his thinning hair. Was that the senator's "tell" Penelope wondered; the little nervous habit he didn't even know he was doing that would tip his hand? She had never seen him this fidgety. Even if it was, she had no idea what it meant. There was obviously a lot more to this story that he was unable or unwilling to share.

"Well," Horn said with a sigh. "Politics is not for the faint of heart."

"So, let me be sure I have this straight. Walker took this Hermes Project underground to keep you from reacquiring it."

"Yes. He completely funded the project from his personal wealth so Walker Industries was protected. Since we couldn't find him to serve a subpoena or give him a notification of reacquisition, he was technically not even in violation of the law. Now that he has been served and has so far refused to reveal the location of the project, we've been able to employ the full force of the federal government in the search for his lab, even though he still hasn't broken any laws."

"What do you mean?"

"As with all legal documents, there is a time frame for compliance. He has 30 days to turn over the Hermes Project and is still within the grace period."

In deference to Senator Horn, Penelope fought the urge to smile; but she had to respect Walker. Whatever he was up to, to have so thoroughly flummoxed one of the most powerful figures on Capitol Hill was no small feat.

"Does the government still have an interest in reacquiring the Hermes Project?"

"When I realized we'd been had by Walker, we attempted to revive the program using the original data and techniques, but we failed miserably. Apparently, this is quite common for this type of research."

"So you won't tell me why the Hermes Project was cancelled?"

"No. Even if you were working for me on this, the actual research and the reason for the cancellation are outside your clearance. Besides, it may all be moot soon."

"What does that mean?"

"The Executive Branch is ready to declassify, but they won't do it without the approval of the oversight committee and Homeland Security."

"Can't they declassify something whenever they want?"

"Technically, yes. But from a practical standpoint it would be potential political suicide. They're looking for some cover in case this blows up in their faces. Walker can be pretty slippery and no one is completely sure what he's up to."

"How does your committee feel?"

"They're in the same boat as the administration. No one wants to be on the wrong side of this one in an election year. But, Walker's influence only goes so far and until I'm replaced on the committee next January, I hold the swing vote."

"So with one phone call you could declassify the Hermes Project?"

"The administration will still need the buy in from Homeland Security. I seriously doubt they would declassify without it." Senator Clayton Horn shook his head. "I would give anything to know if the rumors are true."

Penelope, tired of talking in circles, paused for a moment before something occurred to her. "If Michael Walker is still in the 30-day grace period for compliance, why has he been arrested?"

"He hasn't been arrested. He has been detained."

"Okay. Why has Michael Walker been detained?"

"Homeland Security was able to convince a judge that Walker was a potential threat to national security and a flight risk, so a sealed warrant was issued giving them the right to detain him until the 30 day grace period is up."

"Arrested, detained. It sounds like a difference without a distinction. What will it take for him to get released?"

"He will have to tell us where he moved the Hermes Project, and what he's been up to for the past six months. We also want to know the whereabouts of all of the missing people. A number of them have extremely high security clearances and inside knowledge of many very sensitive projects."

"Do you have sealed warrants out for them?"

"No comment."

"Do you think Walker would have harmed them in any way?"

"I'm a pretty good judge of people, but he is tough to read. I'm guessing that they are fine and will be as long as he still needs them."

"That sounds menacing."

"It wasn't intended to be. It's just that Michael Walker is one of the most exasperating people I've ever come across."

"What do you mean?"

"In one breath, he is the most charming man I've ever met, but before long I feel like I'm in the middle of an Abbot and Costello routine trying to figure out who is on first."

"I don't understand."

"For an obviously well-educated man he has some of the most bizarre ideas I've ever heard."

"I'll have to take your word for that, senator."

"I might be able to help you there."

"How so?"

"If we can come to an understanding, I might be able to assist you with your story."

"What kind of understanding?"

"All I want to know is where all of his people have gone and what he has been doing for the past six months."

"That's the story I'm trying to write."

"I know."

"You'll be able to read all about it if I succeed."

"So you agree that we share the same interests and there would be no conflict in providing me with everything you discover?"

"After publication."

"How about a few hours before you go to press so I can be ready?"

"No prior censorship?"

"I give you my word."

"What's in this for me?" Penelope asked.

Senator Horn's eyes twinkled.

CHAPTER SIX

"It takes two to speak the truth: one to speak, and another to hear."

HENRY DAVID THOREAU

PENELOPE SPENCE WAS delighted to see that Commander Durkin was still on duty and in her office. It had been a while since she had been so roundly dismissed by a mid-level bureaucrat while working on a story. These little gnomes, toiling in obscurity safely away from the glare of a spotlight and scrutiny could, at their whim, make life either miserable or simple for the people who wandered into their domain in search of approval.

The Commander frowned when she noticed Penelope standing near the main entrance as if waiting for someone. Visiting hours were over, and other than a few members of the cleanup crew and a stray officer or two, the expansive waiting area was empty. Durkin sighed. She thought she had made her position clear. Commander Durkin was nearly to her feet when the front door opened and two Navy Master Chiefs entered and surveyed the room. "What the..."

Before she reached her office door one of the military policemen shouted. "ATTENTION! Admiral on Deck!"

Commander Durkin's heart skipped a beat when Air Force Brigadier General Stanley Gibson, Commander of the Charleston Air Force Base and Rear Admiral Joseph Saunders, Commandant of Naval Weapons Station Charleston strode purposefully through the door. In their wake were eight more officers, half Air Force, half Navy, including her CO Captain Fredrick. All were above her pay grade. Everyone in the area immediately snapped to attention and froze in place like statues. Admiral Saunders eyed the room and barked, "At ease." No one relaxed. Senator Horn and Joan Inman were the last to arrive and huddled immediately with the two senior military men and Penelope Spence. Admiral Saunders said something to Captain Fredrick who pointed toward Durkin's office. All eyes turned toward the Commander. Like a wave they moved in her direction; Durkin had to force herself not to tremble.

"Commander Durkin," Admiral Saunders barked.

"Sir."

"Did you tell this woman that Michael Walker is not in the Charleston Consolidated Brig?"

"Yes sir."

"Why?"

"His name was not on my list, sir."

The Admiral held out his hand. Durkin, confused and terrified, didn't move. "Sir?"

"Show me the damned list Commander."

"Yes sir." She turned crisply, returned with a copy of the list and held it out for the Admiral. He snatched it and read it over. "At ease Commander," Saunders said, handing the list to Senator Horn. "His name is not on it."

"What kind of operation are you running here, Joe?" General Gibson asked, furious that his presence had been requested when this was obviously a Navy screw-up. All eyes turned back to Durkin.

"Commander, who omitted Michael Walker's name from the list?"

Before she could answer a voice from across the room said, "That would be me."

All heads turned in the direction of the voice but only Rear Admiral Saunders spoke. "And who the hell are you?"

Before he could answer, Senator Horn said with a crooked smile, "Assistant Director Robert A. Smith, of Homeland Security."

"Senator," Smith said, with a nod.

Senator Horn answered, "Robert. I'm surprised to see you here."

"Not nearly as surprised as I am to see you."

"I can imagine."

"Are we done here?" Admiral Saunders asked. "I'd like to get back to my grandson's birthday party." Saunders was still steaming. You could count on one hand the number of people who had the authority to order him to accompany Senator Horn to the brig on short notice on a Saturday afternoon, and most of those would have gotten at least a few questions. When he'd recognized the voice calling, only two words were required on the Admiral's part. "Yes" and "Sir."

"That depends," Senator Horn said as he eyed Smith.

"Depends on what?" Saunders barked.

"On whether or not Director Smith plans to try and stop us from seeing Michael Walker."

The Admiral turned toward the two armed Master Chiefs that had accompanied them. "If that man," he pointed to Smith, "gives Senator Horn any problems, you are authorized to do whatever is necessary to remove him from this facility."

The two burly enlisted men smiled as they sized up Smith, "Yes, sir."

Joan Inman tapped Senator Horn on the shoulder and handed him a cell phone. "The Secretary of Homeland Security."

Horn smiled as he watched Smith squirm. "Bill. Sorry to bother you on a weekend. I'm at the Charleston Consolidated Brig and I want to chat with Michael Walker." Horn laughed. "Yes, he is still here. I want to have a part-time reporter, part-time staffer of mine, Penelope Spence, accompany me in for the chat." Horn laughed again. "Pulitzer Prize winner, actually, but she does have top secret clearance with a variety of codeword riders, and she's agreed to go off the record...Well, if she found out where he is you can bet the rest of the posse isn't far behind... Trying to put a lid on a boiling pot only makes it worse, Bill... Right... The way I see it you've got two choices. You can tell me no, and I spend the rest of my time in office making your life a living hell, or, you can honor my request and we'll have a nice little off the record chat with Walker to try and see what he's been up to... No. She already knew he was here. There is no way to suppress that you've detained one of the richest men in the world. That's tomorrow's front page... Yes, she knows about Hermes too but by name only. No details... I agree... that works for me. Hold on. Penelope, any conversations you're privileged to here in the brig are off the record until I release you." Penelope nodded affirmatively. "You have to say it."

Horn held the phone up to Penelope's mouth. "This is Penelope

Drayton Spence. Anything I hear in the brig is off the record, until I get a release from Senator Horn." Her eyes danced, deciding to push the envelope. "As long as I get fifteen minutes alone with Michael Walker."

Clayton Horn laughed as he pressed the phone back to his ear. "Yes, she is... I'll tell her." Horn passed the phone over to Robert Smith. "Your boss wants to talk to you." Smith moved away from the group and talked too softly for anyone to hear.

"Tell her what?" Penelope asked.

"Your fifteen minutes is also off the record until I release you, and he would like to meet you sometime."

Robert Smith handed the phone back to Horn, who passed it along to his Chief of Staff. "Senator, Ms. Spence, right this way."

After passing through a series of checkpoints and locked doors, Penelope Spence saw Michael Walker in person for the first time through one-way glass. He was dressed in an orange jumpsuit, sitting with his eyes closed and his hands folded and handcuffed together on the tabletop. He looked bigger than she had expected from the photos. His hair was shorter and he had a healthy dark tan. She was startled when he suddenly opened his eyes and appeared to stare straight at her, then at Senator Horn.

"Get used to it. He does stuff like that all the time." Smith held the door open for the senator and Penelope. Horn blocked Smith from entering the room. "We'll take it from here, Robert," Horn said. "And turn off all of your recording equipment."

"Yes sir."

Horn glared at Walker. When it was clear that no introduction was forthcoming, Penelope said, "I'm Penelope Spence."

Walker didn't speak, but he studied the woman in front of him carefully. She was younger than him, but not by much, fit and healthy. She had hips that were slightly broader than would be expected from a woman of her height and weight. Probably the residual of bearing three children combined with losing some weight recently. He liked her eyes; pale blue, they were the perfect combination of kind and smart. She had the scent of a recently converted vegetarian who occasionally broke down and made a run to the local Hardees for a "Thick Burger." Her skin tone and texture showed she got some sun but not too much, drank plenty of water, and didn't smoke. So far, she was perfect.

Horn pulled a small device out of his pocket that appeared to be a digital recorder and sat it the middle of the table, then pushed the power button.

≈

Assistant Director Robert Smith was in the control room that adjoined the interrogation room. His instructions had been unambiguous. The Secretary wanted to know what was said in that room. On the multiple screens he had clear views of several different angles of Michael Walker, Senator Horn and Penelope Spence. A variety of video and audio recording devices were capturing every word. Smith watched as the senator placed what appeared at first to be a digital recorder between them. As soon as he hit the record button the entire video monitor array began to flicker and distort. The Petty Officer in charge of capturing an audio record of the interview whipped his headphones off and threw them to the floor. Even from six feet away, Smith could hear the crackling and the high pitched buzz.

Stating the obvious, the Petty Officer said, "That's not a digital recorder, it's a jamming device."

"No kidding," Smith answered. He had underestimated the senator.

"Would you like me to go in and remove it, sir?"

"That's a great idea." The Petty Officer began to rise to his feet. "Sit down," Smith barked, "and try to filter out the interference." He knew he couldn't just waltz in and ask the senator to turn off his jamming device because it was causing him problems recording a conversation he had agreed not to record.

≈

"It's good to see you again, senator." Walker's voice was deep and calm, almost soothing.

"I wish I could say the same, Mr. Walker. I've seen enough of you to last a lifetime."

Michael Walker nodded toward the electronic device in the center of the table. "Is that the one I gave you?"

"Yes."

"We have a new prototype that's a bit smaller. I'll have..."

"Don't bother." Horn's tone was the exact opposite of Walker's; he was agitated and hostile. "Is the rumor true?"

"Which rumor?"

"Don't be coy with me, Walker. I don't care who your friends are." Horn's face was flushed and the vein in his neck was throbbing. "You know exactly what I'm asking. Did. You. Do. It?"

"Yes."

Horn slammed his fist on the table. "Damn it!" The senator shot to his feet and began pacing. "You told me you thought it was a decade or more away."

"It likely would have been if we had stuck to Homeland Security's leisurely pace."

Horn began pacing in a tight circle with his hands locked behind his back. "Damn it!" he screamed. In the adjoining room Smith didn't need a working microphone to understand this part of the conversation.

"Do you remember your promise?" Walker asked.

Senator Horn turned and put his hands on the table and leaned so close to Walker their noses almost touched. "Of course I remember my promise, you manipulative bastard. You've orchestrated this from the beginning, haven't you?"

Walker had barely moved since they had entered the room. Having another person in his personal space didn't seem to bother him one bit. His voice was calm; his eyes seldom blinked. "You of all people know this is too big for one person to orchestrate. The wheels are already turning and if we don't get out in front of this, someone else will."

Horn turned ashen. "You're saying the bowls are coming off the shelf and there is nothing we can do?"

"Those are your words not mine, Senator."

Horn's shoulders sagged and his breathing was labored. He braced himself on the desk as he muttered a personal prayer.

"Senator? Are you all right?" Penelope asked, as she helped steady the elderly statesman. He seemed to be getting older and weaker before her eyes. He waved her away and glared at Walker.

"Will you keep your promise, or not?" Walker asked again.

Senator Horn returned to pacing and continued whispering a prayer that only he could hear or understand. Penelope had moved beyond being stunned by Senator Horn's outburst to feeling concern for the old man's health. "Sir, you really need to calm down."

Senator Clayton Horn, facing the one-way mirror, stopped and composed himself. He drew in a deep breath, adjusted his tie and ran his fingers through his thinning hair.

He turned and locked eyes with Walker. "Yes. I'll keep my promise, but you still have to get past Shepherd at Homeland Security. He'll never agree to it. Never."

"Let me worry about Director Shepherd," Walker said calmly.

"You had better start worrying about me. With you locked up, I'll tell the truth before you can start telling your lies." He let the threat dangle before turning his focus to Spence.

"You don't want to end your career like this senator," Walker said gently. "The same confidentiality rules apply to you that apply to me. Give me a week. With her help..."

Again Senator Clayton Horn's face flushed with anger. "If you think I'm going to let you control the release of this story, you're out of your mind." Horn turned his attention back to Spence. "I promised you fifteen minutes alone with Walker. He's all yours. At noon tomorrow I'm authorizing you to use anything you have seen or heard for whatever purpose you choose. I'll have Joan email you an acknowledgement."

Penelope Spence motioned toward Walker. "What about his arrest and detention?"

"You found that out on your own and it is not classified. Homeland Security will try to stop you from reporting about this but they know all they can do is buy themselves a few hours. The genie is out of the bottle on this part of it. However, if you attempt to say anything about the Hermes project before I go public tomorrow you could find yourself in a cell next to his."

"But, senator..." Horn cut her off with the wave of his hand.

Turning back to Walker, he said, "I'll pray every night that I never have to see you again." With that, Senator Clayton Horn turned and stormed out of the room. Through the open door Penelope watched the senator stomp toward the exit without looking back.

Despite the quality of the air-conditioning in the room, Penelope Spence's mouth was dry and her underclothes were damp. What had Walker done? She had a pretty good idea about the senator's promise; he was going to withdraw his objection to declassifying the Hermes Project.

But, what was the meaning of "the bowls" that nearly sent the senator into cardiac arrest. Her thoughts were broken by the sound of Michael Walker's voice.

"Well played, Ms. Spence. I wasn't expecting you for a few more days."

"You were expecting me?"

"Yes."

"Me, personally?"

"Yes."

"Have we ever met?"

"I'm sure I would have remembered if we had."

"Before I walked through that door, did you know my name or anything about me?"

"Yes. I have a complete dossier on you." Penelope Spence was becoming more unnerved with each passing moment, but was not quite sure she believed him. Walker read her expression perfectly. "Interesting, you didn't use the Drayton part of your name when you introduced yourself. I imagine it opens a lot of doors for you in Charleston."

Now Penelope was starting to panic. A man handcuffed to a table in a high security prison, who she had just witnessed reducing one of the most powerful men in the U.S. Senate to Jell-O knew her name and claimed he had been expecting her. This man, who was at the center of a government cover-up and was potentially responsible for the disappearance of over 30 people, and who was up to his elbows in a covert research project had a file on her. What had Mark gotten her into? Trying to maintain her composure she placed her hands in her lap so Walker couldn't see them shaking.

"You only have fourteen minutes left, Ms. Spence. I would suggest you start asking your questions.

"What just happened with Senator Horn?"

"The senator and I had a disagreement."

"That's putting it mildly. Did the senator promise to support declassifying the Hermes Project if you had the breakthrough?"

Michael Walker leaned back in his chair and smiled. "I knew you were the right choice."

Penelope ignored the compliment and plowed ahead. "Was that what he promised?"

Walker nodded his head, "That is exactly what Senator Horn promised."

"So," Penelope said, as she felt the interview getting some traction. "What was the breakthrough?"

"I'm afraid that would take more than your allotted fifteen minutes to explain, and most of it wouldn't make any sense to you."

"Fair enough. Why are you under arrest?'

"I'm not. I'm being detained."

"What does that mean?"

"Someone considers me a threat to national security."

"Why?"

"Probably because of some of the work I've been doing."

"What kind of work?"

"The Hermes Project."

"I see. But you've never been convicted of a crime?"

"No."

"Have you ever been charged with a crime?"

"I've had a few speeding tickets, does that count?"

"Not enough to get you handcuffed to this table, unless you were going really fast." Walker smiled and Penelope's skin started to crawl again. "How did you know I was coming?"

"Because I needed you and I asked you to come."

"You needed me and you asked me to come?"

"Yes."

"I don't remember getting your invitation."

"Apparently you got my request."

"How do you figure that?"

A broad smile covered Walker's face. "You're here."

Penelope stared at Walker trying to decide if he was serious or just nuts. The smart money was on the latter. "What do you need me to do?"

"We need you to write a story about us."

"Who is us?"

"The Hermes Project."

"I thought it had been cancelled by the federal government."

"They cancelled their financial support, but the project is ongoing. You already knew that."

"And you're now personally providing the funding?"

"Yes, but you already knew that as well."

"So, what exactly is the Hermes Project?"

"You're not ready to hear that answer yet."

"What?"

"I could give you a full and complete answer, but you wouldn't believe me."

"Try me."

"No, we really don't have the time now. But I'll make you a deal. I'll answer any questions you have for me, with one caveat. I may not immediately answer a specific question at the moment you ask it if I feel you are not ready for the answer. But I will eventually answer all of your questions."

"Is there a timeframe regarding when you will answer my questions?"

"That will depend on you."

"I don't understand. What does that mean?"

"See. There is a perfect example."

"Example of what?"

"An example of why I may not be able to answer a question when you ask it. You will not be ready to understand my answer."

Penelope bristled. Who did this man think he was? "Are you saying I'm not bright enough to talk to you?"

"Goodness, no. Just the opposite. People with healthy well-developed egos, especially those that are well-read, sometimes are the toughest for me to communicate with. It's because you are so smart that you will have some difficulty unlearning the things you must let go of before you'll be able to truly hear what I'm saying."

Penelope studied Walker for a moment. He didn't appear to be combative and seemed to be sincere. "What are you saying, then?"

"Sometimes it's harder to show a genius a truth than it is to show it to a fool. A fool won't have as many preconceived notions that the genius will feel the need to defend. There are things you know, or think you know, that your mind will refuse to release without a struggle. At present, your mind will refuse to allow you to believe many of the things I'm going to tell you. But you should be able to increasingly grasp them soon."

"You be sure to let me know when we reach a subject my mind won't let me grasp, okay?"

"Sure."

Penelope studied Walker. Again, there was no malice in his comment, as well as no apparent appreciation for sarcasm. "What was the deal with the bowls?"

"Later," Walker said. "Do you still dance?"

Penelope blinked a few times to be sure she hadn't stumbled into the dayroom of the bi-polar wing at an asylum. Walker seemed to shift seamlessly from rational thought to incomprehensible bouts of gibberish. "Where did that come from?"

"I was just curious. I noticed your degree was in journalism with a minor in dance. I thought that was an odd combination. Do you still dance?"

Penelope leaned back in her chair and forced herself to close her mouth. She had to say one thing for Walker, he had done his homework. At twenty-one, living a short subway ride from Broadway, for the briefest moment she had considered a career as a dancer. Her better judgment won out and she stuck with journalism. After college her husband had little interest in, and even less talent on, the dance floor so she seldom got the chance.

"Not as much as I would like."

"Too bad. Dancing is good for the soul. In some religions dancing... "

"Let's see if we can get back on topic. Could you give me an example of something I won't be ready to believe?"

"Sure. You have started to develop skills and knowledge about the power of thought that you do not understand, and instead of accepting the changes you're finding them unsettling. You may even be frightened of them."

"Frightened?"

"Yes. You are starting to see the world and your place in it in an entirely new light, and it is challenging your logical mind. I could explain what's happening to you, but you're not ready to believe me."

Penelope knit her brow as she studied Walker. Not only did he know an awful lot about her, it was almost as if he knew what she was going through. This was silly. It reminded her of the way scam artists hook people. Throw out a few vague observations, then read your reaction. She was not going to fall for it, especially not from a guy handcuffed to a table.

"Can you be a bit more specific?"

"Sure. Odd things are starting to happen around you, and you're remembering things differently than others who share experiences with you..."

"What are you talking about?"

Walker smiled. "For me it was peanut M&Ms."

CHAPTER SEVEN

"Change is inevitable, except from vending machines."

ROBERT C. GALLAGHER

"Peanut M&Ms?"

"Yes. But with everyone it's different."

"What in the world are you talking about?"

"Have you ever gone into a restaurant or grocery store where you know they have a specific food that you really like, but they never seem to have it when you're there?"

Penelope's mind flashed to the great grits/risotto incident the day before, but she wasn't about to tell him how close to the mark he was. "I have no idea what you're talking about."

"Mine was peanut M&Ms. Every store I went to was always sold out."

"You are a very odd person."

"I've been told that before."

"I don't doubt it for a moment."

"Back to M&Ms. Food is an essential of life and the different elements of your mind want to control it. One part of your brain wants something sweet, while another part knows it's bad for you and wants you to avoid it. When they get into conflict, the power of thought just makes it go away."

"Do you know how ridiculous that sounds?"

"Not if you're dying to have a peanut M&M."

"So all of my problems are related to food?"

"Now who's being ridiculous?"

"What?"

"You asked me for examples of things you wouldn't understand and I gave you a general one and a more specific one. I gave no indication that it was an exhaustive list."

"Oh, so there is a list now? And you have all of the answers to my problems."

"Of course not."

"That's reassuring."

"Only you can answer some of the questions."

"So I already have some of the answers."

"All of them, actually. But your mind won't let you accept them yet."

"Yet?"

"Yes."

Penelope propped her elbows on the table, placed her hands under her chin and stared at Walker. He seemed completely sincere. Crazy as a March Hare, but sincere. "If I already have all of the answers, why do I need you?"

"Excellent question. In theory you don't need me at all. There have been many cases where people simply stumble into enlightenment without even realizing it."

"Enlightenment?"

"I told you, you wouldn't believe me."

"You're right, I don't believe you."

"You need to, and pretty quickly. Being around me, even for a short period of time, has been shown to accelerate the growth process. This will put you at risk."

"Just being in your presence is all it takes, huh? No shortage of ego, I see." Walker smiled but didn't answer. "Ok, I'll play along... what kind of risk?"

"Thought is thought. There is no good or evil. A negative thought carries the same moral authority as a positive one. You're in the early stages, and have not yet learned to control your emotions or how to protect yourself from thoughts you don't want. Emotionally charged negative thoughts tend to be more strongly felt than positive ones. You run the risk of manifesting something that you really don't intend or want for yourself or those around you. You need to be very careful."

"So think nothing but happy thoughts."

"Well, preferably positive ones. Especially ones involving uplifting emotions such as love, peace, or joy." Obviously Walker was sarcasm challenged. "Or just think, 'cancel, cancel' after a negative thought."

"Cancel, cancel?"

"Yes."

This interview was not going at all as she had expected. The few questions she had asked and the off the wall answers she had gotten in return had already caused her mind to begin to create a long list of additional questions. She was starting to understand the senator's warning about him being exasperating. "Positive thoughts; cancel cancel, got it." Penelope was starting to feel like she had fallen down a rabbit hole and was now having tea with the Mad Hatter. Then something occurred to her. "Is the uncontrolled acceleration of the, what did you call it, the growth process, what happened on the Hermes Project?"

A broad grin spread across Walker's face as he nodded his approval.

"What?"

"Excellent deduction. That is exactly what happened on the Hermes Project. We inadvertently allowed people to develop too quickly."

"What happened to them?"

Walker's shoulders slumped and his face grew dark. "It was bad, but I'll explain that in due course. Why don't we get to the questions you really want to ask?"

"Okay. Tell me about the Hermes Project and what methods you used to obtain mind control."

"Methods? Mind Control?"

"Chemicals, electric shock, mind-altering drugs?"

"Wow. You make it sound like we're reenacting the CIA's experiments in the 50's and 60's with LSD and drug addicts, prostitutes, prisoners and mental patients."

"When the government is spending this much time and effort to keep something secret, it has been my experience that it is not usually good."

"Have you considered the possibility we stumbled upon something that could change the world for the better but scares the daylights out of a bunch of powerful people who only want to protect the status quo?"

Of all the scenarios she had contemplated while driving back from Columbia, she had to admit this one had not crossed her mind. "What did you discover?" Walker made a face. "Wait! Wait! Let me guess? You can't tell me that yet."

"If I told you we had found a new path to enlightenment that didn't require decades of meditation and prayer, would you believe it?"

"Probably not."

"How about if I told you we have opened a door that will change the entire world as you know it, would you believe that?"

"Definitely not."

"There you have it; I can't answer all of your questions right now."

"Because my mind would refuse to believe your answers?"

"It just did."

She studied Walker for a few seconds as she tried to decide what approach would be the best to get the most information in the shortest amount of time. He had the kind eyes and serene smile of someone totally at ease with himself. Despite her strong initial misgivings, she felt herself not only starting to like this man with the annoying speaking style, but also beginning to feel that he was someone she might be able to trust.

"Would my mind be able to comprehend what you were doing before you made your earth-shattering discovery?"

"I didn't make it. Dr. Carl Altman did the basic research..."

"Who is Dr. Carl Altman?"

"He's a professor of physics specializing in quantum mechanics and chaos theory at California Institute of Technology, and a Nobel Prize-winning scientist. He's actually the one who started the project; I came in later."

"How did you get involved?"

"The decision was made to move the Hermes Project away from the college campus and turn it over to the research wing of one of my companies... "

"That would be the ultra secret group that does work for the Defense Department?"

"This was a request from Homeland Security, not the DoD. Have you always been a conspiracy nut, or is this something you've just recently acquired?"

"During my formative years we had the Vietnam War and Watergate. Forgive me for having a healthy dose of skepticism towards government."

"Healthy? Hmm. Why is it you reporters seem to think everyone in

Washington is channeling Richard Nixon?"

"Because all too often they are. Can we get back to the Hermes Project?"

"Okay. After we had taken over the project, I personally got involved."

"What about it interested you?"

Walker let out a deep sigh. "Let me try to put this in terms you'll be ready to accept. If I start to leave you behind, let me know."

"Okay."

"Two hundred years ago, if you wanted to go from New York City to San Francisco you either spent many months walking or riding a horse across the entire North American continent, or you risked taking a ship all the way around the tip of South America. Both choices were fraught with danger. Today, you can get on a plane with the biggest risk being that you might get stuck next to a crying child for six hours."

"Is there a point somewhere in my future?"

"The point is this. The road to enlightenment has always been either long and difficult, or totally random and immediate. For seekers it often requires decades of commitment to meditation, ritual, or prayer. Many, if not most, people who commit their entire lives to pursuing it never get there. Others who are not pursuing it, and probably have never thought about it, just randomly have it happen. In either case, we're talking about a very small percentage of the overall population, probably far less than one percent. What we're trying to do is use the explosion of knowledge that has occurred in the past 100 years to make the trip easier. Why walk when you can ride? Why ride when you can fly?"

"Do you know how silly that sounds?"

"Maybe now, but hopefully that will change soon."

CHAPTER EIGHT

"Not creating delusions is enlightenment."

Bodhidharma

Penelope stared at Walker looking for a tell or change of expression that would tip his real thoughts, but couldn't find one. If he was lying or pulling her leg, it wasn't on his face. "Where is Dr. Altman now, and the staff for the Hermes Project?"

"They are working at a secret location."

"Why secret?"

"If you want to do research on the government's nickel you have to play by their rules. Every federally funded research project can be taken over at any time and for any reason. But you already knew that."

Penelope ignored his comment. "And you were afraid they would seize your work?"

"They had already done it once; we were all hoping it would be cancelled so we could get it away from the government and into private hands."

"So you admit you intentionally manipulated Senator Horn to take control of the project."

"I suppose from your viewpoint that is how it would appear."

"What in the world does that mean?"

"A group of enlightened people wanted the project out of the hands of the government and it is now out of the hands of the government. To your mind it would appear to be manipulation to mine it is a perfectly logical outcome."

Penelope shook her head and sighed. "Where is this group of enlightened people now?'

"We took everyone involved with the basic research and moved them out of reach of Homeland Security and the guys at Ft. Meade."

"I see. So they are all fine?"

"Of course they are." Walker was a bit taken back. "Do you actually think I would hurt any of them? What kind of a person do you think I am?"

"Oh, I don't know. The kind that wears an orange jumpsuit and is handcuffed to a table in the high security wing of one of our nation's most secure prisons."

Walker pondered her comment for a moment, and then started laughing. It was a throw your head back, straight from the belly laugh that filled the room. He laughed so hard tears glistened in his eyes. "You do have a point. But you need to understand this is all being done for your benefit."

"What?"

"If I had shown up at your door and said I needed you to write a story about a highly classified government project and that, by the way, Homeland Security is looking for me. What would you have done?"

"Called 911."

"Exactly." He let her process this tidbit for a moment.

"So, you're saying you intentionally allowed yourself to get captured just so you could meet me under the right circumstances?"

Walker smiled.

As she gathered her thoughts, Penelope closed her eyes and drew in a large draught of air through her nose, feeling it tingle in her forehead before descending down her spine. While only in this relaxed state for a matter of seconds, she felt the tension leave her shoulders as her body relaxed. When she opened her eyes she found Walker staring at her with a wry smile.

"How long have you been able to do that?"

"Do what?"

"That was pretty advanced Integral yoga."

Penelope was stunned. How could this man possibly know what had just happened to her? "I just closed my eyes for a moment and relaxed."

"You must have an excellent teacher."

Penelope was nonplussed. "I almost always meditate alone and I don't really have a teacher."

Walker drew in a breath to speak but thought better of it and smiled instead. "That makes what you did even more remarkable."

The two stared at each other in an awkward silence for several seconds. "Can we get back to the Hermes Project?" Spence asked.

"Okay."

"Where did it start to go wrong?"

"The day Homeland Security got involved."

"Explain."

"Dr. Carl Altman was doing some remarkable research on expanding human consciousness using sophisticated direct brain stimulation interfaced with fMRI technology to monitor...."

"fMRI?"

"Sorry. Functional Magnetic Resonance Imaging. I don't want to go into too much detail, but the short version is he was able to track different brain activity and was, and is, working on ways to stimulate or cause different sections of the brain to relax or synchronize in certain ways."

"No drugs?"

"Nothing sinister, Ms. Spence."

"Penelope."

"Michael." They both nodded their agreement.

"Dr. Altman was getting mixed results, depending on the person who was involved in the testing. Those who had studied yoga or were creative did better than those who were less flexible in body and mind. He had a couple of people who showed completely unexpected results, and that was enough to get the attention of someone at Homeland Security."

"What kind of unexpected results?"

"In due course Ms... Penelope. At that point the government stepped in and turned the project over to us. At first it was welcomed by Dr. Altman because it meant more funding and better equipment." Walker paused, his face grew more stern, and he shook his head. Penelope noticed the change.

"What?"

"I wish I had found Altman before Homeland Security. I could have financed the entire project and avoided a lot of pain and aggravation."

"What did Homeland Security do?"

"They wanted to use Dr. Altman's techniques to 'improve the quality' of our law enforcement people. He was able to take a sample group of trainees fresh out of one of Homeland Security's training academies and basically teach them techniques to help overcome fears, control emotions, and exhibit more self-control."

"So far, I don't see any problems with this."

"Hang on, we're getting there. Then someone came up with the bright idea of sending Altman the best of the best. People from Homeland Security's various elite SWAT, tactical, and counter terrorism units, who already had these skills, to see what would happen. That was when the wheels started to come off. These people had spent so much time grounding themselves in objective reality that they were not ready to have their consciousness radically altered in the ways Hermes was experimenting with. It was an unmitigated disaster."

"And these were already well-trained law enforcement officers and special agents?"

"Exactly.

"Did any of them leave the facility?"

"No."

"Were they a threat to the civilian population in any way?"

"The only threat they presented was to themselves."

"I don't understand."

"I know. Let's just say there are doors in the mind that need to be opened voluntarily, and that should never be forced open until it is time."

"Time for what?"

"Time for them to be opened."

"That's very Zen but not very enlightening."

"Actually it's very enlightening."

"Let me guess. This will make sense later, after I've opened a few more doors in my own mind."

Walker smiled again.

Now Penelope was convinced that Michael Walker had zero appreciation for sarcasm. "What happened next?"

"That was when Senator Horn cancelled the funding."

"I see. One thing still confuses me."

"Only one?"

Penelope laughed. Maybe he had a sense of humor after all. "Where does Senator Horn fit into all of this? What did he object to in the

Hermes Project, and why the personal animus towards you?"

"Well, there was a completely unexpected side effect."

"What was that?"

"Me."

"You?"

"Yes, me."

"Care to explain that?"

"When people are around me they begin to act differently."

"I can believe that," Penelope muttered under her breath.

"What does that mean?"

"I'm a non-violent person who has only known you for fifteen minutes, but I've already had the urge to strangle you a couple of times."

Walker chuckled and shrugged.

"I'm assuming other people have a different reaction to being around you?"

"Yes. There are those who are already on the path and I seem to illuminate it in a way that makes their journey easier. If you continue to spend time around me you'll start seeing the effects."

"So you think I'm on the path to enlightenment?"

"We all are, in one form or another."

"Okay. I still don't see the problem with Senator Horn."

"Because of some of the things that have happened, he considers me at best a cult leader and at worst a false prophet."

"A false prophet? Why would he think that?"

Walker sighed and leaned back in his chair. "You have to understand that we were doing some very high-end research on the functionality of the human nervous system. Our results were so stunning that two schools of thought formed. The first was that this was too important to keep secret, and the other that it was too dangerous to release. That argument is still raging."

"That doesn't explain the personal animus Horn showed toward you."

"One of the people at Homeland Security wrote an evaluation of the project, and he speculated that I might be an outlier or an extreme deviation from the mean."

"You and every other billionaire. Why is that a problem?"

"When the senator asked him to name previous outliers he gave some examples that really upset Horn."

"Who did he name?"

"Moses, Jesus, Mohammad, Buddha — pretty much all of these types of religious leaders throughout history."

A short whistle escaped from Penelope's lips. "I'm guessing Horn didn't take that too well?"

"That would be a mild understatement," Walker said as he rubbed his chin. "It was meant to be illustrative, that down through history there have been some that see the world differently and who attract followers. He could have made the same point with secular or lesser known examples. Horn went out of his mind and immediately accused me of trying to play God."

"Were you?"

"Of course not. But after he read that report he never trusted me again. He became hyper-paranoid about me and my contact with the governments of Europe."

"Why?"

"The EU Division of Walker Industries is the largest non-government provider of military parts and equipment on the continent. This caused Horn to wonder where our loyalties might lie."

"Why would that be a concern to Horn?"

"Horn is a literalist when it comes to the Bible. When we had oversight hearings he liked to quote various verses. Revelations, especially 13:1, was one of his favorites: *I saw the beast rise up out of the sea, having seven heads and ten horns, and upon his horns ten crowns, and upon his heads the name of blasphemy.*"

"What does that mean?"

"According to Senator Horn, it represented the wealthy and powerful Europeans."

"How in the world did he arrive at that?"

"The Common Market in Europe originally had six members, with France blocking the British entry, but effectively they were the seven 'heads' or leaders. Guess how many royal families there currently are in Europe?"

"You're kidding me?"

"Nope. There are exactly ten 'Crowns', or royal families left in Europe."

"That's a bit of a stretch."

"That's what I told him, but he is a man of strong convictions. He feels there are other reasons to distrust the Europeans."

"For example..."

"Senator Horn firmly believes the past 60 years of peace in Europe has been enforced by American guns and that they are still a powder keg waiting for someone to light the fuse."

"What do you think?"

"I'm with you. I think it's a bit of a stretch. But he does have some valid points. In all likelihood, the worst reaction to the new awakening will come from Europe."

"The new awakening?"

"Yes, the Fourth Awakening."

"The Fourth Awakening? What is the Fourth Awakening?"

"We've reached one of those points you wanted me to tell you about."

"Tell me what?"

"You said you wanted me to tell you when we reached a place where your mind would not be able to understand what I was telling you. We've reached one of those points."

Shaking her head, Penelope said, "Fine. Are there any other things I should know about Senator Horn?"

"There are all sorts of things you should know but we'll take this up further when we get outside."

"Outside? What do you mean outside?"

"We're leaving now."

CHAPTER NINE

"There is no use trying," said Alice; "one can't believe impossible things."

"I dare say you haven't had much practice," said the Queen. "When I was your age, I always did it for half an hour a day. Why, sometimes I've believed as many as six impossible things before breakfast."

LEWIS CARROLL

PENELOPE SPENCE HAD seen and heard many strange and unbelievable things in her life, but this one topped the cake. "You mean to tell me that you and I are going to walk out of possibly the most secure prison in America, and no one is going to try and stop us?"

"Yes."

"With you in handcuffs and dressed in a bright orange outfit with 'Prisoner' written on the back."

"Yes."

"Are you going to take me hostage?"

"Of course not."

"Will my life or health be at risk in any way?"

"No."

"Will I be considered an accomplice or charged with helping you escape?"

"I don't see how. But someone may threaten you later to try to make you talk."

Spence leaned back in her chair, folded her arms across her chest and blinked at Walker a few times. This was easily the most outrageous thing she had ever heard in her life. Every neuron in her brain was shouting for her to stand up and walk out of the room in the off chance that whatever mental deficiency Michael Walker suffered from might be airborne and contagious. She decided to try a different tack.

"If you can walk out anytime you want, why are you still here?"

"I needed to meet you, remember?"

"Me?"

"Yes. I already told you that."

"But you were caught..."

"I wasn't caught. I let them catch me. Big difference."

"So, you're telling me..." Penelope struggled for the exact words she needed. "You allowed yourself to be captured because you knew they would bring you to Charleston and I would stop in to see you?"

"We've already discussed this previously. The only problem was they kept taking me to the wrong prison. I had to get arrested three times before they finally got it right. I think at some level Smith was on to me and was trying to make this as difficult as possible."

"What do you mean, Smith was 'on to you'?"

"As I said, very few people can be around me for any length of time without starting to show signs of advancing toward enlightenment. Somehow, Robert has been able to do it. I would love to know how."

"Enlightenment," Penelope muttered, holding her forehead with both hands as if trying to keep her cranium from exploding. She was getting hit from so many directions with so many unbelievable concepts; her brain was swimming in a morass of irrationality. Instead of trying to sort out all of this at once, Penelope did what she normally did when confronted with multiple problems: prioritize. "You're telling me, you've allowed yourself to be captured three times, and you've escaped three times, so you can meet me?"

"You keep asking the same questions."

"I'm a reporter. It's what we do."

"Why?"

"To see if the answer has changed since the last time we asked."

"I see. Three and two, actually."

"Three and two what?"

"I've been captured three times but I've only escaped twice, so far."

"Okay. Let's try this. You can escape at anytime you want?"

"Yes."

"Do I have to say or do anything for you to escape?"

"No, quite the opposite."

"What does that mean?"

"Since you know I'm leaving, it is important that you don't say or do anything to give the guards a heads up. In fact, I need you to put it completely out of your mind."

"What? Why?"

"Because you're the only one who could stop me from escaping."

"What? What!" For once in her life, Penelope Spence was unable to form any words with more than four letters that didn't begin with "W".

"While your mind is raw and you're just learning how to use the power of thought, you are quite a formidable presence. If you're thinking about me escaping, it might cause the others in the area, particularly Robert, to pick up on it and stop me."

"You are moon-barking mad! People can't just walk out of prisons without being seen."

"Sure they can. A physical prison is easy to leave, once you've allowed yourself to leave the mental prison."

"Mental prison? It sounds to me like you should be in a mental hospital!"

"Once you have mastered the power of thought many seemingly impossible options become effortless. In fact, some of the people who have already become aware of the Awakening are exploiting it for their personal benefit."

"What are you talking about?"

"There are books and weekend seminars on how to get everything you want just by controlling your thoughts."

Penelope's mind flashed back to the book on her nightstand. "The power of positive thinking has been around forever. What's wrong with that?"

"We're not talking Norman Vincent Peale, but something much more significant. Mankind is moving toward the Fourth Awakening, which will cause an upheaval with far-reaching implications." Walker shook his head.

"What?" Penelope asked.

"I would have hoped more people, upon discovering this secret, would aspire to enlightenment instead of a nice vacation, cash, or," Walker locked his eyes on hers, "a better parking place." Penelope flushed slightly. Was it possible that this odd man could actually read her thoughts? Were her thoughts really being projected out into some unseen universe where voyeurs and mental peeping toms were lurking? No. That simply wasn't possible.

"It really is time to go. After all, we've been talking for over an hour."

Penelope checked her watch, which was just about to tick past the 15 minute mark. This guy really is crazy, she thought to herself. On the other hand, she had to admit that the conversation had seemed much longer than 14 minutes.

"Here's the deal. All you need to do is stand up and ask to leave, and I'll meet you at your Prius. If we get separated, meet me tomorrow at noon at the East Bay Street end of the Old City Market."

"How did you know I drove a...never mind. Okay. Show me what you've got."

"One other thing."

"Here we go," thought Penelope. She had been expecting some quibbling, or a potential excuse to be used later.

"If I do exactly what I say I'm going to, will you believe me on some of the other stuff?"

Like so many things involving Michael Walker, this was unexpected. The only answer that seemed to make any sense blurted out of her mouth. "Sure. Why not?"

Just then, the door flew open. Smith strode into the room and indicated that Penelope's 15 minutes were up.

"Ready?" Walker asked.

"I'm definitely ready," Penelope Spence said as she pushed her chair away from the table and stood up. Walker didn't move.

≈

A S I RISE *to my feet I feel a slight dizziness and hear a faint buzzing noise like a conversation heard through the wall of another room. It is as if I stood up too quickly and all of the blood had rushed away from my brain. Walker is still seated and smiling at me. The sensation is like the one I felt earlier in the day at the bank. It wasn't unpleasant, just different. I turn off the electronic jammer, look at the video camera closest to me and head for the door. A burly guard holds the door open for me. As I walk around Smith I catch a glimpse of Michael Walker in the corridor ahead of me. Turning my head, I see him still in exactly the same place he had been during the interview. He smiles and waves to me again. But I know I just saw him in the hallway. Somehow he is in two places at the same time. I feel my knees wobble, but I don't go down.*

Assistant Director Robert Smith begins to walk me out. I feel as if the world is moving in slow motion and an irrepressibly deep inner-peace settles over me. I feel detached from the concerns of my body and daily life; almost like a spectator watching events unfold below from the vantage point of a hot air balloon or while perched on a cloud. I still sense my worries and they seem to matter, just not nearly as much. Reaching my car I discover a man, in an orange jump suit, kneeling next to the wheel well of my right rear tire. It is Michael Walker.

≈

T HE SIGHT OF Walker jarred Penelope out of her peaceful haze and caused her heart to race. He had done exactly what he said he was going to do. How was that possible? The only logical answer; it wasn't possible. Walker pulled a small electronic box off Penelope's car and stuck it on the car in the next parking space.

"Tracking device." He said. "I've found three others on your car. Someone is serious."

"I don't understand."

"No time to explain now. Let's go."

Penelope got behind the wheel but her hands were shaking so badly that she had difficulty inserting the key in the ignition. Penelope's breath was coming in gulps and her mouth was watering. She could taste bitter bile building in the back of her throat, usually a precursor to throwing up. Walker, from the passenger seat, reached over and helped her get the key in the slot. His hand on hers stopped the trembling.

"We really need to get going," Walker said.

"Why?"

"Because in about two minutes, they will notice that I'm gone."

Penelope turned the key and headed toward the front gate. "How are we going to get past the guards?"

"Let me worry about that," Walker answered.

As they approached the guard station, on the inbound side a car rear-ended a pickup truck that had been slow to pull away from the check-in. Both drivers got out of their vehicles and began yelling at each other. The guards manning the gate stepped out of their small building to intervene before any fists could be thrown. Walker ducked down as Penelope's car moved under the video cameras.

"Just keep driving slowly but don't stop," he said.

The only remaining guard at the outbound gate, distracted by the fender bender in the other lane, waved them through without checking the interior of the car. As they cleared the gate Walker let out a sigh. They were only a few hundred yards further when a loud horn and siren began wailing behind them. In the rearview mirror Penelope could see the guards lowering the front gate and a large military vehicle moving in front of the entrance, blocking the path of the black Suburban with heavily tinted windows that had been behind them in the exit queue.

"Apparently, they've noticed I'm gone." Walker closed his eyes and his breathing became rhythmic.

≈

SOMEHOW PENELOPE AND Walker ended up in West Ashley Park. She had driven all the way to the rear area. There was a little used parking lot with a bridge leading across a creek to a small rectangular island, created when they dug the canals for the adjoining neighborhood. When the car stopped, Walker's eyes opened for the first time since they left the brig.

"Well done," he said patting her on the knee. What she might normally perceive as an insincere or patronizing gesture instead filled Penelope with a pride and zest for life she hadn't felt in, well, ever.

"That was the most amazing thing I've seen in my life. I mean, I saw you in two places at once. I saw you. You did exactly what you said you were going to do. I mean, I saw it myself. If someone had told me this was going to happen, I would have laughed at them." Penelope shook her head and laughed. "Come to think of it, someone did tell me it was going to happen and I did laugh at them. I mean you. I didn't laugh in your face, but boy, I sure was tempted." She paused for a moment and shook her head again. "How did you do that?"

Walker let her ramble uninterrupted; the rest and meditation had restored the twinkle in his eye. "It's really not that difficult."

"What do you mean? What you did wasn't some magician's trick. You actually got yourself out of jail. How did you do it?"

"I used the power of thought. I let my conscious mind, subconscious mind and super conscious mind know that getting out of prison was what I wanted... then I released it."

"That's it?"

"It's pretty much that simple. Let the universe know what will make you happy and it will provide it."

"When did you develop this power?"

Penelope could tell from Walker's pained expression that she had, once again, missed his point. "I didn't develop any special powers. I simply released all of the preconceived notions that had been restricting my personal growth, and allowed my mind to surrender."

"Surrender?"

"You can do exactly the same thing anytime you want."

"What?"

"If you can convince the different elements of your mind to agree that being somewhere else is what you truly want, the power of thought will take you there. It's just that simple."

"Right." The euphoria of the escape was starting to wear off and the cynical skeptic that kept her conscious mind on the straight and narrow began to reassert herself. "Just that simple."

"Anyone can do it if they just allow themselves."

"Including me?"

"Especially you."

"What makes me special?'

"You've already shown flashes of mastering the power of thought. When your unconscious mind is convinced something is impossible, then it is impossible. This is why you're having so much trouble getting your arms around all of this. Your intellect and natural skepticism are holding you back." Walker shook his head. "Once you get past that..." His voice drifted off and a heavy silence settled over the pair as he looked deeply into her eyes.

Penelope was torn. Was it possible that everything she had ever been taught was fundamentally flawed? Did she have the ability to do what Walker had done, or was she falling under the spell of a charming conman?

"If I wanted to be in a different place how would I convince my mind to take me there?"

"Don't think about all of the possibilities and obstacles. Simply tell your mind to take over. It will do what needs to be done."

"That's it?"

"That's it, but you really have to be sincere. You can't lie to yourself." After a brief pause to allow his recent bombshell to sink in, he asked, "Where are my clothes?"

"What? I don't have any clothes..." her eyes flew open. "The Goodwill bag I threw in the trunk a few days ago with some of Bill's old stuff." Penelope's face crinkled into a frown as she popped the trunk and they headed to the back of the car. How closely had he been watching her if he knew exactly what she had in the trunk of her car?

Without a hint of modesty Walker stripped down to his birthday suit. His body was rippled with lean muscle and near zero fat; Penelope felt tingles in places she'd assumed had relocated during the menopause remodeling and not left a forwarding address. Ripping open the plastic garbage bag he rummaged around until he found a pair of sweat pants and a golf shirt. On the floor of the car's trunk was an old pair of battered tennis shoes. In his new wardrobe he could pass for anyone they might meet in the park. Walker tied the orange jumpsuit around a softball ball-sized rock that was conveniently next to the car and tossed it into the creek.

"The money." Walker held out his hand.

"What money?" Then she remembered the visit to her bank. As she reached for her purse she also remembered the strange sensations she felt in the bank. Her eyes shot up and met his with a look of astonishment.

He shrugged as he reached out to take the envelope that was still filled with 30 one hundred dollar bills.

"I suppose you're good for it."

Again his smile wrapped her in warmth that made her feel safe and comfortable.

"Wait a minute," Penelope said as she pulled the envelope back. "With all your money, and if you knew you were coming to Charleston, why didn't you plan this better?"

"I thought it was well planned and brilliantly executed."

"What do you mean?"

"We created a diversion at the guard station and timed it so all the people trying to follow you would be stuck inside when they sealed the gate. I thought it went off flawlessly."

"You staged the accident at the guard station?"

"Of course," Walker answered as he adjusted the collar on the borrowed shirt.

A puzzled expression covered Penelope's face. "Let's say for a minute I believe you masterminded this entire escape and timed it down to the last second. You could have cash and a getaway car stashed just outside the brig."

"You're right, I could have. But it wasn't worth the risk."

"What risk?"

"That someone might have sensed what we were doing and thrown obstacles in our path."

"You mean there are others like you?"

"Yes and you as well. As the Awakening builds momentum, there will be more and more of us. "

"God help us all. Was that you I sensed at the bank?"

Walker laughed and shrugged. "If you ever get that feeling again, don't try to rationalize it, just follow where it leads. I'll explain more the next time we meet."

"What?" There was that word again. "You're leaving? Why?"

"We have to establish an alibi that proves you had nothing to do with my escape. I'll meet you tomorrow at noon. You remember where?"

"East Bay Street end of the Old City Market."

"Look," Walker said softly. "What you've seen so far today is a lot to absorb, but you have to shake it off and be on your 'A' game. The next few hours are going to be a bit rough for you. Fortunately, there should be enough media coverage to protect you."

"Protect me? Protect me from what?"

Walker smiled but didn't answer. "Just remember, you didn't have anything to do with my escape. When they ask where you went, tell them the truth. Since I may not have gotten all of the tracking devices, they may know where you are already. Tell them you came here to think."

Walker looked her up and down. "Be careful. Some doors in your mind have already opened today, and you don't realize it yet. Right now you are very vulnerable but at the same time very powerful. I wish I could stay to get you over this hump, but that is not what's best. Do you have someone to stay with tonight?"

"My friend Joey."

"Excellent. You really shouldn't be alone."

He grabbed both of her arms and stared deeply into her eyes. "You must control your emotions and try to be completely positive. It is important that you are not alone tonight. Do you understand?"

He felt her starting to tremble and she broke eye contact. "Yes. I think so."

"You've been amazing." He kissed her gently on the forehead, causing a jolt like a mild electrical shock that started between her eyebrows then traveled down her body, exiting through her feet. Before she could ask any more questions, Walker began to jog away. Looking back over his shoulder he shouted, "Call the best lawyer you know and have him meet you at your house. You're going to need him!" He vanished around a bend in the road.

Picking up her cell phone she had over 20 voice mails, 15 of them from Senator Horn. She dialed the private number the senator had given her and he answered it personally on the first ring. "Penelope, is that you?"

"Yes, senator."

"Are you okay?"

"Yes, why?

"Michael Walker has escaped. He got out right after he spoke to you."

"Really? I had forgotten to turn my cell phone back on."

"What did that maniac say to you?"

"Most of it sounded like gibberish to me, senator."

"It will all be clearer tomorrow."

"Why tomorrow?"

"Watch the Sunday morning political talk shows and you'll find out. I'm going to tell the entire world about the Hermes Project." The line went dead.

CHAPTER TEN

"Adversity is the first path to truth."

LORD BYRON

PENELOPE SLOWED DOWN as she approached the guard station of her gated community, expecting the night man, Lenny, to simply wave her through like always. Instead he got up and motioned for her to stop. Stepping from his tiny air-conditioned building, he had a gun belt and holster around his waist.

"Since when do you carry a gun?" Penelope asked before her window was completely down.

"I always have it with me, Ms. Spence," he answered as he patted the 40 caliber Glock strapped to his waist. "Only wear it on special occasions since it makes the residents nervous."

"So what's the occasion?"

"You have some company at your house. Official company."

"I see," Penelope said with a sigh as their eyes locked.

"They're looking for a guy who escaped from the brig. It's all over the TV and radio," Lenny said as he motioned toward a tiny portable television that was propped up on his desk. Lenny McElroy was a tough old bird. After 30 years as a cop in New York City, he had retired to Charleston to be closer to his only daughter and grandkids. He had been the night guard for the past couple of years; more to fill his time than to supplement his retirement income. There had never been any robberies or vandalism on his watch.

"They wanted me to call them if you showed up."

"That's fine, Lenny. I didn't do anything."

"I figured, but I think I misplaced their number." Lenny motioned toward the small building surrounded with beautiful landscaping to minimize its presence. "They put your name and address out on the local police band." Lenny shook his head and looked like he would have spit on the ground if a lady hadn't been present. "You would have thought they would have used a scrambled tactical channel." He shook his head again. "Bunch of press in there too."

"Thanks for the heads up, Lenny."

"You take care, Ms. Spence."

Penelope turned the corner onto her street and saw what had to be half the police cars in Charleston parked in front of her house. In addition, there were two large unmarked black Chevy Suburbans — the kind favored by the federal government — and what looked to be two unmarked police cars. There were men in a variety of uniforms standing in her yard, and a couple of local cops who appeared to have been relegated to traffic control.

Along with law enforcement and the media, the street was starting to fill with gawkers and the idle curious with nothing better to do. Penelope pulled into the first parking space she could find. Opening her purse, instead of using the untraceable phone Mark had given her she used her normal cell phone and called his office. If they were taping their conversations, she wanted them to hear this one.

"Mark Hatchet."

"It's me."

"I thought I told..."

"I got in to see Walker."

"They were holding him in the Charleston Brig?"

"Absolutely."

"Yes! Yes! Yes!" Penelope could almost see Hatchet jumping up and down in his office and the heads turning in the cluster of desks in the newsroom's bullpen just outside his window. "I knew you could do it. When can...."

"Hold on. It gets better."

"Impossible."

"Walker escaped right after I talked to him."

"Don't tease me, Nellie."

"I'm serious. But there is one small problem."

"No, no, no, no. There are no problems. Military industrial complex billionaire first held incognito then escapes from the maximum security prison we use to hold terrorists. This is the story of the year."

"You want to explain that to all of the police and Homeland Security people tromping on my flowerbeds?"

"Damn."

"My thought exactly. I happen to know there is a recent vacancy in the high security wing at the Charleston Brig but I would prefer to sleep in my own bed tonight."

"You still have those press credentials I sent you?"

Penelope tucked her phone under her chin as she reached again for her purse. "I think they're upstairs on my..." To her surprise, the laminated badge with her name and *The Washington Post* logo was the first thing she saw when she opened her bag. "My bad. Got it in my hand."

"Okay. I'm going to get some people in here and you're going to file your reports over the phone just in case."

"Just in case what?"

"Just in case they throw a black bag over your head and you disappear. They could be hoping to squelch this by detaining you before you can file your story."

"Lovely."

After about fifteen minutes of questions and answers on a quickly assembled conference call Mark Hatchet felt he had enough to run the story if Penelope was arrested and unable to write it herself. "And Senator Horn's office will confirm all of this?"

"He said he would."

There was a rustling in the background and Penelope heard a voice she didn't recognize say, "I've got confirmation from Senator Horn himself that Walker was being held in the brig and that he has escaped. He said we can use him as a named source." A whoop went up in the conference room. Usually a confirmation on that level came from an unnamed "high government official". To have someone as highly regarded as Senator Horn be willing to put his name on it was the absolute gold standard for journalism.

"Welcome back to the big time kiddo. Not one but two front page exclusives."

"Save a couple of inches for me in Monday's edition. Some of the stuff with Horn is embargoed until noon tomorrow."

"Will do, Nellie. You should be safe from the storm troopers now."

"How so?"

"We've got the story and we've got high level confirmation on the record. They can't stop it from getting out. If they arrest you now there will be hell to pay and they know it."

"I think we're just scratching the surface,"

"There is a one Pulitzer Prize winning story per issue limit. We'll worry about that tomorrow. For now, get a good lawyer before you talk to the feds. If anyone asks, you are now officially working for *The Washington Post*, and you can have anyone who questions it call me directly."

"Thanks."

"Call me back as soon as you can." The line went dead.

Penelope gathered her thoughts for a moment as she felt her pulse rate slowly returning to somewhere close to normal. She had been dreaming about this day for years and now that it had arrived it was everything she could have hope for and more. She still needed a lawyer. Drawing in a deep breath, she dialed the phone number she calls the most. Thanks to the joys of caller ID Joey answered without bothering to say hello. "Where are you?"

"Down the street from my house."

"That Michael Walker character has escaped they're looking for both of you. Your name and address are all over the local channels."

"So I heard. I need to ask a favor."

"Sure."

"It looks like I may need an attorney. Do you think your ex might be willing to help me?"

"Willing? Ha! He is currently sitting in my kitchen begging me to call you for him."

Penelope heard a muffled conversation and a struggle for the phone. "Penelope, this is Ron. Where are you?"

"I'm down the street from my house. There are police and reporters everywhere."

"I'll be there in three minutes. Don't talk to anyone."

"Aren't you going to ask if I did anything?"

"I'm a lawyer. I don't care if you shot JFK. Just don't talk to anyone before I get there. Here's Joey."

After a brief pause, the familiar voice of Joey Rickman came back on the phone. "You okay?"

"I'm fine."

"So, did you bust that hunk out of stir so you could have your way with him?"

Penelope was dying to tell Joey exactly what had happened. She knew her friend wouldn't believe a word of it. She knew she wouldn't believe it if their roles were reversed and decided to stick with the truth, or at least parts of it. "I did nothing to help him escape from prison. He did it all by himself."

"So was he all yummy and dangerous?"

"I was there to interview someone for a story; I wasn't cruising a single's bar."

"I know that. So was he yummy and dangerous? The kind of guy you just know you should avoid but can't resist?"

"Oh, you mean a guy like Ron Rickman?"

"Exactly." Joey realized what she had just said. "Hey!"

Before Penelope could respond, there was a tapping on the window of her car. Apparently one of the Charleston policemen who had been directing traffic had recognized her Prius, which was hardly the car of choice in her neighborhood, and was in the process of making his sergeant's day. He was young, maybe 25, and like all members of the Charleston police department, a college graduate.

"Please hang up the phone," he said, while resting his hand on the butt of his 38 Police Special. "And step out of the car."

"There is a nice young man here with a gun that is telling me it's time to hang up. I'll talk to you later."

"How come you're getting all of the men?"

"Bye, Joey." Penelope gathered her thoughts and stepped out of her car.

"Are you Penelope Spence?" the policeman asked politely.

"Yes."

"Would you please come with me Ms. Spence?" he said, more as an invitation than as an instruction. Penelope nodded. They were almost to the edge of her front yard before the press noticed her and began to surge in her direction.

Sgt. Donald Donnelley, an 18-year police veteran who was cooling his heels on the sidewalk in front of the house as a bunch of Feds conducted a search in his district, was steaming. Even though he had been first on the scene, some guy from Homeland Security had waved a federal search warrant in his face and sent him and his men out of the house with their tails between their legs. He saw the press coming and motioned to the six officers who were milling around nursing their bruised pride. They formed a blue wall between Penelope and the media jackals.

"Good job, Johnson," Donnelley said, slapping the young officer on the back. "Damned good job. Captain will hear about it." Officer Johnson knew he would get full credit for, want of a better word, the "collar" because that was the kind of guy Donnelley was. He was one of the most popular shift commanders in Charleston. He was fair, he was honest, and he didn't have a political bone in his body.

Donnelley was an imposing six-six and 240 pounds, which was 30 pounds below the playing weight from his days as an offensive tackle for the USC Gamecocks and three years in the Canadian Football League. Skin the color of strong coffee with light cream, he had an easy smile and a deep voice. "Ms. Spence?" he asked politely. She nodded. Looking over his shoulder, he pulled her further away from the mob of reporters shouting questions at her. "At the present time," he said in a firm, professional voice, "the Federal Bureau of Investigation and Department of Homeland Security are executing a search warrant involving your premises. They are looking for an escaped convict named Michael Walker. There is nothing to be alarmed about..."

"That's enough," Ronald F. Rickman, Esquire said as he and his two assistants, one male, one female, muscled their way through the phalanx of policemen. "Ms. Spence is represented by counsel and has nothing further to say." Rickman's female assistant, Amy Kindle, an intense woman in her mid-30's, leaned in and whispered in her boss's ear. The famous smile that had charmed juries for three decades and made him a millionaire many times over lit his face. He slapped Sgt. Donnelley on the back as if he were some long lost friend. "Hey, Donny, how you doin'? How's Sandy and the kids?"

Donny Donnelley rubbed his mouth before turning to face Ron Rickman. They'd had a symbiotic relationship for years. Donnelley would arrest them, and those with money would hire Rickman and get off. They both looked at it as job security.

"Counselor," Donnelley answered with considerably less warmth than he had shown to Penelope.

"Donny Junior still going to play in Columbia on Saturdays?"

"He hasn't signed his national letter yet, but Florida and LSU are coming after him hard."

"I hope you told him you'd disown him if he went to another SEC team."

It was hard not to like Ron Rickman. He was handsome, rich, funny and, thanks to his assistants, always had a personal word or comment to add to every conversation. He had the power to speak to a room full of people with each one convinced they were the only one he was talking to. An excellent skill set for a trial lawyer.

"Did the best offensive lineman to ever come out of West Ashley High School ask you any questions, Penelope?"

"He was just explaining that the FBI and Homeland Security are searching my house."

"Feds, huh?" He patted Donnelly on the arm again. "Explains why you're out here." He winked at the big cop. "When I get through with them, they're going to wish they hadn't peed on your jurisdiction."

Donnelley smiled. Those arrogant Feds were about to get hit by Hurricane Rickman. Couldn't happen to a nicer bunch of guys.

Rickman motioned for his two assistants to join them, as they huddled out of earshot of the press who were still shouting questions. Turning to Penelope, "I think you know Josh and Amy." Josh Wassermann and Amy Kindle were the two highest paid personal assistants in Charleston, each earning in the mid six-figure range.

Amy was the face person. She had a photographic memory and her primary function was to make her boss look like he cared by remembering personal details about everyone he met. She was also the research specialist of the team and a master of contract law. If she had ever read about a case, she could instantly cite it.

Josh was the legal brain of the trio but lacked charisma in front of a jury. Tongue tied and unsteady in court, he was a whiz when it came to strategy and tactics. He scripted nearly all of Rickman's closing arguments, wrote his briefs, and was always his second chair.

"Penelope, we don't have a lot of time. In 25 words or less, what happened?"

"I went to the Charleston brig. I interviewed Michael Walker for probably twenty minutes..."

"Who are you working for?" Rickman interrupted.

"*The Washington Post*," Penelope said as she held up her press credentials.

"No kidding," Rickman and his posse were impressed.

"I just got off the phone with the Managing Editor, Mark Hatchet. He's going to make some calls to be sure I don't get arrested."

"You don't need to worry about that," Rickman said with a broad smile. Amy whispered something is his ear. "Right." Turning back to Penelope he said, "Why don't you go ahead and pin that thing on." He waited until Penelope had the press pass clipped to the front of her blouse before continuing. "So what happened next?"

"He was still sitting at the interrogation room handcuffed to the table when I left. A few minutes later he escaped."

"Josh?"

"We blame it on the lack of security at the brig. He was there when she left, which they will probably have on videotape." Three sets of eyes turned to Penelope.

For a moment Penelope panicked. What if the videotapes caught the same glimpse of the second Walker leaving the room that she had seen? No, that couldn't be possible or Walker would have told her. Or would he?

"Penelope, video?"

"Sorry," she said, pulling herself back to reality. "They have video cameras everywhere."

"Amy."

"Youngest Pulitzer Prize winning investigative reporter ever. One of only three people to get a perfect score on both their SAT and ACT college entrance exams in Charleston County in the past 50 years. Established Charleston family since before the American Revolution. Pillar of the community."

"Got it," Rickman said. "Showtime." The quartet walked up the front sidewalk of Spence's house. Ronald F. Rickman, Esquire, stood on the top step of the covered porch, next to Penelope. His two assistants melted into the background. He made eye contact with Donnelley and nodded. The big cop smiled as he instructed his men to let the reporters through.

Rickman watched with a twinkle in his eye as the media scrambled to get their cameras positioned and microphones set up. He ignored all of the shouted questions until the last television reporter indicated that he was ready. The press loved him.

"Currently the Federal Government of the United States of America is searching the home of Ms. Penelope Drayton Spence." The way he said 'Federal Government' made it sound as if General William Tucumseh Sherman and Union troops had been sighted in Summerville and were headed south. "Ms. Spence," Rickman placed his arm around her and drew her next to him, "has done nothing wrong, yet she is being forced to feel the full weight of the Federal Government on her shoulders. Why, you ask? Because she was simply doing her job while the Federal Government failed to do theirs." Rickman was an eloquent public speaker. He knew exactly when to pause in his cadence for the fullest effect. His voice could travel from sympathy to outraged indignation within a single sentence. He was currently on a 183-case streak where he had moved at least one member of a jury to tears during his closing remarks.

"Earlier today, Penelope Drayton Spence interviewed a man at the Charleston Consolidated Brig for *The Washington Post*. And for those of you who don't know, Ms. Spence was the youngest person and one of the first females to ever win the coveted Pulitzer Prize for investigative journalism, and has been a pillar of our community for her entire life.

"The Federal Government," he said with a conspiratorial raise of his eyebrow, "has videotape recordings that clearly show that the man she interviewed was still in Federal custody after she had vacated the area. Then why this search, you may ask?" He waited for someone to offer an answer and when none was forthcoming, he provided his own. "Through their own incompetence, the Federal Government allowed a dangerous man to slip through their fingers, and he could be somewhere in our community. 'Armed and dangerous, do not approach', they will tell us." Rickman paused and looked around. "Armed and dangerous, do not approach. Why are they here, instead of looking for a man who may be hiding in your neighborhood, or yours, or yours?" Rickman's outstretched finger pointed at different sections of his media congregation with the fervor of a Southern Baptist minister rooting out the devil. Penelope half expected to hear an "Amen" from Josh and Amy.

"They are here because they are trying to deflect attention from their own incompetence and have you focus your attention on a woman who... was ...only... doing ...her... job."

When it was clear that Rickman was finished, shouted questions pounded the porch. Penelope leaned in and whispered, "You left out the part about my college exam scores."

He leaned in closer and whispered in her ear. "Makes you look like a know-it-all." He leaned in even closer, "Your hair smells nice."

"Do you ever give it a rest?" She didn't need to wait for an answer. She knew at anytime in the past 30 years if she had so much as raised an eyebrow to Ron Rickman he would have had one of his assistants booking them a weekend in the Bahamas. She turned to enter the house. Inside, she saw a familiar face leading the search.

"Assistant Director Smith."

"Ms. Spence. You've been busy. I've already gotten a call from the Secretary of Homeland Security. Round one goes to you."

"Please speak to me and not my client," Rickman said.

"Not many innocent people show up with an attorney," Smith said, handing Rickman one of the two warrants he had in his hand. Rickman passed the search warrant over to Josh without so much as a glance.

"Not many people arrive home and find it filled with Federal law enforcement officers." Rickman glanced at the other document. "What else have you got there?'

"It is a sealed warrant to hold Ms Penelope Drayton Spence as a material witness."

Rickman's face lit up. "You just made my day."

"Relax counselor," Smith said. "The cat is out of the bag now and I've been instructed not to serve it." He turned and stared hard at Penelope. "Yet." Smith's voice was level and calm as he tucked the warrant in his inside coat pocket. "You need to inform your client that, pending the completion of an administrative review, all of her security clearances have been revoked along with access to all password protected federal databases." Smith's cold eyes found Penelope. "And you should remind her of the severe penalties if she should reveal any classified information."

"That sounds like a threat, Assistant Director Smith," Rickman said.

"I certainly hope so, counselor."

The tension in the room was so thick it even chased the smile from Rickman's face as he glanced at Penelope, whose blood had turned to ice and frozen her on the spot. It was broken by the unexpected sound of a high pitched male voice.

"Tell them to stop, right now," Josh said as he read the warrant and whispered something to Rickman.

"Stop!" Rickman shouted as he leaned in to hear what Josh had discovered. All activity in the room ceased and all eyes turned to Rickman. He nodded that he understood and a broad smile returned to his face. "You have violated my client's rights long enough, you will leave now."

"We're not finished."

"Oh, yes you are. This warrant allows you to search the premises for Michael Walker." Josh pulled a digital camera out of his pocket and began taking pictures. "And I'm going to assume that Mr. Walker is of normal height and weight."

"Yes," Smith answered without the slightest hint of emotion.

"Do you think Mr. Walker would fit in the drawer that agent is currently rummaging through?" A flash went off, catching the agent with his hand in the drawer. "I'm sure Judge..." he leaned toward Josh and got his answer, "Mallory will be interested in how you've turned this into a fishing expedition and abused his warrant."

Smith never changed expressions but motioned to one of his technicians, who was holding a small cardboard box that he handed to Penelope.

"I'm sorry, I thought we were doing your client a favor." Turning his attention to Penelope, he continued. "We found these listening devices all over your house. There are probably more but we'll let your lawyer find the rest of them for you."

"What?" Penelope asked as she accepted the box.

"Your house has been bugged, Ms. Spence," Smith said. "And these aren't the kind you buy at Radio Shack or online."

Penelope looked in the box and saw an assortment of listening devices, some smaller than the head of a thumbtack. "Bugged? Who? Why?"

"It happens all the time to people who get too close to Michael Walker." Smith motioned to his crew to pack up and leave.

"They found her car down the street," one of the agents said as he popped back inside. "You want it searched?"

Smith and Rickman both turned to look at Josh who was shaking his head no. "Not covered by the warrant since it is not currently in the house."

"Would you have any objections to our looking in the trunk of your car, Ms. Spence?"

"Why?"

"To be sure Michael Walker is not in there. I can have a warrant in less than an hour," Smith answered calmly.

Rickman looked at Penelope for any clue that a visual search of her car would be a problem. She shrugged. "I have nothing to hide."

"Give Josh your keys," Rickman said. "He will open the trunk and interior of the car to allow for a visual inspection but you are not allowed to touch her vehicle."

Smith nodded his agreement.

"We're done," Rickman said.

"So are we," Smith said as he nodded toward Penelope Spence. "Be very, very careful. You have made some dangerous enemies today and you are in way over your head with Michael Walker. He is not at all what he seems."

Rickman stepped between Smith and Spence. "That's enough. You're scaring her."

"I certainly hope so," Smith said as he handed Penelope one of his business cards. "Call this number any time day or night and my office will connect us."

Penelope frowned as she examined the card with the blue Homeland Security logo, then her eyes turned again to the contents of the box. Where did they come from? Walker was either in jail or with her until a few minutes earlier; he couldn't possibly have planted the bugs himself. But, he could have easily have had someone else do his dirty work for him. The person most likely to want listening devices in her home, Assistant Director Smith, was the one who told her about them. She felt a chill again as she considered another possibility. Was there another player in this game she was unaware of? The prospect sent her brain reeling.

CHAPTER ELEVEN

"To enjoy good health, to bring true happiness to one's family, to bring peace to all, one must first discipline and control one's own mind."

BUDDHA

AFTER ALL OF Smith's people had left, Ron Rickman commandeered the kitchen and was in the process of giving everyone in the media who wanted a one-on-one interview or a sound bite their chance.

Penelope took her cell phone out on the deck along with a hard copy of the two articles that would appear tomorrow under her byline. Mark's reporters were pros and there weren't many things that needed to be changed. These two articles—one about Walker being held in the brig and one about his escape, were just the warm up act. Once Senator Horn's embargo period was us up at noon tomorrow, she would be on the record with the explosive conversation she had witnessed between Walker and the senator, not to mention her interview.

With the image of the box of listening devices that had been removed from her house fresh in her mind, she wanted to be sure no one else was listening to her conversation. She called Mark Hatchet as she strolled out on the elevated boardwalk behind her house toward the dock and river. She had gotten the house; her ex had gotten the boat. They spent a few minutes going over the edits required before the conversation turned more casual.

"So what's Walker like?" Hatchet asked.

"Somewhere between handsome and terrifying. Oh, while they were searching, they found bugs all over my house."

"That's my girl. You made someone nervous."

She almost blurted out that Walker had found tracking devices on her car but caught herself just in time. While she had already shared some of the details of her conversation with Walker and the totally out of character reactions of Senator Horn; she had played dumb about the actual escape. She knew there was no way she could explain what she had seen without coming across as demented, and possibly an accomplice.

"He said he had been arrested three times in the past two weeks, and that they kept taking him to the wrong prison. If you can believe that."

"I didn't even know he had escaped from the brig until you called."

"How's that possible? There are TV crews and reporters all over my house!"

"Man," Hatchet said with a hint of respect in his voice. "They really have a lid on this. They knew that between you and Senator Horn they couldn't keep the story of the arrest and escape quiet much longer, but they're buying a few hours of damage control by not releasing any information on Walker. Very slick."

"What do you mean?" Penelope asked.

"They kept it a local story about an escape only, and apparently they're hoping none of the local reporters will figure out who escaped. Let's hope they stay in the dark until we've gone to press. Once that happens all hell is going to break loose."

"What time do you go to press?"

"Your stuff will go up on our web page around 11 Eastern and the print edition will start hitting the street shortly after that. You might want to turn your phones off if you expect to get any sleep tonight."

"Good thinking," Penelope said as she nodded her head.

"By the way, I had one of my reporters make a few discreet inquiries to news outlets down there and it turns out they all got an anonymous call about the escape."

"Really?"

"Told them that a deranged maniac suspected in the disappearance of 30 people was on the loose and they should check over at your house."

Penelope burst into laughter. "Maybe he does have a sense of humor."

"What does that mean?"

"It would take too long to explain."

"Whatever," Hatchet said as he suppressed a yawn. "All I know is with one masterstroke it started to pry the lid off Homeland Security's carefully crafted cover-up and gave you enough protection to file your story. By this time tomorrow you will be absolutely bulletproof."

"What does that mean?"

"After this story breaks unless they find you in the same getaway car with Walker there is no way in hell they could arrest you. We media people may all be 'jackals' but we protect our own. If they start fitting you for an orange jumper every news outlet in the free world will go nuts."

"Oh," Penelope said as she changed ears for her phone. "That's why Smith didn't arrest me."

"It would have been political suicide. In this case the only thing that could make this worse than the Walker story getting out would be the Walker story getting out and the reporter who broke the story getting arrested. That moves it from a few embarrassing news cycles to a Congressional hearing and the Secretary of Homeland Security announcing he's retiring to spend more time with his family."

"Why is it I'm starting to feel like a pawn in a much bigger game?"

"What do you care? You got the big story you had been wishing for and potentially an even bigger one in the wings. Speaking of which, let's go over your interview with Walker again. Just in case."

"Just in case of what?

"Just in case Homeland Security changes its mind and throws you in the hoosegow."

"Lovely."

For the next few minutes, Penelope recounted the interview, leaving out the parts she barely believed herself and certainly didn't have the strength to try and convince anyone else about.

"What's the deal with the bowls?" Mark asked.

"No idea but it really set the senator off."

"Speaking of the senator, we don't have any conflict here, do we? The only confirmation we've gotten from him was on Walker being in the brig and nothing on this."

"He or his chief of staff is supposed to email me a release to put what I saw in the brig on the record and there was nothing classified discussed. I haven't done any work for him since he announced his retirement and

Homeland Security revoked my security clearance an hour ago. Where does that leave me?"

"I'll run it past legal but you look bulletproof to me. They booted two senators with Presidential ambitions off *Meet the Press,* and they're giving Horn a double live segment in the morning."

"Looks like he's going to blow the cover off of the Hermes Project."

"That would be my guess too. I wonder how he's going to get around the project still being classified," Hatchet asked.

"I don't think he even cares," Penelope answered. "From what I was able to pick up during the conversation between Walker and Horn, the White House is ready to declassify the project, but they were waiting for Horn's and Homeland Security's buy-in."

"That jives with what I've heard."

"From your mystery source?"

"Don't start. Try and get some rest."

"One of the advantages of living in a small town and in a gated community; reporters can't knock on your door in the middle of the night."

Penelope wandered back into the house just as Ronald F. Rickman, Esquire was completing his last interview and her "legal team" was packing up to leave.

"I don't think the Feds will be bothering you again anytime soon," Rickman said with a laugh.

"How much is all of this going to cost me?"

"Are you kidding, this is the best publicity I've had all year." Ron Rickman put his arm around Penelope's shoulder. "But if you really want to show your gratitude..."

Penelope pushed him away. "Why is it every time I get around you I feel like I need to take a shower?"

"Ooh. That works for me," Rickman said with a smile. "But not tonight. I already have plans."

Penelope shook her head as she maneuvered Rickman toward the door. "Thanks, Ron."

"I'll call you about that shower."

"You do that," she said as she shoved him out the door.

Penelope leaned with her back against the front door, drew in a deep breath and let it out slowly. This had been quite a day.

Needing a quick treat to soothe her nerves, Penelope opened the freezer side of the refrigerator and lifted up a bag of frozen organic peas. Underneath was a handful of small Snickers bars left over from Halloween. Despite her best intentions, she hadn't been able to jettison her private stash. She popped one of the frozen treats in her mouth as she went upstairs to check her laptop.

The release from Joan Inman making her conversation with the senator and Michael Walker in the brig on the record after noon tomorrow was, as promised, in her inbox. She forwarded it on to Mark. Where she would normally get two or three emails a day, mostly from her kids, currently she had over 50 unread messages. She decided to keep them unread.

As eleven o'clock approached Penelope kept hitting the "refresh" button on her browser as she waited for her stories to go online. With nothing else to do, she wandered back downstairs, wiped off the counter and put the few coffee cups Rickman and his people had used into the nearly empty dishwasher.

When she came back upstairs, there it was. Her eyes filled with tears as she saw her byline.

Billionaire Detained by Homeland Security Escapes from Maximum Security Facility
By Penelope Drayton Spence
Exclusive to *The Washington Post*

The lead story in the Sunday *Washington Post*. Nirvana. She emailed the link to the page to everyone in her address book, before wandering back downstairs for a celebratory glass of merlot. Out by the pool, a cool breeze swept off the Ashley River, keeping the insects at bay. The moon rippled off the shallow water of the salt marsh and tree frogs were happily singing. This was a perfect ending to the perfect day. If only she had someone here to share the moment.

"Shoot," she muttered to herself, remembering that Walker had told her it wasn't a good idea for her to be alone tonight. It was nearly midnight; well past Joey's bedtime and she hated to have her beauty sleep interrupted for anything short of a Penelope meltdown. She was a big girl. Right now all she wanted to do was get some rest.

The mood was shattered when Penelope heard the all too familiar sucking sound coming from one of the swimming pool's intake. Something had gotten stuck in the filter basket. Again. Damn this place, she thought. Ever since the ugly snake in the basket incident of a few years ago, when she had reached in to clear a blockage only to discover a bloated dead reptile, she had no intention of sticking her hand in to see if this noise was being caused by animal, vegetable, or mineral. This meant yet another pool service call. "God, I'm starting to hate this place," she muttered to herself as she closed her eyes and relaxed. She felt the tension leave her body as she released the anger.

She was shaken back to reality when her land line rang. She smiled when she saw the name of the editor of *The Post and Courier* in the Caller ID box. Now he wanted to talk to her. Where was he when she needed a job? She smiled and let it go to voice mail. Checking the number posted on the wall next to the kitchen phone, she used her cell to call the guard station and told Lenny she wasn't expecting any guests tonight but some people may try to convince him otherwise. He said he understood completely.

Shaking her head, she turned off the ringer to both her cell phone and her landline before heading upstairs.

Despite being exhausted, in her excitement she tossed and turned and was unable to fall asleep. She had her big story and it was everything she had wished for, and more. But doubts kept creeping in. After the story about the confrontation at the brig between Walker and Horn, then what? Was she going to be a flash in the pan, one hit wonder and slide back to obscurity or was this just the first step to something bigger? Would she see Walker again? Would someone else get to break the Hermes Project story? If she really wanted to be a big time reporter would she have to move? What was Horn going to say in the morning on the Sunday talk shows? Her mind kept coming back to the listening devices in her house. She would never think about the house in the same way again. For nearly 30 years this had been her home and her sanctuary; now this. She felt violated. Did they get them all? Why had she stopped Smith's men? For nearly half an hour her mind raced and churned before she was finally able to drift off to sleep.

≈

I WAKE FROM *a deep sleep with the feeling of someone shouting in my ears. In my haze, I can't make out the words or the voice. I strain my ears to listen but all I hear is an odd buzzing sound I can't place but it sounds like it is coming from the kitchen. It is just a bad dream; but when I close my eyes I hear the shouting again.*

Louder.

A man's voice.

Michael Walker's voice.

He is screaming a single word.

"RUN!"

CHAPTER TWELVE

"Most people stumble over the truth, now and then, but they usually manage to pick themselves up and go on, anyway."

WINSTON CHURCHILL

PENELOPE SPENCE DIDN'T hesitate. Throwing the sheet off her bare legs she opened the door to the bedroom. The hallway was filled with smoke and for the first time she realized the odd buzz she had heard in her dream was the blaring of the smoke detectors in the kitchen. The back staircase that led to the kitchen was fully engulfed in flames, while the main staircase was filled with dense smoke but no fire. Dropping low to the floor, she filled her lungs with air and bounded down the stairs, three steps at a time. Flames licked the foyer, forcing her into the great room off to the right. She bolted toward the rear patio door but stopped short when she saw it. The privacy fence around the propane tank was a blaze. It could only be a matter of seconds before the 250 gallons of propane in the recently refilled tank exploded. All doors in the front of the house were blocked with flames and the last place she wanted to be was in the backyard anywhere near the propane tank. Her only chance was the front window.

As Penelope gained speed for the impact with the glass of the oversized front window, she relaxed and thought of Michael Walker's words about letting her mind take her to a different place.

≈

I put all of the things that could go wrong out of my thoughts; as I approach the window, I feel time begin to slow. I feel an inner calmness that this is going to work out just fine and I surrender to this feeling. I close my eyes, jump and wait for impact, but there is none. I open my eyes and discover I'm sitting in the middle of my front yard. A quick inventory shows no cuts or bruises; I don't have a scratch on me.

≈

PENELOPE GLANCED BACK at the plate glass window. No, that wasn't possible; the glass in the front window appeared intact. The groan of sagging timbers accompanying the collapse of her covered side porch into a pile of burning rubble caused her mind to snap back to reality. "The propane tank...!"

Regaining her footing, she charged toward the street and the only object of any size and bulk she had a chance of reaching, her neighbor's silver Buick Park Avenue Ultra that was parked on the opposite curb. If she could just get behind it.

She didn't make it.

As if being lifted by invisible hands Penelope felt herself leaving her feet as the force of the explosion sent her flying through the air. She cleared the roof of the Buick by several inches and had her fall softened by the lush lawn that had been watered only a few hours earlier. She tumbled a few more feet along the wet turf before finally coming to a complete stop in a heap just shy of her neighbor's front porch.

Dogs barked. Car alarms went off. The quiet neighborhood was as bright as midday when the huge fireball erupted from behind the house that had been her home for 26 years, and instantly vaporized most of the walls and roof. Splinters of wood, none larger than a toothpick, began raining down on her. She shielded her face from the heat as flames began consuming what little was left of her home.

≈

IF ANYONE ELSE told her how lucky she was, Penelope vowed she was going to deck them.

What's lucky about losing the only house you had called home your entire adult life? All of the kids pictures, all of her clothes, her beautiful shoes, her computer, purse, shoes, cell phone, shoes. Every material item she had on this planet, including her precious Prius, which she had made a special point of moving into the garage because she didn't want to leave it on the street overnight, were all gone in the blink of an eye.

The sun was just starting to rise in the east, casting golden fingers toward Charleston. As she sat on the tailgate of an EMS wagon with a blanket draped over her shoulders, dressed only in ratty terrycloth running shorts and a sleeveless t-shirt, she knew that ignoring her mom's advice to always wear clean underwear would come back to haunt her someday. All things considered, she was in pretty good shape. Other than smelling like a chimney sweep, she didn't have a mark on her.

The fire was under control but the smell of burnt plastic and rubber would linger for weeks. What hadn't blown up with the house had been incinerated to ash and lay on top of the concrete slab. Other than the chimney and a few wall supports and water pipes, there was absolutely nothing left of Penelope's home. It was odd to be able to look straight into the backyard from the street and see the sun coming up over the Ashley River. She almost cried when she noticed the two-foot high lump of metal on what had once been her garage floor. All non-metallic parts of her car had long since gone up in flames. The heat from the fire had been so intense it had melted the roof supports, and the sheet metal of the car's body was now covering the engine and transmission in a blanket of lumpy scorched metal. The houses of her neighbors on both sides were far enough away they had suffered only minor damage, and thankfully no one was injured. The live oak that threw afternoon shade on the front porch was missing all of its branches on the house side and those that were still attached after the blast were black and charred. Neighbors five houses in all directions had wood splinters and other tiny bits of building material too small to identify littering their roofs and lawns.

Penelope looked up as the Captain in charge of the West Ashley fire station approached. "I'm sorry for your losses, Ms. Spence," he said as he removed his helmet. "Now you say you went through the window in the family room."

"Yes. Why?

"Well, we're all baffled as to how you got out at all."

"How so?"

"You had hurricane-grade windows throughout your home. Those things are designed to take 190 mph wind. Unless you've got solid brick, in most cases those windows are stronger than your walls. In your fire, with the force of the explosion, many of them blew out as a unit with the frame and glass still intact."

"So."

"Ms. Spence. There is no way a woman your size could have broken through a triple pane hurricane-rated window without breaking the glass first."

"I was having a pretty good adrenaline rush."

"I understand, but in the confusion you may have gone out an open window or door somewhere else."

"What are you saying?"

He watched as his men continued to roll up their hoses. "What I'm saying is we found the window you believe you went out but it is still in one piece. The glass is not broken. We don't know how you got out alive."

"Are you accusing me of arson?"

"Lord no, ma'am. We're all just going to call this one of those miracles we see from time to time and leave it at that. But, I'll tell you what, I'd put a few extra dollars in the collection plate this week, if it were me. You've got a lot to be grateful for this Sunday morning."

Penelope was stunned. If she hadn't gone through the window, how did she end up in the yard? Was it possible? No. It wasn't.

"We're going to keep one unit on the scene for a few more hours in case there are any flame-ups. You're a very lucky woman."

Despite her earlier promise to deck the next person to tell her how lucky she was, she had to admit he might be right.

≈

AFTER HER SHOWER, Joey found Penelope some clothes and a pair of running shoes about a half size too big, but they were better than nothing. The two sat in the kitchen sipping coffee with a generous shot of Irish whiskey added. Penelope had managed to reach all of her children to give them the bad news and to let them know she was all right. She hadn't been able to track down Bill, he was probably out on the boat, but she had left a message on his voice mail. Penelope cradled the cup in both hands and was surprised they were not shaking more. A strange feeling was coursing through her body. She didn't feel angry or even sad. Despite everything that had happened, she felt grateful. She was still alive; she wasn't injured, and no one else had been hurt. All of the material things could be replaced, and none of the important things had really changed. Plus now that damn house was gone. Grateful. How odd.

Penelope took a sip from her coffee cup and held it out for Joey to top off with more whiskey. Joey poured another jigger and when Penelope didn't retract her mug, kept pouring. When it threatened to overflow, Penelope gingerly drew the ceramic mug to her lips and sipped off enough of the liquid to ensure it wouldn't spill when she sat it down. She got a mouthful of almost straight Bushmills.

Penelope glanced at the clock on the kitchen wall; it was 8:45. In fifteen minutes Senator Horn would be on *Meet the Press* and she would see exactly how big of a story the Hermes Project actually was. Right now that didn't seem so important. She took another pull from her mug. "You make a great cup of coffee, Joey," she said, finally starting to relax. Joey smiled but didn't speak. They had been friends long enough that times like these didn't require words to lend support.

Penelope and Joey had met in kindergarten at Charleston's exclusive school for young women of proper pedigree, Ashley Hall. For over 100 years, the campus located on the peninsula near the College of Charleston and the hospital complex had provided a well-rounded classical education for those who could afford to attend.

Penelope and Joey were born to be close friends, being sired from two of the most famous bloodlines in Charleston: the Middletons and the Draytons. Middleton Place and Drayton Hall have stood shoulder to shoulder on the west banks of the Ashley River since before the American Revolution. The two women had followed similar paths their entire lives: excelling in school, then leaving promising careers to marry early, have children, and be active in the community. Each watched as the last child left the nest and the man they had expected to grow old with departed as well.

It took Penelope a year to get her legs back under her after Bill announced he was leaving. Her weight fluctuated in a 30-pound range; she fought bouts of depression, with suicide occasionally contemplated. Church didn't help and most of her "couple" friends gradually stopped calling. If it hadn't been for Joey, there's no telling what would have happened. She would drag her to concerts and plays she really didn't want to see. She would take her shopping to "spend the SOB's money." When Penelope tearfully called at midnight, Joey came over with a bottle of wine and stayed the night.

The friends had grown like two vines on the same tree. Sometimes they would grow in different directions for awhile but they always ended up back together. Now their lives were so intertwined, Penelope couldn't imagine her life without Joey.

The last two days were starting to blur in her memory as her conscious mind began rearranging the facts in such a way to have her quit questioning her sanity. The prison escape clearly couldn't have happened the way she remembered. People can't just walk through a wall, although she had appeared to pass through a plate glass window. Maybe Walker hypnotized her in some way; that would explain a lot.

Her concentration was broken as her ex-husband, Bill Spence, charged through the front door and into the kitchen.

"What the hell happened to the house?" Bill was close enough to being the six feet tall that he had put it on his driver's license without feeling like he was fudging. An athlete in high school, but not quite good enough to play any sports at the college level, he had kept reasonably fit until he turned forty. The day he got his first pair of bifocals at forty-two, he started to go to seed. Each passing year or two since had added an inch to his waistline and a bit more volume to his multiplying chins. Now he seldom exercised and his cholesterol score was awful. Normally his complexion was doughboy white from slathering on sun block whenever it was impossible to avoid being in the sun, but right now he was bright pink from agitation.

Penelope took another sip of her "coffee" before glaring at her ex. "Oh, I'm fine, Bill, thanks for asking."

Bill, realizing how stupid he sounded, turned back to his normal pale color. "I'm sorry. I just drove past the house and it's just gone."

The high school sweethearts locked eyes. Where had it gone wrong? They'd had a fairytale life. Three great kids, they were comfortable financially, and she had thought they would love each other forever. Gradually, time and responsibility had sapped it all away. They never actually fell out of love with each other; it had just atrophied. Yesterday, they'd still had two things in common, the kids and the house. Now, another fragile link that had connected them was gone.

Joey, wanting to give them privacy, slipped into the adjoining family room. She turned on the television to hear what the distinguished Senator from South Carolina had to say about Michael what's his name, and maybe explain those bowls.

She flipped one channel. Then another. Then another. Her left hand flew to her heart as she dropped the remote. "Penelope! Get in here!"

The tone and urgency of her friend's request caused Penelope to slip off her stool and immediately hurry towards the family room. When she saw what was on the television screen, Penelope felt the strength leaving her body like the air from a deflating balloon. The ceramic coffee mug slipped from her fingers, hit the Italian marble tile and shattered. She was on her way to the floor when Bill hooked his arm under hers, breaking her fall.

There was a live video feed on CNN originating in front of University Hospital in Columbia. The volume was too low to hear, but a graphic across the bottom of the screen told her everything she needed to know. *"Senator Clayton Horn (R-SC) Suffers Massive Stroke. Not Expected to Live."*

≈

IT TOOK PENELOPE half an hour before she felt she was composed enough to make rational decisions and take any sort of action. She had to reach Mark Hatchet. Picking up Joey's phone she dialed the disposable cell phone number he had given her. He answered on the first ring.

"Nellie? Where the hell have you been? I've been trying to reach you for hours. Did you hear about Horn?"

"Yes. Did you hear about what happened to me?"

There was a long silence. Hatchet could hardly imagine anything Penelope Spence could tell him that would top the sudden collapse of a senior U.S. Senator hours before he was going to lift the sheet covering a secret project he had helped conceal.

"No, what happened?"

"My house burnt to the ground last night."

"My God, are you hurt?"

"I'm fine. I got out just in time." She wanted to give credit to Michael Walker but had no idea how she could explain it without sounding crazy. Walker! That's it! Her shoulders straightened and she tossed aside the maudlin funk she had been about to wrap herself in. "Are you still interested in the Hermes Project story?"

"Are you kidding me? After your story hit the wire and people figured out what Horn was going to talk about this morning the entire town started going nuts. Horn refused to give any details ahead of time, and now every news organization in the world is on this story."

"Will Horn's illness have any impact on my putting everything I saw yesterday on the record?"

"I don't see how. It was a pretty straightforward release, but I'll run it by legal again. What are you thinking, Nellie?"

"Is it still my story?"

"I don't like coincidences. A senator is in intensive care, and your house burns down with you in it."

Penelope Spence pushed aside the fresh cup of alcohol-laced coffee Joey offered and reached for the toast that she had refused earlier. She needed to get some solid food in her stomach. Her voice was firm, her resolve fixed. "If I can get an exclusive interview with Michael Walker and find the Hermes Project before anyone else, is it still my story?"

"Nellie," Mark Hatchet said, "this is getting too dangerous."

"He picked me, Mark. He looked me straight in the eyes and said he had picked me to write this story."

"This is a man who 24 hours ago was in Federal Maximum Security! I can't let you do this!"

Bill Spence and Joey Rickman both gawked at Penelope, trying to figure out what was going on. "Then," Penelope's voice was ice cold. "You are releasing me from my obligation to give *The Washington Post* the story and I will be free to sell it to the highest bidder?"

"Nellie..."

"Are you releasing me from my commitment?"

There was a long silence. "I have already assigned eight other reporters to the story."

"Then I'm freelance?"

"Nellie..."

"I have a noon appointment to meet the most sought after interview in the free world, Michael Walker."

"You have a what!?" demanded Bill Spence.

Penelope glared at her ex-husband briefly, then turned her back on him and continued talking to Hatchet. "Mark, I'm going to do this story with you or without you. It is your call. In or out?"

"I'm not going to talk you out of this?"

"No. In or out?"

There was another long pause. "In."

Penelope checked the clock on the kitchen wall; she had less than two hours. "I need to go. I don't have much time. I'll call you when I can."

"We've already got the basic stuff from your interview with Walker and his confrontation with Senator Horn ready to go but I'll hold ten more inches on tomorrow's front page for you, Nellie. Please be careful."

"I will."

Penelope turned and saw her ex-husband and best friend staring at her with openmouthed wonder. Neither had seen her act like this in years. "Who are you?" Joey said. "And what have you done with Penelope Spence?"

CHAPTER THIRTEEN

"Follow your bliss. Find where it is, and don't be afraid to follow it."

JOSEPH CAMPBELL

"WHAT IF YOU get three steps out the door and you 'accidentally' fall and break your neck?" Bill Spence shouted. For some reason he believed increased volume added weight to a line of reasoning.

"He has a point." Joey couldn't believe she was actually agreeing with the Pillsbury Doughboy. "Your house burns down and there's a senator in the hospital."

"Life is full of risks." She continued rummaging through Joey's closet. She found exactly what she was looking for. A hideous day glow blue jogging suit. "You need this?"

"Not unless disco makes a comeback."

"I have to leave everything of mine here." she said as she pulled off the wedding ring she still wore, for no particular reason other than habit, and a locket her mother had given her that had been in the family for over 200 years.

"Why?" demanded Bill.

"Because something may be bugged or have a tracking device on it."

"What are you talking about?" Bill asked.

"Our house was bugged, and Michael Walker found several tracking devices on my car." As the words left her mouth she wished she could grab them back and swallow them.

"When was Walker in your car?" roared Bill Spence.

"You did bust him out!" Joey slapped Penelope on the shoulder. "And you didn't tell me!"

Bill Spence moved directly in front of his ex-wife and through gritted teeth said, "Penelope, what was this Walker character doing in your car?"

"Bill," Penelope answered. "Your macho man routine didn't work when we were married. What makes you think it's going to impress me now?"

"I'm just concerned for you..."

"That is such BS. You're concerned I might do something to embarrass you. Too late. After Walker broke out of the brig, I gave him a ride to West Ashley Park. When he left the park he was wearing some of your old clothes. What do you think the stuffed shirts on the opera committee will think of that?" Bill Spence fumed but said nothing.

"Should I call Ricky?" Joey asked.

Penelope glared at Bill for a moment until she realized what Joey had just said. Her shoulders sagged. "Ricky? Ricky!" Penelope slapped her forehead. "Josephine Antoinette Middleton, you didn't do it again. I don't believe it."

"It was entirely your fault."

"How in the world could it possibly have been my fault?"

"If you hadn't been breaking people out of prison he wouldn't have been over yesterday."

"Will you ever learn?"

"What are you two talking about?" Bill Spence asked.

"Shut up, Bill," both women said, in unison.

"I don't have time for all of this now. Damn. I really wish I had my laptop." Penelope paced in tight circles as she plotted her strategy. "Joey, I'm going to need to borrow your car."

"No way. I can't lend my Beemer to a potential flight risk."

"I'm serious. I need your car."

"No way."

"Why not?"

"Three reasons. One, you don't know how to drive a stick."

"I know how to drive a stick shift..."

"Tell that to Froggy LeGrange."

"I was sixteen!"

"Yes but as I recall the transmission in his Camaro ended up in the middle of Calhoun Street." Penelope didn't have an answer so Joey continued. "Two, after driving your little soybean-mobile for the last couple of years you couldn't keep a real car on the road. And three," Joey's eyes twinkled with excitement. "If you think I'm going to miss this, you are out of your mind."

≈

PENELOPE SPENCE CHECKED the contents of the backpack for the third time. The biggest problem with her plan was she still didn't know who the bad guys were. And there was always the possibility there were no good guys in this little drama. She didn't trust Assistant Director Robert Smith even a little; she had dealt with his agenda-driven type before. She only had Walker's word that the 30 missing people were alive and well, but no proof to support his claim. And, considering electronic devices were found on both her car and in her house, she had no idea if there was another player or even multiple players she still hadn't met.

All she knew for sure was that Horn had looked awful when she spoke to him, and it was possible that his stroke was from natural causes. Still, either Smith or Walker had the resources to cause illness to Horn and to burn down her house if either felt it was necessary. Plus Horn had made it clear that there were others waiting in the shadows, not to mention one billion people, who somehow had an interest in what was going on.

She hadn't felt this alive in years.

Penelope plopped into the front seat of Joey's Beemer. She was wearing the ugly blue sweat suit from the back of Joey's closet and had the backpack on her lap.

"I feel like Butch and Sundance," Joey said with a laugh.

"I'm thinking more Lucy and Ethel," Penelope answered as she tried to control her breathing.

"Will you settle for Stephanie Plum and Lula?"

The two old friends exchanged smiles and nodded their agreement.

"Buckle up, baby!" Joey exclaimed as she popped a Guns and Roses CD into the stereo and turned up the volume. Axl Rose began screaming as she turned over the ignition and punched the garage door opener on her visor. The door wasn't even fully up when she slapped the car into reverse, dropped the clutch and floored it. The tires squealed as she laid a track of rubber down the driveway. She hit the curb at about the same moment Axl hit the chorus.

When Joey slammed on the brakes, the car slid briefly on some loose gravel; fortunately there were no cars parked on the street. Before the sports car came to a complete stop she jammed the transmission into first gear and floored the gas. A trail of burnt rubber and blue smoke formed behind the Beemer as it screamed down the nearly deserted street. The tachometer jumped to the right, but she didn't bother with second gear until the red flash of German machinery was going over 30 mph. She was doing 60 long before she reached the guard station of her walled community. Tapping the brakes just enough to keep the car on the road, she dropped the gear from fourth to second, as she flew through the stop sign and made a right turn at over 40 mph. Before the drivers of the two vehicles that were assigned to tail Penelope Spence could put down their coffee and donut, Joey was a half mile ahead of them.

Being a Sunday morning, traffic was sparse as she jumped the light at Sam Rittenberg Boulevard. A third of the town was already on the water or a golf course, a third was in church, and a third was still in bed recovering from the previous night's activities. Joey and Penelope pretty much had the road to themselves. As the streaking red car approached the bridge over the Ashley River, Joey's speedometer was passing 100 mph. Joey upped the volume to the max as the next Guns and Roses song kicked in. Axl began screaming "Welcome to the Jungle." At the top of his lungs.

Joey cut off a lumbering SUV in the middle lane, hit the brakes on the Beemer about a hundred yards from the on ramp to I-26 South, and dropped the gear from fifth to third. The tach leaped into the red again as she popped the clutch and let the engine compression slow the car down; the motor screamed in protest. They were still going 60 mph, well above the recommend 35, when she hit the on-ramp. Thank God for German engineering. Not only did the BMW stay on the road, its right front wheel hugged the inside white stripe without drifting.

Once on I-26, she opened it up again. The speedometer topped out at 120 before she began her descent to the Morrison Street exit. She flew down the off ramp and took the stop sign and left turn at 35 mph. She ran the light at East Bay Street and headed toward town before slowing down to a more reasonable speed.

Joey ran her hand through her windblown hair and said, "I've always enjoyed a Sunday drive. How about you?" For the first time since leaving her driveway she glanced over at her friend. Penelope was paler than her ex-husband, and her fingernails were latched to the upholstery of the seat like a cat that didn't want to be picked up. "Was that quick enough for you?"

"Fine, thanks." Penelope felt her blood pressure starting to return to normal, but nevertheless had a difficult time disengaging her grip on the seat. Her knuckles appeared to have gone into rigor mortis and she no longer had any control over them. "By the way, the Hendricks Racing Team called and said they're looking for a driver next week at Talladega."

"Too many left turns for my taste."

By the time they passed Calhoun Street, most of Penelope's normal functions had returned. As they approached the corner of East Bay and Market, she thought the adrenaline from Joey's driving would have started to wear off. The exact opposite was happening. Walker, if he still planned to meet her, had to be close by. Somehow, on some level, she could feel his presence. They missed the light.

Stuck in the middle of one of Charleston's largest tourist attractions, there were too many people and cars for Joey to try anything aggressive, so they waited for the green light. Penelope looked around for any signs of Walker or flashing police lights, but found neither. She was hardly surprised that she couldn't see Walker; she doubted he would stand out. There was still a half hour before they were scheduled to meet.

Joey drove just under the speed limit down East Bay Street, past Broad and pulled into an open spot in front of the Battery at the extreme tip of the Charleston peninsula. This was the exact spot where, on April 12, 1861, the American Civil War began. Beginning at 4:30 a.m. and for the next 34 straight hours the Confederate batteries pounded Fort Sumter until it surrendered. It is a matter of some dispute whether it was one of Penelope's ancestors or one of Joey's who was given the honor of lighting the fuse on the first cannon. Most history books give the credit to Ezekiel Drayton, a fact Mark discovered while they were in college and had never let Penelope forget.

Joey watched her friend grab her borrowed items and reach for the door handle. Penelope had a nagging feeling that it might be a long time before they shared another bottle of wine and a laugh. Tears welled up in her eyes and she hugged her lifelong friend.

"You okay?" Joey asked, surprised by the flash of emotion from her friend. "I'll see you later this afternoon, right?"

Penelope wiped a tear off of her cheek. "Right," she lied. Penelope

Drayton Spence somehow knew that the moment she stepped out of the car her life would change forever. It still wasn't too late to turn back and rebuild her life in Charleston. Racked for a moment with emotion and doubt, she drew in a deep breath and straightened her shoulders. She was doing the right thing. They hugged again and Penelope jumped out of the car and trotted toward one of the benches in Battery Park.

≈

M RS. GLORIA VON Ward had been considering getting up and getting dressed when her cell phone went off. Having just spent the first night of her honeymoon at a bed and breakfast overlooking Charleston Harbor, she couldn't imagine who would be calling her. When the female voice on the phone told her to hold for the Department of Homeland Security's Director of Emerging Technologies, she sat straight up in bed, slapping her husband of 18 hours hands away.

"Agent Von Ward?

"Yes, sir."

"This is Director Noah Shepherd. I need you to respond immediately to an eminent national security threat."

"Yes, sir."

≈

P ENELOPE WAS NEARLY alone in White Point Garden, a tree-filled park at the tip of the peninsula where the Confederate Battery had once stood. She surveyed the area. There was an old man walking his dog with one hand holding a leash and the other gripping a plastic doggy waste bag. There was a young couple in the gazebo that hadn't even noticed her since they couldn't take their eyes off each other. There was a fit young woman stretching her legs, clearly preparing for her morning run. It looked pretty safe to her.

The runner kept her left side away from Penelope's line of sight. She didn't want her to see the Bluetooth earpiece. This was a career moment for Gloria Von Ward, the honeymoon be damned. To have someone at the Director's level at Homeland Security call her, a Field Agent only a year out of the Federal Law Enforcement Training Center, was unheard of. While the woman in the blue jogging suit may have lost her tail for the moment, they'd all start arriving within the next few minutes. If Von

Ward could keep her in sight for five minutes she would be on a fast track that only having a marker from the Director's level could bring.

Penelope Spence began jogging up Church Street. Before the Civil War, Charleston had been one of the richest cities in the country. The area known as "South of Broad", which encompasses the tract between Broad Street and the Battery, has some of the finest examples of early American architecture in existence. Sprawling restored mansions, many with harbor views, help make Charleston one of the top vacation destinations in the country. On a beautiful Sunday morning such as this, tourists and horse-drawn carriages crowd the narrow streets.

It took Penelope less than a block before she realized that the woman from the park might be following her. Looking for confirmation, she took a left on Atlantic and a right on Meeting Street. The other runner was still there, matching her stride for stride. She looked at least 20 years younger and in much better shape; the chances of outrunning her were slim. She would have to outthink her.

Penelope took a right on Water Street and slowly headed back towards the Cooper River. At the corner, she jogged in place until a tourist's horse-drawn carriage moved out of her way, then she bolted full speed up Church, taking a quick right into Stoll's Alley. She knew the woman would not want to lose sight of her and would try to close the gap between them quickly. The third house down, like so many in the Historic District, was in the process of being renovated and a construction dumpster was parked in the driveway. It was exactly what she had been hoping for. Reaching in, Penelope found what she needed.

Gloria Von Ward, seeing the target had made her, kicked it from a jog to a flat-out run. If she had spotted the tail, that would be too bad, but Agent Von Ward was not going to lose sight of her until backup arrived. She spoke into the Bluetooth. "She's turned right into," she squinted to read the sign as she turned the corner. What a day to not have time to put in her contact lens or be able to locate her glasses. Before she could give her location, an oversized burlap sack was over her head and she was being pulled between the buildings. As she struggled, a leather case with her Homeland Security badge tumbled to the ground. Losing her balance on a cobblestone Von Ward fell hard, and didn't stir. That was all the advantage Penelope needed.

Penelope pulled off the hideous blue jogging suit, and instead of tossing it in the dumpster where it would be a clue to her wardrobe change, she stuffed it in the backpack. Underneath she was wearing a bright yellow sun dress. Reaching into the backpack she pulled out a pair of oversized sunglasses and one of Joey's real hair blond wigs that had cost a small fortune. She put on the sunglasses and adjusted the wig until it felt comfortable. Next, she pulled off her running shoes. They were not nearly as noticeable as the jogging suit and she didn't need the additional bulk in the backpack. She tossed the running shoes down the alley before retrieving a pair of sandals from the backpack and slipping them on. She pulled one last item from the backpack, a Charleston Museum shopping bag, and crammed the backpack inside the heavy paper bag. Her transformation was complete and had been accomplished in less than 30 seconds. Glancing back she saw the woman who had been chasing her just starting to stir. The new Penelope Drayton Spence stepped out onto East Bay Street and joined a group of tourists who were strolling toward the market. They all watched as a Chevy Suburban with darkened windows and flashing lights in its grill squealed its tires and turned into Stoll Alley, clearly following Gloria Von Ward's tracking device.

≈

THE CITY MARKET has been a fixture of Charleston since the time of the American Revolution and in constant use since 1788. As Charleston transformed from a sleepy declining city to one of America's favorite tourist destinations, the market gradually evolved. The four blocks of covered but open-air market had moved from selling fresh fruits and produce in the nineteenth century to trinkets and souvenirs today. On this weekend at the height of tourist season City Market was packed.

Outside a coffee shop catering to the tourist trade were three stacks of newspapers; *The Post and Courier*, Sunday *New York Times* and the Sunday *Washington Post*. Each stack had a brick on top to keep the wind from blowing the newspapers away. There it was.

Taking off her sunglasses, she leaned over and read the headlines. She wanted to shout and point to her name on the front page. She wanted to kiss total strangers. She wanted to buy a latte for everyone in sight. Instead she quickly shoved the sunglasses back on her nose and started looking for Michael Walker. Penelope heard the bells chiming at Saint Philips Church, which meant it had to be around noon. Her watch had been a casualty of the fire. She crossed the street and made her way inside the market.

She looked around for Walker but he was a no-show. The only man even close to his general size was a potbellied biker with a dirty blond ponytail, wearing a t-shirt that read, "Lock Up Your Daughters." She wasn't sure if she was relieved or disappointed. As the seconds began to tick away, she suddenly started to panic.

"Oh, God," she thought to herself, realizing for the first time what she had done. She had assaulted a Federal officer. "Oh, God," She whispered softly as she bumped into the biker.

"Sorry," she muttered as she tried to move away, but the crowd and narrow aisles restricted her mobility.

"I see we both prefer blonds," the biker said in a familiar voice. As soon as the biker pushed his sunglasses to the end of his nose revealing his eyes, she knew it was Walker.

"Been eating well on my $3,000, I see."

He patted the pillow under his shirt. "I finally found a store with peanut M&Ms."

He motioned that they should start moving. With a bit of effort, they managed to escape the crowd and head east a short block on Market Street until it dead-ended into Concord Street and the Cooper River. Taking a left toward the South Carolina Aquarium, they walked around the corner to the warehouse district that few tourists ever discover, even though it is only a few steps from the market. They stopped in front of a rusty blue and white Ford Bronco with 10 years of hard use and an interesting assortment of minor body damage including what appeared to be a bullet hole in the rear quarter panel.

Walker took off his sunglasses so he could make better eye contact. "Anyone follow you?"

"Yes," Penelope said. "I figured they would have tracking devices on me and Joey..."

"Joey?"

"My friend Joey Rickman. She was my wheel man this morning." Walker nodded that he understood and that she should continue. "Everything I have on is borrowed. I couldn't do anything about Joey's car, but I had her drop me off about a mile from here and I walked. I'm pretty sure I lost the tail."

Penelope recounted the entire morning, starting with Joey's driving and ending with her "sacking" a Federal Agent, followed by her wardrobe change. Walker listened intently without interrupting.

When she finished, he smiled. "Very nice. What made you think of that?"

"I have a weakness for trashy mystery novels, and one of my favorite characters is Kinsey Millhone. I asked myself, what would Kinsey do?"

"Sue Grafton would be proud."

"You heard about Senator Horn?"

"Yes," Walker said with a sigh. "It's unfortunate. Nice articles in the *Post* this morning."

"Thanks. It will probably be overshadowed by Senator Horn." Walker nodded. "My house burned down last night."

"I know."

"Was that you that warned me?"

Walker smiled. "What do you think?"

"I have no idea."

"As soon as you do, let me know."

"It's going to be like that, huh?"

Walker smiled and shrugged. "Okay. It's decision time."

"Meaning?"

"Meaning, you have two choices."

"Which are?"

"You can turn yourself in, and tell Robert Smith everything you know..."

"Including the prison break?"

"Everything. Trust me. He will understand exactly what you're telling him, he's seen it all before."

"I don't trust him. They found bugs in my house when they were searching it."

"Excellent."

"Excellent?! What is excellent about that?"

"How many did they find?"

"Close to a dozen."

"Interesting." Penelope watched as Walker sifted through the new information. "That probably wasn't Robert, but it could have been any of several dozen groups or agencies."

"What?"

"You hit everyone's radar screen the moment you asked to see me at the brig. One likely candidate is Robert's boss, Noah Shepherd. I'd bet that at least some of those bugs had the earmarks of a Marcus Wolfe black bag job."

"Who?"

"The Department of Emerging Technology is huge and they occasionally push the envelope on what's legal. Wolfe is the director's muscle. Given the number of bugs that were discovered and how poorly they were hidden, they were intended to be found. No doubt others were there that you'd probably never be able to locate. Someone is trying to scare you."

"They're doing a pretty good job."

"They are very talented people."

"So is this bad for the Hermes Project?" Penelope asked.

"Just the opposite. For this to work we need to have the Director personally involved."

"Why?"

"It will be clear, soon enough."

"So you're not going to tell me?"

"You don't need to know, and if you did it could be uncomfortable for you if you turn yourself in."

"Why."

"Because Wolfe would get it out of you, one way or another."

Penelope didn't like the sound of that at all. "Do I need protection?'

"Maybe. Wolfe is not known for his soft touch."

"Am I in physical danger?"

"There are all kinds of danger; you gave them some leverage when you put that bag over the agent's head."

Penelope chewed it over for a second then shook her head. "She didn't actually see me do anything. My lawyer would have a field day with any charges."

"That's the spirit. If you decide to turn yourself in, only talk to Robert Smith, and turn yourself in with your attorney and with the press covering it if possible."

Penelope smiled. "I think my attorney can arrange that."

"Robert will make it much easier."

"Still don't trust him."

Walker sighed. "I worked with the man for nearly a year. I've had dinner at his house and know his wife and kids."

"What do you mean you worked with him?"

"He was the Homeland Security liaison for the Hermes Project."

"What?"

"He's actually on our side. He was our strongest advocate for keeping the program alive. He went with me to the final hearing with Horn's committee and was pretty persuasive."

"Yet he has thrown you in jail three times this week."

"He was just following orders. He would never hurt me or anyone else. It's not in his nature."

"If you say so. You said I had two choices. What's behind door number two?"

"You come with me."

"What?'

"You say that a lot, don't you?"

"I'm a reporter. How about option three?"

"Which is?'

"You stay here and I interview you, then I'm home for dinner."

Walker lowered his eyes and as Penelope realized she didn't have a home to return to, a heavy, awkward silence settled over them.

"You don't want to do that," Walker said softly.

Penelope forced her house from her mind; nothing could be done about that now. "Why not?"

"Because then you won't get to meet Dr. Altman and see the Hermes Project firsthand."

That stopped Penelope dead in her tracks. "You certainly know how to say all the right things to a lady. That's very tempting."

Walker studied her closely; judgment time had arrived. In the next few moments he would know if he had risked his life, and possibly the entire future of mankind, on a fool's errand. "Let me ask you something."

"Go ahead."

"What do you want more than anything?"

"Grandkids," she answered without thinking.

Walker waited until she was ready to be serious. His blue gray eyes bored into her. She knew exactly what she wanted but didn't want to say it out loud since it seemed so petty and selfish. She had so much to be grateful for and it would be easy for anyone, especially her children, to take it the wrong way. Walker continued to wait.

"It sounds so shallow," she said meekly, as tears filled her eyes.

"No, it doesn't."

"You already know what I'm going to say?"

"Yes. That's why I sought you out."

"Then why do I have to say it?"

"I have to hear you say it."

"Why?"

"Because you have to hear yourself say it. Until you declare this to the universe, nothing will happen."

She focused on her shoes as tears began to stream down her cheeks. "I want to be 23 again, and have every newspaper in the world on their knees begging me to come work for them. I want to go back and do it differently." She broke down and began sobbing on Walker's shoulder. "I love my children, I really do. That sounded so awful."

He patted her softly on the back and whispered in her ear. "No, it didn't." She was crying so hard she was shaking. The events of her life and the past two days had finally caught up with her. Here she was, on a public street, wrapped in the arms of a man she barely knew, crying like a baby. Her mother would have been horrified.

Walker waited until the bulk of the storm passed before whispering in her ear. "What if I told you, you could have exactly what you want if you come with me?"

Penelope pulled away and looked in his eyes without releasing her grip. Every bit of logic, all of her intellect, everything she had ever learned told her this man was crazy. But there, trapped in his eyes and feeling the warmth of his body pressing against her, she believed him.

"The 23 again part I can't do anything about," he said with a twinkle in his eye. "That boat has already sailed."

Penelope started laughing just as hard as she had been crying moments earlier. She wiped a tear from her cheek, straightened her shoulders and said, "When do we leave?"

Walker motioned toward the battered Bronco. "Your chariot awaits."

"You got to be kidding? This is what you spent my $3,000 on?"

"I also got a new T-shirt."

"We're going to have to talk about that. I have two daughters."

Walker shrugged as he opened the passenger side door and Penelope Spence climbed in.

PART TWO

The Fourth Awakening

*"If you realized how powerful your thoughts are, you would never
think a negative thought."*

Peace Pilgrim

CHAPTER FOURTEEN

"Once you see things differently, you gain power.
All of a sudden there is enlightenment."

JOAN CHEN

PENELOPE SPENCE GLANCED over her shoulder as Walker turned onto the Ravenel Bridge and headed toward Mt. Pleasant. Opened in 2005 and built at a cost of over $500 million dollars, with a span of 1,546 feet it is the longest cable-stayed bridge in the Western Hemisphere. Crossing the Cooper River just north of the historic section of the Charleston peninsula, its twin spires and miles of graceful cables make a striking backdrop for tourist photos.

Looking back she could see the South Carolina Aquarium and could just about make out the famous "Rainbow Row" of restored Charleston style homes along East Bay Street that have inspired a thousand artists and many more photographers. Far in the distance, at the mouth of the harbor, was Ft. Sumter and just beyond, the Atlantic Ocean. Looming on the Mt. Pleasant side of the Cooper was the USS Yorktown, a World War II era aircraft carrier now converted into a floating museum.

She felt the Bronco reach the apex of the span at the center point between the two massive towers and start the gradual 150-foot descent back down. Charleston, the town she and 14 generations of her family had called home for over 250 years, melted behind her as they headed north on U.S. 17 in the direction of Myrtle Beach. She sighed as she considered the fact that she had no idea when she would see the city again, if ever. More than one bridge had been crossed. Walker understood the whipsaw of emotions she was experiencing and didn't intrude on her thoughts by speaking.

Instead of getting on I-526 as she had expected, Walker continued a few more miles and made a left on State Route 41. The road was poker straight with light traffic. Penelope smiled when she thought about the Bronco. In Charleston, it was a noticeable eyesore, but on the back roads of rural South Carolina it was just another battered truck with a garden-variety redneck behind the wheel. They drove in silence for nearly half an hour before Walker turned on his left turn signal in the small town of Huger— pronounced "Huge Gee"— and headed west on State Route 402.

He finally broke the silence. "What was the last you heard about Senator Horn?"

"Stable, but still critical."

"That's too bad. We really wanted Horn to go on the talk shows this morning."

"Excuse me?"

"Your article today got the ball rolling, and the senator's appearance would have caused a feeding frenzy in the media. That alone could have been enough to force Homeland Security to come clean on our research."

"What do you mean?"

"Classified or not, Horn was ready to go public. That would have put tremendous pressure on Homeland Security to declassify it. You could then have written anything you wanted with impunity. Now we have to go to plan B."

"Plan B?"

"You and I will be spending a great deal more time together than I initially thought."

"Sorry," Penelope said.

"Don't be. I enjoy your company."

"Thanks. What happens next?"

"We have a very narrow window of opportunity here. With your help, we either flip Noah Shepherd, or put so much heat on Homeland Security that the decision is taken away from Shepherd and made by the Secretary of that department. He has much more political exposure, and with what's happened in the past 24 hours he's probably already starting to feel the heat. We have to move quickly before anyone can change their mind."

"How do you propose doing that?"

"Before Senator Horn's stroke I would have said he was going to ram it through for us, with you covering the story. Now it's all up to you."

"Me?"

"Yes. We have to make as much information public as quickly as possible. Right now, because of your story about my arrest and escape combined with the rumors about what Horn was going to say, our opponents are back on their heels. That won't last for very long."

"How long do you think you'll have?"

"I'm guessing we'll need to get Hermes declassified and in the media in the next 48 to 72 hours. If we miss this opportunity, who knows when we'll get another chance. Horn's condition will temper some of the attacks on me and Hermes, since they will appear in bad taste if he's still in critical condition. The only winner here is you."

"Me?"

"Yes," Walker said calmly and without even a hint of regret or emotion "His stroke has greatly increased the value of the stories you're going to write." Penelope wasn't sure how to take Walker's last comment. While it was true that if she were the only source of information on a breaking story it would enhance her value, the thought of benefiting from another's suffering went against the grain of her conscience. Walker's analysis was as cold-blooded as it was accurate. She turned and stared out the front windshield as an uncomfortable silence settled in again.

The Bronco came up on a Ford F-150 pickup, laboring at 15 mph under the posted limit, pulling a bass boat. Walker inched up on the rig, let a Honda Civic headed the other direction pass, then hit the gas. The Bronco's big V-8 accelerated with such force that Penelope was unexpectedly pressed back into her seat. While the Bronco might not be much to look at, with a powerful engine, new tires and a tight transmission, clearly it could hold its own if evasion were necessary.

As the minutes ticked by, something else dawned on Penelope. "There won't be any story if I can't get in touch with Mark Hatchet at the *Post*." Looking around the Bronco for a pen and paper she didn't see any. "I wish I had something to take notes with."

"Look under your seat."

Puzzlement crept over Penelope's face as she felt something thin and metallic wedged under the seat. She pulled out a laptop computer. Her laptop. "Where did this come from!?"

"I got it out of your house last night."

"What?"

"I thought it might come in handy. I bought you a lighter power plug..."

"What?"

"You plug it into the cigarette lighter and..."

"I know what a lighter plug is," she said angrily. "What were you doing in my house?"

"I already told you. I was getting your laptop for you."

"You were in my house last night?"

"Yes."

"Wait a minute," as another thought occurred to Penelope. "I keep my laptop in my bedroom." She glared at Walker. "Well?!"

"Well, what?"

"I keep my laptop in my bedroom."

"That's a statement, not a question."

Furious, Penelope slowly asked her question, enunciating each word carefully. "Were... you... in... my... bedroom... last... night... while... I... was... asleep?"

"Yes... I... was. I told you I was getting it for you since you were going to need it, and it was unlikely you would bring it to our meeting. I did it for you."

"For me? You were in my house. Hell! In my bedroom stealing my laptop so you could give it back to me today?"

"Yes."

"Did you set the fire after you finished looting my house?"

"No. That started hours after I had left."

"Are you the one who told me to run?"

"In a manner of speaking."

"What the hell does that mean?" Walker shrugged and his eyes locked on the road in front of them. "No, no don't tell me; let me guess. I'm not ready to understand."

Walker struggled to keep a poker face and kept driving.

"Do you know who caused the fire?"

"Of course. So do you."

"You're talking nonsense again!"

"Am I? All things considered, you've got your laptop, and you got out of the house uninjured. I would think that would make you happy."

"What would make me happy is for you to have prevented my house from burning down, but for now I'll settle for you telling me what caused it."

Walker shook his head. "Sorry, you're not ready yet."

Penelope grunted and slammed both of her fists on the dashboard of the Bronco. Small clouds of dust and lint came out of the air vents. "You know, I think you are the most annoying person I've ever met."

"Thanks."

"That wasn't meant as a compliment."

"I know." Walker shook his head in appreciation, "You shouldn't be so frustrated. You really need to let yourself relax and be grateful for how far you've come so quickly."

"Having come so far still doesn't mean you're going to start giving me any straight answers, does it?"

"No. But you're a lot closer."

"What does that mean?"

"When you can tell me who started the fire and why, let me know."

Penelope glared a hole though Walker. "I give up." She said, throwing her hands up in despair. "Will I be able to talk to Mark Hatchet and send him an article?"

"You will not be able to speak directly to Hatchet until tomorrow, but you will be able to send him your article. We'll find a Wi-Fi coffee shop and bounce your article around the globe for a few hours so it can't be traced.

"Cool. What happens tomorrow?"

"We'll be at the compound."

"Won't they be able to trace a call from there?"

"Maybe, but I doubt it."

"Why do you doubt it?"

"We'll be using Walker Industries' communication satellite. They tried to hack it before, but I doubt they'll try again."

"Why? What happened?"

"When we detected the hack, we retaliated. It led to quite a bit of messy back and forth with the NSA, some of our government contracts, our..."

"When did all of this happen?"

"About six months ago, when they first started aggressively looking for me. Let's just say they experienced some computer problems."

"Wait a minute," Penelope said with a smile. "That was around the time there was a foul up with Social Security checks and they were late going out. The Secretary of the Treasury was almost forced to resign."

"No comment." Michael Walker smiled, but didn't take his eyes off the road.

"You didn't." Penelope began to laugh.

"I have no idea what you're talking about."

"My God! You did! You hacked the Treasury Department's computers to get the National Security Agency off your back?"

"They were a lot easier than trying to hack the NSA."

"Didn't you get in any trouble?"

"No. But we certainly got their attention. We quietly reached a ceasefire agreement. 'You leave our stuff alone and we'll leave your stuff alone.' The politicians in Washington are more afraid of the AARP than anything I might have been doing."

"You're awful," Penelope said wiping a tear from her eye after laughing so hard. "So, now are you going to tell me exactly what happened with the Hermes Project?"

"No."

"No?" Penelope's smile vanished. "What do you mean, no!?"

"Senator Horn is the big story right now. You were the last reporter to speak to him and you have a pretty good idea what caused his stroke. With everything that happened yesterday now on the record, you've already got a huge story to write. Without the senator, the Hermes Project will have to wait until it's declassified."

Penelope opened her mouth to protest but stopped when she realized Walker was right. It would be a huge build-up piece for when she finally got to the compound. Every news outlet in the world would be waiting for her to file her report.

"Okay. But what if the Hermes story breaks before you get around to telling me about it?"

Walker smiled. "Even if they should somehow find the compound, which I highly doubt they will, I promise you an exclusive interview with both me and Dr. Altman."

"On the record and you'll give me direct answers to all of my questions?"

"Absolutely."

"I'm going to hold you to that." Penelope said as she plugged her laptop in to the cigarette lighter. For the next two hours they rode in relative silence, broken only by Penelope asking Walker a few clarification questions.

She ended up with two articles, one long and one fairly short. Both were a bit wordier then her normal style, but Mark would edit as he saw fit. She wanted to give him everything she had since they didn't have the ability to discuss the copy over the phone. The first and longer piece was a general overview of her day with Horn, what had happened at the brig, and as much as she knew about the Hermes Project. The shorter and most dramatic piece was her recap of what had happened in the interview room with Walker and Horn. She was intentionally vague about the Hermes Project and gave no indication that she was sitting an arm's length away from Michael Walker.

"I'm done."

"Excellent. We're near Florence, South Carolina. We should be able to find a Wi-Fi site somewhere." As if on cue, a McDonald's marquee on U.S. 52 proclaimed "Free Wi-Fi". Penelope was still doing a final proofread when Walker wheeled the Bronco into a space near the door. She was surprised when she felt the passenger side door open. Walker extended one hand for the laptop and the other to Penelope.

"Such a gentleman," Penelope said as she disengaged the laptop from the cigarette lighter and handed it to Walker.

Walker selected a table by the window with a clear view of their vehicle, then pushed a piece of paper in Penelope's direction. "What's this?" She asked.

"That's the email address you should send the article to and the name you should use on the file. But first we need to run it through an encryption program."

"Excuse me, but if the NSA and Homeland Security are monitoring emails wouldn't a document using your encryption be like sending up a flare asking them to come and arrest us?"

"Very nice," Walker said with the nod of his head. "But encryption probably is the wrong word. This is a name substitution program. Any emails, and especially any that originate from the southeastern United States with your name and words like Walker Industries, Hermes or *The Washington Post*, among others, will be instantly flagged. What we're going to do is change them to something else and have them converted back just before the document is sent over to your editor."

"Are you sure that will work?" Penelope asked.

Walker's eyes twinkled and a broad grin covered his face. "I'm pretty confident this will work."

"Oh, Lord," Penelope said with a laugh loud enough that heads turned in the restaurant. Looking around she leaned in and whispered. "You wrote the NSA email search program, didn't you?"

"We might have been involved in that project."

"I can see why these guys don't want you running around without adult supervision," Penelope said shaking her head. "How long before Mark will get this?"

"Four or five hours." Walker motioned toward the front counter. "You want anything?"

Penelope glanced up at the menu board. "A fish sandwich and sweet tea." She turned back to her computer and grimaced; she was having problems getting linked to McDonald's Wi-Fi. "I hate computers..."

Before she could make any further comments on the annoying complexity of modern electronics, Walker had spun her laptop around and his fingers were dancing across the keyboard. "I'm going to freshen up," she said, sliding out of the booth. When she got back the file had been sent and her food was waiting for her. To her surprise Walker had ordered himself a Big Mac combo and a chocolate shake. But, as if to show opening her car door for her wasn't a fluke, he had politely waited for her return before starting to eat.

"Sir," Penelope said in her best Scarlett O'Hara impersonation, "You have the manners of a true Southern gentleman."

"I'm from Miami," Walker said with a shrug. "Which is about 600 miles south of Charleston. That almost makes you a Yankee to me."

"Oh, Fiddle-dee-dee," Penelope said as she shook a napkin into her lap and took a bite of her sandwich. After a few moments of silent chewing she pointed to a dot of special sauce in the corner of Walker's mouth that he immediately wiped away. "With all of this talk about enlightenment I was expecting you to be a vegan."

Walker smiled as he took another bite of his Big Mac. "What makes you think I'm not?"

"You're eating a Big Mac might be a clue."

"Am I?"

Penelope's mind flashed back to her lunch with Joey at the Sunfire Grill and remembered how Joey had a completely different recollection of the meal they had shared. "You are a very odd man."

"Thanks."

"Wasn't a compliment."

"I know."

≈

Back in the Bronco and on the highway, the adrenaline rush from the chase downtown and the jolt Penelope had gotten from writing another article that would be tomorrow's front page was starting to wear off. Running on only a few hours sleep, a deep fatigue crept over her. Not only was she exhausted physically, but she was mentally and emotionally drained. Less than two days ago she had been sitting at home minding her own business and now she had helped someone escape from prison, her house burned to the ground, a man she had worked closely with for six years suffered a stroke, and she had beaten up a federal agent. Here she was in a car, wearing a wig, headed who knows where with the guy she had helped bust out of the clink. All in all, this was not her typical weekend.

Almost as if he was reading her mind, Walker reached behind the driver's seat and tossed her a pillow. Looking in the back to see what else he might have, she saw camping gear, an assortment of tools and some lumps covered with a blue plastic tarp. She tucked the pillow between her shoulder and the window, and in less than 30 seconds was fast asleep.

≈

Penelope Spence's eyes didn't open again until she felt the Bronco slowing to a stop. The sun was low in the western sky. Walker was pulling into a Cracker Barrel Restaurant and she realized that despite the quick lunch at McDonalds, she was famished. Though she had been trying to go vegetarian, the smell of grilling meat and poultry coated in flour and frying in vats of grease set her mouth to watering. This was going to be a real test.

"Where are we?" she asked.

"A restaurant."

"I can see that. A bit more general, please."

"Third planet from the sun."

"If you're going to be like this the whole time," she said with a smile, "then I'm going home." Penelope's smile faded when she realized what she had said, and she lowered her eyes.

Walker noticed the mood change and decided to give her a straight answer. "We're just outside of Mt Airy, North Carolina. We're far enough from Charleston that we can safely get on the interstate now."

Penelope shook off the wave of weepy emotion that was trying to control her. "Where are we headed?"

"Inside a restaurant," Walker said with a smile as he held the door open.

She waved a warning finger in Walker's direction. "I've already kicked one person's butt today..."

≈

PENELOPE SPENCE COULDN'T remember a meal that had tasted better or that she had enjoyed more. Walker must have read her mind. Because of the disruption of her normal sleep cycle, she was more in the mood for breakfast food than a traditional dinner type meal. Cracker Barrel had been the perfect choice; breakfast all day. Sitting across from each other like old marrieds instead of next to each other like lovers, they began talking for the first time. Since each had read the other's bio, they were more like friends renewing an acquaintance than strangers sharing a meal. Walker shook his head whenever she started to ask questions that he didn't want overheard, so they kept the conversation light. His research department had done a heck of a job. He seemed to know an awful lot about her.

"So? Walker asked with a smile. "Do you still dance?"

"You asked me that before."

"Yes, but you didn't give me much of an answer. I was curious. Your first two years of college it looked like you planned to be a dancer, then when you had to declare your major you headed into journalism instead. Was there a reason?"

"Other than the fact that my mother would have come to New York City, dragged me back to Charleston by my hair, then locked me in the room next to my crazy Aunt Martha?"

"That was your mother's reason. What was yours?"

"You're not going to let this go, are you?"

Walker shrugged and waited for an answer.

"In the summer between my sophomore and junior year I got a job on

Broadway. It wasn't much. I was a vacation replacement for some of the girls in the chorus line of *Chicago*."

"Wow! *Cell Block Tango* is one of my all-time favorites." Walker's eyes brightened as he propped his elbows on the table and rested his chin on his fists. Penelope had his full and complete attention. "That must have been exciting."

"If you're going to patronize me..."

"I'm serious, that's one of my favorites."

"It sounds more glamorous than it actually was. The tedium of eight shows a week began to wear on me pretty quickly. As the fall semester approached I had to make a decision. They offered me a full time position, but the experience had made it an easy choice. Dancing was my passion. Turning it into a job took all of the fun out of it."

"Interesting." Walker nodded his head as if he completely understood.

"You seem to know a great deal about my personal life, just how many of your employees have you had stalking me?" she asked as she motioned to the waitress for a refill of her sweet tea.

"A small army," Walker answered as he sipped his plain water—no ice, no lemon.

She had gotten over the embarrassment of their food order and was feeling refreshed. The waitress had used a huge tray to carry the assorted bowls, plates and platters. Four of them—a plate with a large stack of pancakes and three eggs over easy, a bowl with fried apples, another bowl with cheese grits and a side plate of buttered sourdough rye bread—had gone to Penelope's side of the table, while Walker's French toast and side of plain grits had fit on a single plate.

"I didn't want to admit it in the brig but I had been having problems with food, just like you said." She told him the grits/risotto story.

"So," Walker said as casually as if he were asking her opinion on the chances for rain. "You were able to completely change the reality of those around you while maintaining your own reality."

"I don't know if I would have described what happened in those terms."

"How would you have described it?"

"I was going friggin' nuts."

"That's also a possibility."

"You're so reassuring."

When the check arrived, he left a three dollar tip for a $20 bill.

"Last of the big tippers?"

"We don't want to be a big tipper or a lousy tipper. We just want to be another customer at another dinner rush. We don't want to give our waitress a reason to remember us."

In the warm glow of a full tummy and good conversation with an attractive man of her own age Penelope had momentarily forgotten that much of the federal government and probably every state and local police department in the country were looking for them. Walker's caution brought it all back and put a knot in her recently filled stomach. At the cash register, she placed a pack of Tums on the counter, which Walker paid for along with their bill.

≈

T HEY WERE HEADED due north on I-77 in the mountains of Virginia as the sun set over the Allegheny Mountains. It was a Sunday night, and the traffic was light.

"Okay," Penelope said as she adjusted herself in the bucket seat. "What exactly is the Hermes Project?"

"First, a bit of history. We are on the cusp of the Fourth Awakening of mankind..."

"Okay. Let me stop you right there. A news story must deal in facts. My generation, which now controls all of the newsrooms, already survived the dawning of the Age of Aquarius. If you start talking like a middle-aged hippie, I don't care how much traction you've gotten from your arrest and Horn's stroke, there is not a major paper in the country that will touch this story, except maybe the *Psychic Hotline*."

"I know. That's why we need you."

"I don't follow...?"

"You have credibility with the media. We don't. If we try to tell this story we'll be branded as kooks and nut jobs by the people we're up against."

"Ok. Then tell me about Hermes."

"Without the background context, you could be like so many others that get completely hypnotized by the significance of the breakthrough we've made, and miss the bigger story."

"Which is?"

"The Fourth Awakening is coming and there's nothing we can do to stop it."

CHAPTER FIFTEEN

"It is not the answer that enlightens, but the question."

Eugene Ionesco

"T HAT SOUNDS PRETTY ominous."

Walker laughed. "The Fourth Awakening is a natural progression in human development and shouldn't be feared or misunderstood. One of the reasons we sought you out was because you could explain what is going on in language that could be understood by the average person on the street."

"You win, we'll do background first, but I want to establish a few ground rules."

"Such as?"

"No psychobabble or New Age gibberish. I want the five "W's. Who, what, when, where and why."

"I can work with that."

"I'm not done. I need verifiable facts, and not opinions or interpretations based on divine intervention or the reading of tea leaves."

"Fair enough."

"One more," Penelope said with a sideways glance. "If I ask a direct question, could you at least pretend to give me a direct answer?"

A broad smile broke across Walker's face. "Just because you haven't understood an answer doesn't mean it wasn't direct."

"I thought your goal was to reach as broad an audience as possible? If it is too dense for me to translate then we're both wasting our time."

"Fair point," Walker answered with a sigh. "I'll try to rein in my enthusiasm. If I lose you anywhere, let me know." Walker waited for an acknowledgement, which he got in the form of a nod, before continuing. "We are on the cusp of the Fourth Awakening of mankind..."

Penelope chuckled softly. "Here we go."

"What now?"

"How many times have you practiced this?"

"Is it that obvious?"

"Oh yeah."

"What was the giveaway?"

"You used the exact same phrase a minute ago and for the first time since I met you, it sounded like you were reading off of a teleprompter. Why the prepared speech?"

"It is critical that you grasp the historical perspective. Without an understanding of what happened previously it will be difficult to fully grasp what's happening now. We need you to see the big picture."

"You've obviously given this a lot of thought, and you did buy me a nice dinner." Penelope leaned back in her seat and folded her arms across her chest. "The least I can do is listen to your little presentation. Please, proceed."

Walker glanced sideways at Penelope and cleared his throat. "We are on the cusp of the Fourth Awakening of mankind. During these transition periods the entire fabric of societal structures changes and a new way of thinking emerges that is completely revolutionary and results in the abandonment of old ideas and methods of functioning both individually and collectively making it impossible to ever return to the old way of thinking." Walker glanced over at Spence and saw that she was staring at him with her mouth open. "What?" he asked.

"Who wrote this for you?'

"I did, with the help of some of the academics at the Hermes project."

"Academic, huh? That explains it."

"Explains what?"

"I don't think I've heard a sentence that long since college. It does show you are absolutely right about one thing."

"What would that be?"

"If that's the best you can come up with, you guys really need some help telling your story."

"If you think this is bad," Walker said with a laugh. "You should have heard some of the earlier drafts."

Penelope shivered slightly. "I've run across tons of people who believe that just because they got over 700 on their English SAT when they were seventeen it automatically made them the next Hemingway."

"I've seen some of that first hand recently," Walker answered. "What do you suggest?"

"Since I'm a reporter, we could try the interview format. I ask a few questions. We'll see if you have it within your powers to give me some straight answers. Which, by the way, the jury is still out on."

"Hmm," Walker answered as he fixed his eyes on the road.

"Oh, don't get pouty," Penelope said as she rested her hand on Walker's arm. "I'll make you a deal. We try it my way for awhile and I'll promise to read every word of your little speech."

"And view the PowerPoint?'

"Yes, I'll even watch the PowerPoint."

"Okay. Where do you want to start?"

"You claim the Fourth Awakening is upon us; since this is all new to me you'll need to define what constitutes an Awakening."

"I thought I just did."

"Let's try it again, maybe with punctuation this time."

"Okay. An Awakening occurs whenever there is a major shift in people and the way they view the world around them."

"For example."

"For example when humanity moved from compact familial groups of hunter gatherers to the first non-family based small farming communities. From there we moved to even more complex social orders such as city and nation states. Once you've gone from a cave to a hut to indoor plumbing, there is no going back."

"I guess there is a certain logic to that. Why do you call them Awakenings?"

"Are you a morning person?"

"Yes. Annoyed the heck out of the rest of the family. My ex-husband was one of those three cups of coffee before you can talk to me kind of guys. Why?"

"That's a perfect example."

"Perfect example of what?"

"Of one reason I decided to call it an Awakening."

Penelope sighed and shook her head. "We were running along fine there for a few minutes then suddenly you go off the rails again."

Walker laughed and a broad grin covered his face. "The point is people wake up at different rates. Some bounce out of bed at their best while others have to shake off the cobwebs. Some wake up at the crack of dawn while others sleep in until noon. This is exactly what happens in an Awakening. There is an adjustment period before everyone gets on the same page."

"Oh," Penelope said while shaking her finger at Walker. "I get it. Some people take longer to adjust to the dawning of a new day than others."

Walker continued on. "The big question, as you have so artfully pointed out, is how to put this into language that will resonate with the most people. Some of the folks at the compound wanted me to use the currently accepted names for the eras but I didn't think it would fly with the general public. "

"Currently accepted by whom?"

"Some of the most enlightened minds of our time."

"I suppose that would include you?" Walker shrugged but didn't answer. Penelope thought for a moment then asked, "Out of morbid curiosity what did these enlightened minds call these eras?"

"The first era, pre-200,000 BCE, is referred to as the Archaic Structure. After the First Awakening came the Magical Structure which was followed by the Mythical Structure..."

"Ha!" Penelope said with a short laugh. "I guess these folks were all Beatles fans."

"Where did that come from?"

"Sounds like you guys were having your own personal Magical Mythical tour."

"You have a very interesting thought process."

"Thanks."

Walker grimaced slightly. "That wasn't a compliment." They both laughed.

"With that level of verbal craftsmanship," Penelope said. "I can't imagine why you guys don't have people knocking down your doors begging for more."

"Actually there is a large body of supporting work and some truly outstanding books on this subject. Jean Gebser's *The Ever Present Origin*.

Allan Combs' *The Radiance of Being.* Ken Wilber's *Up from Eden.* I'll get you a reading list if you'd like."

"Maybe later. Did they help with your little prepared remarks?"

"I wish," Walker said while shaking his head. "Gebser is dead so unless we have a séance he's not available. As for the others, with every spy agency in the world looking for the Hermes Project we didn't dare try to contact them. I was afraid to even go through Walker Industries' PR department. That left me with a bunch of lab rats and PhD physicists to help me write this. "

"Oh my. Do you think Combs and Wilber could have done better?"

"Absolutely. When you read their stuff you'll understand. They are gifted writers who could have put this into language that even a reporter could understand."

"Hey!" Penelope said in mock protest. Walker shot Penelope a knowing glance but didn't reply. Puzzled, Penelope asked, "What was that look for?"

"When you read their work, you'll understand."

"Whatever," Penelope said. "I think your instincts are spot on about using the Awakening language over the era structure thingy. That's a very elegant way of describing all of this."

"Excellent."

"What kind of a time-frame are we looking at for these Awakenings to completely take hold?"

"It can be hundreds if not thousands of years."

"Thousands of years?"

"Yes. After the first Awakening the adjustment period was over 100,000 years."

"Really? Why so long?"

"There are a lot of factors that can affect the amount of time it takes for an Awakening to be fully engaged. While the progress is always ongoing, environment, weather, geography, food supply and other outside forces have always played a role in human development. Plus, there is the inherent nature of the Awakenings themselves."

"What does that mean?"

"Around the time everyone is just getting used to the current Awakening, the next one starts and the cycle repeats itself."

"The early risers are on a different page than the night owls?"

"Essentially that's correct. Everyone develops at their own pace."

"I see," Penelope said as she rubbed her chin. "What happened 200,000 years ago that merited the First Awakening?"

"That was when Homo sapiens are thought to have emerged in East Africa."

"I guess that would qualify as a pretty big change."

Walker nodded. "Progress in human development was pretty slow back then. It took around 150,000 years before the next Awakening and that is when things started to get interesting."

"Interesting?"

"Are you familiar with Joseph Campbell?"

"Are you kidding? I went to an Ivy League college when he was in his heyday. I stood in the rain for two hours to get tickets to hear him speak."

"Excellent," Walker said as he nodded his approval. "Then just imagine this Second Awakening being the canvas he used as the background for his *Power of the Myth* theory. Spoken language emerged during the time of the early shamans, and great myths were told around the campfire. For the first time, early humans became self aware and while still considering themselves a part of nature they understood they were somehow different."

"What does that mean?"

"We began to explore our spiritual side through myth and the creation of Gods and other unseen forces to explain things we didn't yet understand. Most importantly we became aware of our own mortality. We started to fear death and began to seek a deeper understanding of the cycle of life and how it applied to us."

"How did you conclude that?"

"We started to develop increasingly complex rituals of burying our dead to prepare them for the afterlife."

"Your proof?"

"We moved from simple burial sites during the First Awakening to those big pointy things in the deserts in Egypt in the Second. I would say that is a pretty impressive progression."

"Pointy things? The pyramids?"

"Sure. The ancient Egyptians are thought to have believed the soul would survive as long as the body survived. The body was preserved and wrapped in linen in case the owner happened to return for it later. They put food and gold in with the mummies in case they got hungry or needed cash. Have you ever heard of the terracotta army in China at the grave of the first emperor?"

"I've seen that in person. It's amazing."

"A very different burial ritual but easily on the same scale as the pyramids."

"Interesting."

"Interesting indeed. But without an incredible number of things happening around 14,000 years ago we probably wouldn't be here talking."

"I'll bite. What happened 14,000 years ago?"

"In the middle of the Second Awakening the last great ice age ended and we had the perfect storm for human development."

"And?"

"And, people were physically and mentally in position to take advantage of it."

"Take advantage of what?"

"As the planet warmed it became much more hospitable for human development. Early humans were able to plant crops and keep livestock which allowed for larger fixed population centers. As the food supply grew and became more predictable there was a population explosion in Homo sapiens just as our primary rivals disappeared."

Penelope made a face and slowly shook her head. "Do you work at being obtuse or is that just your default mode?"

"What?" Walker asked.

"Who were our rivals?"

"During the Second Awakening," Walker answered. "Homo sapiens were one of three high intelligence species. The Neanderthals vanished around 30,000 years ago and Cro-Magnon became extinct right around the time of the great thaw."

"Do you think early Homo sapiens did them in?"

Walker shrugged. "What exactly caused their demise is the subject of great debate but as always the winners get to write the history books. The romantic theory is the smarter more nimble Homo sapiens squeezed out first the dumb lumbering Neanderthals then the Cro-Magnon. You can still see that theory everyday in bad insurance ads on television. Considering that Cro-Magnon had nearly the same brain capacity as us and was bigger and stronger, it is impossible to say what happened. The key point is Homo sapiens were ready to seize the opportunity. And they did." Walker smiled and glanced over at Penelope with a twinkle in his eyes. "More importantly, we had the first irrefutable proof that we're all connected through thought."

"What is your irrefutable proof?"

"Art for one..."

"Art?"

"Yes. Art is always a good indicator of an Awakening firmly taking hold. In the middle of the Second Awakening we saw rudimental art in the form of cave drawings and crude figurines."

"Where is your proof?"

"The famous Chauvet and Lascaux caves in France. The Aboriginal Ubirr wall art in Australia. There was the Pachmari Hills in India. The Apollo 11 and Wonderwerk Caves in southern Africa. Fell's Cave at the tip of South America. Is that enough for you?"

Penelope looked at Walker and shrugged. "Enough of what?"

"All of this art was produced at roughly the same time and all are very similar. How do you explain people in every corner of the world who didn't even know the others existed all having the same thought at roughly the same time if we're not all connected in some way?"

Penelope rubbed her chin again. "It could have been a coincidence," she said without much conviction.

"That was my third choice right behind an alien invasion populating the planet," Walker said with a laugh. "Plus there are many others."

"Such as?"

"Metallurgy, ship building, planting and harvesting crops, and astrology to name a few. They all emerged at around the same time worldwide in roughly the same forms. During the last part of the Second Awakening the changes in mankind were stunning. In only a few thousand years humans went from grunting cave dwellers living in small groups to building city-states and writing epic poems. Completely independent of each other, many cultures around the world went through their own Bronze Age and Iron Age at approximately the same moment. This is a clear example of the universal consciousness." The look on Penelope's face told Walker she was not convinced.

"So you're saying some kind of universal light bulb suddenly clicked on 14,000 years ago?"

"It was already on; it just got a whole lot brighter. That's what happens when there is an Awakening; everything changes. Something triggers the change but it can take centuries for all of the rough edges to be smoothed away. From a purely clinical perspective, emerging humans had the brain capacity for hundreds of thousands of years for this type of development but, in my opinion, it took a change in the global climate to trigger the event."

"So," Penelope said with a sideways bemused glance. "You're saying this Second Awakening was caused by Global Warming?"

Walker chuckled and shook his head. "Considering the amount of emotion in that phrase these days, I don't think I would call it Global Warming. But, that is essentially correct. Plus there were internal changes in humans."

"Such as."

"No longer having to live a hand to mouth existence, we began to turn inward and became more spiritual. As we tried to understand our place in the universe we saw the emergence of a shaman or priest class that was held in high regard in these new social structures. Elaborate rituals were created. Cats started liking us..."

"Cats? What?"

"Until this period, cats wouldn't have anything to do with humans. That was a big step in our evolution."

"Cats?"

"Yes." Penelope's mouth opened, but she thought better of it and motioned for Walker to continue. "Cats are some of the most instinctive animals on the planet. When they sensed that we had changed, they started to allow us to live with them."

"Allowed us to live with them?"

"You're not a cat person then?"

"No."

"Ahh."

"Ahh, what?"

"Something else you'll have trouble understanding."

"Cats?"

"You don't choose a cat, a cat chooses you."

"I see. Cats. Anything else?'

"Yes. Humans discovered time."

Penelope closed her eyes and scratched her forehead as she tried to compose her next thought. "So, let me get this straight, you're telling me you believe time did not exist until around 14,000 years ago?"

"Of course it existed, but time wasn't understood in the same way we perceive it. The hunter gatherers noted the things that were important to them but mostly lived in their present moment. After the Second Awakening humans became much more aware of the past and future, which is no minor development. For example, like any agricultural based society, the Egyptians needed to know when to expect the annual flooding of the Nile. They noticed a few days before the spring floods that Sirius, the Dog Star, was visible just before sunrise. Based on that they devised a 365 day stellar calendar sometime around 4,300 BCE that was reasonably accurate even by modern standards. They also used a lunar one for ceremony and festivals the same way we do today."

"What do you mean the same way we do?"

"Easter is always the first Sunday after the first full moon following the equinox. The same logic applies to Jewish High Holidays and Islamic Holy Days. That's why the dates change every year, to correspond with the moon."

"Interesting."

"Plus the entire social structure changed. Hunter gathering societies were largely family based. Farming brought the first small settlements that placed importance on what someone could do rather than who they were related to. Not only were the groupings increasingly larger, we saw the ascension of Pharos, Emperors and Kings who were often considered to be the direct descendent of God. This was a huge change."

"Hmm," Penelope said as a frown twisted her mouth downward.

"What?" Walker asked.

"These are some awfully big leaps of faith based on some pretty sketchy facts."

"Such as?"

"The universal thought thing. That's a bit hard to swallow."

"Why?"

"Suppose it is snowing. It wouldn't take a collective consciousness to tell me to put on a coat. There are some things that people are just naturally going to do."

"I agree."

"Really? That's a first."

"Sure," Walker said with a quick laugh. "That's because it is a perfectly natural progression. It takes everyone a while to get their head around this concept. Just keep asking yourself why do people in different parts of the world keep making the same discoveries, all around the same time? As we move along I'll give you some more examples for you to try to rationalize away."

Penelope gave Walker a playful punch in the shoulder. "I have to admit this is an interesting way of looking at things."

"Good," Walker answered. "Then we're making some headway here. Plus this has been fun."

"I guess that depends on your definition of fun."

"Come on," Walker answered shaking his head in disbelief. "Front page of the *Post*. Helping break a lunatic out of prison. Getting your house blown up." Walker motioned toward the blond wig Penelope was still wearing. "New hairdo. What more could anyone ask for?"

Penelope self-consciously adjusted the hair piece. "You are a certifiable nut job."

"Thanks."

"Wasn't a compliment."

Walker shrugged. "All of that was just the warm up act. This is where it really gets interesting."

"Do tell."

"Around 3,000 years ago we had the Third Awakening. From now on we'll be talking about stuff you already know, or think you know, just presented in a manner you probably had never considered. Since you've studied history and have a quick mind we won't need to go into great detail. What I'll need you to do is start thinking of the facts you learned in school and look at how they support my theory of the Awakenings. If you can do that then all of this will start to make sense."

"Where's the fun part?"

"The adjustment period for the Third Awakening is almost over and it's time for the Fourth Awakening. That's why you're here."

CHAPTER SIXTEEN

"God is Dead."

FRIEDRICH NIETZSCHE

"Nietzsche is Dead."

GOD

PENELOPE BLINKED HER eyes and pulled back. "What in the world do I have to do with the Fourth Awakening?"

A sly smile covered Michael Walker's face. "We'll get to that in a few minutes. Right now we need to get you up to speed on the current Awakening. This will be right down your alley with lots of who, what, where and when's. You want to speculate on why we have so much information about the most recent Awakening?"

"I have no idea."

"Come on. Humor me. There are always huge changes after a new Awakening. What do you think was one of the big ones between the Second and Third Awakenings? I'll give you a hint, it's your bread and butter."

Penelope drew in a breath and stared out the window of the Bronco at the West Virginia countryside as it whizzed by. Suddenly her eyes flew wide open. "Oh my God!"

"I thought you could get there all by yourself."

"Written language! You're right, that is a huge change."

"Precisely," Walker answered, beaming. "Unfortunately it also created some new problems."

"What kind of problems?"

"After the Sumerians began to write on clay tablets, the dominant cultures of the time saw an opportunity."

"What kind of opportunity?"

"The Chinese and the Egyptians were neck and neck in developing the first written language but the folks in power intentionally made this new media difficult to learn."

"Why?"

"By limiting literacy to the ruling classes it helped protect their status. We've seen this type of thing repeated in different ways time and time again throughout history."

"So you're saying that there are people who will exploit an Awakening for personal gain?"

"Absolutely. The Egyptian scribe class was incredibly powerful and secretive; which is unfortunate since they didn't leave any directions on how to translate all those hieroglyphics they created. That has been driving Egyptologists crazy for centuries. In China there are still over 47,000 characters in their alphabet with 4,000 in regular use. All of this was clearly designed to protect those already in power. Fortunately for the rest of us the suppression of emerging knowledge by ruling elites never works for very long."

"What does that mean?"

"Around 3,000 to 4,000 years ago, right at the beginning of the Third Awakening, it became clear a more universally understood written language that wasn't controlled by the elites was needed. This is when we saw the emergence of various Semitic languages, primarily Aramaic. They lead to the Greek alphabet and the rest is, as they say, history."

"That's interesting," Penelope said as she mulled over Walker's latest epiphany. "So the genie was out of the bottle and there was no way for the ruling classes to keep it to themselves forever."

"Precisely," Walker answered with a nod. "That would be one of those rough edges of an Awakening that can sometimes take a while to smooth off. Even after a written language became available, because of the high cost of producing the manuscripts it was still limited to the wealthy, religious and well educated classes. This didn't start to change until around 600 years ago..."

"Gutenberg's Bible," Penelope interrupted.

"Precisely," Walker answered as he nodded his approval. "That is also a perfect example of the time it can take for an Awakening to smooth itself out. It took us 2,500 years to go from alphabetic words to movable type printing presses."

"Hmm," Penelope muttered under her breath as she pondered this latest nugget of wisdom from Michael Walker. Some of his theories were too fantastic to take seriously while others had an implicit logic that was difficult to deny. This was going to be a challenging story to write.

As if reading her mind, Walker gave her a moment to process this new information. When he saw her shoulders relax, he continued. "Another big issue that arose with the written word is that it requires the use of mutually agreed upon symbolic language. This means the language and the descriptions they produce are subject to interpretation and are run through the filter of each individual's experiences and prejudices."

"Sounds like the deconstruction theory that was rampant when I was in college," Penelope said.

"Exactly," Walker said with a nod of appreciation. "Suppose an ancient Egyptian scribe drew a hieroglyph he wanted to represent a tree. Someone else may see it as "shade" and another person as "fruit" and a third may see it as a symbol of summer. Symbolic language is subject to individual interpretation. Communication can be like the old game of "telephone" we used to play as kids. You tell someone something and they pass it on then they pass it on. After the fourth or fifth telling it sounds nothing like the original."

"Like two different people can read the same poem and come away with completely different messages."

"Or no message at all. It comes down to the way the individual interprets the symbolic language and how receptive they are to the idea. If you think about it for a moment, all of your thoughts revolve around symbols. While the changes a new Awakening brings are always easier to see in hindsight; it appears we may be heading to a new era where a non-symbolic understanding becomes the standard."

"You're making words up again, aren't you?"

Walker laughed. "Of course I am but that doesn't make it any less valid. Besides, people do it all the time. Globalization, e-mail, aerobicized, pop tarts, SPAM. The list is nearly endless. "

Penelope chuckled and shook her head. She hadn't enjoyed a conversation this much in years. Walker had the ability to challenge her intellectually with a good natured calmness she found comfortable. "If you had to write the definition for non-symbolic for Webster's, how would it read?"

"You really can't, because that would require symbols. But, people have been trying their best to write about and explain non-symbolic understanding for thousands of years. The concept is probably most familiar to you as enlightenment."

"Enlightenment? You're kidding. Are you trying to tell me that the next phase of humanity will involve all of us becoming enlightened?"

Walker shrugged but didn't answer. "You're on a roll now. You want to take a shot at figuring out the key elements of the Third Awakening?"

"Sure." Penelope curled up in the seat with her feet under her like a cat. "How many key elements am I looking for?"

"Two."

"Just two? That's hardly your style."

"Think big picture here. Another hint. We're still in the adjustment period for the Third Awakening."

"What does that mean?"

"They are still the two most important things shaping our world today."

"That dramatically limits the field." Penelope drew in a deep breath through her nose and allowed it to slowly escape between her lips. "Considering your disdain for Washington I am going to guess politics is not one of them."

"Different forms of government come and go and politicians always think they are more important than they really are."

"Okay. Not politics." Penelope rubbed her chin as she thought out loud. "Economic systems aren't important enough."

"Right."

"What's been around for the past 3,000 years?" Penelope's eyes flew open. "Is it that simple?"

"Yup."

"Oh my!" Penelope's eyes danced as she pondered the possibilities.

"Nothing conflicts with your revered who, what, when, where, and why?"

Penelope's mind continued to race as she mentally thumbed through every book and article she had ever read before she absently shook her head. "Not yet."

"Excellent. Now if we can just get you over the final hump of realizing we are all connected through thought..."

"Slow down, Skippy," Penelope said as her eyes focused back on Walker. "While I will grant that you have an interesting theory here; I wouldn't start fitting me for my choir robes just yet. I have a few more questions."

"Okay."

"First off, I'm not even sure we're talking about the same stuff. What do you think are the two most important elements of the Third Awakening?"

"You first."

A heavy silence settled over the Bronco as Penelope folded her arms across her chest and glared at Walker. "Why do I have to go first?"

Walker shrugged. "We are on the cusp of..."

"Stop. STOP! You win." Penelope shook her head in resignation. "The two key elements of the Third Awakening are Religion and Science."

"Give the lady from Charleston full marks. In the last 3,000 years we have seen the decline of the ancient faiths and rituals and the emergence of every major modern religion. Also, as the grip of religion has waned, the power of science has grown at an amazing rate. These twin pillars are, for better or worse, what hold up modern society."

"None of this supports your core argument that we are all connected through thought," Penelope said with a sigh.

"Did you know that between 800 BC and 400 BC, all around the world there was a religious explosion? This is when the key events in the Old Testament occurred, from which emerged Judeo/Christian beliefs. At the same time Taoism was being followed by Confucianism in China. The same was happening with Shintoism in Japan, and Hinduism and Buddhism in India, and later Islam."

"Your point being?"

"If we are not connected by thought, how did all of these simultaneous religious explosions happen?"

"Surely you can see the logical fallacy," Penelope said with a dismissive wave of her hand. "You're starting from a false premise that we are all connected through thought then using that to draw a conclusion."

"What's false about it?"

"Your job is to convince me that you are right. It's not my job to convince you that you are wrong."

"Fair enough," Walker answered. "Let's try another one. Let's go back to art." Penelope nodded her agreement. "In the early days of Greek art they made some spectacular vases."

"Okay."

"At precisely the same moment the Jomon Culture in Japan and the people on the Korean peninsula were creating nearly identical work."

"Sorry," Penelope answered. "We're running in circles here, Michael. Without some sort of concrete proof I'm more inclined to go with coincidence, unknown trade channels, or some other logical argument over your psychic connection theory."

"I didn't expect this to be easy," Walker said with a smile. "Your pigheadedness is a refreshing change."

"What does that mean?" Penelope demanded.

"Usually I have this type of conversation with someone who is sitting on the edge of their chair hanging on my every word. These are people who want to believe me; sometimes are desperate to believe me."

"Sorry," Penelope said with a substantially less than sincere laugh. "I guess I'm just not one of your Awakening groupies."

"No, you're not. That's why you're perfect."

"Perfect?" Penelope said as she pulled further away from Walker. "That's a bit of a reach."

"What I meant," Walker said with his usual calmness. "Is that you are the perfect person for me to be talking to right now. If I can figure out how to reach you and make you understand; then together we'll be able to reach the world."

"You are a very odd man," Penelope said while shaking her head.

"Thanks."

Penelope didn't bother to correct him; she was lost too deeply in thought. For about five minutes they rode in silence as she mentally poked and jabbed at everything Walker had told her. She had to admit a lot of it made sense, but that's the way con men hook you. They bury a lie within a kernel of truth. She glanced over and studied his profile; he certainly didn't look or act like a nut job. He had a coolness about him that was so sincere it was almost jarring. Penelope rubbed her chin and cleared her throat. "Let me be sure I've got all of this." Walker nodded but did not answer. "200,000 years ago Homo sapiens emerged from the primordial goo. That's the First Awakening."

"Right."

"Over the next 150,000 years they start to slowly develop into something resembling us today."

"Right."

"50,000 years ago there was a Second Awakening where people started to become self-aware and realize they are mortal with all the baggage that entails." Walker nods his agreement. "They begin forming larger social groupings and started looking for spiritual answers through myths and rituals."

"Right."

"Around 14,000 years ago, in the later stages of the Second Awakening, there is a change in the global climate and this process of self-discovery accelerates."

"And continues to accelerate through the present day."

"3,000 years ago is the Third Awakening which is basically the double edged sword of science and religion."

"Religion had been around for a lot longer in a variety of forms. Science was the new comer to the game."

"You're pretty confident the Fourth Awakening is about to happen."

"It has already started."

"Really," Penelope said deadpan. "My invitation must have gotten lost in the mail."

"Received, signed for and opened."

"Here we go again," Penelope said while shaking her head. "This is going to be another one of those things I'm not ready to understand yet. Right?"

"Right."

"I give up. Tell me something to make me believe the Fourth Awakening has started."

"The breakdown of relations between science and religion is a good one."

"What are you talking about now?"

"The relationship has always been a bit strained but it broke into the open when Galileo and the Pope had their little dust up."

"That was 400 years ago!" Penelope protested.

Walker just smiled. "You really need to be thinking in longer time lines. For a universe that is who knows how old and a planet that is over four billion years old, 400 years is the blink of an eye."

Penelope shook her head and sighed. "Amazing," she muttered under her breath.

"What?"

"Nothing. Please continue."

"For the past 500 or so years the political power of the church has waned while the power of science has flourished. With a few exceptions most of the people today live in societies with secular governments."

"So? What does any of this prove?"

"Nothing," Walker said flatly. "And everything."

Penelope closed her eyes, scratched her forehead and then motioned for Walker to continue.

"For many scientists knowledge hit a tipping point about 150 years ago. Universities began to switch from being religious institutions to being based on the German research model. Leading scientists were declaring that soon they would have no new major discoveries to make. While skeptical of religion, before that time all of the great minds were looking to science to prove there was a God, not to disprove it."

"I suppose you have a theory of why they suddenly turned their back on God in the 19th century?"

"Would you be surprised if I didn't?"

"Frankly, yes. And I'm betting it will be a doozy."

"Dinosaurs."

"Dinosaurs?"

"Yes."

"I can't wait to hear this one."

"In the early 19th century, when Western scientists figured out those old bones they had been digging up for centuries were not dragons or animals that had perished in Noah's Biblical flood but animals that had roamed the planet millions of years earlier, it pretty much shot down the theory of Earth being built in six days. To many this was as startling as Copernicus disproving the long held belief that the earth was the center of the universe. At that point, science pretty much gave up on religion as superstition and myth."

"Let me get this straight. You're claiming that the current skepticism about religion got its start because of the discovery of dinosaur bones?"

"No. They've been at each other's throats for thousands of years; that was just the proverbial last straw."

"That moves the bar, even by your standards."

"Thanks." He held up his hand and stopped her before she could reply. "I know."

"Don't let me slow you down. Please continue."

"Recently we've seen a reversal where a large number of truly gifted scientists have returned to the spiritual and the mystical for answers to the big questions science can't answer."

"Big questions?"

"Why are we here, and how did we get here? How was the universe formed, and who or what formed it?" Walker continued, "The advance in human knowledge during this period has been astounding and appears to be accelerating. In the 20th century we went from the first motorized flight to walking on the moon in less than 70 years. Cures for diseases were discovered and life expectancies doubled, then doubled again. The industries that dominated modern society at the end of the 20th century—air travel, automobiles, computers, instant mass communication, motion pictures, television, the Internet—none of these even existed a hundred years earlier."

"Are you ever going to get to the point?"

"The point is our current organized religions are not filling our needs and science is so tied up in symbolic thought it can no longer support its own weight."

"I have no idea what that means," Penelope said while shaking her head.

"Basically it all goes back to how each of us tries to avoid the ending of our existence. Religion offered one solution, often in the form of things that could be done to ensure survival of our consciousness after physical death. Science offers another path; immortality though the knowledge you create outliving you."

"So the idea is that death is the big motivator."

"The possibility of non-existence it brings, actually. There's a long line of schemes for this that probably started not long after we realized the possibility.

"Such as?"

"Well, virtually all culture relates to this. It gives us the opportunity to perpetuate something larger than ourselves that we're tied to and will out live us. Making contributions to one or more of our cultural institutions serves the same purpose. For millennia this was about the best you could hope for, aside from religion. The problem is that it doesn't take a genius to see that contributions made to Sumerian culture didn't last forever. Rather than knowledge relating to a culture, science offers the opportunity to create universally relevant knowledge and thus a higher form of immortality so, practical benefits aside, it's not hard to see why it caught on.

"Go on." Spence said rubbing her chin.

"The basic underpinning of science is universally understood truth. As they have piled more and more on, it is starting to buckle." Walker smiled. "When the big ideas from the previous Awakening start to collapse then a new Awakening is on the horizon."

"That's your proof?"

"I'm guessing that means you are not buying any of it."

"No...no...no," Penelope said shaking her head. "I buy a great deal of it. In fact much of it is hard to argue with. It's just two small parts are giving me trouble."

"Namely?"

"I don't see any great collapse in science or any proof of us being connected through thought." Penelope pursed her lips and shook her head. "Sorry."

As usual, Michael Walker appeared unmoved. If he was disappointed or hurt, nothing in his body language or facial expression showed it. "Are you willing to listen to more arguments?"

"Of course," Penelope answered quickly. "But please don't take this to mean I can't still write your story for you... "

Walker cut her off by patting her gently on the knee. Penelope looked down as she felt a jolt of energy similar to a static electricity shock only more powerful. She froze when her peripheral vision caught sight of a bright violet glow surrounding Michael Walker. It instantly vanished as she gasped and turned her head to look directly at him.

"What?"

"I thought I saw something."

"What did you see?"

"It was nothing, really."

"Penelope. Considering all the seemingly outrageous things I've told you in the past few hours, do you really think anything you could say would surprise me?"

She chuckled. "Good point. I thought I saw you surrounded by a field of light."

"Excellent!"

"Why did I just know you were going to say that?"

"What color was it?"

"Color?"

"Yes, what color?"

"I don't know. Deep blue."

"Purple, maybe?'

"More like violet."

He patted her on the leg again. "That's excellent!"

"What does it mean?"

"It means you're getting close to believing me. Right now your energy field is yellow, which is the color of inspiration, intellect and shared action."

"You can see my energy field?" Penelope thought for a moment then added, "I have an energy field?"

"Everyone has one," Walker answered as if surprised by the question. "Plus, everyone has the ability to see them but few realize it."

"I was only able to catch a glimpse of it out of the corner of my eye, but when I looked at you directly it went away."

"That's common at first. You mentioned earlier that you don't have an instructor or teacher."

"No, I go down to a local yoga class occasionally."

"What did you learn there?"

"Not much; mostly just some stretches and breathing exercises. They seemed more interested in selling outfits and mats."

"They didn't teach you any meditation techniques?"

"Not really." Penelope was a bit embarrassed. "When I was a teenager I had a book on Vipassana Meditation. I just started meditating the way I remember doing it then."

"So," Walker said calmly. "You reached this level of spiritual development basically on your own?"

"Spiritual development? Please."

Walker laughed again. "Carl is going to eat you up with a spoon."

"Carl?"

"Dr. Altman." Penelope nodded that no further explanation was required. "If we can just get you past your pigheadedness..."

"I prefer steadfast."

"I'm sure you do," Walker said with a chuckle that caused the corners of Penelope's mouth to curve into a smile. A Cheshire cat smile covered Walker's face.

"How long have you been doing this?"

"Doing what?"

"Yoga. Meditating."

"Off and on forever. Seriously for about a year."

"Hmm."

"What?" Penelope asked.

"There are Buddhist monks who spend a lifetime in a monastery and never reach your level of development."

"Really?"

"Don't get too full of yourself. There are also uneducated peasants who wake up one morning in a state of enlightened bliss with no idea that anything has even changed."

"So someone can have this handed to them without even knowing they're receiving it, while a monk can spend a lifetime seeking it and never find it?"

"The universe has a great sense of humor."

"You have to admit this entire Awakening concept is a bit hard to swallow in a single sitting."

"I know. Unfortunately we're on a tight schedule, but at the rate you're progressing I'm sure it will make more sense to you soon."

"What does that mean?"

"Your alarm clock has already gone off and the Fourth Awakening has already started, which is the problem."

"What problem?

"So far we've only talked about the benefits of an Awakening. There is a dark side."

CHAPTER SEVENTEEN

*"Don't worry about the world coming to an end today.
It's already tomorrow in Australia."*

CHARLES SCHULTZ

"WHAT DO YOU mean there is a dark side?"

"Let's take a pit stop first," Walker said as he flipped on the turn signal and the Bronco began to slow down. They reached the end of the exit ramp and turned left toward an open Shell Mini-mart. "Besides, I need to make a phone call."

"I thought we couldn't use the phone?"

"I can use it all I want. You, on the other hand, can't call *The Washington Post*, or any of your friends and family, since I know their lines are being monitored."

"How do you know that?"

Walker just smiled and winked.

"Sorry," Penelope answered with a sigh. "What was I thinking?"

Walker pulled into the pumps so that only the front license plate, which had a Confederate flag on it, was visible to the station's video cameras. Walker filled up the Bronco's tank while Penelope freshened up. He paid cash for the gas, bought a prepaid phone card, and was standing at the pay phone in front of the building chatting with someone when Penelope joined him.

Anticipating her question, Walker put his hand over the mouthpiece and whispered, "Senator Horn has stabilized but the next few hours will tell the tale." Penelope nodded that she understood as Walker turned his full attention back to the person he was talking to on the phone.

"Yes. She's standing right next to me... she got in the car around 12:30." Walker laughed. It was that deep, full-bodied laugh which caused all within earshot to smile, and that Penelope had grown to want to hear more often. "You guys never learn." Walker covered the mouthpiece and spoke to Penelope. "Mark Hatchet has your article for tomorrow. We want to send him a heads up that he will be getting a visit from Homeland Security in the morning, and let him know you're okay. Is there some kind of code word or something we can use to let him know it's from you?" He held the phone in her direction.

Penelope thought for a moment. "Yeah. Tell him it's from Nellie 2204. Oh, and ask him to call Joey and tell her I'm okay." Walker nodded.

"Got that?" Penelope could make out a man's voice confirming he had heard her correctly. "Great." Walker hung up the phone and motioned toward the Bronco. "As I suspected, the order to bug your house came directly from Noah Shepherd without notifying Robert Smith."

"What does that mean?"

"That means we need to get you to the compound as quickly as possible because Shepherd is upping the stakes."

"Should I be worried?"

"No. But if you do get caught somehow, offer no resistance of any kind and don't say a word until your attorney arrives."

"What are the odds I'll get caught?"

"Unless something happens at the airport, almost zero."

"Airport? Do you have a plane stashed somewhere?"

"Yes. At the Delta terminal in Cincinnati."

"Isn't that a pretty big risk, flying on public transportation? What if we get seen?"

"Trust me," Walker answered with a smile.

"What are you planning?" Penelope demanded.

Walker continued to smile and shrugged.

"I give up," Penelope said with exasperation in her voice. "How am I supposed to get on an airplane without any identification?"

"It will be waiting for us in Cincinnati."

"I smell like a wet goat. And, I'm not sure I want to be seen on a plane with you and that shirt."

"We'll both get a chance to change before we go."

"Okay."

Once Walker and Penelope were safely back on the interstate, she had to ask. "What were you laughing at?"

He laughed again. "Stu won the pool. You would think they would learn."

"What pool?"

"Some of the people at the compound had a pool on the date and time you would decide to come with me, and a guy named Stu Levy won."

"You had a betting pool on when I would come?" Steam started building under Penelope's collar.

"Yes," Walker said cheerfully as he focused his attention on a slow moving 18 wheeler that had them pinned in the right lane. "We started it up a couple of months ago. Stu not only had today, he had been getting 20-1 that it would be between noon and one. Everyone thought he was nuts..."

"You and your merry band of New Age freaks were betting on me?"

It finally dawned on Walker that Penelope didn't seem to be enjoying the joke as much as he was. "I never personally get involved, but it's perfectly harmless; they do it all the time. It's good practice, really."

"Oh, really? So why was this Stu guy winning so funny?"

Walker's voice got smaller and his eyes focused harder on the road. "Why would you bet with a guy that is possibly the most gifted psychic in the world?"

"Hmm." Penelope folded her arms across her chest and they rode in silence. After about ten miles, she had to admit that was pretty amusing. After twenty, she had trouble keeping the smile off her face.

"So how good a psychic is this Levy character?"

"He went to the Bellagio once and called fifteen out of twenty turns of the roulette wheel correctly."

"The casinos must hate to see him coming."

"No, he doesn't gamble."

"Really? With that kind of skill?"

"Stu is a bit, how should I put this, different."

"Pots and kettles calling each other names again?"

It took Walker a moment to get the joke. "Noooo. You'll just have to meet him."

"And when will that be?"

"Unless we run into a problem, we should be at compound by this time tomorrow."

"Where exactly is the compound?"

"I can't tell you that yet. There is still a chance you might get caught."

"Fair enough..." she said, as she covered her mouth with her hand to catch a yawn. "So tell me about the dark side of these awakenings."

"Whenever there are dramatic changes there are winners and losers. Often the group that prospered in a previous Awakening becomes less important or in some cases completely obsolete as the new one unfolds."

"Let me guess," Penelope said as she stretched and flexed in a vain attempt to find a more comfortable spot in the lumpy bucket seat. "They do not go gentle into that good night."

"That's putting it mildly. The entire history of mankind is littered with the victims of war and suppression by groups unable to change with the times but also unwilling to give up their perks."

"I'm guessing here," Penelope said with a laugh, "that Cro-Magnons, Kings and Popes don't think too highly of these Awakenings."

"Exactly," Walker answered. "The real danger today, thanks to modern science, is that the carnage could be massive."

"So you're expecting a protracted period of wars because of this Awakening?"

"No, quite the opposite. The change will be over much more quickly this time."

"I don't understand."

"The people today who have the most to lose also have most of the weapons, and have shown a willingness to use them. In the first three Awakenings the killing was pretty much done on a one-on-one basis. Modern weapons don't have that limitation."

"What are you saying?"

"Today, someone can push a button and an hour later more people are dead than died in World War II. Unless we can make as many people as possible aware of this, someone somewhere is going to do something desperate to try and stop this Awakening."

"You're serious?"

"That's why we wanted you. You've already started Awakening but you still have your skepticism. You were the perfect choice. You'll be able to explain it very effectively since you're going through it yourself."

"Why is it whenever I start talking to you I feel like my head is about to explode?"

"Raw animal magnetism?" Walker offered.

Penelope ignored Walker's answer and shifted as far as her seat belt would allow as she tried to face him. "What do you think will happen?"

"Unless we can get in front of this Awakening and let the world know what is going on, I don't see those in power taking any options off the table."

"You actually think a government would launch weapons of mass destruction to stop an Awakening? You can't be serious."

"They're not the ones I'm worried about. Most major governments with these kinds of weapons have all sorts of checks and balances built in. My biggest concern is that a fringe group that cuts across cultural and political borders will emerge and somehow gain access to them."

"What kind of group?"

"I don't know. They haven't shown themselves yet. But let's hope they aren't willing to kill for their beliefs," Walker hesitated. "Or worse, die for them."

"What are the odds of this happening?"

"A lot of that will depend on you."

"Me?"

"Yes. The more people we make aware of the Awakening the better."

"What if that is not enough?"

"Then millions of people could die."

"What?"

"Suppose a war breaks out between two high population nuclear powers such as Pakistan and India, then spreads to China? Even the countries that are not involved will feel the environmental and economic damage for decades..."

"Pull the car over." Penelope demanded.

"What? Why?"

"Pull the damn car over NOW!"

Walker steered the Bronco onto the berm of the Interstate but left the engine idling.

"Look at me," Spence demanded, her eyes blazing. A bemused smile was on Walker's face as he turned to face her. "Are you telling me you think this story I'm suppose to write for you could save millions of lives?!"

"Possibly billions," Walker answered calmly. Penelope's mouth moved but no words came out. Walker leaned back against the car door, propped his elbow on the steering wheel and rested his chin on the palm of his hand. "Why do you think we went to all of this trouble to get you here if it wasn't this important?"

"How dare you!" Penelope demanded. "Who do you think you are trying to hang something like that on me?" Penelope folded her arms across her chest and continued to fume. "If I don't believe your silly little fairy tale a billion people will die. How dare you!"

Walker chuckled and shook his head. "That isn't what I meant at all. All I'm saying is if we can make people aware of the Awakening we can potentially save lives. Whether you tell the story or we find another way to get it out really doesn't matter to us. We just need to get the story out."

Penelope started to run her fingers through her hair until she realized she was still wearing Joey's blonde wig. She jerked it off and tossed it at her feet.

"You're still going to need that," Walker said as he pointed to the hair piece.

"Shut up!" Penelope turned and faced the front of the Bronco.

"You're tired and I've hit you with..."

"You can drop me off at the next exit."

"You don't mean that," Walker answered.

"Why not?"

"First and foremost you are an old school pro and a world class reporter. You're not going to walk away from a story this big just because some maniac you've been humoring for the past few days said something that you didn't like. Especially not now since you're sitting on the biggest exclusive of the decade. It's not in your nature."

"I don't like being manipulated."

"Who's manipulating you?" Walker asked with a laugh. "I didn't even ask to read your stories before you sent them off. I don't care what you write as long as you spell my name right."

Penelope glared at Walker.

"Hate me, love me; believe me or not. Just get the story out there where as many people as possible can see it. That's all we want from you."

Penelope leaned back in her seat and contemplated what Walker had just said. He was right; this was too big of a story to simply walk away from over a flip comment that she might have simply brushed off as hyperbole if she wasn't so tired. Walker had said so many unbelievable things, why should she suddenly take him at his word over this? The initial jolt of adrenalin from his verbal hand grenade was starting to wear off and be replaced with a marrow deep fatigue.

Penelope felt the knot returning to her stomach and wasn't sure if it was being caused by too much dinner or the day's conversation with Walker. She rubbed her forehead. A headache was starting to build as well. Penelope had never been this tired in her life. Her eyes fluttered closed and she had to force them to reopen.

After a few minutes of silence, Penelope felt her irritation toward Walker melting away. He had made it clear from the moment they'd met that he had picked her to write this story and made no effort to minimize its importance. He had promised her that she would be the most sought after reporter in the world and, boy, had he delivered. For the moment she was willing to overlook the fact that many of the people seeking her had badges and arrest warrants with her name on them. So far he had done everything he said he would do and to the best of her knowledge he had never lied to her. Plus, he had picked her. In some weird way she almost felt complimented.

The Bronco continued to idle on the side of the Interstate and Walker didn't feel the need to fill the silence with meaningless chitchat; another point in his favor. A car whizzed past and as the headlight filled the interior of the SUV, Penelope could see Michael Walker's eyes were fixed on her. They twinkled with mirth.

Finally, Penelope softly asked, "The Fourth Awakening has already started hasn't it?"

"Yes, but we can't be sure this isn't just another false start."

"False start?"

"It very nearly happened once before."

"Let me guess," Penelope said as she tried to swallow a yawn but wasn't quite up to the challenge. "The Sumerians found Pandora's Box and let the cat out?"

"A little more recent than that. During your lifetime, actually."

"My lifetime?"

"Yes."

"I didn't notice?" Penelope was incredulous. She folded her arms across her chest as she glared at Walker. "I can't wait to hear this one."

"In the early 1960s ..."

"Early sixties! How old do you think I am?" Walker shot her a glance that showed her how futile that gambit was. She threw her hands up in mock surrender.

"Shall I continue?"

"Please. And can we stick to the who, what, when, where, why, format this time?"

"Who, Timothy Leary. What, LSD. When, 1960s. Where, the United States. And why, because Americans like so many before them wanted enlightenment in an easy to take pill, and came very close to finding one."

Walker shifted in his seat, slapped the Bronco into gear and pulled back onto the nearly deserted Interstate highway. "But that can wait for another day."

"So you're not going to tell me the Timothy Leary story?"

"Not tonight. You've already had so much to absorb in such a short period of time, it would probably be counter-productive. You should try to get some rest."

Penelope wanted to protest but realized Walker was right. Reaching in the dark for the pillow between her feet she found Joey's wig instead. With a sigh she put it back on. Retrieving the pillow, she tucked it between her shoulder and the window and stared out into the dark West Virginia countryside speeding by. Overpowering her fatigue, doubts began to creep in keeping her from sleep. Had she pushed back too hard? Had she said something wrong?

"Look," she finally said. "I can be really difficult sometimes..."

"Pigheaded."

"Steadfast."

They both laughed. He stopped her by placing a hand on her shoulder. "You have absolutely nothing to apologize over. I am so grateful you've decided to help us, I really can't express it in words. Get some rest. If what you have seen in the last few days has your head spinning, wait until tomorrow."

"What happens tomorrow?"

"You're going to get to meet Dr. Carl Altman and see the Hermes Project in action."

Just before she drifted off to sleep, she asked, "How did you know that

Homeland Security was going to visit the *Post* in the morning?"

"We have an old friend at Homeland Security."

"You have a spy inside of Homeland Security?"

"Yes."

Normally that type of bombshell would cause her to leave Tired Town and kick her mind into overdrive. For now, she had so many remarkable and terrifying things to consider, it didn't even make her top ten list. People being able to project themselves to another place merely by thinking about it. The destruction of her home. Senator Horn's stroke. Assaulting a federal officer. Risotto. Timothy Leary... With Walker's hand on her shoulder and the whine of the highway in her ears, her eyes closed and she fell fast asleep.

≈

MARK HATCHET, AS usual, was still at his desk. He took a sip from his coffee mug, but the contents were cold and had turned bitter. He reached for the pot on the burner behind his desk and topped off with a brew dark enough and thick enough to seal the cracks in a blacktop driveway. He'd had worse. The Monday edition had been completed and sent to the pressmen, and the City Edition would be hitting the streets in a few minutes. Mark smiled as he wondered, thanks to Penelope, how many congressional interns were standing on dark corners waiting for copies of the paper to hand deliver to their bosses. After tonight, even if Nellie didn't send him another word, she was a lock for her second Pulitzer. The last story to hit Washington with this much impact was Iran-Contra. If she also broke the Hermes Project... Hatchet shook his head. She would be the biggest name in American newspapers since Ben Franklin.

The lead stories were, of course, the two that Nellie had sent him. The only other story on the front page was an article about the condition of Senator Clayton Horn, with several sidebars on his impressive legislative and personal life history. To everyone's amazement, not only had the senator's condition stabilized, he was doing remarkably well for a man of his age. It appeared he would lose some function on his right side and his speech was definitely impaired, but how badly was yet to be determined.

A man dressed in a blue and red courier's jacket tapped on the door and looked at the name on the envelope in his hand. "Mark Hatchet?" The managing editor nodded and the man handed him the envelope. When it was clear that no tip was forthcoming, he turned and headed toward the elevators.

Using a letter opener, Hatchet sliced the envelope open and pulled out a single sheet of paper. There was a handwritten note:

Expect a visit tomorrow from Director Noah Shepherd, Assistant Director Robert A. Smith and Special Agent Marcus J. Wolfe of the Emerging Technologies Division.

I'm with you know who.

I should be at the Hermes Project late tomorrow.

I'm fine. Call Joey.

Leave Wednesday's front page open for me and my interview with Dr. Carl Altman and Michael Walker.

Nellie 2204

Hatchet slapped the piece of paper with the back of his hand and smiled from ear to ear. "That's my girl." He knew it had to be from her; who else would have known the number of his dorm room in college? Hatchet pushed a button on his phone that rang at the desk of his executive assistant, who was in the process of putting on her coat. They made eye contact through the glass.

"I need to set up a meeting with the publisher and legal."

"For when?"

"Within the hour, if possible."

She tossed her coat aside and motioned for an intern to get her another cup of coffee, indicating that a fresh pot was also needed in Hatchet's office. It was going to be one of those nights.

Hatchet was already dialing research. "Call in extra staff if you need it but in the next 30 minutes I want a preliminary bio, and then I want everything you've got or can find by 6 a.m. on the following people, Dr. Carl Altman, Director Noah Shepherd..."

CHAPTER EIGHTEEN

"Enlightenment must come little by little — otherwise it would overwhelm."

IDRIES SHAH

PENELOPE SPENCE AWOKE to find her head resting on Michael Walker's shoulder and her left arm hooked under his, holding it tight. Blinking her eyes, she tried to orient herself. She was wrapped in a soft cotton blanket she couldn't remember seeing before. They were in what appeared to be a rest stop along an interstate highway. The clock on the dashboard said it was just a few minutes before 7 a.m. She tried to untangle herself carefully, but when she did Walker's eyes flickered open.

He cleared his throat before saying, "Good morning."

"Sorry. I didn't mean to wake you."

"I was already watching my body wake up," Walker answered.

"What does that mean?" Penelope said with a laugh.

"It's not important."

"If you say so," Penelope answered while fighting a yawn. "Where are we?"

"We're at a rest stop in Richwood, Kentucky, about 15 minutes from the Cincinnati airport." As if on cue, a large passenger jet in its final approach for landing rumbled overhead.

"How long have we been here?"

"About four hours."

As she stretched and covered a yawn with the back of her hand, Penelope asked, "How long have I been asleep?"

"Long enough."

"I'm going to the powder room."

"Here." Walker handed her a small plastic bag. A puzzled expression crept over her face as she looked inside the bag. It contained travel sized versions of all of her normal personal hygiene products, including her preferred toothpaste and deodorant. In plastic wrap was a new toothbrush, and there was also a washcloth and small hand towel.

For a brief moment she considered asking how he knew exactly what toiletry items she preferred but decided she really didn't want to know. "Thanks."

When she returned from her brief but refreshing trip to the ladies room, she was surprised to see Walker talking to a man who was leaning against the Bronco. He was a younger version of Walker and looked enough like him that he could be his son. Each was reading a copy of *The Washington Post*; a third copy was waiting for her on the hood.

"Who's your friend?" she asked.

"Timothy Ellison, Penelope Drayton Spence."

Timothy Ellison shook her hand firmly, but not too firm, and made strong eye contact. "Ms. Spence, it's a true pleasure." Normally she hated it when men over 25 called her Ms. or Mrs., but there was something gentle and sincere about Ellison that practically made her want to adopt him. He was handsome with a rugged outdoorsy demeanor; the sun had started early smile lines on his face. Like every mother with unmarried daughters, she let her eyes drift to his left hand. There was no ring on the third finger and no shadow of one that had been recently removed.

"Tim has worked on the Hermes Project since the beginning," Walker said. "If I'm ever not around, listen to him and do what he says."

Ellison handed her a copy of *The Washington Post*. "Very impressive, Ms. Spence."

"Please," she said as she spread the paper across the hood of the Bronco so she could get the full effect. "Call me Penelope." To her surprise, Mark had done precious little copy editing. "Wow!" she muttered to herself. Every word on the front page of today's edition had her byline. Mark had even added her as a source for the background pieces on the condition of Senator Horn. For a journalist, this was the equivalent of hitting a grand slam in the ninth inning of the seventh game to win the World Series while pitching a no hitter. It just doesn't happen.

"Here, Ms..," Ellison caught himself. "Penelope." He smiled as he handed her a hotel keycard.

"What's this?"

Walker opened the passenger door and said, "Our next stop."

≈

W ALKER BACKED PARTWAY into a parking spot in the rear of the Airport Sheraton, well away from the view of the front desk and any surveillance cameras. Jumping out of the Bronco, he grabbed a screwdriver, removed the license plate and tossed it into the nearby trash dumpster. Next he opened the tailgate and flipped the tarp back. Underneath, Penelope saw a familiar looking carrying case for a laptop and three pieces of luggage. Her luggage!

"I see you grabbed more than just my laptop." He shrugged as he pulled the four bags out of the Bronco and set them on the curb. This time she wasn't upset; quite the opposite. She was eager to see what he had selected for her. Looking at the offending T-shirt he was still wearing, she didn't hold out much hope.

"So what would have happened to all of my stuff if I hadn't come along?" Penelope asked.

"You'd have found it sitting on your friend Joey's porch," Walker answered with a smile.

Walker jumped back behind the wheel of the Bronco and slowly backed it up until its rear bumper was touching a six-foot high retaining wall. Locking the doors, he tossed the keys in the dumpster.

"What in the world are you doing?"

Walker smiled. "We aren't going to need this car anymore and by making it hard to see the license plate, it is likely the hotel staff will walk around this thing for weeks before they do anything about it."

Leaving the laptop case for her, Walker and Ellison picked up the other three pieces of luggage and nodded toward the rear door of the hotel. By using the swipe keys that Ellison had already secured, they were able to avoid the front desk and any video equipment that might be near it. Their rooms were on the first floor at the end of the corridor. Again using the magnetic card Timothy Ellison had given her, she opened the door to her room and stepped inside.

Ellison had booked them two adjoining rooms. Walker lined up the suitcases and pointed to the door that connected the room. "I'll be in there. Please don't leave the room for any reason, and keep the blinds pulled. If you need anything, tap on this door."

Penelope nodded that she understood.

"How about I give you an hour to get cleaned up and change, then we'll get some breakfast." He was almost out the door when he turned back. "Wear your charcoal skirt, white blouse and the black Manolo Blahnik shoes."

"Why?"

"For once, could you just trust me?"

"It depends on what else I find in my suitcases."

Walker laughed as he pulled the door shut.

Penelope couldn't remember enjoying a bath so much in her life. Walker had done brilliantly. One of the suitcases, the largest one, was filled with some of her favorite shoes; including, of all things, her old college dancing shoes. Men. The other had the perfect mix of casual and formal clothes, just the right amount of underwear and her make-up kit. This man was certainly building up a considerable number of credits in her mental ledger.

Feeling somewhat like a school girl getting ready to go to a movie with a boy she liked, she tried on a series of different white tops, hoping to find the one that best complimented the requested charcoal skirt, before settling on a simple white silk blouse. She was slipping on her black Manolo Blahniks, which also happened to be her favorite pair of shoes, when she heard a soft tap on the connecting door. She opened it and was immediately startled by what she saw.

The man she had driven a third of the way across the country with was gone. No crude T-shirt, no long greasy blond hair and no pillow to give the impression of a budding potbelly. Michael Walker was clean-shaven, and wearing a perfectly tailored, three-button dark blue Armani suit with pinstripes. His shirt was pale blue and custom fitted. Around his neck was a tasteful pale blue Luigi Borrelli tie, and he wore handcrafted Forzieri black leather Oxford dress shoes. With the hint of silver on his temples, he looked like he had just stepped off one of the pages of GQ.

"You clean up nice," Penelope said as she adjusted his tie and smoothed down his lapel. Catching just the faintest whiff of Emporio cologne, she said, "Smell nice too. Did you go to all of this trouble just for me?"

"No," he answered. Penelope pulled away; if Walker noticed he didn't indicate it. "We have to make the right impression at the airport. We don't want anyone slowing us down. We're going to need you to wear the blonde wig and these," he said as he handed Penelope a pair of contact lenses. "They will make your eyes brown instead of blue."

Penelope didn't like either idea, but didn't protest. "I suddenly feel very underdressed."

"You're dressed fine for your role."

She took another step back. "My role?"

"For the next few hours all eyes need to be on Tim and me, not on you."

"Why?'

"If our latest bit of information from inside Homeland Security is correct, they are no longer looking for me." He locked eyes with her. "Their main target is now you."

≈

N OAH SHEPHERD'S ENTOURAGE filled the entire elevator. In addition to Robert Smith and Marcus Wolfe, there were four Homeland Security lawyers. It was his usual approach to display overwhelming numbers and power when dealing with a potential adversary. He wanted to do everything possible to intimidate Mark Hatchet and *The Washington Post*. A surprise visit might be enough to get them to back off from trying to discover the actual work that was being done at the Hermes Project and just leave it as some secret, classified program. If he was successful, this story would blow over in a few days. Especially if he could locate Penelope Drayton Spence.

Shepherd was a fit and elegant man in his early fifties with an air of sophistication usually seen in career diplomats and those running entire departments of government. Coming from old money, Shepherd supported the arts and was also a generous contributor to politicians of both parties. He belonged to all the 'proper' social clubs and contributed to all of the right causes. He was well traveled and fluent in nine languages, including Mandarin, Japanese, and Russian. He was famous for requesting original copies of important documents and doing his own translations.

"Crap," Marcus Wolfe quietly muttered, when the elevator doors opened and they were greeted by twelve men and two women in expensive business suits, all carrying notepads. In addition to Hatchet, the group included the publisher, editor, several senior editors, four corporate lawyers and even more outside counsel.

Mark Hatchet extended his hand. "Director, we've been expecting you. This way, please." All activity stopped in the busy newsroom as everyone's eyes followed the parade of dignitaries down the corridor.

Shepherd was not used to being outmaneuvered and he didn't like it one bit. He had suspected there was a leak in his office and this confirmed it. Worse yet, apparently it was at the highest level. Only three people knew they were coming this morning; Smith, Wolfe and him. He glared at Robert Smith as Hatchet guided them toward the conference room.

After the introductions were completed and everyone was seated, Hatchet, sitting directly across the polished mahogany table from Shepherd, began the proceedings. "What brings representatives of Homeland Security to our offices this morning?"

"We," Shepherd said as he straightened his tie, "wanted to express our disappointment that your newspaper has decided to renege on your agreement not to pursue a story involving national security at the highest level."

Hatchet glanced at the *Post's* head of legal, Leon Steinberg.

Steinberg slid a piece of paper across the desk toward Shepherd, while a secretary moved around the table and handed each of the Homeland Security staff a copy. "I think you'll find that in order, Director Shepherd."

"What is this?"

"This, sir, is a release from Senator Clayton Lee Horn to Penelope Drayton Spence, allowing her to use any and all material from her meeting with the senator and their joint interview of Michael James Walker while he was being detained in the U.S. Naval Consolidated Brig in Charleston, South Carolina, on Saturday afternoon."

Steinberg was a bull of a man with a thick neck and broad shoulders. He'd grown up in Brooklyn and earned his law degree at City College at night while working construction during the day. There was nothing he liked better than a good scrape with some prissy Ivy League elitist. His career was almost exclusively built on eating guys like Shepherd for lunch, and Steinberg considered them his primary source of roughage.

"You will find that this release covers everything published in *The Washington Post* concerning this topic."

"That will be difficult to verify, considering the condition of the senator," Shepherd said.

Leon Steinberg smiled as he passed a second document across the table. "This is a copy of a notarized statement from Senator Clayton Horn's Chief of Staff, Joan Louise Inman, verifying the accuracy of the release." Steinberg waited until everyone had the document in front of them before he reached into his folder again. "And this is notification of *The Washington Post's* intention to withdraw from its agreement not to pursue this story."

"I must admit," Shepherd said, not bothering to wait for the final document to be distributed. "I find this disappointing."

"Sir," Mark Hatchet said, "we do not enter into suicide pacts to remain idle while our competition is looking into something that may not be an issue of national security. At present we consider this story to involve the potential cover-up of a government experiment that, if exposed, would simply prove embarrassing."

"We strongly disagree with that characterization and reiterate that you are pursuing information, and have already published an unacceptable level of detail concerning, a project whose secrecy is of grave importance to the national security of the United States of America."

"We'll be in a better position to evaluate your claims later today after we've talked to Dr. Carl Altman and have had the opportunity to review the Hermes Project firsthand."

Everyone on the Homeland Security side of the table flinched except Director Noah Shepherd. Hatchet and his bosses could tell from their reaction, they had drawn blood. If *The Washington Post* had been able to find the Hermes Project, this was rapidly disintegrating from a containment operation to damage control.

"I'm afraid any information you receive from Dr. Altman will be classified and we'll seek a federal injunction to prevent it from being published."

Before Hatchet could answer, Leon Steinberg jumped in. "You can try, sir. But the federal government hasn't won a prior restraint decision since before the Pentagon Papers, and that was over 30 years ago."

Shepherd rose to his feet, and his entourage to theirs a half-beat later. "Let me again express our deep disappointment and concern over the irresponsibility of the decisions being made on this matter."

In the back of his governmental limo with Special Agents Smith and Wolfe, Shepherd was so furious he almost raised his voice. "We have a leak." Shepherd's eyes locked on Smith. Wolfe he was sure of, and there was no reason for him to have given the newspaper a heads up. Smith, on the other hand, had been close with both Walker and Altman. "Who else knew about this meeting?"

"The other people who were with us?" Wolfe offered.

"No." Shepherd said flatly. "They were not notified there was even going to be a meeting until it was time to leave, and they were not informed of where we were going until we arrived."

"One of your two secretaries?" Smith said.

"Possibly," Shepherd said. "But not very likely. They only arranged our entourage but were as much in the dark as everyone else."

Assistant Director Smith could see where this was headed, and didn't like the direction. "What about the computer guys?"

Director Shepherd thought for a moment. "I don't think so. While it is true Obee is the one who discovered that the Spence woman was working for the *Post* within minutes of her first appearance at the brig, he didn't know about the meeting. Besides, he has no loyalty to anyone in the Hermes Project and he seldom leaves his room."

"What about the other guy?" Wolfe asked.

"I only dealt with Zhack, or whatever he calls himself," Smith said weakly.

A heavy silence settled over the car. Having played political games himself for years, Director Shepherd knew that as situations changed allegiances could as well. Adjustments often had to be made. Perhaps the Assistant Director was feeding Walker information in the hope that when this unraveled he could avoid becoming everyone's scapegoat. That was what he would have done.

"Whatever it takes," Director Shepherd said. "I want Penelope Spence found before she can file her next story."

≈

TIMOTHY ELLISON, NOW dressed just as nattily as Walker, joined them for breakfast, where Walker was already explaining what they were going to do and why.

"We're going to have about five hours of vulnerability, from the time we enter the Cincinnati airport until we leave the Salt Lake City airport," Walker said. "After that we're home free."

"Aren't you afraid we're going to be seen?" Penelope asked. Walker didn't answer but exchanged smiles with Ellison. "What?"

"Trust me," Walker said.

Timothy Ellison outlined the plan. "Since this is a 737, all of the coach passengers will enter the plane and make an immediate right. Our seats are in First Class, which is a left turn at the entry door and directly behind the cockpit. There may be a few others in Business class but we should have most of the front section to ourselves. I booked us four seats together, so this will mean we have a certain level of privacy, and no one will be looking at our faces."

"Four?" Penelope asked. "You're coming with us?"

"Yes," said Ellison. Apparently, he was as fond of one-word answers as Walker.

"They are looking for a man and a woman. Not two men and a woman. We bought the other seat to assure no one sits next to us," Walker answered before she could ask.

Ellison left and went up to the rooms to get the luggage. Before he did, he slid Penelope a wallet that didn't look new but didn't look old either. Inside was a Florida driver's license in the name of Sally Winters with a picture of a woman who looked enough like her to maybe not be her twin but at least her kid sister. There were also a library card and a few credit cards. In the back was around $500 in small bills. He also handed her a passport that made her appear to be a frequent world traveler.

Out front of the Sheraton a black stretch limo with dark windows was idling at the curb; the driver was helping Ellison place the bags in the trunk. When they arrived at the Delta Terminal curbside check-in, Ellison immediately jumped out of the car, grabbed a Sky Cap and handed him a $100 bill as the driver popped the trunk. Ellison placed the preprinted boarding passes on the airport security table along with three passports, before opening the rear door of the limo. Walker, wearing dark wraparound sunglasses, got out talking briskly on the telephone, using his left hand to cover his mouth and keep the conversation private. It had the side benefit of also covering more of his face from the surrounding video cameras. Penelope, with her head down, was right behind him writing furiously on a notepad, never raising her eyes.

"I really don't care what time it is in Singapore. If they want to do this deal then we're going to have a conference call as soon as we get to Salt Lake City."

The TSA agent behind the curbside check in counter watched Walker carefully and compared his passport picture to his face.

"No," Walker shouted as he placed his hand over the mouthpiece of his phone and turned to Ellison. "Are we about done here?"

Ellison, with a kicked puppy look on his face, turned to the man behind the counter, his eyes pleading for help. The TSA guard nodded toward the terminal. "Thank you," Ellison mouthed sheepishly.

The trio walked inside with no one giving Penelope a second glance. "Which part of 'no' is unclear? The word only has two letters in it, apparently the same number of digits as your IQ."

Once they had cleared the front door, Walker immediately closed his phone and tossed it to Ellison. The only carryon bag they had between them was Penelope's laptop, and it was safely over Ellison's shoulder. "Hold on one second." Walker pulled a piece of white thread out of his pocket and stuck it on the back of Spence's skirt.

"What's that for?"

"Later," Walker said as he led the way toward the metal detector. With no keys and no other metal of any kind on them, Walker and Penelope breezed through security. But Timothy Ellison, who had "forgotten" he had a cell phone in his front shirt pocket, caused alarms to ring. The second time through he had "accidentally" touched the side of the metal detector, setting off the alarm again. As all eyes turned toward Ellison, Spence and Walker reclaimed their shoes and moved down the corridor unnoticed. He caught up with them in a restaurant where they were seated with their backs to the people walking by. Ellison sat down facing them and in a position that allowed him to keep an eye on their surroundings.

They waited until the final boarding call for Delta Flight 1712, non-stop from Cincinnati to Salt Lake City, before they left their seats. As Penelope stood up, Walker plucked the white thread off the back of her skirt. She looked at him, quizzically.

"You need to start trusting someone in your life, it may as well be me," Walker said with a weak smile. "When we get to the gate, keep your head down and don't look up, no matter what happens. Also stay close. We're going to be walking at some odd angles which will seem a bit disorienting."

"Why?'

Walker pointed to a video camera on the opposite wall. Penelope nodded that she understood.

Again, as they approached the boarding ramp, Walker was on the phone and Penelope was writing on her note pad with her head down. Ellison handed the three boarding passes to the check-in person and apologized for the late arrival with his eyes. Alone in the connecting tunnel, Walker flipped Ellison the phone and asked if he was ready. He nodded that he was. As they reached the door of the Boeing jet, Ellison tripped and went sprawling face first in the doorway, causing the crew and passengers to focus on him. By the time he had been helped to his feet, Walker and Penelope were already seated in the front row with their backs to the rest of the passengers. Ellison popped into one of the two empty seats behind them.

The flight was one of five daily non-stops from the Delta hub in Cincinnati to Salt Lake City. This was one of the airline's most profitable routes; there were seldom any empty seats on the 737-800. This was good and bad. It's always easier to get lost in a crowd, but with more eyes available it increases the risk someone might recognize you.

Once the jet was in the air, the trio settled in for the three hour and fifteen minute flight.

"So," Penelope said as she sipped her merlot. "Are you going to tell me the Timothy Leary story?"

"Oh, Lord," Ellison moaned from the seat behind them. "Not that one again." Ellison stood up and leaned over the seat. "He's been trying to sell that to the guys at the compound for the last few months."

"Are there any buyers?"

"Fifty-fifty, at best. The consensus at the compound is he wanted to be the one to bring you in so he could indoctrinate you into all of his theories."

"Hey," Walker protested.

"Be quiet," Spence said as she slapped Walker's arm. "So others found some of his stories hard to believe?"

"Are you kidding? Wait until you get involved in the nightly debates. While we all tend to agree on the major points...he's got his ideas, but believe me, there are other opinions."

"I will concede that we don't have total agreement on all..."

Penelope slapped his arm again and held a finger up to her lips. "Will you shush? I'm talking to Timothy and would like to hear what he has to say." Turning her attention back to Ellison, she continued. "So not immediately believing what he says is normal?"

"Absolutely. You'll eventually work it all out for yourself; we all have. I have to admit, in most cases everyone pretty much ends up agreeing with him."

"Thank you," Walker said as he reached for his water and brought on yet another slap.

"Except for the Timothy Leary theory."

"Why?" Penelope asked.

"A lot of us think he's still upset that he was such a serious college student that he missed all of the sex, drugs and rock and roll, so his view of the 60's and 70's is tainted."

Tim Ellison had an easy smile and deep, kind eyes. He looked to be around the same age as her eldest, unmarried, daughter Carrie. Strong-willed and difficult at times, especially when tired or hungry, Carrie still hadn't found the right guy. In high school, her father called all of her suitors "Clarence". When one asked why, he told the boy if he was still around in three weeks he would make an effort to learn his name. From the time she started dating at 15, until she went off to college, Carrie only dated boys named Clarence. Penelope had to wonder if Ellison would have the right stuff to deal with a 21st century woman like her tightly wound little darling. She sighed. Since he probably did, that would mean Carrie wouldn't find him the least bit attractive.

Walker unbuttoned his jacket and took another sip from his bottle of water. "Last count, the majority of the people at the compound have come around to my way of thinking on this, as well, thank you very much."

"I've heard all of this before," Ellison said, "I'm going to try and catch some sleep." He fell back into his seat, closed his eyes, and was instantly fast asleep.

"He's already asleep."

"Sort of," Walker said.

"What does that mean?"

"At his stage of development he is always awake at some level, even while asleep."

"Awake while you're asleep. Just when you were starting to sound sane," Penelope said with a sigh. "Timothy Leary?"

"Are you willing to at least consider that we are all connected through thought, and that there is power in thought?"

"If I say, 'no' do I still get to hear the story?"

"No."

"I wholeheartedly believe we are all connected through thought, and that there is power in thought."

"Your sincerity is touching."

"We've got three hours to kill, just tell me the story."

"Okay. Back in the late 1950's, Leary, who was a psychology professor at Berkeley, began experimenting with psychedelic mushrooms to try to raise consciousness levels. Then along came LSD and he was off to the races. Later he moved to Harvard, which gave him a bi-coastal following. As the number of people exposed to LSD grew, the San Francisco Bay Area and the Boston to New York corridor became hotbeds of psychedelic usage. Soon this fad jumped the oceans and was in the urban centers of Europe and Asia, with LSD as the drug of choice for intellectuals on college campuses across the globe."

"Why was it so popular?"

"Those that took it started to have what appeared, to them at least, as an awakening."

"You mean like your Awakening?"

"Yes."

"Because of Timothy Leary and LSD?"

"There was a renaissance in the realms of music, art, fashion and politics. Leary and his experiments, though incredibly crude, were strong enough that they began having an impact on the collective consciousness. As the usage of LSD spread, so did the problems."

"Problems?"

"As you have so wholeheartedly agreed," Walker said as he cleared his throat. "We're all connected and thoughts have power, but understanding this has to come naturally and can be dangerous if forced on a person."

"Isn't that what you're doing?"

"It's like comparing a chainsaw to a scalpel. We give a gentle nudge while Leary and his followers started a train wreck that had worldwide implications for nearly a decade."

"What kind of implications?"

"It was almost as if the thoughts of those on LSD were being amplified by the drug. Their thoughts were distorted, and in some cases, destructive. LSD seemed to open some kind of spiritual Pandora's Box; the effects started to seep into other parts of society and spread around the world."

"Sounds almost like a virus."

"Exactly. This virus started to affect everyone else on the planet in a negative way. People around the globe became more violent. By 1967 it appeared the whole world had gone mad."

"Are you kidding me? 1967 was the summer of love. Those people were not violent."

"That's the way most people remember it, but consider this; in 1967 and 1968, more than fifty cities had race riots. The Vietnam War was at its height. Martin Luther King and Bobby Kennedy were both assassinated. In Chicago, the Democratic National Convention was disrupted by student protests that were put down violently. College campuses were being shut down. The Weathermen and Students for a Democratic Society were blowing up ROTC buildings. And it wasn't just in the United States. The insanity was worldwide."

"Worldwide?"

"In 1967, OPEC was formed, and the Arab world united and attacked Israel. Former colonies in Africa and other places were breaking away from their European masters. The Soviets and Chinese were saber rattling across their long border. There was the Prague Spring, and around the same time student riots in Paris in May of 1968 nearly toppled the French government."

"You're going to blame all of this on the consciousness level of the world being altered by a few hippies dropping acid?"

"It was a lot more than a few."

"Moon barking crazy." Penelope heard a snicker from the seat behind them. Walker was right; Ellison wasn't sleeping as soundly as she had supposed.

"Am I? During those years the people in power were terrified they were losing control. In the United States, they bought off the cities by creating a wealth of social welfare programs. The Europeans created an even more generous welfare system, and they jettisoned all of their colonies. The two major Communist powers went in the exact opposite direction. The Russians used their military to crush Prague and to send a message to the rest of the Soviet Union by dramatically increasing the size and brutality of their gulags and prison camps. The scariest was what happened in China."

"Oh, you're kidding me? You're going to try and hang that on poor old Timothy Leary?"

"As a representative figurehead, at least. Mao's Cultural Revolution started in 1966. You do the math. The Red Guard killed millions of people and sent millions more to re-education centers."

Concern etched a frown on Penelope's face. "Are these the kinds of things you're afraid will happen because of the next Awakening?"

"You read the newspapers and see the news."

"Lord. What, in your theory, stopped all of this?"

"In this case it was bad chemistry."

"What?"

"A lot of bad LSD started popping up. People began to think they could fly and started walking off rooftops or stood in front of trains convinced of their own invincibility. Considering how it evolved, I suspect the government had a hand in it. They had been experimenting with LSD for years and likely had uncovered many of its nasty side effects. Then they started planting stories that LSD caused chromosome damage and could make your testicles fall off and other nonsense."

"That would certainly put a damper on the summer of love." Penelope scrunched up her face. "The government giving bad drugs to our own kids? I find that hard to believe."

"This was the decade before Watergate, and back then the government did all sorts of nasty things they could never get away with today. The FBI under J. Edgar Hoover had files on nearly everybody, the CIA was going around the world assassinating political leaders, and the Pentagon could pretty much do whatever they wanted. Combine that kind of unchecked power with the fear they may be losing their grip on it, and I wouldn't put anything past them."

"So, let me get this straight. You think the federal government made a concerted effort to discredit LSD because they knew it was having a negative impact on humanity's collective consciousness."

"Yes. They had been experimenting with it for years and had to be aware of the cause and effect regarding the spread of its usage. Had to."

"And you accused me of being a conspiracy theory nut!"

Walker shook his head. "I knew you weren't ready."

"Apparently neither are the rest of us," wafted from the seat behind them amid more snickering.

"How exactly do you suppose the government went about discrediting LSD?"

"They did a frontal assault on the people most likely to be using it. If you've ever seen the movie on Woodstock, you saw the guy who took the microphone and warned everyone about some 'bad acid out there.'"

"When rock stars began dropping like flies—Hendrix, Joplin, Morrison—from drug overdoses in 1970, the popularity of the drugs of choice from the sixties faded and they were replaced by disco and cocaine. After that, things pretty much stabilized and the status quo was restored.

"So you're saying the last act of insanity from the LSD movement was Disco?" This brought yet another snicker from the peanut gallery behind them. "Wow. Now it all makes sense for me. Timothy Leary begot us John Travolta. How could I have been so dense?"

Walker shook his head. "Just give it some thought."

Penelope fanned her face with both hands. "Are you kidding? This is the epiphany I've been waiting for my whole life. For the first time, with total clarity, I understand Disco."

"Pigheaded," Walker muttered under his breath so only Penelope could hear. He picked up a copy of the *Wall Street Journal* from the stack of newspapers Ellison had bought at one of the airport gift shops. Penelope smiled when she saw her byline on the lead article of the morning edition of the *Cincinnati Enquirer.*

≈

THE SEAT BELT light had gone on indicating final approach for Salt Lake City when the cockpit door opened and the co-pilot stepped out to use the restroom. Glancing over at the trio, he stopped dead in his tracks. "Mr. Walker?"

CHAPTER NINETEEN

*"I know God will not give me anything I can't handle.
I just wish that He didn't trust me so much."*

MOTHER TERESA

MICHAEL WALKER DIDN'T flinch when he realized he had been recognized. All of their efforts to conceal their faces had been focused on the 180 people behind them so they hadn't considered the risk of being recognized by one of the people in the jet's cockpit. Walker rose from his seat and stepped into the aisle so he could stand up without being hunched over.

"Hello, Martin."

The co-pilot, Martin Lundberg, was in his mid-forties. Too many layovers far from home had added a few inches to his waistline. He had a full moon face, with a good tan, and thinning brown hair. His eyes danced over to Penelope and stayed there long enough she shifted uncomfortably. "I heard something about you on the news. Didn't catch all of it. Were you arrested or something?"

Walker laughed. "Obviously if I had been arrested I wouldn't be on this flight."

"Good point. I must have heard it wrong," the co-pilot said with a smile as he again sized up his chances with Penelope and decided it was probably a lost cause. "Look, Mr. Walker. I really need to get back, but it was great seeing you again."

Penelope leaned and whispered, "Who is this guy?"

"For three years he was a pilot for one of my corporate jets."

"You have multiple corporate jets?"

"I don't, the corporation does."

"There's a difference?"

"According to the IRS, there is."

"How come we're not on one of those?"

"Because we needed you to walk through the Cincinnati and Salt Lake City airports."

"Why?"

"Trust me."

Martin Lundberg had hustled to the restroom and taken care of his business so quickly Penelope was sure he hadn't had time to wash his hands. Yuck. The sound of the landing gear lowering could be heard as Lundberg passed back through the cabin.

"He's kind of creepy."

"He was a decent enough pilot but we had to let him go."

"Why?"

"We kept getting some interesting charges on his hotel bill. Plus he looked at every woman in the company the same way he was looking at you."

"Do we have a problem?" Ellison asked as he leaned over the seat.

"We'll know in a few seconds."

"What's going on?" Penelope asked

"If we suddenly go back up into the holding pattern instead of landing that means Lundberg radioed ahead that we are onboard. If we land, then we should be okay."

Timothy Ellison turned and glanced back into the coach section of the plane and pointed to the luggage rack.

"What's going on," Penelope asked.

"Plan C," Walker answered with quick laugh. Looking around to be sure no one was watching, he asked, "May I have your wallet and passport, please?" She handed them over without question. Walker removed all of the cash and handed it to Ellison. "Give her the other set."

Ellison handed Penelope another complete identification package

Penelope looked at the Ohio driver's license. "At least I'm not a blonde anymore."

The wheels of the jet touched the tarmac and the plane began to slow down. The minutes seemed like hours as the plane taxied toward the terminal.

Not waiting for the seatbelt light to go off and with their seats in the tiny first class section close to the exit, Walker and Timothy were able to position Penelope so she would be the first one off.

"If we get separated, someone will find you and take you to the compound," Walker whispered in her ear. "Walk straight out into the terminal and do not look back for any reason."

She nodded that she understood. Her eyes focused on the door, which seemed like it was never going to open. With a faint whoosh, one of the Flight Attendants released the handle and the door swung open.

A commotion broke out to Penelope's left as she heard an angry voice shout, "Hey! That's my laptop."

Before she could turn to see what was causing the uproar, she felt Walker's hand gently shoving her out toward the terminal. "Don't look back," he whispered.

Suddenly Walker was at her side with his arm hooked under Penelope's encouraging her to pick up the pace. They walked briskly through the terminal until they were well away from the gate but could still see Ellison standing near the door at the top of the tunnel.

Back on the plane one of the passengers was apologizing profusely to the air marshal and the passenger he had accused of attempting to steal his computer. It seemed they had nearly identical laptop cases and they were both in the same overhead bin. The people began slowly filing off the airplane when the co-pilot Martin Lundberg joined the flight attendants and the air marshal who were chuckling in the galley near the exit.

"I thought that guy was going to clock the other guy," the marshal said with a laugh.

"This has been a strange one," Lundberg said as he interjected himself into the conversation. "First I see Michael Walker on the plane and..."

"Michael Walker!?" The marshal shouted. "Are you sure?"

"Of course I'm sure," he smiled and winked at one of the flight attendants who rolled her eyes. "I was his personal pilot for 3 years and...."

"You idiot." Anger flashed in the air marshal's eyes as he turned his full attention to the co-pilot. "Who else was with him?"

"He was sitting with a good looking blonde and the guy behind them may have been with them."

The Air Marshal reached for his cell phone and started trotting up the tunnel pushing the disembarking passengers aside. "This is Preston. I've spotted Michael Walker; he just deplaned at Gate D-11 of the Salt Lake City International Airport."

Walker had Ellison stay back just in case someone from the plane followed them. As usual, Walker's instincts were correct. The marshal burst through the doorway and scanned the terminal while still talking on his cell phone. "The woman is wearing a dark skirt..."

That was all Ellison needed to hear as he reached into his pocket and pulled out a wad of cash, nearly $4,000 in fives, tens and twenties. The gate they deplaned from was at the end of a concourse arm with four waiting areas in close proximity to each other. Since this was a peak time of day, the terminal was packed. Even with several hundred seats in the general area, people were milling around waiting to board various flights.

Ellison vaulted to the top of a ticket counter and grabbed the microphone out of a startled gate attendant's hand.

"Who would like some MONEY?!" He shouted into the microphone, as everyone looked up.

He took about a third of the bills and tossed them as high and far as he could across an area where nearly two hundred people were waiting for a Seattle bound plane to begin boarding. As expected, a near riot started as people began diving for dollars and fighting over possession.

The air marshal was swept up by the surging crowd and prevented from going any further. Ellison jumped down and snaked his way to the gate on the opposite side of the aisle. Bounding up on the now deserted counter, he grabbed the microphone and shouted, "There's more money over here!" as he threw another handful of bills into the air. A healthy portion of the mass of people on the other side of the terminal surged across the aisle and began struggling with the people waiting to board a flight to Dallas.

The airport security guards who were sprinting toward the end of Concourse D expecting to be looking for a man in a suit and a blonde woman in a dark skirt were confronted instead with a full-scale insurrection. There were now nearly 500 people pushing, shoving, and cursing. Ellison saw them coming and tossed the last of his bills in the air. Women were screaming, babies were crying. Men were exchanging punches. Ellison melted into the crowd and disappeared.

Walker and Spence, standing in a West of Brooklyn gift store, watched the security guards sprint past them without a second glance. Walker grabbed a Zion National Park t-shirt off the rack and a Utah Jazz baseball cap. He quickly paid for them and handed them to Penelope.

"Go into the bathroom and put these on," he said, handing Penelope the shirt and cap. "Toss the wig in the garbage can."

Penelope, her breath coming in short gulps, nodded. Her eyes were the size of saucers and all of the color had drained from her face. If the sudden change of events frustrated Walker in any way, it certainly didn't show.

"We've made provisions for something like this." His voice was soothing and his demeanor had the same serenity he had shown since the moment they had met. The man was imperturbable. "Go straight out the door of the main terminal and next to the car rental area and baggage claim you'll find a shuttle service." He pressed a boarding ticket into her hand. "Get on the shuttle to Jackson Hole, Wyoming. Just visualize yourself on the Jackson shuttle. Okay?"

"Okay."

"Nothing but good thoughts."

"I'll try."

"Remember to release."

"Okay."

Walker locked eyes with Penelope. "This is critical. You must convert all negative ideas and images to positive ones and try to stay released. When you feel them starting to creep back in they must be replaced with good thoughts. Remember to stay released. Don't just release the negative thoughts, make absolutely sure that you transform them first."

"Why?'

"A negative thought has just as much power as a positive one. And in the early stages of development, even more."

"Look..."

"No, you look." Walker's voice was still calm and soothing but had a firmness she hadn't heard before. "This is not some pretend problem, or something to be sneered at by your reporter friends at a cocktail party. This is real world serious, and you have to do what I tell you."

"How in the world is what I'm thinking going to influence anything?" she snapped back at Walker. "All this New Age..."

"Were you upset Saturday night?"

"Of course I was upset."

"And at some point during the day did you have strong negative feelings toward your house, and then totally release them?"

Before Penelope answered, she remembered how she had wished the house would just go away. Or just burn down. She felt a chill tingle down her spine. "You're not saying..."

"Yes, I am. Your negative thoughts, amplified by being agitated, and then released are why your house burned down. That's why I didn't want you to be alone that night."

"You're saying I burned my own house down?"

"Yes. When we get you to the compound, we will have people who will show you how to control this, but right now you're like a loaded gun in the hands of a toddler."

Penelope's hands started shaking and her mind was reeling. "What should I do?" She asked meekly and fearfully.

"You can start by not being so pigheaded and trust me just a little. Relax your mind and envision yourself on the Jackson shuttle. Do not allow any negative thoughts to slip in, and if they do just think 'cancel, cancel' and your mind will disregard the thought." He patted her on the arm, and could feel her trembling. "Stay released and you'll do just fine."

"Okay."

"When you're moving through the airport, walk slowly. Don't seek out people's eyes but don't avoid them either, and smile at everyone who makes eye contact with you."

He pulled her close and wrapped his arms around her. A surge of energy rushed through her as his lips again kissed the middle of her forehead. Surrounded by chaos and thousands of people, she felt as if the two of them were in an energy sphere that was floating a few inches above the floor. Time stopped. There was no noise. There was no one in the universe but them. Her fear and confusion melted away. As he loosened his grip on her, she felt her knees starting to buckle but he didn't allow her to fall.

Steadying her on her feet, he said, "I'll see you in a few hours. Jackson Hole shuttle." He turned and melted into the crowd.

Penelope went into the ladies room, pulled off the wig and put on the t-shirt. In the mirror she caught a glimpse of her face, which made her stop. Flushed with rosy cheeks, she hadn't looked this healthy in years. What kind of power did this man possess?

Stepping back into the concourse she stopped when she caught a glimpse of Walker only a few hundred yards away. Instead of running away he was standing as if waiting for someone. Walker nodded toward someone around the corner but out of Penelope's line of sight. Walker walked briskly away and vanished into the crowd. A few seconds later three airport security guards came barreling down the concourse in pursuit of Walker.

Before she could react, she noticed two airport security guards were walking straight at her. They were each holding what appeared to be a photograph and they were studying every woman they approached.

Penelope tried to focus on the instructions Michael had given her. She closed her eyes and relaxed....

≈

L ESS THAN 10 seconds after the air marshal made contact with Homeland Security, Zack "Zhack" Obee was already in motion. Obee, one of the "Twins" — computer whiz kids at Homeland Security's Division of Emerging Technology — thought he might have Michael Walker in his electronic crosshairs for the first time since he had escaped from the Charleston brig. Looking for confirmation he pulled up the security cameras from the check-in at the Cincinnati Airport. Walker and the woman had managed to stay on the fringes of the camera's viewpoints and both kept their faces covered or their eyes down. "Clever," Zhack muttered.

"What?" Troy Sabrinsky, the other "Twin" asked, looking up from his computer.

"Just some geriatric who thinks he's smarter than me."

Sabrinsky chuckled. "As if."

Obee and Sabrinsky formed the backbone of cutting edge technology at Emerging Technologies, or "ET", as it was known by the other resident geeks. Obee, a world class hacker before he turned fourteen, was still three weeks shy of his twenty-first birthday but had been working for Homeland Security for nearly three years.

Sabrinsky was two years younger but he had already graduated from Caltech with a triple major in Mathematics, Computer Science and Physics. To the best of anyone's knowledge, from kindergarten through college, he had never answered a math question wrong. Sabrinsky had only been with the agency for seven months and his hiring was considered a major coup for Director Shepherd. No one could understand why anyone with his skill set would want the job. The real money these days was in programming video games. Any number of high-level bureaucrats at the Department of Defense and National Security Agency would have given up their firstborn to have either on staff. Emerging Technologies had both.

Zhack wanted confirmation before he notified the Director. He got the pictures he needed from the camera at the metal detector at the security checkpoint in the Cincinnati airport. Obee was able to get a full facial image from the security camera for Walker, Spence, and their traveling companion. He sent the pictures through the department's face recognition system with a request that it look for known Hermes people first. It took just under three seconds to positively identify both Michael Walker and Timothy Ellison. Penelope Spence took only a few seconds longer since Homeland Security had started a dossier on her, including photos that were less than 24 hours old, within moments of her requesting to speak to Walker at the Charleston brig.

"Okay, rich guy, you made a mistake."

"Dude," Troy Sabrinsky asked, "You need me?"

"No, this old fart is burnt."

"Whatever." Sabrinsky shrugged and returned to his online Sudoku game. He was playing at the "Evil" level and tying to improve his personal best time of fifty-four seconds.

Zhack called the Director to give him the good news.

≈

IT HAD TAKEN one of the Homeland Security jets a bit under five hours from the time Walker and Spence had been spotted to travel from Washington to Salt Lake City. As per instructions, the two detainees were held under tight guard and no one spoke to them until Assistant Director Robert Smith arrived. He was accompanied by Special Agent Marcus Wolfe and his prisoner transport team—eight of the scariest men imaginable.

Because of the "Early Christmas", as the news media was calling Walker's diversion, the airport was still crawling with camera crews and reporters. "This doesn't make any sense," Smith said to Wolfe as they headed down the security tunnel to the holding center. "It is so unlike Walker to set up an elaborate diversion and still get caught. Especially when he's with the woman he has to know we're looking for. This is way out of character. "

"You give this guy entirely too much credit," Wolfe sniffed. "It's not like he can move mountains or walk on water." Smith wasn't so sure anymore. They were greeted outside the door of the interrogation room by the head of airport security, Hank McGee. McGee, a retired thirty-year veteran of the Salt Lake City police department, had built a tight crew during his eight years at the airport. He had managed to get rid of most of the bullies and hotheads with rent-a-cop mentalities, and had replaced them with former cops or recent college graduates.

McGee pointed through the one-way glass. Walker was facing the window; Penelope Spence was sitting opposite him with her back toward the glass. Both were completely relaxed and both appeared on the verge of sleep. Walker's eyes opened and he smiled and waved at Smith and Wolfe. "You made good time, Robert. I see you brought Marcus," Walker said, his voice sounding tinny as it came through the intercom speaker next to the door.

"Damned creepy," McGee said. "He says hi to me every time I walk by. I have to get that glass checked."

"Did they ask for a lawyer, or make any other requests?" Smith asked.

"None," McGee answered.

"Did he give you any trouble?" Wolfe said as he glared at Walker through the glass.

"No. They allowed us to fingerprint and photograph them with no complaints."

"Anything else we should know?" Smith asked.

"No. He did all of the talking; not a peep out of her. Said he wanted to wait and talk to you, which was fine by me. The sooner we can get these people out of here, the better."

Smith didn't like this. Walker wouldn't have gone to all of this trouble just to allow a few airport cops to catch him with Spence. What was he up to now? Wolfe handed McGee the transfer papers for Michael Walker and Penelope Drayton Spence. "They are no longer your problem," Wolfe said as he reached for the doorknob.

The Chief read the papers and frowned as he leaned back against the wall. "There may be a problem." Wolfe and four of the prisoner transportation team entered the room. Walker and Spence offered no resistance as heavy leather belts were strapped to their waists.

"What kind of problem?" Smith asked.

"This isn't Penelope Drayton Spence."

CHAPTER TWENTY

"The thing you fear most has no power. Your fear of it is what has the power. Facing the truth really will set you free."

Oprah Winfrey

"Vacation?"

"I'm sorry, what?" Penelope asked.

"Are you going to Jackson for vacation?"

"Yes. Vacation."

Looking around, Penelope found herself in a middle seat of the Jackson Hole shuttle and looking up at a smiling woman about her age. The shuttle was starting to fill as new passengers boarded and stowed their suitcases.

"Do you mind?" Penelope still wasn't tracking very well. Once again her internal system had experienced a shock that baffled her intellect and left her numb. "May I sit with you? You never know what you're going to get, otherwise."

"Of course," Penelope said as she slid over.

"I'm Paula Simpson."

Penelope panicked. She had forgotten the name on the new identification Walker had given her. What was she going to do?

Paula leaned in and whispered. "Your name is Elizabeth Hart from Akron, Ohio. I'm a friend." Penelope Spence stared at the woman with openmouthed wonder. "He sent me to watch over you." A guardian angel?

Penelope was finding it difficult to form words, much less sentences.

She didn't remember boarding the bus or how she had avoided being arrested. Paula leaned over and patted her on the arm.

"The first couple a times you do that can really take the starch out of you. We've got a long ride, so why don't you try to get some rest now? You've had a rough couple a days."

~

"WHAT DO YOU mean, this isn't Penelope Spence?" Wolfe demanded as he spun the woman in the chair around. She certainly looked like Spence to him. Smith's shoulders sagged.

"According to her fingerprints," Security Chief McGee said, "she's..."

"Sally Winters," Smith said, cutting off McGee in mid-sentence.

"Hi, Robert."

"You know her?" Wolfe demanded.

"Of course I know her." Smith wanted to add, 'You idiot' but swallowed the urge. "She is one of Michael Walker's personal staff."

"Senior Vice President of Communications for Walker Industries, actually." Walker corrected.

"She used her real name and passport when she checked in," McGee stated.

Without another word, Smith turned on his heels and left the room. Caught off guard, Chief McGee and Special Agent Marcus Wolfe were left standing in the middle of the interrogation room and unsure of what to do next. Michael Walker offered some advice.

"I think Robert is waiting for you in the hall." The two men, realizing he was probably correct, left the room.

In the corridor, Smith was already in the middle of a call to the Director. "No, sir. I have no idea what he's up to. We have no reason to hold the woman. She is the head of public relations for Walker Industries and you can pretty much bet she's not the only Walker Industries PR person here in the terminal. The airplane ticket was booked in her name and she is not on any of our no-fly or terrorist watch lists." Smith began pacing in a tight circle as he focused all of his attention on the phone at his ear. "Sir, Walker Industries has over 85,000 employees. We couldn't put them all on the no-fly list, and until this moment we had no idea that she would be a concern." He listened again. "This place is crawling with media, and if we arrest her I'm sure someone on her staff will tip them off. Do you really want to see the head of Walker's PR department holding a press conference right now?" Smith's head bobbed up and down slightly as he listened. "I agree."

Assistant Director Smith put his hand over the mouthpiece of the phone, looked at McGee and said. "The woman is free to go."

"What?" exclaimed Wolfe, freezing the Chief in his tracks.

"Which is it?" McGee asked.

"She's free to go." Smith turned back to his cell phone. "Yes, sir. We can try to bring him back to Washington but I doubt we can hold him..."

"I'll guarantee it," Wolfe said.

A bemused smile covered Smith's face as he glanced up at Wolfe to see if he was serious. He obviously was. "Hold on, one second." He turned and faced Wolfe, then held his cell phone close enough to the other agent's face that the Director would be able to hear the words directly from his mouth.

"Director. I personally guarantee the delivery of Michael Walker to Washington."

Smith shook his head and grinned. "You heard it straight from Special Agent Marcus Wolfe that he personally guarantees the delivery of Michael Walker to Washington." Smith chuckled, "I agree. Okay."

Smith closed his phone, turned to Wolfe and smiled again. "The Director has given you full authority and responsibility for getting Michael Walker to Washington. This is your operation now. I'm just an observer."

"Finally," Wolfe thought to himself. The three previous escapes had occurred after they had turned Walker over to Smith. His guys would never let him escape. Wolfe pushed the button on the intercom and barked to his men. "The woman is free to go." A few moments later Sally Winters emerged from the interrogation room and smiled at Assistant Director Smith.

"Good seeing you again, Robert," she said cheerfully, as she headed down the corridor escorted by two airport security men. Wolfe shook his head as he watched Winters walk away.

"I can't believe this," Wolfe muttered. "You're just letting her walk out of here like this."

"If I were running this operation instead of you, Marcus, I probably would have put at least two of my men on her," Smith replied.

Wolfe glared a hole through Smith before pushing the button to the intercom. "Parks, Taylor." The door opened and two burly men stepped out of the holding room. "Go follow the Winters woman and don't be afraid to let her know you're there." The men nodded, then sprinted down the corridor after her.

Before the door to the holding room fully closed they heard the sounds of shouts and the scraping of chairs. The door flew open and one of Wolf's security crew was standing in the doorway ashen. "Did you stop him?"

"Stop who?" Wolfe demanded.

"Walker," he said, "One second he was there, the next second he was gone."

"What do you mean, gone?" Wolfe shouted, as he stared through the one-way glass at the spot where Michael Walker had just been. The heavy leather belt that moments earlier had been around their prisoner's waist was folded neatly on the chair.

The two agents Wolfe had sent to trail Sally Winters were hustling back down the hallway. "Sorry, sir, but we lost her."

"What do you mean you lost her?" Wolfe demanded.

"It was like she just vanished."

"That didn't take long," Smith said as he tossed his phone to Wolfe. "Just hit redial to get the Director."

≈

PENELOPE SPENCE, AKA Elizabeth Hart, had been asleep long enough that the sun was starting to set.

"Hello, sleepyhead," Paula Simpson said. The shuttle bus was pulling into an airport, and for the briefest moment Penelope was afraid they had returned to Salt Lake City. But, this airport was much smaller. The elevation seemed higher and the mountains were in the wrong place. Seeing the puzzlement on Penelope's face, Paula said, "This is the Idaho Falls airport. The shuttle stops here before heading over the pass to Jackson."

Penelope ran her tongue across her teeth; they were covered with film, and the inside of her nose felt like it was full of tiny, hard cockleburs. "Here," Paula said as she handed Penelope a liter of bottled water. "It's a lot less humid here than what you're used to, and you'll need to stay hydrated. At this elevation, and with it being so dry, you're going to think you're not sweating. But that's not the case, it just evaporates instantly."

Less humid was an understatement. Having spent nearly her entire life at sea level in the oppressive humidity of Charleston, Idaho felt like it was trying to suck every drop of liquid out and dry roast her.

"You're going to need to use more moisturizer, and you're definitely going to need some of this." Paula handed her a small tin of lip balm.

"Thanks, ah..."

"Paula." The shuttle pulled to a stop and the driver opened the door and announced that they would be leaving in half an hour. "Here," Paula said as she handed Penelope a small plastic bag. Looking inside Spence found a nearly identical set of toiletries to the ones Walker had given her earlier in the day.

"Does Walker buy this stuff in bulk?"

Paula bristled slightly and looked around to be sure no one was listening. Everyone else on the shuttle had already left the bus or was in the process of gathering up their things to exit and no one had heard the exchange. She leaned in and whispered, "No names when we're out among the general populace. Understand?"

Penelope Spence nodded that she did, wondering when the cloak and dagger stuff would start to become more second nature.

"The things he remembers to take care of is friggin' amazing sometimes."

The two women stood up to leave when Penelope noticed that Paula had left her purse. When Penelope reached for it, Paula stopped her and shook her head no. The two women left the shuttle and the automatic doors of the terminal opened as Paula exclaimed, "Nuts! I forgot my purse." She turned on her heels and jogged back to the shuttle. A few moments later she rejoined her traveling companion.

"What was that about?"

"I was checkin' to see if we were being followed. If you do a quick and unexpected 180 you can usually spot a tail instantly. They're so surprised they will usually do something stupid to expose themselves."

Penelope looked around the terminal with suspicion. "Well?"

"Well what?"

"Were we followed?"

"Naw," Paula said with a laugh. "And since Smith and his boys are tied up in Salt Lake City..."

"You know Smith?"

"Sure! I worked with him for six months."

"You were part of the, ah..."

"Yup, the ah. I'm one of the 'Dirty Dozen'".

"Dirty Dozen?"

"That's what they call us at the 'resort'. We're the ones who have been with him for years. You'll be meeting everyone soon enough."

"I can't wait."

"You've already seen many of us but didn't know it."

"What do you mean?"

"Timmy, you met. Four others were on the plane with you. Another four were in the terminal, and three others from my team are on the shuttle with us."

"What?"

"The four who were on the plane are in a car that has been following the shuttle. We had six different contingencies ready to go. The money one was everyone's favorite. We all liked it so much that's probably why you guys got spotted."

"The power of thought?"

"Absolutely. With that many people at our stage of consciousness thinking good thoughts about something, it's bound to happen." Paula pointed to a TV screen where CNN had an update on the condition of Senator Horn. They were too far away to hear what was being reported but across the bottom of the screen was 'Miracle Recovery.' "He has had all of us praying for the senator."

"I thought he was the one who shut down the, ah..."

"He was. But every one of us who came in contact with him simply adored him. Besides, we all were hoping he would cut the funding."

"So you could take it private?"

"That allowed us to get this out of the hands of the military types."

Paula pointed to the screen again and laughed loud enough that heads turned. When they followed her finger to the mounted television, they joined in with the laugther. CNN was showing footage of the riot in the Salt Lake City airport. "The man has a wicked sense of humor," Paula said.

Penelope pulled back a bit. Around her Walker had shown flashes of having a sense of humor but nothing she would hardly describe as wicked. "I guess I haven't seen that side yet."

"He was probably on his best behavior."

"I hear he's a good dancer too," Penelope said sarcastically.

Her attempt at humor bounced right off of Paula. "Oh, my God. He makes Gene Kelly look like he's got two left feet. He won an International Tango competition in Buenos Aires a few years ago."

"Really? That wasn't in his bio."

"He went in under the name of Inigo Montoya to avoid any publicity."

Penelope chuckled. "Inigo Montoya, seriously?"

"Isn't that hilarious?"

Penelope nodded her agreement. Maybe he did have a sense of humor. "I did some dancing in college."

"Believe me," Paula rolled her eyes. "We all know that."

"What do you mean?"

"That was all he talked about for the past two months. He couldn't wait to meet you in person."

"You're kidding."

"Nope. He tried to get a ballroom dancing night going at the compound, but no one was really interested. Out of pity, a few of us showed up as a take one for the team kind of thing, but he ran us out after about half an hour. Said we had no passion."

"Interesting." Penelope's eyes flew open. "What do you mean he's been talking about me for two months? I only met him two days ago."

"Time is very different for him than for most people." Paula grinned, hugely. "When you're around him and he has a plan working, a day can feel like a month and a week can feel like a year."

"I imagine it can be exhausting."

"Actually it's exhilarating."

Having reached the ladies room, the two women headed in to get freshened up.

Penelope Spence was astounded. "My hair has never been this straight in my life."

"It'll get even straighter once we get east of the Tetons," Paula answered. "I used to have to wash my hair every day, now two or three times a week is enough. You won't need to shower as often either; body odor doesn't seem to exist out here in the high plains. Come on let's grab something to eat."

They found a small restaurant with decent looking salads and claimed one of the tables.

"You seem to know a lot about this part of the country," Penelope said.

"We've been livin' here for a while now."

"We?"

"The Project members. He moved us here about six months ago."

"So Jackson Hole is where the compound is located?"

"Just Jackson. Calling it Jackson Hole tags you as a tourist. The compound is a few miles out of town."

"I can't wait to see it."

"It's friggin' awesome. I mean, everybody loves it out here, but I do miss my nieces, and I'm sure my mom is going mental by now."

"What do you mean?"

"We all had to drop completely off the grid for a few months."

"That has to be hard."

"Yes and no. Wait until you see the compound. He didn't cut any corners, believe you me. The food is kickin', and there are all kinds of outdoors things to do, like hiking and horses. I mean, I'm like in the best shape of my life."

"That would explain why you all look so fit and tanned." Penelope drew in a breath as she contemplated her next question. "So, Paula, do you consider yourself awakened and enlightened?"

"Awakened, yes. Enlightened is still a work in progress."

"What does that mean?"

"You're talking apples and oranges." Paula could tell by Penelope's expression that she wasn't following. "Knowing something exists, that would be the Awakening part, doesn't necessarily mean the universe is just going to hand it over to you on a silver platter. It's different for everybody." Paula patted Penelope's arm. "We all went through what you're going through; this must be scarin' the bejesus out of you."

"A little."

"It'll be over soon enough."

"How soon?"

"No telling. But I guarantee it'll jump up and bite you when you least expect it."

"When did it happen to you?"

"I was up at Goodwin Lake. Sorry. There's this alpine lake near the top of one of the mountains just outside Jackson. I was camping alone, and decided to go for a hike to the top when I found myself in the worst possible situation you can be in if you're alone and unarmed and miles from the next nearest person."

"What happened?"

"This little Jersey girl had managed to walk between a mother bear and her two friggin' cubs. Those little bundles of joy took one look at me and started crying for their mommy, who just happened to be a 600 plus pounder that was not overly pleased to see me."

"My God! You must have been terrified."

"Ya think?" Paula leaned back and laughed. "I was so far beyond terrified... It was a three-day walk to get back. I couldn't run. I couldn't fight. I was convinced that little Paula Jean was toast. That's when it happened."

"What happened?"

"A calmness settled over me. I looked at the bear and the bear looked at me. The bear, I swear, shrugged, rounded up her kids, and they just went on their way like I wasn't even there."

"That's amazing."

"I know. But I'll tell you what, it's no fun when there isn't any doubt at all about who is at the top of the food chain and it ain't you."

"What was it like?"

"What was it like?" Paula scratched her chin, drew in a large draught of air and allowed it to exit slowly through her lips. "It was like dying and being born again as a different person. It completely changed my life."

"Do you think something like that will happen to me?"

Paula shrugged. "Who knows? A lot of different things can trigger it and not all of them require a change of underwear like mine did. Near-death experience is one way. Some get there through meditation, others prayer or ritual."

The two women sat in silence for a few moments while Penelope absorbed this new information. Finally, her reporter instincts kicked back in. "So, Paula, why is all of this happening now? What has changed from six months ago?"

Paula pulled back and looked at Penelope with a confused expression. "The breakthrough, of course."

"What breakthrough?"

Paula looked at Penelope like she had suddenly grown a second head. "You mean he didn't tell you yet?"

"No. What was the breakthrough?"

"Ha!" Paula said while shaking her head. "If you think I'm going to go there if he didn't tell you, you're nuts. No. No. No, girl."

Penelope wadded up her napkin and threw it down in disgust. "I would love to get a straight answer just once from you people."

"Hang in there, the tough part is already over."

"What do you mean?"

"Have you gotten the lecture on the other Awakenings?"

"Yes."

"And he explained what's going on inside you."

"Sort of."

"Super, then get ready to get knocked on your butt."

"A hint maybe?"

"Naw, I don't want to ruin the surprise."

"I can hardly wait."

"Neither can we. I mean the compound has been in total chaos for a couple of weeks. People have been running around like crazy tryin' to get ready."

"Ready for what?"

"Ready for you. Of course!"

CHAPTER TWENTY ONE

"Before Enlightenment, chop wood carry water;
after Enlightenment, chop wood, carry water."

ZEN PROVERB

PENELOPE LEANED BACK in her chair and let this new information soak in.

"Me?"

"Yes, pumpkin. You. And you can pretty much expect a rock star greeting, by the way."

"Why?'

"He has told everyone that when we get you to the complex we'll all be able to see our family and friends again."

"What?" Penelope was stunned.

"It's been rough on some of the crew, especially the married ones that for one reason or another couldn't have their spouses join us. Walker kept them informed as best he could, but it has been rough."

"I still can't believe you all volunteered to leave your family and friends behind."

Paula pulled back and gave Penelope a quizzical look. "Of course we did. You know how important this is."

Penelope shook her head.

Something between a snort and a laugh escaped from Paula. "You still don't get it, do you?"

"Get what?"

"If you have to ask, then you have to ask."

"You're starting to sound exactly like..." Penelope caught herself before saying Walker. "He who must not be named."

Paula sat back and was visibly flushed. "That is like the nicest thing anyone has ever said to me."

For the first time Penelope studied her traveling companion. They were close to the same age, with Paula maybe three to five years younger. Incredibly buff, with next to no body fat on her five-six frame, her complexion was dark and windswept like someone who spent most of the daylight hours out of doors. That healthy glow that went deeper than just a good tan seemed to be a pattern with all of the Hermes Project people she had met. She had milk chocolate brown eyes that twinkled when she smiled, but could turn serious quickly. Her auburn hair was close cropped and sun streaked, and her nose looked as though it had been broken a time or two. Attractive, but not pretty by any standard, she carried herself with confidence and a "take me the way I am or kiss my backside" attitude. She had not noticed before, but Paula was also wearing a different color "Zion National Park" shirt, similar to the one Penelope had on. *The man thinks of everything.* Anyone who saw them would assume they were old friends on vacation together.

Paula flipped their trash in the garbage can and motioned toward the main entrance of the concourse. "We should be hittin' the road; the shuttle will be leaving in a couple of minutes."

They walked in silence for a few moments as Penelope continued to digest all of this new information. Michael Walker was undoubtedly the most complex and multi-layered person she had ever met. He seemed to be completely sincere in his beliefs, plus he was handsome and rich. *Why,* she thought, *was this man walking the streets unattached?* They were nearly to the terminal door when Paula glanced over at Penelope and smiled.

"What?" Penelope asked

"When are you going to ask me?"

"Ask you what?"

"What you're thinking right now."

"What?"

"Does he have girlfriend? Is he gay?"

"Who are you talking about?" Penelope walked a few more steps when it hit her. "Oh."

"Oh," Paula said with a mischievous smile. "Lord Voldemort."

"How did you know that was what I was thinking?"

"Good Lord, you've been shoutin' it so loud and so often it is startin' to get annoying."

"Really?"

"Ya. Really. When you're sending out thoughts to the universe that loudly people like us can't help but hear 'em. Soon you'll be, too."

"So you're saying soon I'll be hearing voices in my head?" Silently Penelope wondered if Walker had been hearing her thoughts on this issue as well.

"Yep, well sort of."

"Isn't that an early sign of insanity?"

"It's on our list."

"What is?"

"To see how many people are in mental facilities who don't belong there."

"You're kidding?"

"No. Those who believe God is telling them to go out and kill someone are probably right where they belong. But the rest may have been awakening, but made the mistake of mentioning the wrong thing to a mental health professional. It's much worse if this happens to you in a place like Western Europe or the United States which has its head buried so deep in science they wouldn't recognize a non-symbolic state if it bit them in the ass."

"Non-symbolic. He tried to explain that to me without much luck."

"Enlightened was getting so over used around the compound we sorta came up with a new way to describe it better," Paula said with a laugh. "That's the first one to stick."

"Doesn't help me understand it any better."

Paula sighed and scrunched her face as she tried to find the right words. "Okay. Try this. We use language to communicate, right?"

"Right."

"Our language is based on symbols. "Words such as sky, tree, sun, clouds all help us form a visual image so we can make ourselves understood by other people."

"So far so good."

"When you move into a non-symbolic state—some will call it

enlightenment but that barely scratches the surface—the symbolic world is replaced."

"Replaced with what?"

"A non-symbolic consciousness."

"The logic here escapes me."

"Spoken like a true Westerner. It is much easier to grasp the concept if you live in an Eastern culture."

"Care to explain that?"

"Sure. Take India for example. They're much better at recognizing enlightened souls since they aren't so committed to rational thought as the end all to reality. In Western cultures they want everything proven scientifically. Over here we might look at someone as a crazy homeless guy muttering to himself. Over there he is a holy man and the folks look after him."

"Hmm," Penelope said. "I did a paper on the Sadhus Holy Men when I was in college."

"Really? Why?"

"Far Eastern religions were very hip back then."

"I had kinda dropped that one down the memory hole," Paula said. "Come to think of it I still have my Ravi Shankar albums somewhere."

"So what you're saying is there could be people who are Awakening and don't know what's happening to them?"

"That's exactly what I'm saying. Haven't you felt like you were goin' nuts for the past few months?"

"I've wondered a bit off and on."

"And what if you had shared those feelings with your shrink?"

"I probably would be taking Thioridazine."

"There you go."

Penelope tucked her arm under Paula's and pulled her closer. "Let's get back to what matters, so does he have a girlfriend? Is he gay?"

"Definitely single and available. His first wife died about ten years ago, and before the Project he apparently was quite the ladies' man. Since then, not so much."

"Hmm," Penelope said. "Interesting." Finally a straight answer.

"Interesting. That's a good word for it. About every woman above the age of consent that stumbles across his path gets the hots for him." Paula let her get on the shuttle first and checked behind them before boarding.

"I've almost been tempted."

Penelope thought that was a bit of an odd thing to say. "You don't find him attractive?"

"He's not exactly my type."

"Really? What is your type?"

"You, actually." Paula had a huge smile as she watched the blood drain from Penelope's face. She patted Penelope's arm. "Don't worry, pumpkin, I'm not hitting on you. At my age I don't have the time or energy anymore to try and convert a straight chick like you. Too big of a project, and it never works out for more than a few months anyway."

Penelope Drayton Spence, suburban housewife and mother of three, was speechless. There had been a moment in college with a friend named Melissa when she had briefly considered the possibility, but her Southern sensibilities and upbringing had ensured she let the opportunity pass. When she finally recovered the ability to speak she said, "I'm flattered. I guess." Penelope thought for a few moments and then her reporter's instincts kicked in again. "What makes me your type?"

"You're pretty and feminine but tough enough that you don't fold up like an accordion when things get rough. You were great in the airport, by the way. Those two guards walked right up to and all you did was smile and keep walkin'. Very cool. The articles you've written so far have been absolutely kickin'. You're smart as hell and, most important," Paula waited until Penelope made eye contact. "You wouldn't be surprised that Paul McCartney was in another group before Wings."

They both laughed.

"My son is gay."

"Really?" Paula patted her on the leg. "Some say it's genetic. Maybe there's hope for you."

≈

THE MOOD ON the Homeland Security Gulfstream was gloomy. The Director had ordered Marcus Wolfe and his team to return to Washington immediately for a personal debriefing on how a restrained suspect, surrounded by law enforcement officers, had been allowed to escape. In the past hour, there had been nearly a dozen reported sightings of Penelope Drayton Spence from Portland, Maine to San Diego, California and pretty much every place in between.

≈

ASSISTANT DIRECTOR ROBERT Smith had elected to stay in Salt Lake City on the remote possibility that one of the tips from the Mountain or Pacific Time zones panned out. Smith was sitting on one of the four barstools in the Club Room of the Radisson Hotel, located about halfway between the airport and downtown Salt Lake City, nursing a second scotch and water, and waiting. He had been there for about forty-five minutes and was just about to give up when he felt someone slide onto the stool next to him. He didn't have to look up.

"I've been expecting you."

"Hope I didn't get you into too much trouble," Michael Walker said.

"Actually this last one worked out great." Smith took a sip of scotch. "You escaped about five minutes after Marcus took full responsibility for your safe delivery to Washington."

Walker chuckled softly. "He's never lacked for self-confidence."

Smith took another pull from his scotch. "Shepherd knows you have a mole in the agency, and he's sure it's me."

"You're the perfect candidate. I would suspect you, too."

"Thanks, that makes me feel much better."

The two men sat in silence for a moment before Walker said, "They have to know the lid is about to blow off all of this one way or the other."

Smith leaned one elbow on the bar and turned toward Walker. "You wouldn't throw the Spence woman to the wolves by letting her release classified information..."

"I don't think it will come to that." Walker said interrupting.

Smith turned back and faced forward toward the bar. "I wouldn't be so sure. For starters, there's a group at the Pentagon that's adamant about not declassifying this thing."

"True, but they're not the ones taking the heat."

"Shepherd is certainly starting to feel it. He's made Wolfe Agent-in-Charge, reporting directly to him."

"It was only a matter of time."

"I just don't want to see any of your people get hurt."

"Marcus Wolfe doesn't scare me. He may be a thug, but at least he is a completely predictable thug."

"He's a very dangerous man, and if the Director told him to, he wouldn't hesitate..." Smith let the last of the sentence dangle in the air, unspoken.

"I know, and I appreciate your concern, but it's you I'm worried about. Shepherd is setting you up to take the fall."

"I know. They're already moving me out of the loop."

"The offer is still open. I've got a spot for you whenever you're ready."

"Judi and the girls would kill me if I asked them to move again."

"Then don't move."

Robert Smith turned to face Walker. "What do you mean?"

"If everything goes as expected, we'll be opening a liaison office in Washington next week. I'd like you to run it."

"Are you serious?"

"Yes."

"I meant the part about being in Washington."

"Yes."

"Out in the open?"

"Yes."

Smith shook his head and took another sip from his scotch. "Just when I didn't think you could surprise me anymore. This Penelope Spence must be quite a lady."

"You have no idea, and neither does she."

"Has Altman gotten an fMRI yet?"

Walker grew serious and his smile vanished. "No. Not yet."

"Does she know the danger she's in just by spending so much time around you?"

Walker sighed. "No, but she's being watched 24/7."

"No repeats of the last time?"

"Not if I can help it."

"Shepherd still thinks he can stop you."

"I know." They both chuckled this time.

"Where does the Secretary stand on all of this?"

"He's never seen the big picture on the Hermes Project, and he has enough on his plate that he just wants this to go away. It won't take much of a push to get him to big foot Shepherd and declassify Hermes."

"Excellent. That's exactly what I wanted to hear. If you don't want to work for me," Walker said, "how would you like Shepherd's job?"

"Too political for my taste. Besides, I don't see him stepping down for this when he's got me to blame."

"Things can change."

"I don't think I want to hear this."

"I wouldn't tell you, anyway. You're too damned loyal." Walker patted Smith on the shoulder. "Think of a number, Robert, that would get you to move over to our side, and don't undersell yourself." Walker reached into his pocket and placed a $50 bill on the bar. "Give it some thought. I'll be in touch."

Robert Smith didn't bother to look up or turn around; he knew that Walker would be gone. The bartender, seeing the cash on the bar walked over and picked up the fifty. "You ready to pay out?"

Smith nodded as he started to reach for his wallet and said, "That was from my friend."

A puzzled expression covered the bartender's face. "Sir, you've been alone the entire evening."

Smith finished the rest of his scotch with a single gulp. "Of course I have."

≈

ZHACK WAS REPLAYING the surveillance video from the Cincinnati Airport, again. Instead of wide angle security cameras that produced grainy images, the ones by the security gates were of higher quality and covered a much smaller area. The cameras were placed so it was impossible for passengers to conceal their faces without drawing suspicion from the security people.

It was definitely Penelope Drayton Spence; of that he was one hundred percent certain. After that, he wasn't so sure. The only clear camera angle he had was just moments before Walker and the second Spence were arrested. The rest of the time, Walker and she had managed to cover their faces when they passed by, or they avoided the surveillance cameras all together. The guy had definitely done his homework. Somewhere, somehow, they had made the switch between the metal detector in Cincinnati and the main concourse of Salt Lake City. The big question was had they made the switch at Cincinnati or Salt Lake City? When he knew the answer to that, he would have a much better idea where to search for her. It was a long shot, but Zhack began checking the other departure gates that had flights leaving around the same time from Cincinnati.

Troy Sabrinsky wandered out of his room and began watching the 120-inch HD monitor. "Sup?"

Zhack put up the video of Penelope Spence as she went through the metal detector in Cincinnati. "This lady went through airport security in Cincinnati around noon Eastern. Somewhere between here and Salt Lake City, they made a switch to a woman who looked like her."

Troy watched the loop intently. "Got any other angles?" The image on the screen changed as it showed Walker and Spence putting on their shoes and walking down the corridor. Sabrinsky had him play the video loops several times. "What else is there?"

"Here they are getting on the flight to Salt Lake City." Zhack began playing the videos from the departure gates at 4X, slowing back down to normal speed when he saw Walker and Spence enter the frame.

"This the only shot?"

"Yeah. The chode did his homework. We got zip until here."

The two watched as the trio scrambled to get on the jet. "Dude," Sabrinsky said pointing. "Looks like her to me."

"The Director is all over my case since they arrested the wrong woman in Mormon Town. I'm not going 0 for 2."

"What about video from other flights boarding?"

"I didn't see anything."

"Run it."

"k."

When the video of the Miami flight boarding began to play, Troy shouted. "Stop!"

"What?"

"Go back."

Zhack ran the video backward until Troy held up his finger. Troy walked up to the screen where the people were nearly life-size as the video played. "Give me three shots. This one, the one of them boarding the Salt Lake City flight, and a view of Spence's ass after she cleared security in Cincinnati."

"Buttboy eh?" Zhack goaded. With a few keystrokes, the three images were side by side up on the screen.

"You blind geezer, they made the switch at Greater Cincinnati." Troy Sabrinsky motioned toward the three images on the HD screen in front of them.

"WTF are you talking about?"

Sabrinsky picked up a laser pointer and used it to circle the white thread on the back of Penelope's skirt after she had passed through Cincinnati security, then on the skirt back of the lady boarding the flight with Michael Walker. "Dude. You got a one hundred percent positive ID, right?"

"Right, so?"

"When she went through security she had a white thread on the back of her skirt, and it wasn't there when she boarded the flight to Salt Lake City."

"It could have fallen off."

"And happened to land on the exact same spot on somebody else's ass?" Sabrinsky muscled Zhack out of the way and took charge of the keyboard. The frame of the trio boarding the Salt Lake City flight vanished and the other two frames claimed the open space. He zoomed in on the back of the skirt in both frames. "Right there, dude. She's getting on the Miami flight." Sabrinsky circled the thread on the back of the woman's skirt. While the woman headed for the Sunshine State had on a different blouse and a floppy hat, she wore the same shoes, the same skirt and, more importantly, the same white thread.

Zhack, not liking to be upstaged, was visibly pissed as he reached for the phone to call the Director.

"Who's your daddy?" Troy started gloating and did a little victory dance that would have earned him a "Geek of the Week" award at any dance club in America.

≈

THE FIFTEEN-MILE TRIP over the pass between Victor, Idaho and Jackson Hole, Wyoming would probably have been more impressive during daylight hours. In the dark, and with no moon, it was closer to a ride on Space Mountain than a Chamber of Commerce photo op. The shuttle swayed and groaned as it labored up the pass, then swayed and groaned as it went down the other side with the driver riding the brakes. At the bottom of the pass she could see a few lights, then quite a few more some distance away. Penelope was expecting to be in Jackson immediately when they got over the mountain, so she was surprised to see a sign saying "Wilson, Population 1412". They drove for another ten minutes before they arrived at anything that could remotely be considered a town. Taking a left on US 89/US 26, she saw the first indication they had returned to civilization. The street sign said they were on "Broadway", but it wasn't much like the one Penelope had gotten used to during her years at Columbia. There were fewer fast food restaurants than she had expected for a tourist town, only a McDonald's on the right side of the road and a Wendy's on the left. She noticed that many of the buildings were constructed from logs instead of brick and siding. None were more than two or three stories high. Off further to the right she could make out the shadow of a mountain and thought she caught glimpses of ski lifts. It was hard to tell in the dark.

"That's Snow King," Paula said as she motioned toward the mountain.

Penelope never cared much for cold weather. Fourteen generations living in South Carolina had bred it out of her DNA, and her ex-husband had felt the same. On the few occasions they had taken a winter vacation, they had always opted for the tropical rather than the arctic.

The shuttle arrived at what could generously be called the heart of town and took a left at North Glenwood, pulling up in front of the Wort Hotel. The historic landmark was located in downtown Jackson just a block off of the town square. Stepping inside, Penelope found the hotel with the unfortunate name decorated with lodge pole furnishings and bright western style fabrics. A sweeping staircase that split halfway up, forming an impressive "Y" on its way to the second floor was similar to the style in many Southern plantations. It was unlikely, though, that any of the antebellum mansions of the old Confederacy would have had a stuffed buffalo head mounted on the wall of the foyer.

Paula handled the check-in; Penelope found their double room to be smaller than she had expected, but comfortable and very clean. The room was rustic with two full-sized beds and an assortment of Western style decorations. Paula claimed the bed closest to the door.

"Do not leave this room without me under any circumstances. Period. Understood?" Paula said firmly.

"Understood.

"Good." Paula opened her carry-on, handed Penelope a pair of pajamas, and smiled. "The rest of your clothes will be here soon."

"What?"

"Don't worry about it. Get some rest; you have a huge day tomorrow."

"What happens tomorrow?"

"We're taking you to the compound, and you're going to get to see the Hermes Project first hand."

CHAPTER TWENTY TWO

"There are many paths to enlightenment. Be sure to take one with a heart."

LAO TZU

THE HOMELAND SECURITY Gulfstream had just passed through the St. Louis, Missouri air corridor when they received the change of destination. Marcus Wolfe had never been so relieved in his life. Letting Walker slip through his fingers, after he had personally guaranteed his delivery to the director, was a nightmare. His men immediately losing Sally Winters in the Salt Lake City airport was just more icing on the cake. Walker had made his handpicked team look like a bunch of amateurs. Someone was going to pay.

Miami, home of the world headquarters of Walker Industries, made a lot of sense. While they had searched every corner of both Miami and Dade County, they had never found the hidden Hermes Project complex. It would probably turn out to be in the Everglades or a Walker-owned warehouse they had missed. They refueled in Knoxville and landed in Miami just past midnight.

Wolfe called his eight-man team together. "I've had about enough of Michael Walker and his people. We're going in hard and fast, and don't feel any need to be gentle." They all understood exactly what Special Agent-in-Charge Marcus Wolfe was saying, and nodded their agreement. What had happened in Salt Lake City reflected badly on them as well.

Wolfe had been in constant contact with Washington, where Zhack and Sabrinsky had been able to track a video of Spence getting into a cab. The oversized hat she was wearing concealed her face from all of the camera angles but made it easy to spot her in a crowd. According to the cab records, she had been taken to an address in an upper middle class neighborhood heavily populated with Cuban-Americans. The home was owned by a holding corporation that was so multilayered Zhack figured it had to be a safe house owned by Walker Industries. Plus, it was not far from Walker's Miami Beach mansion.

Miami, between the port, airport and other divisions, had a Homeland Security staff of over 1,400 local agents. This made it easy for Wolfe to have the address staked out until he could get a search warrant. Glimpses of a woman matching the general shape and size of Penelope Drayton Spence could be seen between the partially drawn curtains. Facial identification was impossible since the window shades were lowered so nothing above the shoulder was visible. One thing was certain. The hat the woman had been wearing in the airport was now sitting on a table on the covered front porch. That was enough for Wolfe. It took rolling a Federal Judge out of bed at 4 a.m., but just before sunrise they had the "no knock" warrant in their hands. Wolfe checked his watch again.

"Where the hell are they?"

"No idea, sir," said a terrified young man in a Homeland Security windbreaker who had been sent over and ordered to watch the house. Normally, he spent the 11-7 shift checking cargo containers at the Port of Miami. His hands trembled as the gear was unloaded from the rear of the twin black Suburbans idling at the curb.

"How many people are in the house?"

"I've only seen two, sir."

"Did you see any weapons of any kind?"

"Not that I've seen, sir."

"I'm not waiting for the damned SWAT Team," Wolfe barked as he nodded to his men. At just a few minutes before 6 a.m., along with his best eight men, Wolfe was ready to take the house.

Timing their entry perfectly, they used battering rams to knock in the front and back doors simultaneously. "Music to my ears," Wolfe muttered to himself as he followed the first wave into the house. The assault team, armed with automatic weapons and bulletproof vests, swarmed into the home shouting and kicking doors open. The startled man in the master bedroom jumped up in boxer shorts and a t-shirt and demanded, "What's going on?"

He was roughly tackled by two of Wolfe's men and planted face first in the Oriental carpet, then handcuffed. "Do you have any idea who I am?" the man shouted.

Wolfe didn't know and didn't much care. His interest was focused on the figure hiding under the sheet on the king-sized bed. Wolfe triumphantly pulled the bed linen back from the now hysterical woman. His shoulders sagged when, instead of Penelope Spence under the sheet he found an attractive dark-skinned woman in an oversized nightshirt who looked to be in her mid-forties.

The prone man on the floor growled again. "I'm the mayor of Miami, get your hands off me!"

Special Agent Marcus Wolfe's blood ran cold. "Get those cuffs off of him. Mr. Mayor, we are so sorry...."

Rubbing his wrists, the barrel-chested man in his late fifties, his eyes flashing with anger, said, "Not nearly as sorry as you're going to be."

"Then who is this?" One of Wolfe's men asked without lowering his weapon.

"That's my wife, you idiot."

One of Wolfe's team, who had been in a different part of the house, pulled his boss out of the room. "Sir, we've got a situation." He nodded toward the front yard which was lit up like a football stadium and was already filling up with camera crews and reporters. "It looks like someone tipped them off."

"Walker set us up." Wolfe mentally processed his options and none of them were good. "Get everyone out of here as quickly as possible. No one comments to the press." Wolfe grabbed the local agent in the Homeland Security windbreaker, "Go out there and tell the press you have no comment."

"Sir, I make $10.58 an hour, I didn't..."

"Just say no comment, and I'll get you a press liaison officer as soon as I can."

Wolfe shielded his eyes from the glare of the camera lights as he tried to return to his vehicle. He had to run a gauntlet of reporters and shouted questions.

"Are you Special Agent Marcus Wolfe?"

"Unbelievable. They know my name," Wolfe thought to himself, as he muscled his way through the crowd of reporters. Overhead he heard the whump, whump, whump of a helicopter. On the side was written "Channel 4 is Always On." It was the CBS affiliate's news chopper. Great.

"Who is the Mayor with?"

"Is it true the Mayor is in there with a woman who isn't his wife?"

"Why is Homeland Security involved?"

"Was the woman sent by al-Qaeda?"

"Is there more than one woman?"

"Is the Mayor under arrest?"

"What is he being charged with?"

"Are drugs involved?"

"Will there be Federal charges brought against the mayor?"

Special Agent Wolfe jumped in a black Suburban and disappeared into the night. Across the street, unnoticed in the growing crowd, a woman in a charcoal skirt and Manolo Blahnik shoes flipped open her cell phone and dialed a number.

"The fish took the bait." In less than 10 minutes, CNN, MSNBC, and Fox News had all broken into their regularly scheduled coverage with the story of Homeland Security breaking down the door of the Mayor of the City of Miami. The Mayor's wife, Michelle, who was the daughter of one of Miami's richest real estate developers, was reported to be in shock and admitted to Jackson Memorial Hospital for observation. The Mayor, who was in the midst of a tougher than expected primary challenge, had been one of Homeland Security's harshest critics for their recent budget cut involving the Port of Miami. This was the kind of sensational story the cable news channels would run 24/7 for days.

At that exact moment, the fax machine in the office of the Director of Homeland Security's Department of Emerging Technology came to life.

Director Shepherd:

I can make a phone call that will save your career, but you must agree completely to all of the items below. These terms are non-negotiable.

For the next 24 hours the only member of the media you or any member of your organization will speak to is Penelope Drayton Spence or her designee.

You will not attempt to make Robert Smith the scapegoat.

You will move to completely declassify the Hermes Project.

You will restore the good names of all members of the Hermes Project.

Michael Walker

Director Shepherd, who, as usual, had arrived precisely at 6:00 a.m., smiled. How did Walker get the number to his private fax line? The damned leak again, no doubt. Shepherd reread the fax and smiled. The arrogant bastard, he thought to himself, who the hell does he think he is? Did he think his little ragtag group of misfits and oddballs were a personal threat to him?

Shepherd's office door opened and one of his flustered assistants stuck her head in the office. "Sir, you need to turn on the television."

"Which channel?"

"It doesn't matter."

Director Shepherd picked up the remote control from his credenza and turned on the TV in one of his bookcases. On CNN a reporter was standing in front of a house in Miami. The volume was off but across the bottom of the screen was a headline. "Homeland Security Raids Mayor's Home." Director Shepherd's mouth went dry and his hands began to tremble as footage of Special Agent Marcus Wolfe emerging from the house filled the screen. Worse yet, on the bottom of the screen was "Agent Marcus Wolfe of Homeland Security's Department of Emerging Technology." Turning up the volume, he discovered it was worse than he thought.

"...however, it is unlikely a raid on a political figure such as the mayor could have happened without authorization from someone higher up." Shepherd hit the mute button. They already had the name of the agent in charge and that the order had come from his department. It would take an ambitious reporter just a few minutes on the Internet to figure out where the buck stopped. In this case it was squarely on his desk.

The Secretary of Homeland Security had given Shepherd an ultimatum. Make the embarrassing stories in the media stop at any cost or not only was he was going to withdraw his objection to declassifying the Hermes Project but he was also going to find himself a new Director of Emerging Technologies.

A very public blunder in the largest city of one of the most important Presidential electoral states, and home to Walker Industries, was a nightmare beyond belief. Instead of just having to charm a Senate Select Committee in closed session, he was likely now facing very public hearings that would be broadcast live on C-SPAN. He could feel his carefully constructed empire turning to clay and beginning to crumble around his feet. In his career he had made more than his share of enemies. Within hours there would be blood in the water and the sharks would start circling. Shepherd's mind raced as he stared at the picture on the television screen and considered his options. None of them were good.

Before he reached his chair, his intercom buzzed. "Sir, the Secretary of Homeland Security is on line one, the Attorney General is on line two, a Michael Walker is on line three, and the Governor of Florida is on line four. Also, sir, the main switchboard is being flooded with calls from reporters. All of them are asking to speak to you personally."

Shepherd looked at the fax and smiled. Smith had warned him not to underestimate Michael Walker. He pushed the button on his intercom. "Jean. Get Wolfe on the line immediately." Next he pushed the button on his phone for the most important person waiting to speak to him. "Mr. Walker?"

"Director Shepherd."

"What is it going to cost me to make this problem go away?"

"Do you have the ability to restore the funding cut from the Homeland Security budget for the Port of Miami for this fiscal year?"

"What is the amount?"

"Forty-seven million dollars."

"I think that can be arranged."

"I need a yes or a no, not I think."

"Yes."

"Yes, what? This call is being recorded, and I don't want any ambiguity."

The Director had no choice. Shepherd was in a box and Walker could either let him out of it, or seal it up and throw him overboard. "Yes, I can arrange to have the forty-seven million dollars cut from the Port of Miami in this year's Homeland Security budget restored."

"It must be restored by noon today."

"I don't see a problem with that."

"Cut the weasel words, Shepherd. Yes or no. Will it be restored today?"

"Yes, it will be restored today."

"And the rest of our terms?"

"I don't have the authority to declassify the Hermes Project. That will take an executive order."

"I have it from an unimpeachable source that it will be declassified as soon as you make the request to the White House."

"Are you sure about that, Mr. Walker?"

"Yes."

As if on cue, Director Shepherd felt a faint vibration and heard a low buzz. Glancing up he saw the light on the red phone on the corner of his desk was blinking. The phone, a gift from his grandfather who had worked as an Under Secretary at the State Department for President Eisenhower, had never rung before. Only two people in the world could make that phone ring; one of them lived at 1600 Pennsylvania Avenue and the other at the Naval Observatory.

"I agree to your terms, Mr. Walker. Please make your call."

Michael Walker, sitting in the front passenger seat, flipped his phone shut as the SUV chugged up the back roads of Wyoming toward Jackson. The other three passengers couldn't read his expression.

"Well?" Timothy Ellison asked.

"Why don't you give your mom a call, Tim?" A whoop went up and high fives were exchanged all around.

In the backseat, restricted by the limits of their seatbelts, Timothy Ellison and Sally Winters exchanged a hug. The driver, Lucas Haley, Walker's personal bodyguard for a dozen years, said in his deep baritone, "Man, when you put a plan together, it stays together." Haley offered his massive right hand to Walker, who accepted it with relish.

Walker dialed another number that was answered on the first ring. There was so much noise and confusion in the background that Walker placed his finger in his other ear to hear better. "Miguel?"

"Michael," boomed the voice of the Mayor of Miami. "Hold on a second." After a brief delay the Mayor moved to a quieter spot. "Michael, Michael."

"So, anything new going on in your life?"

Miguel Cortez's laughter boomed in the phone, loud enough that the others traveling with Walker could hear. "Your plan has worked brilliantly. Last week I was two points down in the polls and now the phones at our campaign headquarters are ringing off the hook."

"So you think our little ploy might work?"

"Are you kidding! I've got—what do the kids call it—major street cred. There is a rumor going around that it took six agents to get me cuffed and that I put two of them in the hospital."

"Gee, I can't imagine where a story like that might have come from."

"It's a total mystery." Both men laughed. "There isn't anyone with a Hispanic surname who would vote against me now. Heck, I may run for governor."

"How is Michelle holding up?"

"Are you kidding me? She hasn't had this much fun since Buenos Aries. Paparazzi have actually been trying to sneak into her hospital room. She's in seventh heaven."

"I need a favor."

"Anything, my friend, anything."

"You need to let Director Noah Shepherd of Homeland Security off the hook."

There was a pause. "That's a very large request. Is there a reason why I should grant this favor?"

"I can think of forty-seven million reasons."

"Are you serious?

"Absolutely.

"Our full funding restored?"

"In time to call a four o'clock press conference. Of course, you will have to deny a quid pro quo, and be totally forgiving that mistakes involving warrants sometimes happen."

"Of course."

"Then we have a deal?"

"Yes." There was a long pause. "I am still in your debt."

"I disagree, Miguel. If you hadn't let me borrow Michelle for three months we never would have won the dance trophy."

"That was some night, my friend."

"She was radiant." Walker hung up from the call with his old friend in Miami and dialed Director Shepherd's office again.

"This is Michael Walker."

"Hold, please."

Shepherd picked up the phone almost instantly.

"Shepherd."

"Have you made your calls?"

"Yes. The Secretary has agreed to restore the funding to Miami immediately out of discretionary funds, and to withdraw his objection to declassifying the Hermes Project. The Executive Order to declassify the Hermes Project is being drafted as we speak and should be signed within the hour."

"Excellent."

"All members of the Hermes Project and Walker Industries have been removed from the no-fly list, and any existing warrants for their detainment have been revoked."

"And your news blackout?"

"No one from this division will speak to the media in any capacity until 6 a.m. tomorrow, except to Penelope Drayton Spence or her designee."

"Excellent."

"As for Robert Smith..."

"He was not my source. He has been 100% loyal to you."

"Interesting. I can now assume that the Mayor will take no action against the agency or me personally?"

"None and there is no reason for your name to even come up in this matter."

"Brilliantly played, Mr. Walker. You know, there is no reason for us to be enemies."

Walker laughed. "We were never enemies, we just had different goals. Politics makes for strange bedfellows. I have a feeling we're going to be seeing a lot of each other."

CHAPTER TWENTY THREE

"When history tells the story of time, the truth will be known!"

ZIGGY MARLEY

PENELOPE SPENCE WAS awakened by a light tapping on her door. It took her a few seconds to orient herself and remember where she was. She was surprised to see that Paula had not actually been sleeping in her bed but had been sitting in a chair watching her. Paula opened the door and Walker, Timothy Ellison and several people she didn't know burst into her room. Sally Winters held out her hand and introduced herself. "Sally Winters. I was your body double at the Salt Lake City Airport." Ellison flipped her suitcases onto the bed and said, "You probably should change so we can get going."

"Going where? And what time is it?"

"7:30 Eastern," Walker said. "We need you to wear something that will look nice on television." Sally Winters already had her suitcases open and had picked out a nice professional business suit with a pale blue silk blouse.

"What's going on?

"Remember the promise I made you day before yesterday?"

"God. Has it only been three days?"

Walker smiled and said, "I'm ready to deliver. You are about to become the most important reporter on the planet."

Walker pulled her aside so they could not be overheard and squared her up so their eyes locked. "I know how pigheaded you can be."

"Steadfast still sounds better."

"But isn't nearly as accurate." She hadn't realized how much she had been enjoying his company until he had left. "Until this storm blows over, you are going to need to let these people make all of the decisions for you that don't involve the story. At first you're not going to like it, but you'll get used to it pretty quickly. When they tell you to eat, you eat. If they tell you to sit down, you sit down. If they tell you to take a nap, you take a nap. If you put your full focus on this story, by this time tomorrow you will have every newspaper in the world begging you to come work for them."

"Okay. But when are you going to make me twenty-three again?"

"I told you, that boat has already sailed."

It suddenly hit Penelope that while she had been talking to Walker, Sally Winters had stripped her down to her bra and panties. It was like one of the costume changes from when she was working on Broadway. None of the men in the room seemed to notice and for some reason she didn't feel the least bit self-conscious. "Arm," Winters said. Penelope stuck her right arm in the sleeve of her blouse, followed by her left. The other woman had her completely dressed in less than two minutes.

Another person Penelope had never seen before stuck his head in the open door. "The cars are ready."

"Let's go," Walker said.

Out front of the Wort, two V-8 Jeep Cherokees were idling. Painted on their doors was "Lazy S Ranch". As Penelope breezed through the lobby, the day desk clerk who had just come on duty strained to see the person at the center of the entourage. No one had told him a celebrity had checked in overnight. Walker and Penelope took the backseat of the lead 4x4 with Sally Winters riding shotgun and Lucas Haley behind the wheel.

"I have Mark Hatchet on the line." Winters leaned over the seat and handed the phone to Spence as the car pulled away from the curb.

"Mark?"

"Nellie? We haven't heard from you in over 24 hours. We were starting to get worried. What the hell is going on?"

Walker motioned for the phone. "This is Michael Walker. Please listen carefully, since the clock is running. I'm going to put you on speaker. If there is anyone else with you, I would recommend you do the same. This call is being recorded."

Winters leaned over the seat again with some kind of mobile cell phone speaker that Walker placed between himself and Spence. They could hear rustling on the other end. "This is Mark Hatchet, managing editor of *The Washington Post*. With me in the room are the publisher, Bill Flickling and our lead legal counsel, Leon Steinberg. Our CEO Franklin Mitchell is on his way and should join us momentarily."

"On this end we have Ms. Penelope Drayton Spence and I'm Michael James Walker. Ms. Spence has been my traveling companion for the past two days. We are currently in Jackson, Wyoming. I would strongly recommend you get out here as quickly as possible."

"Why is that, Mr. Walker?" Hatchet asked.

"Through the efforts of Ms. Spence, she has secured for *The Washington Post* a twenty-four hour window wherein you will have the only media access to Director Noah Shepherd of the Homeland Security Division of Emerging Technology, and any and all information with reference to the Hermes Project. This exclusivity will last until 6 a.m. tomorrow. This means your papers will be on the streets before any other news organization in the world has the story."

"Nellie, is this correct?"

Walker and Winters both shook their heads "yes". Walker began writing feverishly on a pad. Spence read the message and nodded she understood.

"Yes, Mark; that is correct. I am currently in transit to interview Dr. Carl Altman and view the actual Hermes Project. This will be the first interview by Dr. Altman in over two years, and the first and only interview related to the Hermes Project."

"This is Leon Steinberg. Will we be getting into any issues with classified documents?"

"As of this morning," Michael Walker said. "The Hermes Project is no longer classified. The President should be signing the Executive Order as we speak. But the people on this call are the only ones who know that."

"What? How in the world..." Pandemonium broke out on the speaker. "Nellie, I'm going to put you on mute while we discuss this."

Walker patted Spence on the knee. "So, you having fun yet?"

"It'll do," Penelope replied with shrug.

For the first time Penelope Spence looked up at the surroundings whizzing by. Jackson was beautiful. To the west the Teton Mountains were still snowcapped, and the sun rising in the east cast a golden glow on them. The Jeep's right blinker turned on as it approached the Gros Ventre turnoff and they headed into the rising sun.

Her thoughts were interrupted by the sound of Mark Hatchet's voice. "What do you need from us?"

Walker had been ignoring the scenery; instead, he had been working out a list of items for her. He handed her the notepad. "I'll need at least five more reporters; ten would be better; fifteen would be perfect. A minimum of two must be from the science and technology beat to handle background, but I'll take everyone you've got with a science degree. I'll also need whoever you have working the religion beat, as well."

Walker scribbled a name on the pad. Penelope silently mouthed "Why?" Walker wrote "Trust me" on the pad. Penelope shrugged.

"Also, be sure to bring Aaron Joseph."

Penelope recognized Hatchet's voice. "Why do you want Aaron?"

Walker tapped the words on the pad. "Trust me," Penelope answered. "Okay."

"I'll need at least two photographers and a video crew."

"Video crew?"

"It will be for your web page," Walker said. "Trust me, you're going to want this video. It will be the most watched thing ever posted on the Internet." Spence crooked her head, smiled and mouthed, "Are you serious?" Walker indicated that he was.

"Nellie," Mark asked. "How much space should we reserve for tomorrow's paper?"

"The entire front page for sure and four to five interior pages should be enough," Penelope answered.

"What?" Mark Hatchet said. "Are you serious?"

"If you don't want the exclusive," Walker interjected. "I'll call the *Times*."

"Ms. Spence, this is Bill Flickling, the publisher. I have already called the airport and they are fueling two jets for us as we speak. We will be there in five hours with everything you've requested and much more. I understand from Mark that you are not under contract with *The Washington Post* for this story and we would like to know what compensation you expect."

Penelope looked at Walker who shrugged. "$250,000."

"That's acceptable."

"I'm not finished yet. I want the lead byline on the main story, and my name to appear first on all background stories. All future stories about this will contain a line between the headline and body copy indicating it is based on the story I broke. I'm sure Mr. Steinberg and my lawyer Ronald F. Rickman of Charleston will be able to agree on the wording."

"I don't have a problem with any of that, Ms. Spence."

Walker shoved his pad in front of her again. She smiled and gave him a thumbs up. "In addition, I will retain all book and movie rights."

"I don't see any problems here. Anything else?

She thought for a moment. "And I want a new Prius."

"What color?"

CHAPTER TWENTY FOUR

*"The real meaning of enlightenment is to gaze with
undimmed eyes on all darkness."*

Nikos Kazantzakis

The Lazy S Ranch is located on Gros Ventre Road, about fifteen miles outside of Jackson and three quarters of the way to Slide Lake. Built on the edge of Bridger-Teton National Forest with over a mile of frontage on the Gros Ventre River, it was originally a hunting lodge for a rich banking family that bought the land for peanuts in the late 1920's. In 1925, a massive landslide upriver had blocked the valley and created Slide Lake. The slide held for around two years before breaking and flooding the valley. Those in the small town of Kelly that survived were eager to sell and crazy Easterners were a godsend. Over the years the ranch had been expanded, and now it had 20 bedrooms in the main house and 14 additional cabins. Combined with an assortment of outbuildings and stables, it had proven to be the perfect place to keep the Hermes Project going after the government cancelled the funding.

It wouldn't raise any alarms for a ranch this size to have people coming and going constantly at odd hours. It was also far enough out of town and enough off the beaten path that few people ever drove by without a purpose. The project had been able to hide in plain sight. Walker, through a series of lawyers and interlocking companies, had purchased the property without leaving any clues. For the past four months the only people in any of the rooms or cabins were project members.

When the two Jeeps pulled up, as Paula had predicted, they were given a rock star welcome. A group of 25-30 incredibly fit men and women, mostly men, were waiting for them as they drove into the horseshoe circle in front of the main house. When in the "Stroke Belt" of South Carolina—lots of fried food and little alcohol to clear the arteries—Penelope Spence looked lean and fit. Here she felt like an out of shape, overweight lump. "I'm so fat compared to these people I could qualify for handicap parking," she muttered to Walker under her breath.

Walker patted her hand. "You have no time for negative thoughts today. Stay positive and stay focused." He pushed his door open and stepped out. Lucas Haley opened Penelope's door for her and escorted her around the SUV where she joined Walker on the curb. A wave of applause echoed off the mountains. Walker motioned for silence, which he instantly received. "As I'm sure you all have already guessed, this is Penelope Drayton Spence." Another, louder round of applause interrupted him. He motioned for quiet again. "A couple of announcements for those who have not heard, the Hermes Project has been declassified and none of you are wanted by the feds anymore." Silence. "Apparently all of you have already heard. Moving on." Walker glanced over his shoulder at Sally Winters who was on her cell phone. She leaned in and whispered in his ear. A broad smile crept over his face.

"Here is some news you haven't heard. In addition to commandeering all of Walker Industries' aircraft, we have chartered a 737, and it will be arriving here tomorrow. It will be filled with friends and family. Who, I'm sure..."

A roar went up, drowning out the rest of his comment. Walker motioned for silence. "But there are some things that can't wait." Puzzled expressions covered the faces of all the members of the Hermes Project. "I know this has been a difficult time for many of you, but for some it had to be nearly unbearable." Walker's eyes fell on a lean young man with fierce red hair who was 28, but often still got carded in bars. Following Walker's gaze, the rest of the people turned and looked. "Frank, I wanted to let you know that one of our corporate jets has just gone wheels up. Your long-suffering bride and Trent Allen McCarthy should be here within four hours."

Frank McCarthy was buried under a sea of hugs and back slaps.

Penelope leaned over and had to shout in Sally's ear to be heard over the din. "I don't understand."

"Trent Allen McCarthy is only four months old." Winters could see from Penelope's eyes that it still wasn't tracking. "Frank has been here for the past six months."

It finally hit Penelope like a thunderbolt. "He missed the birth of his son?"

"Let's just say his wife was less than pleased."

Walker motioned for quiet. "We are expecting a large group of people from *The Washington Post* here in a few hours." Walker pointed to a young man in the front row. "Kevin, are the phone connections and Internet access in place?"

"Available and will be in place within the hour."

"Stevie." A Nordic blond with a deep tan stepped forward.

"Yo!"

"Is the web page ready to launch?"

"Absolutely."

"Bandwidth issues resolved?'

"We're still working on it. Right now we have locked in 80 percent of the projected capacity with server redundancy. We might run slow at times, but we probably won't crash."

"I want that probability turned into a certainty by 9 p.m. local time."

"That shouldn't be a problem. If push comes to shove we'll steal capacity from Walker Industries."

"Guys, you know what is at stake. If we miss this opportunity today it could take us years to get back to this moment. Any questions?"

Silence.

"One additional point. For the next 12 hours you leave this woman alone." Walker pointed to Spence. "Don't tell her your name or distract her in anyway. Right now she is the most important person in our world. Let her do her job." He looked around at every face in the group. All were confident and smiling. "Let's get to it."

"Thanks for not putting any pressure on me," Spence whispered to Walker as he walked past.

"No problem."

The inside of the main house was similar in design and style to the Wort Hotel. Apparently, every building in Wyoming was constructed with knotty yellow logs, and every rug and wall hanging was required to have a Thunderbird or other "Old West" design. Walker led the way into the main dining room. It had large heavy tables with knotty yellow logs for legs. A crew of six men and one woman were busy running phone lines and computer cables across the floor and placing them on a long table designed to seat twelve, six on each side. Another crew of three men was running electric extension cords with surge suppressors on the end to each of what appeared to be ten workstations. The crews were quick and highly efficient, with no wasted movement.

Sitting at a smaller table was an elderly man with a gray goatee and thinning hair. As Penelope got closer she saw that, while his body looked frail, his eyes were keen and bubbled with mischief.

"Dr. Carl Altman, Ms. Penelope Drayton Spence."

"I've been looking forward to meeting you." Altman extended his hand. His grip was surprisingly firm.

Sally Winters appeared with a plate of three eggs over easy, toast, and cheese grits that she placed next to Penelope's elbow along with a mug of strong coffee with cream. The eggs were prepared exactly the same way as the ones she had enjoyed a few days earlier at the Cracker Barrel restaurant. "I'm really not..."

"When she tells you to eat, you eat," Walker said sternly.

Chastened and repentant, she unwrapped a cloth napkin. Penelope removed the silverware that was inside and placed the napkin in her lap.

"I'm sure Michael has told you all about the Hermes Project."

"Actually, not very much at all. We mostly discussed previous Awakenings and Timothy Leary."

"I see," Altman said, a bit taken aback. "I'm sure Michael has his reasons, but they would seem to elude me at the moment."

Michael Walker smiled and said, "Ah!" Running toward them was a young man in his early twenties. "Here's the reason now."

Altman turned stiffly in his chair and announced the arrival, "My grandson Jerold." Altman leaned in and said to Penelope, "He could be a brilliant scientist, but he believes he has the soul of a journalist." The old man was obviously proud of his grandson and having him close seemed to give him added vitality. "He's quite enamored with you."

As he got closer Jerold looked remarkably like a movie star. Unfortunately his double was the guy who played Napoleon Dynamite. All he needed was a "Vote for Pedro" t-shirt. Stacked in his arms were a laptop computer and a small box.

"Sorry. I was just trying to get everything perfect."

"Jerold, this is Penelope Spence."

Jerold Altman ran his hand across the side of his pants before extending it to Penelope. It was still clammy. "This is such an honor. Those articles you wrote..."

"Let's stay on message, Jerold," Walker said.

"Oh, right. Right." Opening the box, he placed a stack of documents next to Spence's breakfast. "What I've done is compile some basic background research on the Hermes Project, and the written bios of the major players involved." Pulling the top document off of the stack he said, "Here is a chronology with a complete timeline of major accomplishments. Next, an executive summary of the project itself, followed by a more detailed analysis."

Spence began reading the chronology and then the summary. "These are excellent, Jerold." The young man flushed noticeably. Turning to Altman and Walker, she asked "And you have both signed off on these as being 100% accurate?" Both men nodded that they had.

"Perfect." Spence began reading the detailed report. "This is going to save me a ton of time. This is really outstanding stuff." Jerold Altman went from flushed to bright crimson.

"How long do you think it will take you to absorb all of this?" Walker asked.

Penelope wasn't expecting a question and had already crammed half a piece of toast in her mouth in an attempt to finish her breakfast as quickly as possible. She put her hand over her mouth to catch any crumbs that might attempt to escape and said, "A our." Swallowing the bread and washing it down with a gulp of water she tried again. "An hour; sooner if Jerold can stay here and answer any questions I might have."

"Excellent," Walker rose to his feet then helped Altman to his. The doctor walked with the aid of a cane. "We'll meet back here in one hour, and then take the grand tour."

As the two men slowly walked away Penelope heard them bickering like two old married people. "I can't believe you spent all that time with her and didn't discuss the Project."

"I figured Jerold would be able to speak her language, since they are both journalists."

"Yes. Yes, but..." Their voices faded in the distance.

"Are they always like that?" Penelope asked as she shoved the last of the eggs in her mouth.

"Pretty much," Jerold said. He appeared to become more and more relaxed the further his grandfather got from the table.

Penelope pushed her plate aside and the dishes instantly disappeared. Sally Winters acknowledged her approval and handed Spence a lip balm, which she applied liberally to her lips without protest.

"How soon before I can have a place to plug in my laptop and get to the Internet?"

One of the men said, "Right now." Ellison appeared out of nowhere with her laptop and placed it in front of her.

Another man appeared over her other shoulder. "We have a wireless router online." He motioned toward her computer. "May I?"

She slid her chair back and allowed him access to her laptop. He entered the encryption code for the router. "This will get you on the internet and give you access to your email. Everyone in the room will be behind the same firewall, so they technically could...."

Sally Winters pushed the laptop back in front of Penelope. "I want a secure hardwire connection to this laptop, ASAP."

"Five minutes?"

Sally nodded that that was acceptable.

"I'll need a phone, printer — laser if possible — and a fax machine."

"They're already on their way, Ms. Spence," came a male voice from under the table, where one of the crew was already working on her hard line connection. Penelope reflexively crossed her ankles and pressed her knees tightly together.

Penelope dialed Mark Hatchet's cell phone but it immediately clicked to his voice mail. "Damn." She shouted across the room to the work crew. "Do we have any way to get in contact with the people on *The Washington Post*'s jet?"

A man in his late twenties came over with a clipboard in his hand. "I have all of the contact numbers for both of the jets. We can also send them a fax or an email."

"Good." Spence pointed at the young man. "Don't go anywhere. Oh, what's your name?"

The young man glanced at Sally Winters; he had a look of panic on his face. He remembered what Walker said earlier. "This is Danny," Winters answered. "He's a member of my staff. You'll be seeing a lot of him." She recognized him from earlier in the day in her hotel room at the Wort. He had seen a lot of her already.

"Okay." Turning her attention back to Jerold, she motioned to the stack of background material on the table and asked, "Do you have this information on your laptop?"

"Yes."

"In a Word format?"

"Yes."

"Danny, get these files emailed to both jets as soon as possible. Jerold will show you which ones I want sent." Penelope handed Jerold's laptop to the techie. "Then get a copy of the files onto my machine." Donnie pulled a flash drive out of his pocket, plugged it into the USB port on Jerold's laptop, and began the file transfer.

"I need to speak to Mark Hatchet on the Gulfstream. Can I do that?"

Danny handed her a cell phone and said. "Just hit one and it will speed dial directly to his plane."

"Cool." Penelope pushed "one" then "enter" and the phone immediately dialed. A man's voice answered that she didn't recognize. "I need to speak to Mark Hatchet."

"Sorry, he's not on this plane." Looking around, she saw that Danny had taken Jerold's laptop and moved to the other work area to send the emails. "Danny. He's not on plane one."

"Try the second speed dial," he said.

"Thank you." She disconnected, then hit two on the cell phone.

"Mark Hatchet."

"It's me. I'm going to be emailing some files to you. It has all of the background material on the Hermes Project, and bios of all of the major players. This should give your background and science guys something to work with while they're in transit."

Penelope was excited. She had her big story. She had a deadline. She had support people falling all over themselves to help her. Walker was right, she was rapidly reaching the point where it wasn't even annoying to be handled. Life does not get any better than this.

"Just an FYI, Walker set up the whole thing in Miami to force Homeland Security to declassify the Project."

"Get out of town!"

"No. Seriously."

"That certainly explains why Director Shepherd has been so cooperative."

In the doorway leading to the dining room, Dr. Carl Altman and Michael Walker stood together watching Penelope Spence work. Walker smiled when he heard her laughter echo around the room. Dr. Altman patted Walker on the shoulder, "Interesting choice, Michael."

"She's perfect Carl."

"I want to get her an fMRI as quickly as possible."

"I know."

"Have you seen any of the warning signs?"

"Yes. During the interview in the prison she elevated her awareness substantially in less than five seconds of meditation."

"That's rare, but not worrisome." Walker shook his head and frowned. "And?"

"Well," Walker continued. "Her house burned down Saturday night."

Anger flashed in Dr. Altman's eyes. "She was left alone after meeting with you?"

"I didn't have a choice. She needed an alibi, and being seen with me would have pretty much shot that down, don't you think?"

"I'm not going through this again Michael," Altman said curtly.

"I told her to have someone stay with her, but she forgot."

Altman froze. "You mean you wanted her to do something and she was strong enough to do something different?"

"Yes."

"You have to tell her what kind of danger she is in."

"She has been under constant surveillance since yesterday."

"Have you told her why they shut down the project?"

"Only in general terms."

Dr. Altman was starting to become agitated. "Good Lord, Michael. What did you two talk about for the past two days?"

"Carl, she has had a lot to absorb. If anyone can appreciate the risk of going too quickly it should be you."

"If anything were to happen to her because of us..." Altman's words drifted off.

"I know. But what we're doing is larger than the life of one person."

Carl Altman was horrified. "You sound like those government fools when you talk like that."

"I don't like this any more than you do, but we have to be realistic."

"Have you told her about the big show we're going to be putting on for the media?"

"Not yet."

"She doesn't know about Hermes or what went wrong with it. She doesn't know about the demonstration. What exactly does she know, Michael?"

"She's been through quite a lot in the past few days and I didn't want to overwhelm her."

"Good Lord." A light flicked on in Dr. Altman's eyes. "She still doesn't completely believe what you've been telling her and showing her."

"She has doubts."

"Doubts! This is just great."

"I know. We've discussed the risks before, Carl, and decided that an outsider was our best choice."

"This could degenerate into a nightmare, Michael."

"I'm not going to let her get hurt."

"Her personal safety is only one part of the equation. From what you've told me and what I've seen already for myself, she has the ability to neutralize the event if she is not in the proper state of mind."

"I know." Walker reached into his pocket and brought out a small leather case containing a hypodermic. "We will do whatever is necessary to make the event go off smoothly."

"What have we wrought, Michael? Let's hope it doesn't come to that."

CHAPTER TWENTY FIVE

"Of course it is happening inside your head, Harry,
but why on earth should that mean that it is not real?"

J. K. ROWLING

INSTEAD OF TRYING to clean up a stable or converting an outbuilding to house the sophisticated equipment used in the Hermes Project, they had constructed a 120 by 40 foot steel shell. The building was functional, sterile and boring. It had its own diesel power generators so any sudden increase in electric consumption wouldn't raise eyebrows at the local power company.

Dr. Altman was like a proud papa as he showed Penelope his fMRI machine. The fMRI took up half of the room; next to it was an area with a gurney and a wall of machines that Penelope couldn't identify. After removing all metallic objects, Penelope laid down on the table and felt totally relaxed. "This is the room where we do all of our initial work with subjects. What we're going to do, Ms. Spence, is get a baseline fMRI of you. This will allow us to track any future changes and, based on the results, determine which programs would be most beneficial for you."

Spence flinched when she felt the table she was lying on begin to move. "Just relax. This is just a preliminary scan and won't take very long."

Walker and Altman both stared intently as the magnetic re.sonance equipment thumped to life and the image began to build. Altman gasped audibly.

"Is there a problem?" Spence asked.

"No," Walker said calmly. "We just spilled something on the desk. Please remain still."

Walker flipped off the intercom so Penelope could not hear. "I warned you that this was a possibility," Altman said, his face bright crimson. Walker placed a firm hand on Altman's shoulder.

"Not now, Carl."

After a steady stream of chatter the sudden silence was a bit unnerving. "What are you two talking about over there?" asked Penelope.

There was faint click as the intercom was reactivated. "Okay. We're all done." Walker entered the exam room and helped her off the table. Dr. Altman, limited by his cane, was slow arriving.

Spence smiled. Dr. Altman reminded her of her late grandfather. He told wonderful stories of his wild adventures from his younger days, and had a speaking style similar to Altman's. He used crisp precise language and full enunciation of each word. Walker had been correct to wait and let Altman explain the process. Without context or being able to see the actual facility, the effort would have been unproductive. Dr. Altman kept using terms such as "k-space formalism" and "inverse Fourier transform" and at one point Altman put a complex math formula on a chalkboard that was perfectly logical to a Nobel Laureate such as him, but to Penelope was nothing but squiggles and lines.

"In a nutshell, Penelope, different parts of the brain serve different functions. Here," Walker said as he touched the upper back portion of his head, "is one part that is very important to our work, for example."

"This is the part of the brain," Dr. Altman said, "the posterior superior parietal lobe, that assists with determining your reality and orients you to the physical world, thereby clearly defining what is you and what is everything else so that you can function...."

"Carl," Walker said softly as he saw the confusion cloud Penelope's face. "Let me try." Altman bowed slightly from the waist and yielded the floor to Walker.

"That part of the brain is always busy determining distance, interpreting sounds, checking the temperature. It is what lets center fielders catch fly balls. People who have had this part of the brain damaged due to injury have difficulty functioning. They will try to lie on their bed and end up on the floor instead."

"So far, so good," Penelope acknowledged.

"It has been well established that when people are in deep meditation, activity in this part of the brain changes significantly." Walker drew in a deep breath and let it out slowly. "Scientists currently believe that this is one of the gatekeepers that separates you from the carefully crafted world this part of the brain has created, and the larger universal world that we are all a part of."

"Whenever a person starts to glimpse the greater world that we all share," Altman interjected, "this is one of the key parts of the brain that immediately wants to pull the curtains shut and go back to the reality it has created for you."

"I'm not sure I understand..."

"We can go into this aspect later," Walker said as he glared at Altman. "For now let's just say this is a part of the brain that is constantly working to fine-tune your perceived world."

"Okay," Penelope said, watching Altman struggle to keep from jumping in.

"The brain is a complex biochemical system. What we've done is isolate some very precise electromagnetic, or EM, wavelengths that affect certain parts of the brain. By sending very carefully tuned electromagnetic pulses, we are able to cause different parts of the brain either to relax or to be stimulated. We have found that when we alter the input the posterior superior parietal lobe receives from other key areas of the brain, as well as other sections such as the left temporal lobe, all sorts of interesting things start to happen."

"For example." Walker and Altman exchanged worried glances. "When this section is ..."

Dr. Altman couldn't restrain himself any longer. "Occupied trying to figure out what is going on due to the stimuli we are providing. The other parts of the brain are more responsive to other stimuli."

"What Carl is saying... without certain gatekeepers to stand guard, various parts of the brain start doing remarkable things."

"Such as?"

"With the proper combination of EM pulses, we can give the test subject a brief spike in psychic ability."

"We," Altman added, "can even give them a glimpse of Enlightenment."

"That was the breakthrough Senator Horn was so worried about?"

"No," Walker answered. "Researchers have been doing this at a clinical level for years, mostly with drugs and by implanting wires and electrodes in people's brains. Our breakthrough is that we are now able to do this without any physical contact, and without the subject ingesting any drugs."

"What?" Penelope's eyes and mouth were both wide open. "So you're saying you have developed some type of a ray gun that can alter a person's reality without touching them or attaching any wires?"

"I don't think I would characterize it as a ray gun, but the answer to your question is yes. This also isn't new, the government has been able to do this for decades, but it never occurred to them to use it in the way we have. Some of our results have been rather stunning. That's what we want to show the people from *The Washington Post*."

"So people don't even have to volunteer; you can just blast them as they walk down the street."

"Pretty much." Walker answered.

"I can see why this was classified. Can it be used as a weapon?"

"Yes," Walker said. "But only against people and not military targets."

"What does that mean?"

"Most high-end command and control facilities are already shielded to block the EM pulse from a nuclear blast, so our pulses couldn't get through even if we wanted them to. It would be like trying to throw a spitball through a brick wall. But it can be used to affect unshielded populations."

"What does that mean?"

"In the early stages of this research Dr. Altman did a demonstration with an auditorium full of students. He used one of his early prototypes to make half the room think they were freezing. They were huddling up with their teeth chattering."

"You are kidding?"

"He always had a flair for the dramatic," Walker said with a laugh as he glanced over at Altman. "Those on the unaffected side of the room thought it was a trick until it was their turn."

"Why didn't I ever hear about this?"

"Altman had touched the third rail of science..."

"The what?"

"You know? The third rail on a subway train that if you touch you get electrocuted..."

"I know what the third rail is, but what on earth is the third rail of science? It sounds like one of your Timothy Leary theories."

"Not quite," Walker said while shaking his head. "There are certain things you simply don't discuss among other scientists if you want to be taken seriously within your peer group. If you touch any of those rails, your funding will dry up and no one will publish your findings. They send you into intellectual purgatory and you become an outcast."

"Do you have any examples?"

"Tons of them. Scientists are some of the narrowest minded people on the planet and if you question the current scientific consensus they will turn on you like a pack of wolves."

"Once again you are talking gibberish. Are there any examples in my future?"

"How much funding do you think a climatologist would get for research into global warming being caused by a natural solar cycle instead of manmade pollution?"

"Okay. That's one."

"What about a geneticist who wanted to do a comparative study to see if race is a factor in a person's intelligence?"

"That's settled science and borderline racist."

"Perfect example."

"What do you mean by that?"

"That is the exact argument the scientific community would use. Political correctness is killing science."

"Political correctness?" Penelope shook her head in disbelief.

Walker shrugged. "In any case it is well off the point. Dr. Altman had the nerve to touch the biggest third rail out there."

"Which is?"

"He is doing research like the Hermes Project. Very few scientists would have the courage to do this type of research, much less talk about it."

"Why?"

"It would be impossible to get tenure at any major university. Funding would be out of the question..."

"He got funding."

"True, but he is a unique case."

"Why?"

"He had actually gotten measurable results, plus he doesn't give a damn what his peers think about him. He believes they should be more worried about what he thinks about them."

"What gives him that luxury?"

Dr. Altman couldn't keep himself from interjecting himself in the conversation. "Sometimes I feel like Gulliver in the land of the Lilliput. Why should I care for one moment what someone who would struggle to even get a passing grade in one of my classes thinks of my scholarship?" Walker put his hand on Altman's arm.

"Plus he's 81 years old and has already won every award available in his field, including the Nobel Prize."

"He must drive the scientific community nuts."

"There isn't much middle ground. The scientists who do their best work in the faculty lounge and cocktail parties hate him; those doing cutting edge research or dealing with anything the slightest bit controversial love him."

"Would shining a mind control ray gun on an auditorium full of hapless students fall under the controversial category?"

"Ray gun?" Altman folded his arms across his chest and glared at Penelope.

"What would you call it?"

"A precision controlled microwave pulse," Walker answered.

Penelope shrugged. "Still sounds like a ray gun to me and I'd be more than annoyed if you used it on one of my kids."

"We had full disclosure and signed consent forms from everyone," Altman offered in his own defense. "There was even a waiting list. Besides, it's relatively easy to shield against these pulses, even for individuals."

"How?"

"We're working on a special hat..."

A smile broke across Penelope's face. "So you're saying those guys who wrap their heads in tin foil might be on to something?"

"The Pentagon has been working on special liners for their combat helmets for years."

"Really?" Penelope scratched her head. "So people without their little protective caps would be at risk to being exposed to your ray... EM pulse..." Penelope paused then smiled. "That's why you want this technology made public, so people can protect themselves, or at the minimum know what's going on."

"Knowledge is power, Penelope," Walker said with a smile.

"The power of thought?" Penelope answered with a wry smile.

"Exactly," Walker answered.

Penelope glanced at the clock on the wall. "We're on a very tight deadline. I already have an overview of the project, which I got from your grandson's excellent work. What else should I know before the people from WaPo start arriving?"

"I suppose," Dr. Altman said with a sigh. "I could show you some progression fMRI images that show..."

"Dr. Altman," Penelope cut him off. "Do you have any before and after shots, preferably in .jpg format that will be easy for the average reader to see the difference?"

"Of course." Dr Altman took Penelope's arm and started to guide her toward his office. "Please. Call me Carl."

"Only if you will call me Penelope."

"Penelope. That's an unusual name."

"I was named after the wife of Malcolm Drayton, who signed the Declaration of Independence and represented South Carolina in the first Continental Congress."

"Michael told me you were from a well-established and wealthy family in Charleston."

"Well-established, yes. Wealthy is another matter."

"I thought..."

"In the South, Carl, the real wealth passes to the oldest son, not to the youngest daughter."

"I see."

"Can I see those files now?"

"I'll have Jerold fetch whatever you need. For now I want to show you the pièce de résistance," Altman said as he ushered Penelope down the hall to a large room. There was slight swooshing sound as he opened the door and announced, "I give you the Hermes Project. This is where we've made all of our more recent breakthroughs."

She wasn't sure what she had expected but this was certainly anti-climactic. The room was partitioned in two. One section appeared to be a control room, and in the other section of the room was a 12-foot-by-12-foot plastic cube. Inside the cube were several resin lawn chairs and a plastic deck table; the kind you would expect to find next to a backyard swimming pool.

"The exterior walls, floors and ceiling, as well as the control room, are all electromagnetically shielded with Mu-metal that absorbs nearly all of the stray EM. The chamber," Altman motioned toward the cube, "has no metal components that might affect the magnetic resonations we use. You may notice your ears popping since we closely control the temperature and barometric pressure in the room."

"Why is that necessary?" Penelope asked.

"As far as we can tell, it's not. But it is always important to eliminate as many variables as possible when doing science. The better you control the experiment, the purer the results."

"I see."

"You will note there are no electrical outlets or wiring of any type that might possibly generate a stray electromagnetic field." Altman pointed to the ceiling and a series of translucent panels. "The same applies to lighting fixtures."

"What about those?"

"They are fiber optic, they collect light on the roof and distribute it in here."

"Does that mean you can only work during daylight hours?"

"Yes," Altman answered, "we don't want to risk any chance of contaminating the results." Dr. Altman pointed to a heavy black shoe-box sized container mounted near the ceiling in the corner. "That little dime sized hole is the only spot that is not 100% multi-layered shielded. The box contains the video camera we use to monitor the activity in the chamber and the hole is for the lens. The feed goes straight into the control room so nothing escapes."

"Are you going to show me how it works?" Penelope asked.

"We really don't have time right now," Walker said.

"Yes. We are short of time," Altman added quickly.

Penelope studied the two men carefully. Walker was a much better liar than Altman. Something about her being in this room made both of them uneasy, but she wasn't sure why. Penelope finally asked the big question.

"Why did Senator Horn shut down your project?"

Altman and Walker exchanged worried glances. The moment of truth had finally arrived. They didn't have time to sugarcoat or avoid the subject any longer.

"Initially," Altman said, almost apologetically, "we were working with an entirely new technology."

"We were in completely unknown territory," Walker added.

"It took us months to refine our screening process to be sure someone was psychologically ready for our program."

Penelope Spence started to feel a chill; she didn't think she was going to like what she would be hearing next.

The mood was broken when Sally Winters and Jerold Altman joined them in the control room. "Sorry," Winters said when she realized she had interrupted something important. "The people from *The Washington Post* should be here in a bit over an hour." She nodded and was just about to leave when she caught Michael Walker's eye; he shook his head about an eighth of an inch but didn't say anything. He didn't need to. Sally Winters took up a position behind Penelope.

"What happened," Penelope asked softly.

Altman and Walker looked at each other; neither wanted to add the final piece to the puzzle. Penelope Spence waited. No one in the room was willing to make eye contact with her. She knew that what they had to say was going to be bad. Very bad.

Michael Walker broke the awkward silence. "All of the people who willingly volunteered for the program were fine. The people sent over by Homeland Security were another matter, entirely."

"They reacted very badly to our efforts," Dr. Altman added.

"What kind of reaction?" Penelope looked back and forth between Altman and Walker. Jerold and Sally had shrunk into the background. Finally, Walker gave her the answer.

"We had twenty volunteers," Walker said. "Three of them came through the process with amazing results and three of them showed no long term effects."

"And the rest?" Penelope asked softly.

Walker's shoulders sagged. "Fourteen of the volunteers suffered profound psychological damage; eleven of them are currently in mental health facilities."

Penelope Spence could see the pain in Walker's face. "What about the other three?"

Walker drew in a deep breath. "They committed suicide."

"I see," Spence said softly. "What is the current status of the remaining eleven volunteers?"

Walker sighed. "Seven of them appear to be in a total non-symbolic state of consciousness from which they are unwilling or unable to return."

"What does that mean?"

"They have found, for want of a better word, enlightenment. We've spoken extensively to the three from the original 20 who achieved this state and have returned, and they assure us we shouldn't worry about the others. Each told us separately that while the seven appear to be in a near vegetative state, they are happier than they've ever been."

"Like the Sadhu Holy Men of India?" Penelope asked

Dr. Carl Altman clapped his hands and laughed. "Excellent, Penelope. Excellent." His eyes twinkled as he glanced in the direction of Walker. "You were spot on, Michael. She was the perfect choice. Not one in a thousand would have made that connection. "

Penelope ignored the compliment and plowed on. "By my count, there are still four people we haven't talked about."

"Yes," Walker answered. "Two of the people appear to drift between the non-symbolic state and someplace else. They will have brief periods where they are lucid enough to recognize friends and family then drift away again. The last two," Walker lowered his eyes. "The last appear to have profound Kundalini damage that we have no idea how, or even if it is possible, to fix."

"Kundalini?" Penelope said as she processed all of this new information. "You mean like the Kundalini they talk about at yoga classes?"

"Exactly. We're concerned that the combination of their ego driven resistance and our applied pressure to move them to a non-symbolic state may have caused some thing to break that cannot be repaired."

"Like a willow verses an oak tree in a wind storm," Penelope said softly.

Walker's eyes twinkled but Altman looked confused. Michael Walker touched his friend's arm. "Some, like the willow, bend with the wind and survive the gale. While the oak remains ridged and gets uprooted."

"Brilliant," Altman said with a nod toward Penelope. "That's the perfect symbolic analogy."

A thick silence settled over the room. They were now down to the brass tacks and it was no time to be bashful or overly concerned for hurt feelings. Penelope wanted the answer to the question Walker had managed so far to avoid answering. "Senator Clayton Horn strongly opposed your project on religious grounds. Why?"

"Horn, as I said earlier, is a literalist. He believes the Bible says what it means and means what it says and doesn't have much room for interpretation."

"I know. How does it apply here?"

Walker wiped his mouth and looked at Altman, who shrugged. "As our screening process got better so did our results. Those of us who went through the program started to develop a connection. Not just to each other but to plants and animals. With our consciousness more receptive to a greater world that our mind normally ignores or minimizes, we're able to see and do things that are baffling to many, and frightening to devout people such as Senator Horn. By the last few oversight hearings, he didn't even want to be in the same room as me."

"What if he's right and you're wrong?"

"Then, as he feared, the end time is here. This genie is not going back into the bottle. The Fourth Awakening has already started, and not just with the Hermes Project. There are other countries working on this and it is happening spontaneously all around the world."

"What scared him so much?"

"Let me give you an example." Walker motioned for them to follow him back out into the hallway and a small lobby area used by people waiting to enter the room while an experiment was in progress. He opened the shades of the window. Outside, there were a few people milling around but everything looked normal. Walker sat down in a chair facing the window and closed his eyes. He drifted into the meditative state she had seen before. Doors in other buildings flew open and everyone was racing full speed toward the lab.

Sally Winters placed her hand on Penelope's shoulder. "He used his mind to tell everyone they were needed in the lab immediately."

"We've been unable to ascertain the transmission medium," Dr. Altman said. "But there is no doubt we are not alone on this."

"What about the hats?" Penelope inquired.

"They can protect from our electromagnetic research, but not from this."

Walker opened his eyes, saw that his message had been received, and closed his eyes again. All of the members of the project broke stride and headed back to what they had been doing.

"Good Lord," Penelope muttered, as she felt her knees weaken under her. Winters kept her from falling.

"It can be a bit unnerving the first time you see it."

"That's not it. I knew exactly what was going to happen because I felt the request."

"Everyone in the universe felt it," Walker said. "It's just that most did not have it register on a conscious level."

"I don't understand."

"Imagine you're in Central Park in New York."

"Okay."

"At any given moment the signal from fifty radio stations, a dozen television stations, countless cell phones, police radios, and taxi cabs are passing through your body. They are also passing through the body of every other person around you but no one hears them. Just because they are not heard doesn't mean they don't exist. Thoughts are the same way. Right now we're all being hit with an infinite number of thoughts, but our brain is very selective as to what it will let us hear. Now imagine you're in a crowded cocktail party where you don't know anyone and you're alone."

"Okay."

"All you hear are murmurs and fragments of conversations. Your ears hear a familiar voice calling your name from across the room and your mind quickly begins to filter out the background noise so all you hear is your friend's voice."

"Okay."

"The same is true with thoughts. You told me you have a close relationship with your son. That would be a familiar voice that you would recognize and respond to if you heard him shouting for help. The only difference is you're in the world of thought, not at a cocktail party."

"You're saying you're a telepath?"

"Yes and no, depending on how you define your terms. We really don't have the vocabulary yet to completely explain what is happening."

"I don't follow."

"Imagine trying to explain the space shuttle to someone who has never seen an airplane or a computer, or an iPod to a person who has never seen an electric light bulb. We have no symbolic language yet to describe what's going on." Walker returned to his feet. "That's not all. We started to discover that we were not alone. There were others who could also share our thoughts."

"A thought has power, Penelope," Altman said. "When you send out a powerful thought it is like a shout in the night. You never know who will hear you."

"This is when we discovered that the field really exists."

"The field, what field?"

"I won't bore you with the details," Altman said. "But I shared my Nobel with a gentleman in Prague that, at the time of the discovery that led to that award, I had never heard of nor met. Yet we both had exactly the same idea at the same time. Without knowing it, we were sharing the energy from the same thought. This happens all the time in science. Have you ever heard of Elisha Gray?"

"No."

"He filed his patent for the telephone the same morning, but an hour later than Alexander Graham Bell," Altman said.

"As we gained a better understanding of what we were dealing with," Walker added, "we realized that all the thoughts of all people are in the field."

"What are you talking about?"

"It's almost like the Internet. You surf the Web right?"

"Of course."

"All of the information on the Web is just sitting out there, waiting for you or anyone else who might want it. All that is required is a connection and the right address."

"So you're saying all of my thoughts and all of the thoughts of the other people in the world are in this giant field of energy just waiting for someone to connect into them?"

"Not just people, but plants and animals; and not just this world, but the entire universe. And not just our time, but every time."

"That's absurd."

"Is it? There are times you sense things about your son. How do you explain that?"

"I don't."

"Let me try."

"Michael," Altman snapped. "You are on dangerous ground."

"I understand. But if she is going to write the story we need told, she has to understand what's happening to her."

"Me?"

"I will have no part of this." Dr. Carl Altman turned and shuffled down the hallway.

Penelope was torn between her curiosity and being terrified of what

Walker might say next. Walker drew in a breath and gathered his thoughts before continuing.

"The power of thought. Have you ever heard of someone who is sick suddenly getting well after people have prayed for them?"

"Of course. People who have gone into unexplained remission of a cancer that should..." Spence felt a chill going down her spine that iced her blood and froze her vocal cords. "You ordered your people to pray for Senator Horn. That's why he improved."

"Yes."

"You have that kind of power?"

"We all have that kind of power."

CHAPTER TWENTY SIX

"The words that enlighten the soul are more precious than jewels."

HAZRAT INAYAT KHAN

"SENATOR HORN THINKS you were trying to elevate yourself as an equal to God."

"Yes."

This concept sent her mind reeling. The magnitude of what she was trying to absorb became too heavy for her legs. Penelope Spence blinked and fell into one of the waiting area chairs facing the window. Horn had told her that every major religious organization in the world would try to stop Walker. The implications for organized religion were far-reaching and dangerous, at least to them. If common people could connect directly to a higher force, why would they need expensive churches, or to pay the bills of ministers, rabbis, Imams and priests? Organized religion around the world could become superfluous, and every place of worship a quaint remembrance of different times.

If what Walker was saying were true, then they were about to enter the Fourth Awakening and the entire social fabric of the world could be shredded. To some religious leaders and their followers it might appear to be the end of the world. And they would be correct; it could very well be the end of *their* world. Penelope shivered as she remembered what Walker had said earlier. He was right. They would not give up their power and position without a fight.

"What we've shown you in the past few days..."

Penelope jumped. The sound of Walker's voice drawing her back to reality was like a heavy book hitting the floor of a quiet library.

"...We usually spread out over a longer period of time to allow your mind and body to adjust to the new reality." Walker gripped Spence's arms, lifted her to her feet and turned her to face him. Penelope felt her heart flutter and her cheeks flush. "It is critical that you stay focused and positive. Do you understand?"

"Why is it so critical?"

Walker gathered his thoughts and chose his words carefully. "Because of what you've been through in the past few days and the fact that, while you started down this path willingly, we may have pushed you too fast."

"What are you telling me?"

"Your fMRI is showing some of the same markers as the people we lost."

Penelope Spence's mouth fell open and her body turned to ice. "What have you done to me?"

"I'm sorry to expose you to this risk but it was necessary."

"What kind of risk?" Any thought of remaining positive was being pushed further and further from her mind as the anger and the fear began to build. He had betrayed her, and possibly put her life in danger. Walker sensed the change in Penelope; he glanced up at Sally Winters.

"Calm down, we won't allow anything to hurt you," Walker said. Behind Penelope and out of her sight line, Sally Winters had quietly opened a small leather case and had taken a syringe in her hand. If it became necessary, she could inject the sedative in Penelope's neck in less than a second. Sally Winters' eyes locked on Walker's, awaiting the signal.

"Don't tell me to calm down. What kind of risk?"

"Enlightenment is like a pyramid. The wider your base the higher you can go. What has happened is you have developed faster in certain areas, and you may not have a sufficient base to support this growth."

"What have you done to me?" Penelope felt hot tears forming in her eyes and streaming down her cheeks.

"Nothing has happened, and nothing is going to happen. You're in the compound now, and we have people to help you get over this last barrier."

Walker glanced up at Sally Winters, who moved to within mere inches of the shaking woman, as she removed the cap from the needle of the syringe. Following his eyes, Penelope saw the syringe poised next to her throat, a drop of clear liquid already on its tip. Penelope tried to run toward the door but Walker held her arms too tightly.

"You betrayed me! YOU ALL BETRAYED..." Unable to fight or flee, circuit breakers in her mind began clicking off as she slumped forward.

"Penelope. PENELOPE!..."

Penelope Drayton Spence didn't hear anything else.

≈

THE FEAR IS *gone and has been replaced with an overwhelming bliss. A sense of total peace and calmness settles over me.*
I hear a familiar voice.
"Please come back."
"Why would I ever want to leave this place?"
"Trust me."

≈

MARK HATCHET, READING glasses perched on his nose, reread the executive summary. This obviously wasn't Nellie's work; it was too clinical and bloodless. It had no flow, and whoever had written it managed to bury the lead that the Hermes Project had experienced some kind of breakthrough in expanding human consciousness. Still, it gave the crew he was able to round up on short notice something to do during the four plus hours they were in the air, besides drink coffee and stare out the window.

The two reporters he really wanted on this story weren't here. The obvious first choice because of his personal relationship to Walker, Kent Lazlo, was on assignment in London at a G-8 Conference. His second pick, a young fire breather named Stacey Grover, who reminded Hatchet of Nellie in her prime, hadn't made it to the airport on time. He had her booked on the next commercial fight out to Jackson Hole but she wouldn't be there in time to contribute much before deadline.

He had known that even giving Spence the initial contact was risky, but now he was in career jeopardy territory. With this huge buildup, if she didn't deliver she could run back to Charleston and lick her wounds. He, on the other hand, was in the corporate jet with his boss's boss and the CEO of the paper. If this didn't go well, the blame would rapidly run downhill in his direction. He still had his big trump card, the confidential source he still hadn't revealed even to his boss. Even a pipeline straight into the Oval Office might not be enough to save him if things went south.

In her day, Penelope Drayton Spence had been the finest investigative reporter he had ever met, including some of the legendary ones on his own staff. But did she still have it? The first two stories she sent him on the Hermes Project were impressive, and would likely win her every award in journalism this year. This was something very different. This was the kind of story that defined a career, the kind Hollywood makes movies about. Mark Hatchet popped another Tums into his mouth.

≈

PENELOPE SPENCE'S EYES flew open. Standing in front of her was a terrified Sally Winters. "Are you all right?" Penelope was unable to speak but nodded that she was okay. "Are you sure? Who am I?"

"Sally Winters," Penelope said in a barely audible voice.

"Where are you?"

"Jackson, Wyoming at the Hermes Project."

"Thank God." Winters hugged Penelope tightly. "We thought we had lost you like the others." That was when Penelope saw Michael Walker on the floor. Jerold Altman was pushing on his chest and counting. He stopped, then breathed into the prone man's mouth.

"What happened?" Penelope tried to shout but her voice was like a clarinet with a broken reed. Tears streamed down her cheeks. "What happened?" she finally asked in a soft husky voice. She tried to move toward Walker, but in her weakened state she was no match for Sally Winters.

"You fell into a complete non-symbolic state."

"What does that mean?" Penelope asked as she realized she was too weak to struggle and gave up the fight.

"You completely let go of your ego and for a flash you were completely enlightened."

"I have no idea what that means."

"I know," Sally Winters said as she stroked her hair. "I know."

"What happened to Michael?"

"We have no idea. He muttered 'trust me' then fell to the floor. No one has ever seen anything like this before."

The room began filling up with people; instructions and shouts were ringing in Penelope's ears. She barely heard them. Dr. Altman came in and the crowd parted as he made his way to his fallen friend. Turning to Penelope he asked softly, "What happened?"

"He spoke to me," Penelope's voice cracked.

"What did he say?"

Sally Winters gave Penelope a liter of water from which she sipped enough so she could speak above a whisper. The room fell silent. All eyes in the room, except for those belonging to those giving Walker CPR, turned to her.

"He asked me to trust him."

"My God," Altman shouted as his mouth fell open. "He did it. He did it!" He fell to the floor next to Walker and gave him a shake. "Don't you die on me now! Do you hear me!"

Walker's eyes fluttered open. "I think everyone in the state heard you."

"Well?" Altman demanded. "Is it scalable?"

Walker was helped into a chair and the color was starting to return to his cheeks. He waved away offers of further assistance and rubbed the middle of his sternum. "Your grandson is stronger than he looks."

"Yes, yes," Altman made no effort to hide his annoyance. "Is it scalable?"

"That depends."

"Depends on what?' Altman demanded.

"Her." All eyes in the room turn to Penelope. "How are you?"

Penelope did a quick personal inventory and was satisfied. "I'm fine." She crinkled her nose and looked at her different body parts and nodded her head. "I would say I am much better than fine. But you already knew that," she said with a smile.

"Yes, yes," Altman said impatiently. "We can all plainly see you've had a glimpse of the non-symbolic state and are none the worse for wear. Welcome to the Hermes Project. But that is not the question on the floor," Altman turns back to Walker. "Can you do it again?"

"With a bit of work, I would say yes."

"Hallelujah!" Altman dropped his cane and danced a little jig. Everyone in the room watched in bemused wonder. Altman came over to Penelope and took her hands. "Madame, prepare yourself," he said, pulling to her feet. "I am going to kiss you full on the lips." And kiss her he did.

No one had ever seen Nobel Lauriat Dr. Carl Altman in such a state.

Walker rose to his feet and motioned for Jerold Altman. "Take your grandfather to his room and get him ready to go to the airport before he hurts himself." As Jerold Altman began to walk toward his grandfather, Walker tugged on his arm, turning him back around. "And for future reference, I was fine. I just used too much energy and couldn't move." Jerold nodded. Walker smiled. "I appreciate the effort."

"What is going on?" Penelope demanded.

The smile on Walker's face would clear a cloudy day. "We did it."

"Did what?"

"What we've been working on since the accident."

Walker surveyed the room where fifteen members of the Hermes group had gathered and more were coming through the door. A flicker of recognition began to light the eyes of the others in the room. Excited whispers turned into shouts of "YES!"

"Is someone going to tell me what's going on?"

"For the past year we have been looking for a way to repair the damage we inadvertently caused. And you were the missing element."

"Why me?"

"Because, thanks to you and your pig..." Walker caught himself. "Because of your steadfastness we now know where we made our biggest mistake. Since the incident we have been overly cautious. Because of circumstance, you are the first person we have allowed to develop this rapidly. By fighting me every inch of the way, the same way some of them did, I was able to find the path to rebuild their egos and bring them back into balance."

"Will you be able to restore them all?"

"Possibly. It depends on if they are just residing in a non-symbolic state of enlightenment or if there was permanent Kundalini damage. The important thing is, for the first time in a long time, there is hope."

"Did you hit your head when you fell?"

"I did not."

"Then what in the world are you talking about?"

"Remember the place you were?"

"A little hard to forget."

"I'm confident that at least seven are at that place or even deeper, and possibly two more of them as well. Because of your glorious steadfastness they will have the option to return to their families."

"They will have options?"

"Of course, we all get to select our own path," Walker said with a smile. "Some may choose to not come back but it will be by their choice and not ours to make. Thank you for trusting me by the way." Penelope felt her cheeks flush and she lowered her eyes. Walker kissed her in the middle of the forehead and she felt the now familiar jolt of energy surge through her body buckling her knees. He swept her into his arms before she could fall.

"Do you tango?"

"Not in the past 25 years."

"It's like riding a bicycle. When this is over, we dance!"

CHAPTER TWENTY SEVEN

"Any sufficiently advanced technology is indistinguishable from magic."

ARTHUR C. CLARKE

MICHAEL WALKER'S TEAM had arranged a fleet of rental cars and vans that were lined up at the south end of the tarmac of Jackson Hole Airport, waiting for the trio of corporate jets to arrive. Judging by the row of private planes and jets parked near the terminal, it was hard to dispute that Teton County has the highest per capita income in the United States. Sitting in a hole, with mountains on three sides and Teton National Park and the National Elk Refuge to the north, land is at a premium in Jackson with the average home costing well into seven figures. The airport itself is within the boundaries of Teton National Park and on certain days and weather conditions, is one of the most difficult places in the world to land an airplane.

Today the fog had burnt off early and the winds were light. As usual, miles from the nearest industrial center and too early for forest fire season, the air was a pristine blue that was so intense sunglasses were required. On a clear moonless night the sky can be so clear, that if the angle of the sun is right, you can actually see satellites orbiting the earth. The first Gulfstream to land was not from *The Washington Post*. It had the Walker Industries company logo on the tail fin.

The door opened and after the stairs were extended a tiny woman carrying a baby wrapped in a blanket came down the steps. Frank McCarthy ran across the tarmac to see his infant son for the first time. All that was visible of the lad was a shock of bright red hair. Taking the boy in his arms, he motioned toward the main party while he and his wife began marching purposefully in that direction.

"Mr. Walker, this is my wife...."

Before he could finish his sentence, Cindi McCarthy had slapped Michael Walker hard enough across the face to rattle his fillings. "Pleased to meet you," she said, as she walked past the CEO and leading shareholder of a Fortune 50 company. The others in the Hermes Project had to cover their faces or turn away to keep Walker from seeing their laughter.

Walker flexed his jaw. "I deserved that."

"Yes, you did," Penelope agreed, making no attempt to suppress her glee. "Wanted to do that a few times myself," she muttered to Sally Winters, who nodded her agreement.

"What was that?"

"Nothing."

Another jet touched down and taxied toward them. This one contained the brass of *The Washington Post*. Mark Hatchet was first off and greeted Penelope with a hug. He held her at arm's length and examined her from head to toe. "Wow, you've lost some weight."

"Thanks for noticing." She patted his potbelly and said, "Looks like you found everything I lost."

"Hotel food."

"We need to find you another wife."

"Yeah, you know what they say, the sixth time's the charm." Mark Hatchet was nearly seventy pounds heavier than he had been in his college days. Years of living out of a suitcase, covering everything from natural disasters to presidential campaigns, had taken a toll. Moving off the news beat and into the editor's chair hadn't helped. He still kept to his four basic food groups of caffeine, nicotine, alcohol, and fast food. Though he was only three months older than Penelope, no one would guess they were nearly the same age. What was left of his thinning hair was more gray than brown and the years had etched canyons in his face.

"Mark Hatchet, this is Michael Walker and Dr. Carl Altman." After a wave of introductions and handshakes, Penelope Spence pulled Hatchet aside and handed him a suggested car assignment sheet. Mark's boss and the CEO would travel with Dr. Altman; Hatchet would be in the car with her and Walker.

The second Gulfstream had landed and *The Washington Post's* worker bees were now milling around on the tarmac gawking at the Grand Tetons.

"Where do you want Aaron to ride?" Hatchet asked.

"Who is Aaron?" Penelope asked.

"Aaron Joseph. Our Senior Technology Editor?" Hatchet pulled back with a look of puzzlement that Penelope was drawing a blank. "You specifically asked for him by name."

"Oh, right." She motioned for Walker to join them and he broke away from another group and headed in their direction. "Where do we want Aaron Joseph?"

"It really doesn't matter. Anywhere is fine. He'll have plenty of time to catch up with Dr. Altman in the next few days." Walker read their blank looks. "He was one of Carl's students at Caltech."

Penelope broke into a wry smile. "If I hadn't gotten in the car with you in Charleston?"

"Yes." Michael Walker answered calmly. "I would have driven to Washington, instead of to Cincinnati."

"Do you always have a plan B?"

Walker smiled at Spence. "And C, and D, and... "

Penelope squeezed Walker's arm. "I'm glad I got in the car." Walker nodded.

"I'm grateful you did as well."

"What's going on?" Hatchet asked.

"Nothing," Penelope said, as she held the door open for her old friend.

≈

THERE WAS A steady din in the large dining room of the main house as the staff and managers from *The Washington Post* and the members of the Hermes Project mingled. At the north end of the room was a tall, rail thin man dressed in black. He had a mane of golden hair and skin so pale it appeared nearly translucent. Gathered around him were three men and one woman, also dressed in black; none of them taller than Penelope.

"Is that James Steerforth?" Mark Hatchet asked.

"Yes," Michael Walker answered after a quick glance over his shoulder.

"Who is James Steerforth?" Bill Flickling, the publisher of *The Washington Post*, asked.

"He's that famous illusionist who makes tigers and airplanes disappear in Las Vegas," Hatchet answered.

Franklin Mitchell, CEO of *The Washington Post Group* crossed his arms and glared at Hatchet. "I get the feeling we're getting set up here."

"He's much more than that," Michael Walker said with a smile. "He has made a career out of debunking other illusionists and so called psychics."

"We did a story on him recently," Hatchet looked around the room and motioned for a reporter to join them. "Jeanette Wilson wrote the piece."

Wilson, concern on her face at being summoned to a private conversation of all of the top brass of *The Washington Post* and the Hermes Project reluctantly joined them. "Yes, sir?" she said softly.

"Sir?" A bemused grin covered Hatchet face. "That isn't what you called me yesterday when I assigned that story you wanted to somebody else."

Jeanette Wilson's eyes danced from person to person and she appeared on the verge of losing control of her bodily functions. She never for a moment thought telling off the managing editor over a story assignment would merit a dressing down in front of the publisher AND the CEO of *The Washington Post Group*.

"Oh for heaven's sake, Mark," Bill Flickling said. "You're scaring her to death." Flickling pointed at James Steerforth. "Did you write a story about him recently?"

"Yes sir," Wilson answered softly.

"Mr. Walker here says he likes to debunk illusions. Is that the case?"

A great weight lifted off of Jeanette Wilson. "Yes sir. He seems to think he's Harry Houdini and..."

"What the hell does Houdini have to do with any of this?" Franklin Mitchell demanded.

"Houdini, sir," Wilson said as she turned to face the CEO. "He made a career out of exposing frauds such as fake mediums and phony séances. James Steerforth has gone one better. He has a standing offer of one million dollars to anyone who can do a magic trick he can't figure out. All of the other magicians hate him with a passion."

"And," Michael Walker said as all eyes turned to him "I went him one better. I've hired his team and offered them a five million dollar bonus if they can prove we staged any of what you're about to see."

"So," Mitchell said. "He's on your payroll." An unexpected girlish giggle escaped from Jeanette Wilson. "What's so funny, Ms Wilson?"

"Sir," she answered with a hint of panic in her voice. "James Steerforth is one of the highest paid entertainers in the world with a personal net worth in the hundreds of millions of dollars. He even owns his own island in the Caribbean."

"So?" Mitchell demanded

"For him five million dollars would be a slow month. Plus he has an ego that could fill the Grand Canyon."

"Your point?"

"What she's trying to say," Walker said. "Is that it would be worth much more to him to prove me a fraud than any money I might pay him."

"Exactly," Wilson added. "I agree with Mr. Walker one hundred percent. His ego would never allow him to think someone was smarter than him. Combine that with all the publicity this story is generating, if he could expose Mr. Walker as a fraud his market value would explode. There is no way he could be bought off." She shook her head firmly. "Never happen."

Mark Hatchet put his hand on Jeanette Wilson's shoulder. He could feel her still trembling beneath his touch. "Thanks."

Michael Walker made eye contact with James Steerforth who nodded that he was ready. Walker motioned to the group that they should head to the north end of the dining hall. Everyone had to pass between two rows of tables covered with small boxes.

"Please," one of Steerforth's male assistants said with a slight German accent. "Place all electronics and metallic items in one of the boxes. Just like the airport, no metal allowed."

The other three assistants were running handheld metal detecting wands over everyone before they were allowed to enter the roped off section of the dining room. In the middle of the space, Steerforth's people had constructed an elevated platform with a seven-foot high, eighteen-inch thick wall separating it into two equal parts. Suspended above the platform was a shimmering metallic cloth like material that cast a shadow over the platform. On either side of the wall was a small table with a single chair. Positioned around the table were three video crews. One belonged to Walker, one to *The Washington Post*, and one had been flown in by James Steerforth.

After brief introductions, Walker asked Steerforth, "Are we ready." He nodded yes. "Why don't you explain exactly what we have here?"

"Of course," Steerforth answered as he brushed his hair off his face. "We constructed this wall to be sure there is no communication between the people on either side." Steerforth with a flick of his wrist motioned toward the material tenting the area. "This canopy is a special composition of my personal design that will block any video equipment mounted above from..." Steerforth paused for dramatic effect and waited until all eyes in the room were locked on him. "Shall we say assisting the participants?" A confident smile covered his face as his eyes locked on Walker. Walker's bemused grin caused him the briefest moment of hesitation but it quickly passed as his master showman instincts kicked in. "The platform has special sensors to detect any movement, several additional sensors that we cannot talk about for competitive reasons are also in place, and we are monitoring radio frequencies in the immediate area."

"Who built this thing?" Franklin Mitchell asked.

"My staff and I," he answered softly. "Before you ask, either I or one of my assistants have been here the entire time since we began construction. None of Walker's people have been allowed near the arena."

"Tell them about the two people we're using," Walker suggested.

Steerforth had cold gray eyes that seldom blinked. "They have been with us for the past two days. We have taken them to an outside medical facility where they had full body X-rays and no metallic implants were found. We have monitored what they have eaten and they are wearing only clothes which we've provided."

"Are you satisfied?" Walker asked

Steerforth drew in a deep breath and slowly released it. "Yes. I am satisfied."

The members of the Hermes project fell back and let the people from the newspaper have the best vantage point to watch the show. From the rear of the room, another of Steerforth's assistants escorted the two Hermes graduates toward either side of the table. Both were barefooted and each wore thin black silk pajamas that clung to them as they walked. In one chair was a wiry woman who appeared to be in her mid-thirties and across from her was a sun baked young man in his late thirties.

"To welcome you, what we're going to do," Dr. Altman explained as he faced the bank of video cameras, "is give a brief and very minor demonstration of a fraction of the potential in the research we've been conducting. As a bit of introduction, the two participants in this demonstration are Laura Banks who has worked for Michael Walker for over a dozen years and Stu Levy who has been associated with me for a similar amount of time. To help us is noted illusionist Mr. James Steerforth." With a smattering of applause Dr. Altman yielded the floor.

"Thank you, Dr. Altman." Steerforth held up a deck of playing cards. "Mr. Walker and Dr. Altman allowed me to select the demonstration to be used and no one here knew what we were going to do until this moment." Steerforth slowly looked around the room as he flicked the hair from his face. "I decided to make this quite simple." He paused again for dramatic effect. "These cards have been in my constant possession since before our arrival. We will show a single card to one of the participants and ask the other to identify it."

Steerforth covered the deck with his right hand as he selected a card with his left, pressing it to his chest so no one could see it. Leaning in close to the woman on his side of the partition he showed her only the slightest corner of the card. On the other side of the partition he immediately heard, "Jack of Clubs."

Steerforth's eyes, for the briefest of moments grew large before returning to their normal size.

"Well," demanded Mitchell, "let's see it." Steerforth held up the Jack of Clubs. "I'll be damned."

Moving to the other side of the partition, Steerforth repeated his selection process and showed a card to Levy. He immediately heard a female voice say, "Three of Diamonds." Steerforth glared over at his assistants who were manning a bank of equipment scanning for radio signals on all frequencies and they all appeared horror struck.

After six more correct answers Steerforth motioned for his video crew to quit filming. "There are a thousand ways you could have done this trick. I'm sure when we analyze the video tape we will discover how you did it."

A bemused smile covered Walker's face. "One more card, Mr. Steerforth." James Steerforth glared at Walker but didn't move. "Please. It may change your life."

Reluctantly Steerforth showed another card to Stu Levy who was seated next to him. Thirty voices, every member of the Hermes Project, said, "Eight of Clubs." Steerforth glared at Walker.

"Well?" Walker asked casually. "Are you going to show everyone the card?" Reluctantly, Steerforth held up the eight of clubs.

"Son of a..." Mitchell looked around the room at all of the smiling members of Hermes. "Okay I have to admit, that was pretty impressive, but I'm still not convinced."

"Nor am I," said Steerforth.

"Would you like to try another demonstration?" Walker offered.

Steerforth nodded as he pulled a silver dollar out of his pocket. "But this time I would like to use him." Steerforth's long delicate finger pointed in the direction of Franklin Mitchell.

"Why me?" the CEO asked gruffly.

"Because," Steerforth answered. "You may be the only other person in the room I trust beyond my personal staff. If you were to run this fairy tale as fact and then later have it proven to be false it could destroy your newspaper."

"You got that much right."

"Any objection, Mr. Walker?"

"Nope," Walker answered with a smile.

The woman, Laura Banks, who had been involved in the first experiment stood up and Mitchell took her seat. "Now what?" Mitchell asked.

One of Steerforth's assistants appeared out of nowhere with a thin velvet pillow and a heavy metal cup. "Please place the silver dollar in the cup, shake it then put it down on the pillow. Do not lift the cup until I ask you. Do you understand?"

Franklin Mitchell shook his head at Steerforth. "I think I can manage that."

Steerforth turned back and addressed his "audience". "This cup was manufactured to my specifications and even the most powerful X-ray cannot penetrate it. The pillow is of similar construction. When the cup is upside down on the pillow, no currently known methods of detection can breech them." Glancing back over his shoulder at Mitchell he said, "Please proceed." Franklin Mitchell placed his hand over the mouth of the cup, gave it a shake then flipped in over on to the pillow.

Steerforth stepped off of the elevated platform so he could see both sides of the wall. "Please lift the cup and tell us whether it is heads or tails."

"Okay." Mitchell lifted the cup. "Heads," he announced.

"Please do it ten more times," James Steerforth requested.

After eight flips there was a buzz in the room, by the tenth flip it had gotten so loud, Mitchell nearly had to shout to be heard. "What's going on?" he demanded.

"Franklin," Bill Flickling said. "The man on the other side of the table has a ping pong paddle in each hand. The one in his right hand says "Heads"; the one in his left says "Tails."

"So?"

"Not only did he pick every one right; he made his selection before you lifted the alleged impenetrable cup."

"What? That's impossible; it has to be some kind of a trick."

"We thought you would say that, Mr. Mitchell." Walker said. "We would like a volunteer from your staff."

Immediately, a dozen hands shot up.

"Volunteer for what?" Franklin Mitchell demanded.

"We've progressed through several types and levels of training and learned a variety of techniques to enable someone to reach the states of consciousness you've seen demonstrated," Walker said calmly. "For example, our outdated Level One modification, if you'll excuse the term, was direct and intense while the newer Level Two techniques are more of a gentle nudge."

With a cross between a demand and a question, Bill Flickling interrupted, "What on earth are you talking about Walker?"

"I assume you've all read the summary of our work," Dr. Altman said. "For Level One we delivered direct stimulation to specific parts of the brain to enhance certain functionality. Level Two requires no contact with the subject."

"Is this dangerous?" Mark Hatchet asked.

Dr. Altman answered. "We have refined our techniques and the risk is now negligible."

"Define 'negligible' for me," Mitchell said.

"You have to realize," replied Walker, "that Dr. Altman is a scientist. His world is not black and white. Safe to us is 'negligible risk' to him."

Altman continued, "This will be a small application, and the results will be temporary. It shouldn't last more than fifteen minutes to an hour."

"I'll do it," Penelope said, stepping forward.

"No," Mitchell said. "If we do this, it will have to be someone else."

"Why?" Penelope demanded.

"To be blunt, Ms. Spence," Mitchell answered, "you've been with these people for the past two days and I don't know you from Adam."

"I'll do it." All eyes turned toward Mark Hatchet.

"No," Mitchell said. "There is only one person in this room I will trust. I want someone with as much skin in this game as I have."

All eyes turned to James Steerforth. As the consummate showman he milked the moment to let the tension build. With a click of his heels and a nod of his head, he agreed.

≈

JAMES STEERFORTH, DRESSED in light blue surgical scrubs, was lying on the gurney next to the fMRI. An elite handful of *The Washington Post's* people, along with Altman, Spence and Walker had crammed themselves into the control room. Everyone else was outside watching the progress on monitors.

"What we're going to do," Dr Altman said addressing the room and not Steerforth, "is to apply direct stimulation to a precise part of Mr. Steerforth's brain. Then..."

"Is this going to hurt?" Steerforth asked, with as much confidence as he could muster.

"No," Altman answered. "You may feel a slight tingling and be a bit disoriented. In most cases there is a release of certain neuropeptides, so you may also feel an overwhelming sense of euphoria. With the methodology we use this feeling will only last for a limited period of time. Are you ready, Mr. Steerforth?"

"Ready as I'll ever be."

There was a loud "thump, thump" that increased in speed and volume as the equipment came to life. All eyes were focused on James Steerforth, who laid motionless on the gurney. Penelope glanced at a broadly grinning Walker.

After only a few seconds, Dr. Altman flipped some switches and announced, "We're finished."

"That was it?" Franklin Mitchell was incredulous. "That's all there is to the Hermes Project?"

"No," Walker said. "This is just a small, controlled example of what Hermes can do." Walker stopped short, but the twinkle didn't leave his eye.

The control room emptied as the equipment fell silent. The gurney holding James Steerforth slid back from the oversized donut and everyone looked down at him. He was blinking his eyes and having difficulty focusing on the faces.

"Let's give him a few minutes to get his bearings," Walker said gently as a Hermes project nurse started taking the illusionists vitals. After a few uncomfortable moments of silence, James Steerforth pulled himself up into a sitting position and accepted the offer of a drink of water.

Penelope was about to speak again, but Michael Walker's hand on her shoulder stopped her.

"Give him a few more minutes to reorient himself. Let him acknowledge you first."

James Steerforth's eyes moved from face to face without the slightest hint of recognition. He looked around the room as if he had awoken from a long nap and found himself transported to another planet. His eyes drifted back to one of his personal assistants who was fidgeting nervously, shifting his weight from one foot to the other. "Bruno," Steerforth said with his first sincere smile since arriving in Wyoming. "That was amazing."

A collective sigh went up from the people who knew Steerforth best.

"Where are you?" Walker asked.

"I'm in Jackson Hole, Wyoming," Steerforth answered slowly as if the simplicity of the question puzzled him. Gone was the hard to place accent that was a cross between Eastern European and British. In its place was something that would have been more at home in Brooklyn. He pulled back as he studied Michael Walker carefully. "I'm thinking the better question would be where the heck are you?"

A smile broke across the faces of Walker and Altman as they exchanged pleased glances.

"What does that mean?" Franklin Mitchell demanded.

"It means he's fine," Walker answered. He motioned for the assembled party to return to the "arena" in the dining hall. "We'll give him a few more minutes to get his feet underneath him, then we'll get started."

After being helped to one of the small tables, one of Hermes Project people handed Steerforth the head and tails ping pong paddles. "Cool. I call first game." He began swinging them like a kung fu master. "Ah, grasshopper..."

"How long will he be like this?" Penelope asked

"It varies," Walker answered. "When we get time I'll show you some of the videos."

"You have your own outtake reels?"

"Yes. This is tame compared to some of the more intense sessions. They're hilarious."

Steerforth's eyes found Jerold Altman and he rose to his feet swinging the paddles. "Women like men with nunchuk skills." Walker pushed him firmly back into his chair.

"We will have time for that later, James. Right now, you need to focus on telling us whether the coin flip will be heads or tails. Can you do that?"

Steerforth examined the paddles as if he had just become aware that they were in his hands. "Sure!"

Walker motioned for the CEO of *The Washington Post Group* to return to his position on the opposite side of the wall from Steerforth. Altman handed Franklin Mitchell the silver dollar and the heavy cup he had used in the earlier demonstration. Before he could get the cup to the table, Steerforth held up "heads;" Franklin Mitchell flipped tails.

"Let's focus, James," Walker said gently. Steerforth turned his head and winked at Walker. Walker patted him on the shoulder as a broad grin crossed his face.

Steerforth held up "heads" again. It was tails. After eight straight wrongs there was a murmur in the room as concerned whispers were exchanged. Franklin Mitchell glanced up at his publisher, Bill Flickling, with displeasure.

After ten more incorrect, the murmur in the room had turned into a roar. With each additional miss there were groans and even a few shouts of encouragement to Steerforth.

Penelope leaned in to Walker with concern etched on her face. "You need to stop this."

"You're right," Walker answered. "I think we've made our point." Walker stepped over and placed a hand on Steerforth's shoulder. "Thanks James. I couldn't have come up with a better demonstration myself. That was perfect."

"Perfect!" Mitchell roared. "He missed every damn one!"

As usual, Walker was nonplussed. "You flipped the coin, by my count, 21 times."

"So?"

"With a fifty-fifty possibility of each flip being either heads or tails.

What do you think the odds are of getting that many wrong in a row?"

A voice in the back of the room said, "Two million ninety-seven thousand one hundred fifty-two to one." All eyes turned to Jerold Altman, who immediately turned bright pink. "Two to the power of twenty-one," he said, surprised that no one else in the room knew it off the top of their heads.

"You guys didn't seem to be impressed when they got all of them right earlier," James Steerforth said as he shook the cobwebs out of his head. "So I thought it might get your attention if I got them all wrong."

"Mathematically," Walker added, "getting them all wrong is the same probability as getting them all right." Walker patted Steerforth on the back. "That was inspired."

"Thanks." Steerforth motioned for one of his assistants who handed him an oversized golden envelope. "After what I saw earlier, I thought I might be needing this." Steerforth rose to his feet and waited until he was confident he had everyone's attention and the video equipment was running. A hush fell over the room.

"I'm James Steerforth and I never thought this day would arrive. I have spent my entire adult life debunking fakes and charlatans. I was so confident I have issued a challenge to anyone to prove me wrong." Steerforth motioned for Walker to join him. "This is Michael Walker. By now I'm sure all of you have heard of the Hermes Project. I'm here to tell you, it is not a trick, it is real. I have seen it for myself first hand." Steerforth handed the envelope to Walker. "Inside is my check for one million dollars." As the room exploded in applause, Steerforth leaned in and whispered in Walker's ear. "Anything I can do to help, just let me know."

A smile covered Walker's face. "There might be one thing you can do for me." The two walked away together with Steerforth nodding his agreement.

"So," Franklin Mitchell said to Dr. Altman. "This is the Hermes Project."

"That was the appetizer, Mr. Mitchell. The part of our project that has everyone so excited is in the next room."

CHAPTER TWENTY EIGHT

*"An Enlightened Master is ideal only if your goal
is to become a Benighted Slave."*

ROBERT ANTON WILSON

AFTER THE PERFORMANCE by James Steerforth, there was no shortage of volunteers from *The Washington Post's* crew to participate in another demonstration. With the heavy shielding and limits on space, everyone had to be either shoehorned into the windowless control room or watch the demonstration on video monitors in the waiting area outside. There was only enough space for the senior *Post* brass, Penelope, Walker and Altman in the control room. There were three chairs in front of the control room console. Altman took the seat in the middle with Flickling to his left and Mitchell to his right. Walker, Spence and Hatchet stood behind them.

"This entire area is heavily shielded," Dr. Altman said.

"Is that to keep interference out?" Hatchet asked.

"Initially, that was the idea," Altman said turning to make eye contact with Hatchet. "With our recent advances it is more important to keep our experiment contained. We used to have thick glass here in the control room but we had to replace it with something more resistant to our experiments. As we got better it started to affect this room as well. That's why we will need to observe this via video."

"That sounds ominous," Flickling said as he adjusted himself more comfortably in the chair. The plane trip and the long day were wreaking havoc on his lower back. "Is it safe in here?"

"The risk is negligible," Dr. Altman assured him. "We have gotten more and more skilled and better able to focus our efforts."

On multiple viewing screens inside the control room, they all could see four reporters from the *Post*; two men and two women. Dressed in blue surgical scrubs, their body language said everything anyone needed to know about their relationships. Each had claimed a corner of the cube and was as far away from the others as possible. Their eyes kept darting around like mice looking for the cat. Each kept shifting his or her weight uncomfortably from one foot to the other. Both women had their arms folded across their chests and the two men refused to make eye contact with the other.

"Normally I wouldn't put those guys together in such a small space," Hatchet said. "Are you sure this is what you want?"

"They are bitter rivals?" Altman asked.

"That's putting it mildly. We had to break up a fist-fight between Steve and Alex in the newsroom last week over a story assignment. Joan and Celeste work the Capitol Hill beat and have been at each other's throats for years."

"Then they're perfect," Walker said. "Let's get started."

Altman turned on the microphone. "We're going to begin now. Will each of you please be seated?" The four moved gingerly in the direction of the wobbly plastic table in the center of the cube and each claimed one of the white chairs each. None made eye contact with any of the others. Altman flipped a switch and, other than a red "In Use" indicator light blinking on the control panel, nothing seemed to be happening.

"You may feel a slight dizziness. That is to be expected. Sit back and relax, this will not take very long." Altman turned off the microphone and addressed the people in the control room. "We should start seeing a reaction in just a few moments."

"What kind of reaction?"

"They are being hit with a very specific magnetic wave that will cause some portions of the brain to become less active."

"Is this the part you have to quiet first?" Franklin Mitchell asked.

"Exactly," Altman answered. "All of these subjects have strong and well-developed egos. Decreasing activity in this part of the mind will cause them to experience the early stages of enlightenment."

"What the hell does that mean?" Mitchell demanded.

"They will start to experience a level of contentment they have never thought possible." Walker pointed toward the cube. "It has already started."

In the cube, the four people around the table no longer looked like mortal enemies. Their body language had gone from defensive to relaxed and open. They were actually smiling, possibly even at each other.

Altman flipped on the microphone. "How are you all doing in there?"

"I've never felt better in my life," answered one of the male reporters.

"Amazing," said one the female reporters as she glanced around the table. The other three heads nodded their agreement. "I feel like a weight has been lifted off of me..." They all began to talk at the same time and only bits and pieces could be distinguished.

"I'm happier than..."

"...total peace..."

"...relaxed..."

"....feeling of absolute serenity..."

When they realized they had been talking over each other, all conversation stopped. They glanced around the table and all burst into laughter. They all began talking again, this time apologizing for their rudeness, then started laughing again.

"I didn't think I'd ever see this day," Hatchet said as he watched the interplay with his mouth hanging open. "That's amazing."

"That's the future of mankind, if we can survive the transition."

"One of you better start explaining this," Mitchell insisted with the tone of a person at the pinnacle of their worldly influence.

"I think that's enough, Carl," Walker said. Altman nodded his agreement and the "In Use" light clicked off. Immediately, four members of the Hermes Project entered the test room and joined *The Washington Post* reporters in the cube. They offered the test subjects bottles of water, which they quickly accepted. As the room began to fill with the rest of the WaPo people, loud animated conversations and laughter echoed off the walls as each of the reporters tried to describe to their compatriots what it had been like.

"Gentlemen," and with a nod toward Penelope, "and Lady," Walker said. "We are on the cusp of the Fourth Awakening of mankind." Walker pointed toward the cube. "And that is a perfect example of the potential. All we did was give each of them a nudge and shine a bit of light on the path; their innate nature did the rest. In one hundred years or so, the way they are reacting and interacting will be the norm."

"So," Hatchet said, "this will work on anyone?"

"This is a much lower level of stimulation and considerably less focused than what James Steerforth went through. All that happened is we briefly sped up a process that has already started. All four of those people have experienced something they may have found on their own tomorrow, next week, next year or decades from now."

"Is this a permanent change?" Mitchell asked.

"Possibly, but not very likely in this case," Dr. Altman said. "They would have to spend much more time with us at this point to permanently rewire their neuropathways and stabilize the brain processes involved."

"It is important that you understand that this phenomenon is occurring spontaneously around the world, as we speak," Walker interjected.

"You're saying the whole human race is moving in this direction?" Hatchet asked.

"Yes. It's the Fourth Awakening that was mentioned in the material we sent you. What we're hoping is, with your help, we can get out in front of this and let people know what's happening before it is too late because there is a potential dark side."

"That is why it is so urgent," Dr. Altman added. "This technology can be used to enhance the human experience or, in the wrong hands, stifle it.

"I'm sorry," Bill Flickling said, "I don't see a problem here. If this can make the world a better place, then I just don't see a problem."

"The problem," Walker answered, "if we had shined a light on a slightly different path, some of them may have turned into monsters."

"What the hell does that mean?" Flickling demanded.

"Some people," Walker answered calmly. "When they reach the non-symbolic state of consciousness..."

Franklin Mitchell cut Walker off in mid-sentence. "What the hell is this non-symbolic whatever you said and what does it have to do with the Hermes Project?"

"Non-symbolic consciousness is difficult to describe since the vocabulary is still evolving and most of the current words are just placeholders. But generally speaking, in Eastern religions it is called enlightenment. In Western religions it is God's divine grace." A smile broke across Walker's face. "To Luke Skywalker it was the Force. And it has everything to do with the Hermes Project."

"Look, Walker," Bill Flickling said as he tried again to get himself more comfortable in his chair. "Everything I've seen today is damn impressive and you've got tomorrow's front page. But if this is all you've got..."

"The problem is," Walker answered calmly. "Some people arrive at this state and still have personal and psychological baggage. Some of them are the exact people Senator Horn is afraid of; people who think they are God and the rest of us are just their play toys."

"What Michael is trying to say," Dr. Altman interjected. "This Awakening is occurring and there are people that can use this technology for their personal or political advantage. We know or suspect at least six other groups that are currently involved in similar research to ours. It is important you understand with just a few minor changes of the settings, I could have had your people at each other's throats instead of having a group hug."

"There's going to be a transition period," Walker added. "We're afraid a great number of people will get hurt or worse if we don't get out in front of this."

"Okay," Franklin Mitchell said as he stood up and tried to start pacing but gave up for lack of space in the control room. "You're saying there may be other people out there whose intentions are not necessarily good and somehow this technology can be used as a weapon."

"Exactly," Walker and Altman answered in unison.

The senior managers from *The Washington Post* exchanged worried glances. Mark Hatchet spoke for all of them. "I understand what you're saying," Hatchet said. "But until I see it, I'll have trouble believing it."

"I won't put any of my people through that," Walker said flatly.

"You don't have to." Hatchet answered, his eyes locked on Walker's. "I'll do it."

"No." Walker said.

"Without a demonstration," Flickling said, pulling himself out of his chair, "we've spent a great deal of time and money on a story that, while interesting won't survive a 24 hour news cycle. In three days the Hermes Project will be forgotten."

Walker looked at Altman, who reluctantly nodded his approval.

After Hatchet had changed into a blue surgical gown and removed his watch, he joined Walker in the plastic cube. All of the furniture except for a single plastic chair had been removed.

"This is for your protection," Walker said as he bound Hatchet's wrists to the arms of the chair with white medical tape.

Hatchet looked down at his wrists. "I don't think that will hold me for very long."

"It doesn't need to. We are only going to give you a short burst, but you will find it terrifying. One aspect of this will trigger your natural fight or flight instincts on a level that's far beyond what you've experienced before. You will want to run but not be able to so you may try to fight. Do you understand?"

"Yes."

"After that we will flood the room with a different blast that should nullify the first one."

"Should nullify?" Hatchet said as he checked the tape on his wrists. "Don't like the sound of that."

"The worst case scenario is you wrestle a bit with Timothy and his friends," Walker nodded toward Ellison and the two others in the cube with him. "Just remember, you know what's coming and the unknown is often the most frightening. It takes a few seconds to change the settings in the control room and depending on how you respond, it could feel like hours. Try to relax and go with it. Okay?"

"Okay." Hatchet forced a smile and waved to a ghost white Penelope who was standing by the door to the control room. Penelope could hear her heart pounding in her ears and her palms were clammy. The reluctance of both Walker and Altman to allow any of their own people to do this demonstration concerned her mightily. They both knew exactly what was about to hit Mark. How would he take it? Was it possible he would react like the men from Homeland Security and end up insane or worse? Penelope closed her eyes, drew in a deep cleansing breath, and allowed herself to relax. Mark was going to be fine.

Walker chatted privately with Timothy Ellison and two of the youngest and largest members of Hermes. Their faces were grim but all nodded that they understood what to do. Ellison opened a storage case and removed three motorcycle style helmets that appeared to be larger and thicker than the off the rack versions. The three donned them, fastened the chin-straps, and took up positions inside the cube as far from Hatchet as space would allow. Walker joined the others in the shielded control room and nodded in the direction of Dr. Altman. "The headgear they are wearing will block the pulse," Walker stated.

The "In Use" light blinked on. At first there was no reaction by Mark

Hatchet. Then his eyes grew wild and his breathing started coming in gulps. He pulled his wrists to his mouth and started tearing the tape that was restraining him with his teeth. "I want out of here!" He screamed in a voice that sent chills up Penelope's spine. With an unexpected burst of strength, he tore the last of the tape from his wrists and tossed the chair aside. Seeing his path to the door blocked, he started backing away from the other men in the cube. A guttural growl was heard as Hatchet's eyes danced between the other men in the cube.

"My God," Penelope gasped. "Is that what happened to those men you lost?"

"That's enough," Walker shouted as he burst out of the control room. Walker, along with Ellison and the two other men in the cube all spread out and gingerly approached Hatchet.

"Mark," Walker said in a soothing voice. "It's all going to be fine. Just hang in there for a few more seconds."

Hatchet's eyes danced between the four men until he backed into the wall and could retreat no further.

"Carl!" Walker shouted as Hatchet grabbed the chair he had cast aside and threw it at the men who were closing in on him. It missed Ellison by inches. Altman worked frantically to change the setting on the control panel.

The "In Use" light clicked on.

"You won't take me alive!" Hatchet shouted, as he lunged toward Walker who grabbed him in a bear hug. As the new pulse started to fill the chamber, the rage began to leave Hatchet's body. Walker, with the help of the others, lowered Hatchet gently to the floor where he curled up into a fetal position softly muttering, "You won't take me alive."

Penelope pushed her way past Franklin Mitchell and ran into the cube. "Mark!" she shouted. The sound of her voice caused him to stop mumbling, and instead he began rocking on the cold concrete floor. "Mark," she said softly. "It's me, Nellie."

"Nellie?" His eyes slowly focused on the woman kneeling in front of him. A smile broke across his face. "Nellie! Wow. And I thought my last divorce was bad."

A huge smile covered Penelope's face. "He's okay. He's okay!"

Hatchet and Spence turned toward the control room door and saw Flickling and Mitchell on their feet, both white as a sheet. Neither moved and neither blinked until Walker rejoined them.

Mitchell cleared his throat before speaking. "You're telling us there are other people and governments who are working on this technology?"

"Yes," Walker answered. "The people have a right to know."

A grim Franklin Mitchell turned to Bill Flickling and nodded. Flickling, his hands trembling, pulled out his cell phone. All of the shielding kept him from getting a signal. He pointed to a phone on Dr. Altman's workstation in the control room and asked, "Can I get an outside line?" Altman shoved the phone in his direction. Quickly dialing a number he said, "This is Flickling. Clear the front page and I want a minimum of four interior pages..."

≈

FOR THE NEXT six hours, the Lazy S dining room was the western annex of *The Washington Post*. Walker's team had anticipated everything the newspaper people could need, from a good selection of wonderful food and drink, to high-speed Internet connections. At around six o'clock Jackson time, 8 p.m. Eastern, someone announced: "They've got footage up on YouTube of James Steerforth with his ping pong paddles doing his kung fu shuffle..."

Another voice added, "Some of the forums are already starting to go nuts."

As eleven o'clock Eastern time approached, a hushed crowd began to form around the workstation Mark Hatchet had claimed for himself. Sitting next to him, her eyes flying across the screen, sat Penelope Drayton Spence as she finished one last proofread.

"We good to go?" Hatchet asked.

"One second," Spence answered.

For the past six hours, Penelope Spence had directly supervised the writing of over fourteen articles that would be appearing in the next edition of *The Washington Post*. In addition to the expected material on the history of the Hermes Project and what it had discovered, there were individual profiles on both Michael Walker and Dr. Carl Altman. Altman had worked with his old student Aaron Joseph, who had written a passable feature on exactly what they were doing and how it was accomplished. In addition there were articles titled, "*Are you Awakening: Five Early Signs*", "*What the Awakening Will Mean to You*", and "*Protecting Yourself from Unwanted EM Pulses*". Each of the four reporters who had been in the cube wrote outstanding stories about their experiences. Mark Hatchet even wrote a rare feature, in which Penelope allowed him to have a solo byline, on what had happened to him.

The religious beat writer, who was mesmerized by Michael Walker, wrote a detailed history of the previous Awakenings, and a top-shelf analysis on how this Awakening and previous ones did not actually conflict with the world's major religious texts. Needless to say, Timothy Leary didn't make the cut.

Hatchet's cell phone rang. "Hatchet." He listened intently, and then jumped to his feet. "*The New York Times* has just gone to press with this headline for their lead story." He let the tension build for a moment, but with the tears in his eyes and the grin on his face he wasn't about to bluff anyone. "I guess they need to start reading *The Washington Post*. Their lead headline: *What is the Hermes Project?*" A roar went up from the room full of tired journalists. It died down quickly as all eyes turned back to Penelope who, oblivious to what was swirling around her, still sat staring intently at the computer monitor.

The CEO of *The Washington Post Group* was sitting with the publisher and Michael Walker, sipping a single malt whiskey, neat. "That's quite some lady you've got there," Mitchell said, his voice slightly slurred from single handedly finishing an entire fifth of the golden liquor in one sitting.

"She is that."

Franklin Mitchell put his arm around the shoulder of publisher Bill Flickling. "I want you to hire her."

"After tomorrow, I don't think we will be able to afford her."

"Did I stutter, Bill? I said hire her, I didn't ask how much it was going to cost. Back up a damn Brinks truck, if you have to. Her name on the masthead will add five dollars a share to the value of our stock."

"Many of the old warhorses won't like it if we pay her more than them."

"Then tell them to quit living off their past glory and go out and write something new. I want to see her name in my newspaper."

"Yes, sir."

Penelope finally finished the article and nodded her approval.

"We're good to go?" Hatchet asked again.

"Yes."

With a flourish he hit the send button on his workstation. "We just went to press! Congratulations everyone! Great work!"

Pandemonium broke out in the room. Paper was tossed in the air; hugs and back slaps were exchanged. The doors at the far end of the room burst open and six members of Walker's team rolled in carts with bottles of champagne on ice. Everyone there knew they were part of the biggest scoop in the history of publishing.

Unlike the previous Awakenings, thanks to Penelope Drayton Spence, this one was going to be documented completely. With the way Walker and Altman were making the world aware of the changes that were coming, there would actually be a chance to avoid the slaughter that had followed previous Awakenings.

The corks began popping and, like a locker room after a team won a world championship; soon the spraying and drenching began.

Walker made eye contact with Kevin and Stevie, his Internet brain trust, and gave them a thumbs-up. With a few keystrokes, the "under construction" sign came down on FourthAwakening.com and the webpage went live. In multiple languages, complete information about the Fourth Awakening was presented, along with opportunities to join an online global discussion involving it. In the first 24 hours the site got over ten million hits; by the end of the week it would be second only to Yahoo! News as the most popular news URL on the World Wide Web.

Mark Hatchet, his hair dripping wet from the many showers of champagne that had ensued, came over to Spence with a bottle in one hand and a glass in the other. "You did it, Nellie!"

"I'm so grateful you called me, Mark!" She clinked her glass against his bottle and took a sip. Mark Hatchet climbed up on the table and called for quiet.

"Let me have your attention, everyone." The big dining room fell silent. "I'm sure no one in this room needs to be reminded that they will be able to tell their grandkids they were part of the biggest scoop of our time!" A whoop went up in the room, and as it ebbed Hatchet again motioned for quiet. "Please join me in raising a glass to Penelope Drayton Spence— the best damned investigative reporter in the world."

A roar of "Hear! Hear!" went up, followed by a chant of "Speech! Speech!" Her cheeks flushed slightly as Mark helped her up on top of the table.

A prolonged and sustained round of applause followed and everyone in the room crowded in closer. Penelope tried to quiet them but they were not having any of it. "Thank you, thank you," Spence shouted over the noise. Glancing in Walker's direction she saw that he, everyone from the Hermes Project, and the senior management of *The Washington Post* were also on their feet applauding. "Thank you, thank you."

The din finally died down enough for her to be heard over the people still applauding.

"I would like to thank one of my oldest and dearest friends, Mark Hatchet, for trusting in me." Penelope kissed Mark on the cheek, which drew oohs and ahhs from the *Post* staff. "And mostly I would like to thank Dr. Carl Altman, who doesn't appear to be here, Michael Walker, and the entire Hermes Project." Penelope turned and raised her glass to Michael Walker, who nodded slightly. "If it weren't for their work, there wouldn't be a story." Penelope gathered herself for a moment before continuing. "And to all of you." She looked around, her eyes glistening, at all the flushed faces in the room. "This is the kind of night that every journalist dreams of." The room fell silent. "This is the big exclusive that everyone will be talking about tomorrow, and for weeks and even years to come. It was a team effort, and I owe each and every one of you a deep debt of gratitude that will be difficult to repay. Thank you so much." Another roar erupted.

Hatchet checked his watch and shouted, "The online edition should be up by now. Let see how long this takes to get some legs."

In keeping with the rustic style of the lodge, televisions were few and far between at Lazy S, and were never allowed in the dining room. This night they made an exception. Earlier, Walker's men had brought in six TVs that, using the satellite dishes in the back yard, were displaying WNBC, WABC, WCBS, CNN, Fox News and MSNBC. A small group was huddled around the TVs when another whoop went up.

"CBS just preempted Letterman."

"Ms. Spence, CNN is reading your lead article, word for word off the Internet."

"Fox News just broke in."

"There goes MSNBC."

"They cut off the Tonight Show in the middle of the monologue."

Another round of excited congratulations followed as Nightline also gave way to the Penelope Drayton Spence show.

Slapping herself on the forehead, Penelope grabbed her cell phone and called Joey. In all of the excitement she had forgotten to call.

"Hello," said Joey, somewhere between sleepy and irritated. Closer to irritated.

"It's me. Sorry I didn't call but I've been busy."

"No problem."

"Really?"

"Sure. That nice Sally Winters has called a couple of times to let me know you were fine. So have you jumped his bones yet?"

"I've been busy."

"Busy doing what"

"Turn on your TV."

"What channel?'

"Take your pick."

"I see you're still timeless." CNN was displaying a file photo that was taken years before when she won her Pulitzer.

"Oh, my God!" She was wearing a puffy-sleeved dress, and her hair was teased with bangs. "Sally!"

Sally Winters appeared instantly. "My assistant already has them on the phone. They have had the new media package for over four hours, but sometimes its amateur night at the cable networks after all the adults go home for dinner." Sally Winters pointed to the screen, which was already displaying a head and shoulder shot of Penelope with the Tetons in the background that had been taken earlier in the day. "We're going to go live on satellite in 20 minutes." On cue a set of lights clicked on at the far end of the dining hall where a table had been set up in front of a huge banner that had the football sized *The Washington Post* logos all over it. "We need to get you over to make-up."

"Joey, I have to go."

"I guess. Are there any awards bigger than a Pulitzer?"

"A few." Penelope hung up the phone and smiled in the direction of the bar. All of the noise had awakened Dr. Carl Altman. He was standing, dressed in a bathrobe and slippers, next to Michael Walker.

Dr. Atlman looked at Walker. "Savor this evening Michael. Now that we've revealed ourselves to our enemies we're at much greater risk."

"I know. At least now, between the news coverage and our webpage, people who have already started experiencing the Awakening will have a place to turn."

"How long before the jackals turn on us and start to discredit our little exercise today?"

"I'm sure it is already underway. A lot will depend on her." Walker nodded toward Penelope. "We might make it through the Sunday talk shows, but I wouldn't think much longer than that."

"I'm going back to bed." Altman patted Walker on the shoulder. "Do you think what we did today will be enough?"

"No. Not nearly."

EPILOGUE

"Truth has no special time of its own. Its hour is now—always."

ALBERT SCHWEITZER

"WHAT'S NEXT?" PENELOPE Spence asked.

"We're done," Sally Winters answered.

"Done done?"

"We are finished for the day."

"Thank God." Penelope pulled the annoying piece of plastic out of her ear, as one of Sally's assistants disconnected the microphone attached to her lapel. Starting with *Good Morning America* and the *Today Show*, the entire day had been a blur of interviews. She had spoken to all the major networks and all the cable channels, even C-SPAN. And, she had done dozens of radio interviews with everyone from NPR to Rush Limbaugh.

"Some people are here to see you," Sally said.

Penelope's shoulders slumped. "I thought you said we were done."

"I think you're going to want to talk to them."

Through the door burst fifty pounds of sniffing, wiggling fur. "Sam?" Penelope said. Hearing a familiar voice and seeing a familiar face, the chocolate lab bounded to her side and leaned against her leg while she rubbed his ear. A few feet behind were her three children: Carrie, Kelly and William.

"Oh, my God!" Penelope shrieked. They shared a bouncing group hug that got Sam so excited he began to run circles around them, barking with joy. "How did you get here?"

As usual, Carrie spoke for all of them. "Apparently, Mr. Walker personally called each of our bosses and requested we get some time off, and then he had us brought here by private plane."

"How long have you been here?"

"Just a few hours," Carrie said. "Talk about organized chaos..."

"A few hours!" Penelope glared at Sally Winters, who just shrugged and kept talking into one of her multiple cell phones.

"Joey said you were busy." Kelly added.

"Joey is here, too?"

"Along with Mr. Rickman," Kelly added, with the innocence only her middle child had ever successfully mastered, and been able to maintain her entire life. "He said something about a book deal and a movie deal. This is so exciting."

"Oh he did, did he?" Looking over her shoulder Penelope saw that Sally Winters had moved a bit further away. Leaving the cabin that had been converted to a makeshift "studio", they stepped outside and Penelope had to put on her sunglasses. The transition in the past few hours had been startling. The area in front of the main building was crowded with people she recognized as Hermes Project members showing their friends and family around.

Two large tents had been erected and caterers were busy setting up tables and chairs in one tent, while carpenters installed a dance floor in the middle of the other, along with a bandstand at each end. At the east end at least 20 roadies were hustling around setting up and testing equipment. Six large men were busy rolling into place in front of the bandstand what was obviously a full-sized grand piano covered in white satin. Others were setting up enough chairs for what looked like a full orchestra. At the west end a five-piece local cover band was tuning their equipment.

"This is going to be some party, Mom." William said.

All eyes turned when the woman screamed. "AHHHHHH!"

Standing at the bottom of the steps of the main house was Joey Rickman. On her right arm was Franklin Mitchell the CEO of *The Washington Post Group* and in her left hand was a Grey Goose martini.

Penelope screamed back.

"AHHHHH!"

Handing her drink to her new friend, Joey ran down the sidewalk as Penelope ran up. Meeting in the middle, both women began screaming at the top of their lungs. They hugged and bounced and screamed again as everyone within earshot laughed and pointed.

"You did it! You did it! YOU DID IT!"

"This has been an amazing couple of days."

"Angelina Jolie."

"What about Angelina Jolie?"

Reclaiming her martini from Franklin Mitchell who had just joined them, Joey said "That's who should play me in the movie."

"Movie?"

"Ron is in there talking to some guy from Sony or NBC/Universal, or whatever."

"Ron is negotiating a movie deal! He's a criminal lawyer!"

"Don't worry, Amy is doing all the talking."

"Amy." Franklin Mitchell shivered. "I've never seen anyone beat up Leon Steinberg like that. I thought he was going to cry."

"You know Frankie. Of course you do, he's your new boss."

"He is?"

"As soon as you sign the contract, Ms. Spence."

"Please, call me Penelope. What contract?"

"Ron was in there, all full of himself. You know how he gets. Apparently, you are the now the highest paid print reporter in the world."

"And then some," Franklin Mitchell added glumly.

"Really?"

"Ron got you all types of perks too. Tell her, Frankie."

"Normal stuff for high-end talent."

"High-end talent," Penelope thought to herself that she liked the sound of that.

"First-class air travel, an apartment at the Watergate for when you're in Washington, a twenty-four hour driver; it's a pretty extensive list."

"I have to move to Washington?" A frown darkened Penelope's face.

"No," Franklin Mitchell answered. "You can live anywhere you like. We'll work around your needs."

"Frankie is taking me to the Kennedy Center next Saturday night. He says he is going to introduce me to the President."

"Really?"

"We would love to have you and, if possible, Michael Walker join us," Franklin Mitchell said.

A mischievous grin covered Joey's face as she nudged Penelope gently in the ribs. "I think she would like that." A sheepish grin covered Penelope's face as she lowered her eyes and felt her cheeks get warm.

"Excuse me," Sally Winters said softly as she tugged on Penelope's arm.

The mood broken, Penelope's shoulders sagged as she sighed. "What now?"

"I've had a request, and if you don't want to do it everyone will understand."

"What's the request?"

"I know you're exhausted but some of the people really want to get home and they will be leaving early tomorrow and this might be their only chance."

"Chance for what?"

"All of the members of the Hermes Project and the people from the *Post* would like to have individual photos taken with you. You know, for the walls in their offices." Penelope's mind immediately flashed back to the pictures on the wall behind Senator Horn's desk. She was flattered.

"Of course..." Penelope turned to her children. "If it's okay with you guys."

Carrie kissed her mother on the cheek. "No problem. This is your day, Mom, enjoy it."

Sally arranged the photo shoot so that the Teton Mountains were in the background, and her staff soon had it organized like a well-oiled machine. Each member got a one-on-one pic holding up a print copy of *The Washington Post* and, if they wanted, a group picture with their friends and family. It took less than an hour.

"Let's go," Sally Winters said.

"Where now?"

"A hot bath and a nap, followed by a late and overdue dinner."

Penelope dropped her head onto Sally's shoulder. "Thank you."

Before Penelope even had her shoes off, Sally had the bath water running. "If you need anything..."

Penelope maneuvered her out the door. "Thanks, I'll be fine."

Alone for the first time in what seemed like months, Penelope savored the quiet. After a long soak she decided to check her closet to see what she should wear to dinner. Hanging inside the door was a garment bag with a handwritten note attached. "Please wear this tonight. Michael." Pulling the zipper down, inside she discovered a shimmering dark blue silk dancing dress with a plunging back. As she lifted the bag off of the hook she noticed that her old dancing shoes, cleaned and polished, were on the floor waiting for her.

Smiling, she sat on the end of the bed and tried on her old shoes. Not only had they been cleaned and polished, someone had taken the time to somehow soften the leather and make them as good as the day she had bought them. To her delight, they fit perfectly.

≈

THE SUN HAD dropped behind the Tetons and the food and drink had been amazing. During dinner, the local cover band had played a variety of tunes to satisfy all tastes. After the dishes were cleared away, Michael Walker tapped a water glass and asked for quiet.

"If everyone would please move into the other tent, thanks to the efforts of James Steerforth, we have a surprise for you."

It took about 5 minutes for everyone to be relocated. James Steerforth, dressed in one of his Vegas outfits, was standing in front of the satin covered piano doing magic tricks to the delight of a dozen small children. After everyone had settled in, he picked up a microphone. "Ladies and gentlemen." He glanced lovingly at the group of children who were now sitting cross-legged on the floor at his feet. "Boys and girls." The spotlight narrowed on Steerforth as he moved away from the piano. There was a hustle of activity behind him but in the dark, no one could quite make out what was happening. "At the request of Michael Walker, I have imposed on a dear friend of mine to perform for you this evening."

A murmur began to build as those closest to the stage caught a glimpse of the man now seated on the piano bench. Not wanting to be upstaged, James Steerforth shouted, "Sir Elton John!"

All of the stage lights clicked on and for a moment the 450 people in the tent weren't sure they believed what they were seeing. After the first bar of "Take me to the pilot of your soul" they were all on their feet cheering. For the next 90 minutes, Elton John and his band dazzled the crowd with his seemingly endless stream of hits. After the third encore, Elton John yielded the bandstand to a 16-piece swing band that began playing old favorites.

About 15 couples, including "Frankie" and Joey, were slow dancing to "Moon River." Hearing a familiar laugh, Penelope noticed Carrie and

William sharing a joke with Timothy Ellison. Penelope, self-conscious in the all too revealing silk dress, had thrown a shawl over her shoulders; it was finally getting cool enough that she didn't feel overdressed.

She had barely seen or spoken to Michael in the past 24 hours. Catching a glimpse of him across the dance floor, she smiled when she saw that he had changed clothes since dinner. He was wearing a Roaring Twenties-style tuxedo that would have been perfect for the doorman at a Prohibition-era speakeasy.

As the song ended and the dance floor emptied, Michael Walker pointed to the band leader who nodded his head. All of the lights in the tent went out, drawing a gasp from everyone there. A spotlight clicked on putting a tight circle of light on the clarinet player. He rose to his feet and hit a note that Benny Goodman or Artie Shaw would have been proud to claim. The circle of light moved over to the drummer who took over for the clarinet player. As the heavy drum beats reverberated through the valley, two more spotlights clicked on; one on Michael Walker, the other on Penelope Spence. A roar went up in the tent.

Michael Walker glided across the floor to Penelope and held his left hand out, palm up.

"Ms. Spence."

"Mr. Walker."

"I believe you owe me a dance."

"I believe I do."

With a flourish she tossed the shawl aside, took his hand and joined him on the dance floor. Another, louder, roar echoed off the mountains.

He spun her away so that the silk skirt twirled like a top, then pulled her back so that his chest was pressing against her shoulders and his mouth was next to her ear.

The drummer stopped playing; the tent fell silent. All eyes were on the couple in the spotlights.

"Tango?"

"Of course."

"Argentine?"

"Is there any other kind?"

He pushed her away hard. Spinning twice, her heels clicking on the hardwood dance floor, she moved about six feet away from Walker and froze with the index finger of her right hand pointing at him; their eyes locked.

"Wooo, go Mom," Carrie shouted as the crowd roared again.

"Maestro, if you please!" Walker shouted. "A Tango!" The crowd erupted again.

The band began playing a steamy tango and the couple began circling each other. The only sound now was from the band as everyone in the tent was mesmerized. Suddenly they moved together, then began moving as one.

For the next two minutes all Penelope Spence saw was Michael Walker's eyes; all she heard was the music. Her heart was pounding and between the exertion and the elevation, her breath was coming in small pants.

"Are you ready for the big finish, Ms. Spence?"

"I am indeed, Mr. Walker. You know, you were wrong about one thing."

"Really? What?"

Penelope didn't answer. As the song ended, her right ankle rested gracefully on Michael Walker's shoulder and her hair was brushing the floor. She was twenty-three again.

The story continues online and with the next book in the series!

THE GATHERING DARKNESS

by
Rod Pennington
&
Jeffery A. Martin

Get a special sneak peek at:
FourthAwakening.com/peek.htm